My Heart's
in the
Highlands

About the Author

Amy Hoff is a Scottish historian and folklorist who went from living on the American road to living in the centre of metropolitan Scotland. She lived in Glasgow for over a decade, where she earned her master's degree in Scottish Studies and wrote her thesis on Sherlock Holmes. She founded and ran a film and theatre company, taught Scottish folklore at the university, and hosted many cultural events in the city. She also lived on Islay, where she worked for the Gaelic college. She's always loved whisky, leather jackets, and muscle cars and had a keen appreciation for adventure.

My Heart's
in the
Highlands

Amy Hoff

BELLA
BOOKS
2020

Bella Books, Inc.
P.O. Box 10543
Tallahassee, FL 32302

Printed in the United States of America on acid-free paper.

First Bella Books Edition 2020

Editor: Medora MacDougall
Cover Designer: Kayla Mancuso

ISBN: 978-1-64247-127-4

Dedication

For Rachel and Sabrina, on the occasion of their wedding, and with a wish for many happy years together.

CHAPTER ONE

Edinburgh

The high, thick wooden heels of her sensible leather boots landed right in a puddle with a splash.

Of course, she thought.

"Fuck," she said.

The cab driver raised an eyebrow both startled and admonishing. She waved him off irritably and he flicked the reins, shaking his head as the cab disappeared in the impossibly dreich weather.

Edinburgh was a watercolour, because what other kind of painting could it possibly be? The striations of grey across a sky that always seemed a bit too close to the earth matched the grey Gothic sobriety of the castle and the rabbit warrens of wynds that wound their way up to the Royal Mile with ominous names like Fleshmarket Close, the joining of Old and New Town in a symphony of rain-drenched stone beneath the shadow of Arthur's Seat.

Lady Jane Crichton arranged herself, an enormous folder tucked under one arm, her long skirt and buttoned blouse just as sensible as her shoes. She had large, very dark brown eyes like a doe, under heavy dark eyebrows, and long, dark chestnut-brown hair, nearly black, that came tumbling down over her shoulders when it was unpinned. Now it was pinned up, the ruff of her starched collar touching her jawline.

She looked every bit the scientist she was, or was trying to be, if she hadn't stepped directly into a puddle and sworn like a sailor. But such was life in Edinburgh; the cost of being at the centre of scientific invention meant putting up with God's worst weather.

Doctor Jane Crichton was her real title, but the men persisted with "Miss." Still, they'd invited her to the scientific convocation today, so she let it slide.

She pushed open the door, which was either far lighter than she'd expected or she didn't know her own strength; it ricocheted off the wall. Fortunately, she caught it before it could hit her, but the noise caused the men in the room to turn in their chairs and stare at her. Starched-suits, young men who were already old, taking on airs as if they were peers in the House of Lords instead of her medical colleagues.

"Ah, Doctor Crichton," said the man currently at the podium. "So nice to have you join us."

He smiled warmly and she returned his smile, hesitant. He'd called her "Doctor."

She always did like Joseph Bell. Whether or not he thought highly of women she did not know, but he respected scientists.

Bell, although just past fifty years of age, had the aura of youth about him. He had bright eyes and a mischievous smile, a razor-sharp wit, and a mind that outshone everyone present. He had angular features and a sharp, hawklike face. He possessed a great energy, evident in the way he moved with barely contained enthusiasm, walking with a strange, jerking gait that identified him from a distance. His mild personality and unassuming air meant that people were all the more astounded by his deductions, a habit of surprising people in which he took particular delight. His passion for scientific enquiry and his love of a mystery like a hound on a scent made Joseph Bell the youngest man in the room, although he was older than most of the men in it.

"As you will see," Dr. Bell resumed, taking the attention away from Jane as he read her silent plea correctly, "there are a multitude of uses for fingerprinting in police investigation. The work of Dr. Henry Faulds will illustrate some of the ways in which this type of scientific advancement has led to the identification and sentencing of criminals."

Jane found her seat and arranged her skirts around her, then opened her messy document folder and began to page through it. After a while, she noticed that Dr. Bell had gone silent. She looked up slowly.

"Doctor Crichton, have I bored you today?" he asked. "Is there something more pressing than the capture of criminals?"

Some of the men snickered but were silenced by a sharp look from Dr. Bell. He returned his gaze to Jane, who held it.

"What about catching criminals before they ever commit the crime?" Jane asked.

This caused a commotion; a whisper went through the assembly.

"Even if that were possible, there is the ethical dilemma inherent in arresting a man for a crime he did not yet commit," Dr. Bell said. "Deduction is an important skill, but even if it can at times predict intent, it certainly cannot be said to imbue the practitioner with psychic abilities. It is not enough to be able to do something. We must consider whether the thing should be done at all. A moral question, to be sure, but a scientist always considers the possible ramifications of his or her actions."

The men in the room chuckled, but Jane, encouraged by Dr. Bell's treatment of her as a human being, was emboldened by the discussion. She spoke to him as if they two were alone in the enormous assembly hall.

"I'm not talking about precognition," she said, a grin starting to spread across her face. "I'm talking about time travel."

Dr. Bell grinned back, as if he too thought this conversation between them alone.

"Indeed," he said. "And if time travel could be used to discern the criminal activities of the mind or return to the precise time before the event to prevent it—whether or not that means the guilty party is still guilty, having not committed the crime—there's still the matter of our not having the slightest notion of how to go about it."

"That's just it, Professor," said Jane. "I think I do."

"Theoretical knowledge regarding time machines is—" Bell began.

"Oh, no, Doctor," she interrupted. "You misunderstand."

"How do you mean?" he asked.

She smiled, triumphant.

"You see, I've already built one."

CHAPTER TWO

Up the Waverley Steps

A hush fell over the assembly. Dr. Bell just stared at her, his mouth in a thin line.

Then the laughter began, swelled and rose across the crowd as a wave.

Jane was not disheartened. She could see that look in Dr. Bell's eyes.

He believed her, and he was a hard man to convince.

* * *

He approached her after the presentations had concluded.

"That was quite a performance," he said.

"Yes, well, I can't help my flair for the dramatic," said Jane.

"Listen, Jane," he whispered urgently. "You and I both know how ridiculous all this is—no truly intelligent man or woman capable of deductive reasoning would posit such a false concept as gender making a whit of difference when it comes to a bright scientific mind—but you know the prevailing belief of the day and what they will do. You were one of the Edinburgh Seven, after all."

Jane smiled. She had seen Sophia's advertisement in the newspaper and written immediately, despite her mother's misgivings on the subject. She had always acted first and considered later, but she also felt that time spent in consideration was time wasted. Had she not jumped at the chance, she would not be the only woman standing in the convocation hall with the other scientists. Even though it was ruled that the university did not have to grant the degrees the women should have attained in 1873, Jane was still a doctor. But for many of the Seven, their treatment and the related public shaming had soured them on Edinburgh forever. As it was, over the past fifteen years, many of them had moved to England and other places. Jane had always been stubborn. She would not let men chase her away from her passion for science and medicine, and she certainly would not let them run her out of Scotland or Edinburgh. After all, Edinburgh was her home too.

"I still talk to Sophia and Margaret from time to time," Jane said sweetly. "Do you?"

Dr. Bell sighed, exasperated.

"Please take this seriously, Jane!" he said. "Edinburgh may be more advanced in egalitarian pursuits than London, but only just."

Jane sighed, scratching at her collar and then one of the multiple pins holding up her hair, which was quite heavy. She looked at Bell's short hair, simple coat, and trousers with jealousy. She shook her head and sighed.

"Yes, Joseph, all right," she relented. "I understand. Or rather, I don't understand at all, because it is absolutely illogical and so fundamentally goddamned *stupid*—"

A few of the other men still lingering in the hallway raised their heads to look over at the pair, as Jane's loud voice started to echo off the bricks.

She lowered her voice to a whisper.

"I understand the danger," she said. "Thank you for the warning."

"Good," said Dr. Bell, rubbing his hands. "Now, to the matter at hand: is it true?"

"You tell me," she said, holding his gaze. Dr. Bell studied her, and his eyes went wild with excitement.

"So it is," he said, barely able to speak. "Will you show me?"

Jane nodded, finger to her lips.

* * *

Jane was always *too*.

She was *too* tall, *too* loud, *too* stocky, *too much*.

She tried to hunch, to hide, until it became obvious to her that a woman of her stature was always going to take up space. This is not to say she was particularly powerful or muscular; there was just a

Lord David Crichton would not usually greet visitors in his dressing gown, but he hadn't known there would be any. He was normally an impeccably dressed man, in his formal brown suits with his blond hair combed flat down against his skull in a severe part. He was certainly some variety of handsome, although Jane couldn't say which; she thought him a bit dull at times. However, she adored his eccentricities; he was very kind, a sensitive soul, and he supported her efforts unfailingly, so Jane felt she had made a good match. All in all, it was a good marriage and allowed her the kind of time and money necessary to pursue scientific interests.

"Now then!" David said. "I expect Janie here told you about her time machine? Absolutely wonderful stuff! She's a genius, our Janie."

"I have to say I agree," said Joe Bell mildly, taking a sip of his tea.

"Gentlemen," said Jane. "You flatter me without knowing a thing about it. You haven't even seen it, Joe. You wouldn't accept that from any of the men in the society."

"Quite right! Quite right!" said David, clapping his hands. "Capital! Janie has always been better at the old women's rights wheeze. Absolutely spiffing is our Janie!"

Jane smiled indulgently at her husband. Harmless with a head full of air, David was nevertheless one of the best cheerleaders a woman could ask for. He'd come from a very well-to-do family. "Serious old Scottish stock, Janie, bore the head off a Highland cow, so they would," he often said. "Absolutely no fun in them at all."

Jane set down her cup of tea.

"It's time," she said, indicating that they should follow.

Joe stood, nearly knocking over the tray in his haste, with David following languorously after, puffing smoke all the way.

* * *

The shed in the back garden was a little worse for wear, as the relentless damp of Edinburgh got through all the cracks and crevices and peeled the paint right off the wood. But none of that mattered; it's what was on the inside that counted.

Jane pushed open the door. There beyond it sat a truncated icosahedron with a small window, a strange contraption that resembled a 20-sided spherical submarine with the texture of beaten copper.

"Here it is," Jane announced proudly.

Joe inspected it eagerly, looking through the window and then opening the hatch and peering down.

CHAPTER FOUR

Highlands

Jane blinked.

Once.

Twice.

Her vision was blurred—or, no. It was the fog.

Distantly, she became aware of rough ground beneath her, the twigs and dirt underneath her hands. Floating in this strange dream, which looked to her like one of the snowglobes she had seen in a London shop window, was the looming shadow of a mountain, white-capped in the distance, so high above her she felt almost dizzy with it and, in the foreground, on a rocky outcrop, a…bonfire?

She pushed herself into a sitting position, and what had seemed like a fire in the distance resolved itself into the figure of a woman with fiery ginger hair, her body wrapped in the woman's version of the long tartan blanket-like garment that men wore as the more recognizable great kilt. Jane knew the word for it, earasaid, although she'd never seen one; that type of clothing was viewed as impossibly uncouth and savage these days. The woman's back was turned to her. A large sword was at her side.

Jane suddenly noticed, to her horror, the broken, twisted remnants of her machine. She covered her mouth to stifle a scream; she had no idea where she was, or when she was, or who her companion might be. She only thought of getting away as fast as she could; something had gone wrong and she needed to find a way to get in touch with David or Joe Bell as soon as possible.

She rolled to her feet and started to creep away silently, her eyes all the while on the silent woman seated at the cliff's edge. She reached the treeline at the edge of the clearing, congratulating herself on her stealth.

"The Argyll are in there, ye ken," said a rich, rolling deep voice.

Jane froze.

"Aye, I'm speakin t'you," said the voice. The woman on the cliff hadn't moved or even looked around. "The daft lassie tryin' to skewer hersel on a Caimbeul dirk."

"Excuse me?" said Jane, insulted.

The woman stood and turned around.

Jane's heart was in her throat, beating like butterfly wings.

If Jane was tall and stocky, this woman was absolutely huge. Her long shock of ginger hair was held in an enormous braid, with a few other narrow braids hanging down on the right side, framing her face. She wore a gold circlet on her forehead and a gold torc around her neck. She seemed to be in her late thirties, close to Jane's age, or a little older. Her skin was pale and freckled, an intricate design drawn onto her face, a tattoo of dark-blue ink in a knotwork pattern; sharp cheekbones swept down to full soft lips tinted pink. Her eyes were large and forest-green, and her stern expression was terrifying. She was incredibly muscular, from the corded lines of her neck to her strong arms and the solid build of her body. She crossed her arms and stared at Jane.

Jane found she was having trouble breathing.

"What happened?" she asked, trying to circle around the woman and distract her with talk.

"I was waitin' to ask ye the same question," said the woman. "Fiery ball fell oot o' the sky, the seer-women will mak merry with this for months."

"And you came to find me?" Jane continued, edging away from the woman, toward the forest.

"Aye, of sorts," the woman said. "Attracted a fair bit o' attention, too, frae the local Argyll dafties."

"The, er, what now?" asked Jane.

Now the woman was surprised.

"The...Argylls?" she said. "What, ye've never heard o' the Caimbeulaich?"

"I, er, I know a Catherine Campbell from Leith," said Jane.

"You're fae Edinburgh?" asked the woman, and when Jane nodded in the affirmative, she snorted. "That explains the fancy talk, maybe even the clothes, but what're you doing this far west?"

"West?" asked Jane, puzzled, nearing the cliff's edge and about to make a break for it, "Where did I land, then?"

Suddenly, the woman threw her down and was on top of her in an instant, pressing Jane face-first into the dirt. The woman covered her with her entire body, the earasaid unfolded as a canopy around them. Jane felt aware of every aspect of the woman's body, from her heavy breasts against the curve of her upper back to where her hipbones had slotted against the rise of her bottom. Her heart hammered wildly in her chest.

"Ye've really got no sense at all, have ye?" the red-haired woman growled in her ear. Jane felt a delicious shudder run through her entire frame and was startled at this unknown feeling. "I'll have to teach ye to obey me if ye won't listen to sense. Stay *down*."

Jane trembled with an emotion she could not define.

"Are you going to..." she began. "Are you going to take advantage of me?"

The woman recoiled.

"Of course not, ye silly wee thing," said the woman, sounding horrified. "Where I come fae, there's a harsh penalty for that, not tae mention it'd be certain death for those fool enough tae try it. What sort of backwards place are you from?"

"Then what the *bloody hell* do you think you're doing?" hissed Jane. She tried to wriggle away, but the woman's strength was like an iron vise holding her still.

"There's Caimbeulaich over the ridge," she whispered, hot against the shell of Jane's ear, "an' if ye're lookin' fer your ain death then that's your choice. If ye want tae keep breathin', ye'll still an' ye'll do as I say."

Jane stopped struggling.

"You could've asked," she hissed petulantly.

"Would ye hae listened?" the woman asked, and Jane felt her huff an amused, soft laugh against her skin.

"If ye'd have kept goin'," the woman continued, "ye'd have given away our position. Lamb tae the slaughter as ye are. Cannae protect ye if they spot ye first, now can I?"

"Protect me?" asked Jane, mindful to whisper now. "Why?"

"Law of Highland hospitality," said the woman, whose soft lips kept grazing Jane's ear. "You are under my protection."

"Am I?" retorted Jane. "And you are?"

There was a pause before the other woman spoke.

"Ainslie nic Dòmhnaill, daughter of Dòmhnall mac Raghnaill, grandson of the great Somhairlidh, and the rightful heir to the title of MacDonald, Lord of the Isles."

CHAPTER FIVE

Island

Jane hastily did the math in her head. She never had been good at history.

If this was…Somerled's great-granddaughter… Then that put the year at around…

The thirteenth century!

Which meant she was currently trapped underneath one of the most powerful people in the most powerful clan in Scotland. According to her father's stories about growing up on the Kintyre Peninsula, the Donalds had never taken kindly to the Campbells. Apparently the animosity went back a very long way.

Jane groaned. Ainslie shushed her.

"Are ye mad?" she said. "Look up—wi' your eyes *ainly.*"

The two women looked up, keeping their heads down. Just over the rise, she could see a number of men searching through the forest, for her time machine, no doubt. Ainslie held her still, and Jane could feel her heart beat faintly through her thick clothes, she was so close. She smelled of pine, and the sea, and the rich, fresh earth…Jane found herself closing her eyes.

"They've gone," Ainslie said, standing suddenly in a single, fluid motion. Jane missed her warmth and then shook her head at her own silliness.

She stood up. Ainslie took in her outfit and stared at her boots. "Those'll do ye no good here, lass," she said. "Best get up so we can cover your…boat? an' protect it frae any prying eyes."

She walked off, and Jane was startled to see she was barefoot. Ainslie rolled the machine over with ease, right into a deep ravine where its dull bronze fit with all the other rocks. After she piled pine branches, leaves, and other forest detritus on it, even Jane couldn't make out where it was from a distance.

Ainslie climbed the ravine and smiled an improbable grin full of pearl-white teeth.

"Weel," she said. "Ye're free tae choose where to go, but as it seems ye're a lang way frae hame ye might want to accept my offer o' hospitality."

Jane thought quickly. The sun would set in a few hours, and she needed time to think. Where would she get equipment to fix the machine in this time period? She sighed deeply.

"Fine," she relented. "But the shoes stay!"

Ainslie looked at the high-heeled boots and then up at Jane, an amused smile playing at the corners of her lips.

"If ye say so."

* * *

"A boat?"

Jane stood on the shore, staring in consternation at the small vessel run aground.

"Aye, a boat," Ainslie said. "How'd ye expect we'd get there?"

"I thought you lived locally!" said Jane.

"Aye, I do!" Ainslie replied. "There, on that island!"

She pointed to a dark outline on the water, nearly obscured by mist.

"Anyway, you came here in a wee boatie just like the rest o' us!" said Ainslie, then looked at Jane's shoes again, much the worse for wear after tramping through the thistle and nettles of the forest. "Weel… maybe not *just like* the rest of us."

Ainslie led her down to the water, where a small clinker-built boat with a dragonshead prow sat low in the water. It was sturdy enough and looked well loved, but it had clearly enjoyed a long life.

"I am not getting in that thing!" protested Jane, stamping her foot.

"I'm an excellent sailor, I assure ye," Ainslie said. "Ye'll be perfectly safe."

"You can assure me all you like! That vessel is not seaworthy!"

Ainslie drew up to her full, impressive height and puffed out her chest.

"How *dare* ye say that about Malcolm?" Ainslie demanded, her eyes narrowed. "He's a faering and a very good one!"

"Malcolm? You named your boat Malcolm?" Jane exclaimed.

"Aye, an' he's sensitive. Ye're hurtin' his feelings," said Ainslie. "Anyway, you crashed yours. Ye've got naethin' tae teach me about seamanship!"

"I'll have you know I—" Jane had a ready retort when Ainslie held up a hand.

Voices could be heard faintly through the trees. Ainslie shook her head.

"Wasted too much time," she said to herself. "There's naethin' for it."

She pushed the boat out into the water.

"What the hell are you doing?" demanded Jane. "That's our only— oi!"

Jane squealed in protest as Ainslie lifted her bodily off the beach and carried her, kicking and struggling, out into the deeper water and dropped her unceremoniously into the boat.

Jane sat up, furious, her hair in disarray from this and their previous scuffles. Ainslie hopped into the boat with ease, and she lifted the oars, pulling steadily. When they had finally emerged from the lee of the land, she hoisted a square sail. The wind filled it, and they sailed off toward the island. The mist draped itself around them, hiding them from view.

"How—how *dare you*—," spluttered Jane.

"Argument was taking too long," said Ainslie.

"You—ugh," Jane groused. Her feet hurt, she was covered in dirt, and her clothes were all but destroyed.

Ainslie reached over and hauled her up with one hand, so Jane's face was suddenly very close to her own.

"Sound carries on water," Ainslie whispered, dark green eyes holding Jane's own. "Or do they no' teach you that in the city?"

Jane breathed, the wrinkles on her blouse rising and falling. She held the challenge of Ainslie's gaze until Jane finally dropped her eyes demurely. She could feel the warmth of Ainslie's breath on her skin. *It must be fear*, Jane thought. *This must be what it is to be terrified.*

But it was unlike any fear she'd ever known. Not really, she realised, much like fear at all.

She stared at Ainslie's mouth, those soft rose-pink lips and the white teeth barely visible behind them. Her breath caught.

"Do ye ken how tae swim?" Ainslie said then, startling her.

Jane shook her head.

"Then ye best stay in the boat," Ainslie said and dropped her into the centre once again.

The strange spell broken, Jane kept silent and watched the island loom up in the mist, as Malcolm plied the water.

CHAPTER SIX

Islay

Jane found the silence of the boat gliding through the water unnervingly quiet. The plip, plip of the water against the hull was the only indication they were moving forward.

"Lady Jane Crichton," she said suddenly.

"What?" asked Ainslie, who seemed to be focused on a horizon Jane could not see.

"It's my name," she explained. "Lady Jane Crichton. I never told you."

"*Lady*," said Ainslie, rolling the word around her tongue as though she did not quite like the taste of it. "And I take it ye live a life of leisure, wi' nae care in the world for others?"

"Well, I wouldn't say that," Jane said, piqued.

"These fancy ladies and gentlemen," Ainslie all but spat. "The English are insufferable, and then the Scots put on their airs and graces. The English tell the Scots, we're the same, ye're like us, all the while patting themselves on the back for pullin' the wool over their eyes again. A Scottish lady or gentleman is a monkey in a hat tae the English. We tell them, join wi' us, but the lure of money is too great."

Ainslie's mouth snapped shut as if she'd said too much. She looked out to sea, resolute.

Jane coughed politely.

"What were you doing all the way on the other shore anyway?" Jane asked, to make conversation. The sea was eerily silent, the shroud of fog a coverlet over the shoulders of the world. Jane had no idea how Ainslie knew where she was going, but it was either stay in the boat or take her chances in the cold waters of the grey sea.

"Fishing," said Ainslie.

"Fishing," Jane repeated.

"Aye," said Ainslie. "Do you find it strange?"

"Well...you're a—a woman," said Jane.

Ainslie's brows drew together.

"Aye?" she said, as if prompting a further explanation. When none was forthcoming, she shook her head. "Edinburgh is a strange place if they think their women won't fish, given half a chance."

"No, it's, er, mostly forbidden," said Jane.

"What, fishing?" said Ainslie, surprised. "What do ye eat?"

"No, not fishing," Jane clarified. "*Women* fishing."

Ainslie looked puzzled.

"What a strange law," she said. "Perhaps a woman stole a fish recently. No matter. When I become Lord of the Isles I will convene a meeting and the women will be allowed to fish. I shall make it a part of my treaty with their lords. I am sure the women will be forgiven and then they can fish again."

Jane stared at Ainslie for a long time.

"It's not, er. It's not just fishing," she said, a bit timid now that it had come to things she held near and dear. "I'm a scientist, you see, and they wouldn't let women attend the university—that's a kind of school. I was one of the first women trained as a doctor, but they wouldn't grant us degrees even though we went through the entire course and graduated."

Ainslie tried to follow this string of unfamiliar words without much success.

"I too am educated," she said. "Father sent me to travel the world and learn what I could. Edinburgh's war against women must end. Whatever woman was unjust to them cannot be held against all women."

Jane despaired of ever making her understand but was starting to see herself that the type of society she had always believed to exist might not have a mere few centuries ago.

"It's not Edinburgh, it's everywhere," said Jane.

"Good fortune for ye to end up with the heir to the Lord of the Isles, then," said Ainslie. "We are not like the Scots."

"Pardon?" asked Jane. "You *are* Scots."

Ainslie's eyes flashed.

"We are *the Dhòmhnaill*," she said. "Ancient rulers of the kingdom of the Gael."

The challenge there was clear. Jane chose not to engage.

A slight hiss told her that the boat—Malcolm—had made it onto the beach, although with the thick mist coiling around the shoreline, it otherwise would have been impossible to tell.

Ainslie hopped out and dragged the boat onto shore, securing it. She went and lifted Jane out of the vessel in a bridal carry, and now that she wasn't surprised by the gesture, Jane marveled that Ainslie could lift someone of her height and size with as much ease as if she weighed no more than a feather.

Ainslie set her down on the beach, where she wobbled a bit unsteadily in her high heels in the sand. Ainslie put out a supporting hand, warm against her back.

"Lady Jane Crichton," said Ainslie. "Welcome to Islay."

CHAPTER SEVEN

Heather Island

Jane followed Ainslie up the path from the beach. The way was steep and rocky, with not much to see on the way. She felt anxious about leaving her machine on the other coast but supposed there wasn't much to be done for it.

"Here we are," Ainslie announced, as they crested the ridge.

What Jane saw was...not what she had expected.

The fields glowed a preternatural green in the setting sun, where the mist had burned away. Jane had thought there would be a small hamlet of some kind, the sort of rude gathering of buildings she imagined when she encountered one of the poor Highlanders begging on the Edinburgh streets, thin as a rail and sallow-cheeked—a place where the cattle shared a home with their owners and where poverty and ragged clothes matched Ainslie's bare feet.

Instead, a busy metropolis of sorts met her eyes; it was not a metropolis built of stone like Edinburgh, but it was a metropolis all the same. The streets were thronged with people, laughing and hauling things, leading cattle here and there, sewing and knitting and doing all the sorts of things people find necessary to life.

And here, too, were sights she found odd: a young man holding a child, a woman working in the glow of the blacksmith's shop, a few old men knitting and weaving. It was not that there weren't men doing "men's jobs" or women doing "women's jobs," it was that there seemed to be no such thing to these people and one was as likely to find a man running a nursery as a woman at the plough.

"City folk always think they've the monopoly on the guid life," said Ainslie, as though she could hear Jane's thoughts. "Île is the capital of the Sea Kingdom. Not that any of ye 'Scots' bother wi' us."

"Why do you speak English?" asked Jane.

"Why don't ye speak Gaelic?" asked Ainslie pointedly. Jane hung her head. "As I said, ye dinnae tak us seriously. No' as seriously as ye tak the English, anyway."

"Where are we headed?" asked Jane.

"There," said Ainslie and pointed.

In the last rays of the setting sun, the world had gone purple in the gloaming-light, and Jane saw a small island on which stood an enormous castle set as a jewel in the surrounding dark blue of the sea. Boats plied the water back and forth from the castle to the land on both sides of the sound.

"Claig Castle, on Fraoch Eilean," said Ainslie. "Built by Somhairlidh, my grandfather, and the stronghold of the Dhòmhnaill, rulers of these islands."

CHAPTER EIGHT

Castle

The castle interior was warm and inviting, an unfamiliar experience for Jane, who was accustomed to the drafty and chill houses of Edinburgh. Fires leapt in enormous fireplaces, and people walked here and there as they passed through the castle. Jane marveled at how full and busy this place was, both the city and the castle, as she had been led to believe her ancestors lived in isolated communities with little contact with the outside world. She could see through the window a number of ships going to and fro on the water outside and wondered if even the Edinburgh of her own time was quite as busy as the island of Islay in this one.

Ainslie came to a large wooden door and knocked.

"Come in," said a voice, also in English. Jane was extremely puzzled; wouldn't everyone speak Gaelic?

Ainslie opened the door and they were standing in an enormous room with a tall ceiling that disappeared beyond the rafters. There were two floor-to-ceiling windows flanking a man seated at a desk.

The man was enormous, with a great long beard he seemed to have tucked under the desk. He was writing something with a fountain pen. The entire thing was so incongruous to Jane that she glanced sharply at Ainslie.

"Father," Ainslie greeted the man.

"Ainslie!" he boomed and stood, walking around the table and embracing her. "Who's your friend?"

Jane was well aware of the picture she made, with her clothing in disarray, dirt and twigs in her hair, which had started to come unpinned.

"Lady Jane Crichton, your majesty," she said. She attempted an aborted curtsy. It did not go well.

Ainslie's father stared at her for a while, chewing on his beard.

He suddenly roared with laughter.

"Dòmhnall is fine, Lady Jane Crichton," he said. "Is there one out of those names that's your own?"

"Jane, your m—Dòmhnall," she said. Dòmhnall smiled and then turned to Ainslie.

"Father, Jane says they forbid women to fish in Edinburgh," said Ainslie. "I'd like tae work on that wi' ye when ye hae time."

"Hmm," said Dòmhnall. "Do ye ken the name o' the woman who caused this?"

"Nae, but we can find out," said Ainslie. Jane didn't have the heart to point out that it wasn't just fishing. "Jane's the one that fell oot the sky today."

"Good thing ye found her before the Argylls," said Domnhall. "We'll hae to find her a cottage."

Jane was surprised that they didn't seem to think a woman falling out of the sky was odd, but she kept quiet.

Dòmhnall beamed at the two of them.

"She's beautiful," he said. "Have ye proposed yet?"

Jane's jaw dropped.

Then, to Jane's utter shock, Ainslie went very red in the face.

"*Da,*" she complained, and Dòmhnall laughed again.

"All in good time," he said, patting her on the shoulder. "Why don't you get her cleaned up? Dinner will be served in an hour."

"Aye, Father," Ainslie said. She hurried Jane out of the room as her father returned to his paperwork.

* * *

Ainslie led her into a smaller room off of the castle's great hall. Night had fallen, so the room was lit only by the fire, and yet it was warm enough.

Ainslie grabbed an apple from the side table and threw herself into a chair.

"Strip," she commanded and bit into the apple, juices dripping down her chin.

"Pardon?" asked Jane.

"Is tha' the ainly word ye ken, Lady Jane Crichton?" asked Ainslie.

"I—I," Jane stammered.

Ainslie rolled her eyes.

"It's tae check for wounds, broken bones, bruises," she explained. "Ye city people, sex is all ye think about."

"You did kidnap me," Jane pointed out.

"I did nae sic thing," said Ainslie. "I offered ye a choice an' ye nearly got us killed wi' yer arguing, an' noo we're nearly gaun tae starve. Do as I say. *Strip.*"

The command in Ainslie's voice went through Jane like an arrow.

It's these savage people, she thought. *Uncouth*, as she removed her boots and began to loosen her corset-strings.

"Savages," said Ainslie, and Jane was horrified; she must've spoken out loud. Ainslie just shook her head and gestured to Jane to continue.

She had stripped off everything and unrolled her stockings, stepping out of them onto the warm flagstones.

"Turn," said Ainslie. Jane did so. "*Slowly.*"

So Jane rotated, the flames bathing her skin in golden light. She looked at Ainslie and thought she saw hunger in the woman's eyes. Or perhaps it was Jane's own presuppositions about life here, among the clans of old. She stared at Ainslie, but the woman's expression was now unreadable.

"Some bruising, but ye'll be fine wi' a bit o' rest an' food in ye," Ainslie decreed. "Noo, yer hair."

"What?" asked Jane.

"Your hair," Ainslie repeated. "Take it down."

"I don't see what this has to do with checking me for injuries," Jane muttered, facing the fire, her back to Ainslie, but she pulled out the first pin, and her rich, chocolate-coloured hair fell down across her shoulders. This time, she swore she heard a sharp intake of breath, but she couldn't be sure. Pin after pin fell to the floor until the entirety of the long waves of her hair fell loose.

"Satisfied?" asked Jane, crossing her arms.

"Aye," said Ainslie. Jane thought the word sounded a bit strained, but as she was not facing the other woman, she couldn't tell.

"May I dress again?" Jane demanded.

"Nae," Ainslie said.

"Pardon?"

"Ye want tae eat dinner wi' the ruler o' a nation when ye're sae filthy?" Ainslie asked. "Nae, ye'll be bathed first. I'll no hae ye offending all o' society wi' yer stink."

"My 'stink,'" said Jane.

"Aye, an' it was on ye afore today," said Ainslie. "How long has it been since ye bathed?"

"I'll have you know I bathe monthly," said Jane. "I *am* a lady, after all."

"Monthly!" Ainslie parroted. "Nae wonder ye stink like a byre."

Jane made an indignant squeak.

"They'll have filled the bath," said Ainslie. "Time for a good scrub."

Jane crossed her arms.

"Am I gauntae have to carry ye there and drop ye in, like I did wi' Malcolm?" Ainslie asked.

"You wouldn't dare. I'm naked," said Jane.

"Your choice," said Ainslie. Jane wouldn't budge. "As ye'll have it."

Ainslie scooped her up, Jane squealing and struggling all the way. Ainslie's strong arms held her secure. She opened the door and kicked it closed with a foot, Jane's punches landing feebly on her arms and shoulders.

Ainslie dropped her carefully into the steaming tub, the water sloshing over the side onto the flagstones. The copper bath and soft white towels surrounding the tub surprised Jane, even as she crossed her arms insolently. She willed herself to stay angry, although the water was deliciously soothing.

"All right, I'm in the bath," said Jane. "Will you go now?"

"Nae," said Ainslie.

"I demand that you leave!" Jane said, in the most imperious voice she could muster. "I am a lady!"

Ainslie lowered her face to Jane's, so they were nearly nose to nose.

"And I am the daughter of the Lord of the Isles!" she said. "An' I'll no hae ye stinking like slurry in the ha' o' my fathers!"

"Fine," said Jane, disgusted. "And who is going to bathe me, as you seem to distrust me to do it myself? Some servant?"

"Nae," said Ainslie. "I am."

"Pardon?"

CHAPTER NINE

Feast

The bath had not been, much to Jane's surprise and consternation, exactly the intimate affair she was expecting. "You are disgusting," Ainslie had complained, scrubbing her so hard with some kind of rough sponge that she felt raw. "Is this how the fancy fowk in Edinburgh walk around? Ye'd smell that stink for miles."

Jane made the mistake of telling her about how the chamberpots were dumped out of upper windows on the Royal Mile, with the bastardised French cries of "Gardyloo!" to keep anyone below from an unpleasant experience. This did not always work, of course.

Ainslie had stared at her as if she didn't believe her, then shook her head as if to say "No wonder."

"Right," she sighed. "Oot the bath. It's time for dinner."

Ainslie wrapped her in a towel and then stopped her going after her clothes.

"Ye're no wearing those things tae dinner," Ainslie said sternly. "Ye shouldna wear them again. They should be burnt. Nae, ye'll wear tha'."

Ainslie pointed to an earasaid much like her own, and a saffron shirt to match it, draped over a chair.

"Ye need practical clothing," said Ainslie. "An' ye'll be much warmer in that. The wind an' cold rise up here like they dinna in Edinburgh."

Ainslie finally turned to leave.

"Ainslie?" said Jane, a bit shy.

"Aye?" Ainslie said.

"Thank you," Jane said in a quiet voice.

Ainslie didn't reply, but a somewhat fond smile softened her features, which up until that moment had been so stern and proud.

* * *

Jane stepped into the earasaid and wound it around her waist and shoulder the way she'd seen Ainslie do it. She marveled at the soft warmth of the outfit, how easily she could move in it, how comfortable it was to wear.

Don't get used to it, she told herself. *Once you get the machine fixed, you're going home.*

She looked around for her boots but couldn't see them anywhere. Ainslie's disdain for them was obvious, so she probably hadn't thought to bring them. Jane wondered at people who frowned upon her own hygiene but were perfectly willing to go everywhere barefoot, including dinner in a castle.

* * *

The great hall had a long table that was absolutely groaning underneath the weight of all the food. Lamb, goose, duck, potatoes, neeps, beer, wine, and whisky. Jane hadn't realised how hungry she was until she took a seat at the table beside Ainslie and could smell the food. Dogs played in the corner near the fire, and the entire room was alive with movement and merrymaking.

"We have a new guest tonight!" Dòmhnall announced. "The Lady Jane Crichton of Edinburgh Town!"

Everyone nodded politely to her, some asking when she'd arrived and how long she planned to stay at the castle.

"Would you like to hear a joke, Jane?" asked Dòmhnall. Ainslie stared at him in horror.

"Da, no!" she warned.

"Yes, sir," said Jane, who knew her manners.

"Do you know why Ainslie likes fishing more than hunting?" asked Dòmhnall. "When I sent her out hunting for one of the red deer, the fog must have been heavy because she mist."

Everyone stared at him. Jane snorted and then covered her mouth in horror.

Dòmhnall roared with laughter, and Ainslie put her head in her hands.

"I hope you'll enjoy your stay with us, Jane," said Dòmhnall, after the commotion died down. "Ye're awright."

CHAPTER TEN

Moonlight on Caol Ìle

The feast went on for some time, and people drank themselves silly on French wine imported from Calais. Dòmhnall seemed to have an endless supply of terrible jokes, and Ainslie was suitably embarrassed by them; Jane was surprised and somewhat warmed by the exasperated but fond expression they put on her face. Ainslie was also adamant about leaning over and telling Jane in a low voice that she could hunt, and hunt well. It was clear that it was very important to her that Jane knew she was a good hunter.

The rest of Ainslie's immediate family would be returning from Barra the following day, so the dinner was not quite as raucous as it could have been. Ainslie assured her that dinner would only become wilder as the nights wore on into winter and there was less to do outdoors.

Then Ainslie had led her to a room in the castle and told her that she would help find her a cottage in the morning. Ainslie had taken her leave and gone to her own chambers, or so Jane assumed.

Now she was standing in the moonlight thrown in patches from the tall window. Jane still marveled at how warm the castle was; she'd been in castles before but they were always drafty. It seemed as though something had been lost between these days and her own.

She held a cup of warm drink in her hands, which she sipped as she stared out over the water, where the moon made a trail to the heavens. So much had happened in one day, it was difficult to put it together. She was thankful for the silence, as it gave her time to reflect on the things she had seen and done. Tomorrow she would get Ainslie and some of her fellow clanspeople to help bring the machine over so she could work on fixing it. The idea that the machine may be beyond all repair was one she did not allow herself to entertain.

Jane glanced over at the fire in the bedroom fireplace, where logs were crackling merrily. She thought of the fireplaces in the great hall and the bathroom, wondering if this was the source of all the warm, cozy heat. She drew the tartan shawl over her shoulders; although barefoot and wearing a simple white shift now, she still didn't feel as chilled as she would have in her own manor house back in her own time period. The black flagstones on the floor were just as warm as the rest of the room, and the same was true of the entire castle.

Since she was alone, she allowed her thoughts to stray to the strange sensations she'd felt. Something about Ainslie was different, she was sure of it. Jane was not a fool. She knew women who were lovers, like Sophia and Maggie. Her own husband was a man who loved men. Yet for Jane, there had never been *anything*. None of the feelings the penny romance writers talked about, nothing like the kinds of things some of the more hellfire-and-brimstone preachers talked about repressing. Jane just assumed she didn't have any of those thoughts at all, which she found relieving because she frankly believed romance was a snare to entrap women into subservience. Her arrangement with David suited them both down to the ground, as she didn't want anything getting in the way of her scientific pursuits.

And yet, here… She was aware of something new, when it came to Ainslie in particular. She didn't know how to categorise it. Perhaps she would eventually find an explanation, but she shut down the idea that it might be attraction she was feeling. Sophia and Maggie notwithstanding, it was not the kind of pursuit a lady indulged in; there was a reason David's secret was only known to her and now Dr. Bell, who was far too much a realist to make bones about it.

She shut down these lines of thinking as she walked over to the bed and drew back the covers, sliding into the cool, welcoming, clean white sheets. The weight of the duvet rested comfortably on her, and she fell asleep to the crackling of the fire's low embers and the crash of the waves on the distant shore.

CHAPTER ELEVEN

Fishing Off Gigha

Against everyone's expectations in Scotland, in general, the sun was shining on a clear day and the sea was a deep blue touched with white here and there.

The sun streamed into Jane's bedroom, turning the flagstones nearly white in its silvery brilliance. Jane woke up, hair mussed, and stared sleepily out at the water. She blinked a few times and felt the deep ache of her body, all the way down to the bone. Time travel was apparently rough on the body—or perhaps it was the crash. Still, she silently congratulated herself as she had built a design that had kept her alive and without a single broken bone.

There was a tap at the door.

"Come in," she said. Ainslie's red hair was like a corona in the bright sunlight of the day. She didn't wear the circlet or torc she'd had on the day before.

"*Madainn mhath*," said Ainslie. Jane stared at her, puzzled; it sounded like "mechin vey."

"What?" Jane asked, yawning sleepily.

"It's Gaelic," said Ainslie, walking to the fireplace and placing more peat onto the dull embers of the night before. "Ye'll best start learning it."

Jane made a mental wild grasp at something in her memory.

"I thought 'good morning' was *madainn mhath*," said Jane, pronouncing it like "matten vha."

Ainslie snorted, as she stirred the fire.

"It is if ye're frae the city," she retorted. "That's no how we say it here."

Jane got out of bed and put on her earasaid. Ainslie glanced at her over her shoulder.

"We're going out today."

"Out where?"

Ainslie stood.

"You, my lass," she said, "are gonnae learn how to fish."

* * *

Outside, despite Jane's protests that she didn't want to learn how to fish, really, Ainslie's insistence that "Edinburgh women ought tae break the law sometime" would brook no argument. So Jane found herself back aboard Malcolm, learning how to fish. Or rather, she was watching Ainslie fish. It was not a particularly thrilling occupation.

"An' see, ye wait til ye feel a wee tug," Ainslie was saying. "Ye let him think he's won, see, an' let him carry it oot a while. Then—pull!"

She demonstrated by yanking back on the rod a little. Jane nodded. Nothing had attempted to bite on her line at all. She thought this must be the dullest activity anyone had ever devised and wondered why men went on about it so.

They were in a small inlet near a dazzling white-sand beach. The water was so clear and blue it reminded her of stories David used to tell her about his father's adventures in the Caribbean. "By Jove, Janie," David used to say, "the water was bluer than the sky."

Jane felt a sudden pang of loneliness. She missed David, sham marriage or not. He was always so sunny and ridiculous, where she was studious and serious.

"Where've ye gone aff to?" Ainslie asked. Jane looked at her, but there was no malice in it. Her expression was curious and a little sad.

"I miss my husband," Jane said simply.

Ainslie seemed to stiffen at her words.

"Oh," she said.

The silence was suddenly tense where it had been companionable before.

"Would ye like to get yer boat today?" Ainslie said, her usual raillery subdued.

"Yes," Jane agreed. They reeled in their lines and set the rods aside. Ainslie turned Malcolm toward the distant shoreline.

* * *

Upon landing on the opposite shore, Ainslie put a finger to her lips. She hopped out of Malcolm and dragged him up onto the sand, gesturing for Jane to wait in the boat. Jane complied; she certainly wasn't ready to face down a possible enemy clan.

Ainslie disappeared into the forest and was gone for some time. The clouds scudded across the sky above Jane, and the world was mercifully quiet. She wondered at that; Edinburgh was so noisy, with the bustle of people, and the trains, and the hansom cabs going to and fro throughout the street all day and night.

She saw Ainslie poke her head out of some bushes, waving to her. Jane got out of Malcolm after some difficulty in the dismount and walked across the beach to join her in the trees.

"The Caimbeulaich must've gien up," said Ainslie proudly. "It's still there. There's naebody around."

Jane was grateful, and she took the hand of Ainslie, who helped her down into the ravine.

There it was, glowing dull and bronze among the ginger pine needles and leaves. She dusted it off with a delicate touch it did not really need or deserve, but she loved to look at the burnished metal, its variance in dark and light hues, and its beaten-copper surface, no one part the same as another when passing a hand over it.

Then she saw it—a wire had shorted and broken, possibly in the crash. She examined it. Yes, it was a mere miscalculation—a tiny one, but enough. She sighed.

"What is it?" asked Ainslie. "Can you fix it?"

Jane bit her lip.

"If I was—back home, yes, I could," said Jane. "It's simple damage. Easy enough. I just don't know if I'll be able to fix it now."

"We can send to Edinburgh for a replacement," said Ainslie. "Ye ken we have trade wi' ports across Europe. We arenae 'savages,' whatever Edinburgh claims."

"It's not that," said Jane. She thought about what she could possibly say to make Ainslie understand.

"I'm a time traveler," she said, finally deciding on the unvarnished truth.

"Oh aye," said Ainslie. "Ye're a Druid."

"No," said Jane. "It's not magic, it's… I'm not sure how to explain. I am from the nineteenth century—six hundred years in the future."

Ainslie shrugged.

"Ye think ye're the first woman we've seen fall oot o' the sky?" she asked.

CHAPTER TWELVE

Crossing the Sound

Jane stared at Ainslie.

"You mean to tell me that there are other women who've fallen out of the sky?" she demanded.

"Well, no' women exactly, but aye, the Fae'll do that frae time tae time," said Ainslie. Jane raised an eyebrow.

"And you've personally seen this?" she asked, sceptical.

Ainslie looked a bit put out.

"Weel, nae, no personally, but..." she said. "When I was wee, my mum an' da said they saw a bright light in the sky, an' it fell; tae the earth or ocean they didna ken. They said it was the Fae, an' one day I might see one too."

"Is that why you were all the way over on this shore, 'fishing'?" asked Jane.

Ainslie rubbed the back of her neck.

"Wasnae gonna let the Caimbeulaich hae the first look at ye," Ainslie muttered.

"Hmm," said Jane. "Well, let's haul it out."

They rolled the machine together easily; Jane had made sure the design moved smoothly on land. It was the work of a few minutes to get it down to the beach and a bit of careful maneuvering to get it to Malcolm without grinding sand into its gears, but they managed.

The machine fell into Malcolm with a plop. Ainslie stood with her hands on her hips, surveying how much more deeply Malcolm was sitting on the water.

"It'll have to do," said Ainslie. "Now, let's get back to fishing."

She pushed Malcolm into the sea while Jane groaned in dismay.

* * *

Later, Malcolm was drifting through a small inlet on Gigha, the sun still shining brightly in the late afternoon. The two women were lying on their backs across the boat, on the opposite end from Jane's machine, their knees over the gunwales and toes dangling in cool water. They both still held their fishing rods but were laughing together, the sport forgotten.

"Nae, no' like that. Ye sound like a seal," Ainslie laughed.

"I'll have you know many seals have lovely voices," said Jane.

"Aye right," said Ainslie. "Let's try again."

She laughed a little through the opening of the song, but her voice gained strength as she sang on, in a rolling, deep alto:

Ho ró, mo nighean donn bhòidheach
Hi rì, mo nighean donn bhòidheach
Mo chaileag lagach bhòidheach
Tha phòs mi ach thu.

Jane joined in on the *Ho ró's* and *Hi rì's* and eventually was able to parrot a little of the ending, before she laughed again.

"It's beautiful," she said, when she caught her breath.

"Is it aye," said Ainslie.

"Yes, it really is," Jane replied. "What does it mean?"

Ainslie looked up at the sky.

"It means 'my beautiful brown-haired girl, my beautiful brown-haired girl, my girl with a gorgeous soul.'" Ainslie cleared her throat, as her voice had gone strange. "I will only marry you."

She looked at Jane, who stared into Ainslie's bright green eyes in the summer light off the shores of Gigha, hundreds of years before the world would even dream of her existence.

Ainslie began the song again.

Ho ró, mo nighean—

—when there was an unmistakeable tug on Jane's fishing rod.

"Oh!" Jane cried, sitting up suddenly. "Ainslie! I got one!"

Ainslie leapt up in a graceful, single motion Jane wouldn't have believed possible if she hadn't seen it herself.

"That's it!" she said. "Just like I told you—reel it in now!"

"It's strong!" Jane said.

"Aye, but ye're stronger!" said Ainslie. "Dinnae let it win!"

Jane's jaw set determined, and she pulled on the rod. She decided standing up would help her get leverage with the fish, but she hadn't reckoned on the time machine's effect on Malcolm.

With a cry, she was in the sea—but she hadn't let go of the rod!

Ainslie fished her out, the waters around Gigha being quite shallow, and hauled her up by her earasaid, laughing the entire time.

She stopped laughing when she saw that Jane had successfully hauled in a large sea trout.

"I didn't let go! Ha!" shouted Jane.

"Well done," said Ainslie, suitably impressed. "Let's get back; the family will want tae meet ye an' it's nearly time for dinner."

Jane sat in the bow as Malcolm cut through the waves on the way back to Am Fraoch Eilean, proud of her catch and loving the sunlight on the water as they approached the green island.

"I did it, Ainslie!" Jane shouted, grinning back in the spray as the trout jumped and wriggled at her feet.

"Aye, good girl!" Ainslie replied from the stern, where she steered Malcolm towards the island.

And then, under her breath, "My wee faerie."

"What?" Jane shouted.

"Naethin'," Ainslie replied and received the quick white flash of Jane's smile and a raised eyebrow in return.

Because, you see, she'd heard it.

CHAPTER THIRTEEN

Return from Barra

"Ye'll be bathin' again just now," Ainslie was saying, as they walked up the path to the castle.

"What? I just had a bath last night," said Jane.

"Aye, and we *savages* bathe aince a day," said Ainslie. "Twice, sometimes."

Jane sighed.

"I'm sorry I said that," she said, blushing.

"Ye may well be, but ye still believe it," said Ainslie. "There's less than—oof!"

A blur of blond hair and tartan had taken Ainslie down. They rolled down the hillside into the bracken. Jane followed after, shouting, and had picked up a rock to hit the person attacking Ainslie when she saw that her friend was giving as good as she got.

"Never do that again, ye mad wee bastard!" Ainslie was shouting, raining punches down on her assailant.

"Ow! I'm telling Mum!" said the man, which was…new.

"Och, *you're* tellin' Mum?" Ainslie said, releasing him. "Tellin' her whit? Ye ambushed me an' got your arse kicked for it? Ye deserve it, ye weapon."

"Nice to see you too," said the man, grinning. "Aw, c'mon, Ainslie."

Ainslie grinned back and threw her arms around the man.

"Welcome hame, Aonghus," said Ainslie.

The two looked up at Jane, still holding the rock, confused.

"I, uh," she said, dropping the rock. "I suppose this isn't needed?" Ainslie beamed.

"This is Aonghus Mòr, my little brother," said Ainslie.

"I'm your younger, bigger brother," said Aonghus Mòr.

"Cheeky!" said Ainslie. "Ye've a half inch on me at most."

"Shortarse," said Aonghus. Ainslie looked at him in mock horror.

"What have I told you about language in the presence of a lady?" she asked him.

"*Pòg mo thòin*," said Aonghus, and Ainslie punched him again.

"What? It's language!"

"Mind your manners," said Ainslie. "This is Lady Jane Crichton."

Aonghus smiled up at Jane. He was blond, with a smattering of freckles across his nose and bright mischievous blue eyes. His skin had pinked in that way of people who cannot be in the sun for more than five minutes without turning lobster-red. Whether or not he was slightly taller than Ainslie was impossible to tell, as he was clean-limbed and quite slender compared to her muscular frame.

"Pleasure, I'm sure," he said to Jane, hauling himself up the hill, Ainslie following suit.

"She fell oot the sky while ye were on Barra kissin' lassies," said Ainslie.

"Did she aye," said Aonghus. "An' I'll have ye ken I didna kiss any lassies, on Barra or anywhere else!"

"Listen tae that," Ainslie said to Jane. "He does aw the work for me. Walked right intae that, so ye did."

Aonghus whacked her upside the back of the head. She easily strongarmed him until he yelled for mercy.

"Little brothers, aye," said Ainslie. "Have ye any, Jane?"

"No," Jane said, smiling. "I was an only child."

"I dinna recommend sisters," Aonghus said, and Ainslie whacked him back.

Jane shook her head and followed them into the castle.

* * *

The sun was falling in the sky to the strange lavender of the gloaming, when they say the Fae and human worlds touch. The light turned the sea to a deep purple grey, and the world felt at once first-heartbeat and magic. The gloaming lasts a long time in the summer, especially in the islands, and gives the world a warm and strange look, like anything is possible.

This particular gloaming-time, however, was the backdrop out of the castle windows while absolute pandemonium reigned inside.

If Jane thought the previous night's dinner was extravagant, she was unprepared for the craziness of this celebration.

The fires had been stoked to their heights, and the dogs were running around with their tiny claws ticking across the flagstones and scrabbling as they tried to execute turns and slipped; they were well aware of the excitement that everyone was home.

Jane had thought Ainslie's family was small. Here, in the castle, with her mum and brother back, they seemed to have brought the entire clan with them, as well as many inhabitants of the settlement on Islay. The noise was incredible; people were shouting, laughing, singing; one man was even dancing around his sword in what Jane recognised as something like a Highland sword dance but more like the kind of thing you do when you're drunk to impress your mates. Jane wondered if that was how the tradition started, after all.

"JANE!" boomed Dòmhnall, parting the crowd as though it were the Red Sea. "Come along, meet my wife!"

Jane grinned and followed him up to the table, where she looked up...

And up.

She must have had her mouth open, because Ainslie was suddenly there and nudged her.

Ainslie's mother was everyone's dream of a Viking woman. As tall as she was broad, physically larger than all the men present including Dòmhnall himself. Her long blonde hair fell in a plait over her shoulder, and she had Ainslie's bright green eyes.

"She's no a Viking, she's a *gallowglass*," Ainslie whispered.

"A what?" asked Jane, wondering when her mouth had started speaking her thoughts without her permission.

"Later," Ainslie whispered back.

Ainslie's mum grinned at the two of them. This was somehow even more terrifying.

"Hi, Mum," Ainslie said. "This is my new friend, Jane."

"Hello, Jane," said Ainslie's mum. "I'm Christina. Welcome to the island."

"Thank you," murmured Jane, quite out of sorts.

"Have you found Jane a suitable cottage yet, Ainslie?" asked Christina.

"Aw, no, Mum," said Ainslie, embarrassed. "We were fishin', an' had tae get her wee boatie afore the Caimbeulaich found it."

"I hear you caught an excellent fish, Jane," said Christina.

"Oh aye!" said Ainslie proudly. "One of the biggest I've seen, Mum!"

"We're having it for dinner," she said. "I—Aonghus Mòr, you take your hands off that pie right now!"

Aonghus, caught red-handed, startled and ran off cackling with a piece of pie in his hands. Christina shook her head and sighed.

"I thought he'd grow out of that," she said to herself. She turned to Jane.

"You make yourself at home as long as you need," she said. "Ainslie will attend to finding you a cottage with a garden so you can work on repairing your boat. Let us know if you'll need tools or assistance. We are at your service."

Jane thanked her profusely as they went to sit at the table. The dinner was spectacular, and this time, champagne was involved. Jane marveled at this world she'd never known existed, even though she was Scottish herself. She wondered what else people hadn't told her.

The night grew late, although the light outside stayed the same deep lavender colour. Ainslie traded jokes and more punches with her brother, and the old men of the clan talked to her in Gaelic although she couldn't understand, and Jane wondered if she really needed to get back to Edinburgh so soon. She was a time traveler, after all.

CHAPTER FOURTEEN

The Women of Innse Gall

After dinner, Ainslie had a bath prepared for her again. This time, she did not accompany Jane into the bathroom.

"What, you trust me to clean myself?" Jane teased. Ainslie looked at her.

"Already showed ye how," said Ainslie gruffly. "Ye're a fast learner."

Jane bathed and returned to her room. She was surprised to see Ainslie sitting there.

"Ainslie?" she asked.

"I'm tae tell ye you've tae meet the Council in the morning," Ainslie said. "Then we'll find ye a cottage so ye can start work on your boat."

"The Council?" asked Jane, sitting on the edge of her bed.

"Aye," said Ainslie. "The Council of Druids. They advise my parents on political matters."

Jane sighed.

"Ainslie, it's not magic, what I did," she said. Ainslie cocked an eyebrow, puzzled. Jane just shook her head.

"Ye said ye come frae the future," said Ainslie. "Do ye ken if the Dhòmhnaill or Caimbeulaich win these lands?"

Jane thought of everything she knew of Scottish history, which admittedly wasn't much, but she knew the salient points—like the end of the clan system and the loss of independence from England and the various tidbits she'd learned over the years.

She also knew that none of these things would happen in Ainslie's lifetime and there was not much she or her family could do to prevent it. The fall of the Lords of the Isles would come much later.

Besides, some selfish part of her wanted to live in this peaceful little paradise with Ainslie for a while, fishing the sound, talking. So she decided that prudence was the best course.

"I've never been good at history," Jane confessed. "Science—that's what I understand best."

"Aye," agreed Ainslie. "Ye're a Druid, like I said."

"If you say so," said Jane.

"I do," said Ainslie gravely.

"You said your mum was a *gallowglass?*" asked Jane, to change the subject. "What does that mean?"

"It means she's a warrior," said Ainslie proudly. "One of the best. An elite mercenary. Da says he's very lucky to have her."

The gears of Jane's mind ground to a halt.

"You mean to tell me that they let women fight?" Jane exclaimed.

Now Ainslie looked at her like she had three heads.

"Ye're very concerned about what women can and can't do," said Ainslie. "Just what kind o' future will the people of these lands be facing?"

"It's very advanced," Jane said, unsure why she was feeling suddenly defensive of her own time period. "There are…trains, telegrams… motorised carriages and instant communications."

Ainslie snorted.

"I dinna ken how advanced it can be if they've decided to make women into slaves," Ainslie retorted.

Jane started to say they weren't slaves and then sat for a while and wondered.

"But, aye, women fight," Ainslie resumed. "As do I. As will you, if it comes to that."

Jane wondered about this possibility.

"But I've never fought," she said. Now Ainslie was really surprised.

"What, never?" she asked. Jane shook her head. "Then *claidheamh mòr* training begins tomorrow as well."

"I'm surprised," said Jane.

"About what?" Ainslie asked.

"Well…we've always been told that only men had political power, only men could fight, or teach, or fish, or hunt," said Jane. "Or…well, anything really, except for having or raising children."

"Sounds like something a cabal o' men would invent, if they wanted to consolidate power," mused Ainslie. "The same thing happened a few years ago wi' two of the clans on the mainland. One clan strategised to undermine the leadership o' the other, an' eventually mair o' the clanspeople drifted to the enemy clan because they believed it was stronger. Not that it was, mind, but they convinced the clanspeople they were in the weaker clan and so were absorbed into the other one. People are most easily led when they think it's themselves doin' the leading."

Jane was taken aback by these ideas. She wondered when this societal shift had happened and who had caused it to come about if it wasn't the natural order of things.

"Ainslie," said Jane. "What year is it?"

Ainslie smiled.

"The year of our Lord 1293," she replied.

Jane nodded, suddenly feeling exhausted underneath the weight of time. Ainslie noticed this and stood to take her leave.

"Good night, Lady Jane Crichton," said Ainslie.

Jane smiled, sleepy.

"Good night, Ainslie nic Dòmhnaill," she said.

CHAPTER FIFTEEN

The Druid Council

Jane awoke the next day filled with trepidation. She had always been a sceptic and didn't know how she would put up with a meeting of fantasists.

Ainslie came to fetch her early in the day. She led Jane out of the castle and, instead of walking towards the hills or woods as she expected, they arrived at a low white building with a thatched roof.

When they entered, an argument was in full swing.

"Pythagoras writes that we must admit the existence of the immortal soul."

"On this I do not debate you," said a woman, evidently in a disagreement with the man speaking. "However, what evidence have we of this? Nothing! I posit that the soul dies when the body dies."

"It seems that there will need to be some kind of unique revelation for us to understand this question," said another woman. "A fundamental shift in the way we think. Or *proof*, Liam. We have neither at the moment."

"Nor do we have proof to the contrary," argued the first, apparently Liam.

"Excuse me," Ainslie announced. The company turned to look at her.

The building was open to the elements, the sky and wind; thankfully the day was pleasant. Those assembled wore white robes, and there were men and women among them of every age and colour.

"Welcome, Ainslie," said the woman who had initially argued with Liam. "What can we do for you?"

"I've brought you another *druì*, like yourselves," said Ainslie. "This is Jane Crichton. Though in her time, they call you 'scientists.'"

Jane couldn't believe it.

"I thought they were religious?" she asked Ainslie.

"We occasionally argue religious matters, as you have heard," said the woman. "But mostly we discuss philosophy, politics, discoveries. Navigation. That sort of thing."

"You're scientists," she said doubtfully.

"Yes," said the woman. "And lawyers and judges. There are a few priests among us, as there often are among the learned."

Jane's mind was ticking over very quickly.

"And you teach people?" she asked.

"And each other, yes," said the woman. "My name is Morag. How can we help you, Jane?"

Jane, however, was rooted to the spot.

"This is a university," she said.

"Of sorts," agreed Morag. "Not everyone can afford to travel, so the teaching remains here. The Druid Council often sends people for further education, particularly when it comes to scientific discovery."

"And you allow women?" Jane asked. Morag nodded, puzzled.

"Why wouldn't we?" she asked.

Jane turned to Ainslie.

"Can we sit down? I feel faint."

* * *

Morag, it turned out, was one of the current heads of the Council, but these were voted on every so often. The Druid Council, she explained, offered the opportunity of pursuing scientific knowledge to the clan chiefs and chieftains, as well as advising them on various aspects of warfare and navigation. This was often based on the weather, which they were able to predict by a means of rude meteorology; a battle fought on a sunny day was much different than one fought in the mud and rain. Knowledge, Morag said, in itself was a power, and as scholars they spent a great deal of time conducting experiments and learning new things about the world.

Very little about them was particularly religious, on the whole. They were philosophers and scientists, just as Ainslie had said.

"If you need help fixing your machine, there are many engineers among us that would be grateful for a chance to learn more," said Morag. "And further knowledge you may have of the scientific discoveries of your time would make you an invaluable member of the group. However, that is up to you, as participation in the Council is quite a commitment. You're under no obligation; just consider our offer and let us know."

Jane thanked her, and the Council at large. Ainslie indicated that it was time to go, as they still needed to secure Jane a cottage and had not yet had the time.

* * *

They walked through the town. Or rather the city; it was certainly busy enough to be called such a word. Jane was very quiet, thinking to herself. Ainslie cast her a few curious looks until she finally stopped her in the street.

"Yer thoughts are bangin' on sae loud I can hear 'em," Ainslie said. "What's going on wi' ye?"

Jane collapsed against a nearby wall.

"Everything I've been told is a lie," she said. "The Druids were supposed to be these, I don't know. Magic men who lived in the woods, mistletoe, trees. Women are supposed to be the weaker sex and must be protected. Bathing is supposed to be infrequent because smell discourages disease."

"I happen tae ken that Morag is a strong proponent of handwashing before an' after meals," said Ainslie.

"That's just it!" cried Jane. "These...women are fighters, philosophers, doctors, fishermen. The men are different, too. I saw a man just yesterday feeding a baby!"

"Well, I dinna ken what they tell ye in your time period," said Ainslie slowly, "but the babby is also the man's."

"I know," said Jane. "That's just it! The fight is also the woman's! Just like healing, or learning, or food! When did all this change?"

"I couldna say," said Ainslie. "But I dinna like the sound o' your Edinburgh."

"It's not just Edinburgh," said Jane. "It's the whole world."

"Is it aye?" asked Ainslie. "Or is it the world as ye've made it? I ken well if ye tell someone somethin' lang enough, it becomes true for them. I also ken that a clan taken over by another adopts its culture. Tell me, Jane. Has someone else taken over the culture of Scotland and made it their ain?"

Jane couldn't speak, couldn't tell her about the ultimate fate of Scotland, of England, of the Lords of the Isles. But the look in her eyes was answer enough.

"Aye," said Ainslie, "an' it's why the word 'savages' beats sae hard in yer breast. Because even after all this, that's what ye think, isn't it? These rude, uneducated people. Weel, it sounds tae me like we aren't the savages. Not by a mile."

Ainslie nodded towards her feet.

"Like they shoes," she said. "Why do ye insist on wearing them? Torture. They wish tae mak their women weak, but first they convince the women they want the things that hurt them. Just like the enemy clan convincing the other of its weakness. If ye ask me, Jane Crichton, everyone fares better here than there. Savages or no."

Jane was overwhelmed. She had no answer.

"Right," said Ainslie. "Ye'll be thrilled to know that you're leaning on your new cottage. I hope ye like your new hame."

CHAPTER SIXTEEN

Bonfire

The interior of the cottage was warm and cosy, just as the castle had been. Jane still marveled at the difference, and as she looked at Ainslie stoking the fire, she wondered if she'd ever feel warm again if she went back to her own time.

Ainslie looked over her shoulder and smiled at Jane. Her heart did a strange little flip in her chest. She pressed it, wondering if she'd come down with something and whether there would be doctors she trusted as much as Joe Bell in this time period.

"Do ye like it?" Ainslie asked. Jane raised an eyebrow. "The cottage."

"Oh!" Jane said. "Yes. It's lovely, thank you."

The cottage was a single room, with a bed to the left-hand side and a fireplace in the wall opposite the bed. The front and back doors faced each other. There was cookery equipment hanging on and around the fireplace and mantel and a table on the right. A hobgoblin stool held pride of place next to the fire. A few windows let in the mid-morning light, washing over black slate flagstones just like the ones in the castle.

Jane thought it was delightful. It would be like camping, she assured herself. She could cook for herself like her father had taught her back when he had taken her around the Highlands. She found the prospect utterly charming.

"There's a wee garden out back," said Ainslie, indicating that Jane should follow.

When the door opened, Jane gasped.

The walled garden was filled from end to end with ivy and leaves climbing up and over the surrounding buildings. Red flowers bloomed as exclamations here and there among the green. It was stunning and private, more than Jane could have reasonably expected.

And there, in the centre, was her machine, glowing slightly in the green dusk of the garden, where sunlight filtered through the leaves.

It was less a garden than a bower, and for that, Jane was eternally grateful.

"It's wonderful, Ainslie," she said. "Thank you."

She couldn't be sure, in the shadows of the garden, but she thought she saw Ainslie blush and smile.

"I'll bring food and provisions," said Ainslie. "My family will be away again soon, and there won't be a feast in the evening at the castle, so I'll bring dinner and drinks to share in a few days. I've got work that needs seeing to, an' you'll need time tae work on your boat. An' maybe meet some o' the ither clanspeople down here awa' from the castle. Dinna worry, Jane; we'll get ye back tae yer husband as soon as ye like."

Jane nodded.

"Awright," said Ainslie. "Weel, if ye're set here, I'll go fetch someone tae deliver food. I'll be working for the next few days, but will see you at the third sunset for dinner."

"Thanks again, Ainslie," said Jane.

"Of course," said Ainslie, who seemed ready to fly from where she stood in the garden. She seemed uncomfortable, so Jane let her go. She had taken up a great deal of her time and hospitality, after all.

Ainslie nodded and left in a bustle of tartan.

Jane stood alone beside her machine, hands clasped together, unsure of what had just happened.

Sighing, she turned to the machine and began to pull out the wires and cords in the guts of the copper sphere.

* * *

The following days came and went in a pleasant sort of way. Jane had walked in the neighbourhood for a while after Ainslie had left, surprised that the place was always such a busy hive of activity.

She made friends with a fishmonger who had been impressed with her catch, and the local woman blacksmith had shyly handed her a little collection of rings she had beaten into a curious pattern. Jane felt welcome and a crucial part of the neighbourhood, as if she had always been there.

One evening, there was a knock at her door. An old man she had seen in the street the day before gestured to her, and she went outside.

Around the corner of the cottage lay the beach, where a large bonfire was blazing. Many of the townspeople were sitting around it, drinking and laughing. Jane was invited to sit, and so she did; her rudimentary Gaelic notwithstanding, the people talked to her anyway and smiled, handing around the whisky as the sparks danced into the night sky. She gladly accepted, and the old man sitting near her kept explaining something and showing her his knitting needles and what looked like a long scarf he was working on. He draped the scarf around her neck and clapped with joy, continuing with the knitting as the gathered crowd started up a *puirt-a-beul*, some mouth music she had never heard but tried to join in with anyway since everyone was encouraging her to sing.

She knew, then, that there was a peace to be found in camaraderie and that the word "clan" meant so much more than "family."

* * *

It was rather late in the day when Jane woke to a knock on the door.

She opened one eye and sorely regretted it.

"Jane?" asked Ainslie, poking her head in. She saw the state Jane was in and rushed to her bedside. "Jane, what happened? Tell me this instant!"

"Shhhh," said Jane. "Ow."

Ainslie cupped her face and looked into her eyes.

"Are you all right?" she asked, softer. "Tell me whaur he is an' I'll batter him for ye."

"Him? Who? Dougal?" asked Jane, puzzled.

"Dougal?" asked Ainslie and then narrowed her brows. "*Dougal.* Did ye go tae the bonfire last night?"

"Yes," said Jane, burrowing back under the covers.

Ainslie rolled her eyes fondly.

"Ye've got the liver o' a wee lamb, so ye do," said Ainslie. "But Dougal ought tae know better, he—ugh!"

She could hear Ainslie leave the cottage and dimly heard a discussion in rapid-fire Gaelic out in the street, Dougal's voice raised in defensive tones.

Ainslie returned after a while, shaking her head.

"Says he just wanted tae make ye feel welcome," said Ainslie. "Knitting ye a scarf, o' all things! Ye'd think ye were the queen o' Scotland with aw this carry-on."

"I feel awful," Jane complained. "I felt wonderful last night."

"Aye, I'm sure ye did," said Ainslie. "Next time dinna drink wi' the lads an' lassies at the fire, awright? No' afore ye've had a chance tae convince yer liver it's no needed."

"Okay," mumbled Jane. Ainslie sighed.

"Right," she said and set about to cook soup for Jane over the fire.

* * *

A few more days passed, and Jane wondered if she'd dreamt the entire thing.

She remembered, dimly, Ainslie holding her while she slept, curling fingers in her hair, singing in soft, low Gaelic tones.

She remembered being woken and fed soup, Ainslie muttering that it wasn't just a hangover, but something else.

The worried look in her green eyes when Jane's had fluttered open to look up.

And then, just like that...

The fever passed, and she was alone, as if Ainslie had never been there.

Maybe she had dreamt it.

Jane found that she was able to walk around again and enjoy the day, although it was now foggy and overcast again. Dougal had seen her and apologised profusely, but Jane tried to soothe and reassure him that none of it had been his fault. Travel often made her ill; time travel apparently even more so. And yet Ainslie remained conspicuously absent.

She'd gone back to work on her machine now that her head had cleared and she'd gained some strength back. She wondered if the exposure to the elements in the back garden may have had a deleterious effect on the machine's copper exterior. Moreover, she wondered if she would be able to jury-rig the wiring she needed; there wasn't going to be much available in the local area. Idly, she wondered if Aileen the blacksmith would be able to help her create something that would do well enough to bring her home.

"You're killing me here," Jane sighed, as she caressed the sphere. "What do you need?"

"I thought I was the only one who talked to their boat," said a voice behind her, making her jump.

"Ainslie!" cried Jane, embracing her without thinking. "Where have you been?"

"Plannin' the next meeting," said Ainslie. "Sorry I was away sae lang, but it'll be a larger gathering than the Dhòmhnaill have ever seen; it took mair time than I could have predicted."

Somehow, Jane got the sense that Ainslie was hiding something.

"That's all right, you're here now," said Jane, shrugging off the feeling.

"How are the repairs coming along?" asked Ainslie.

Jane sighed.

"I think I've found the problem, but I'm not sure how to fix it," she said. "It's going to take some time, and hopefully I'll figure out some invention or another."

"Weel, it's time ye took a break," said Ainslie, lifting a bottle.

"What's that for?" asked Jane.

"Ye dinna remember?" she asked. "I told ye, when my parents left for their journey, I'd come by your cottage. Dinner and drinks?"

"Is it a date?" asked Jane, regretting the sentence the moment it left her mouth.

But Ainslie beamed.

"If ye want it to be," she said. "Let's eat."

CHAPTER SEVENTEEN

Whisky and Cranachan

Ainslie brought a tartan blanket and spread it out in front of the fireplace. She began to unpack everything she'd brought with her and set it out, along with plates and cutlery.

"What about the table?" asked Jane, sitting down with her.

"What about it?" asked Ainslie. Jane didn't have much of an argument for that; it was oddly more comfortable sitting on the floor in front of the fire.

"So, we have my da's famous goose," Ainslie said, setting out box after box, "an' the tablet that Aonghus likes to make, an' the pies fae my gran."

"Men cook?" asked Jane. Ainslie shot her a puzzled look.

"Aye, how else will they eat?" she asked, then shook her head. "The future is strange."

She brought out a couple of bottles of wine and then another bottle wrapped in paper and string. She treated it with such reverence, and it looked so different from everything else that Jane was curious.

"What's that?" she asked, moving closer to see.

"*This,*" said Ainslie with pride, "is the first whisky the Dhòmhnaill ever bottled, after learning from the French. We use barley instead of grapes, o' course, as we cannae grow grapes here."

"You trade with the French often?" asked Jane.

"Aye, they are our allies," said Ainslie. "The clan wants to make it a military allegiance too, but we haven't yet achieved it."

"The Auld Alliance," Jane marveled, nearly to herself, but Ainslie caught it and shot her a quizzical look. "I'll tell you someday."

The centuries-long alliance between the French and the Scots, leading to many crests and mottoes written in the French language, was the kind of future detail that Jane feared might result in her changing things. Ainslie was the inheritor of the chiefship, and this was the kind of political information that could change the course of history forever.

Fortunately, Ainslie had found herself a distraction.

"Anyway," Ainslie said, unwrapping her prize. "This is twenty-five-year-old heather honey whisky. It's for dessert."

She set the bottle down and dished out plates for the two of them.

* * *

"This is *incredible*," moaned Jane through a mouthful of food. "What is it?"

"Do they no teach ladies no' tae talk wi' their mouths full?" asked Ainslie. Jane smacked her lightly on the arm and she laughed. "That's a family recipe."

Jane stared at her.

"*You* made this?" she asked. Ainslie grinned and shook her head.

"Nae. Aonghus did. Slow-roast lamb in sauce," she said. "Dinnae look so surprised. I like to eat good food."

"I'm just surprised you got Aonghus to do something for you," said Jane.

"Ah, weel," she said, "he's a good brother, sometimes."

Jane finished her bite before she spoke again.

"This isn't just good," said Jane. "This is…"

She searched for the right word and found her wineglass instead.

"Is it aye," Ainslie teased. "Carefu' wi' the wine now. I'll no be takin' care of ye again."

"Oh, but you would," said Jane, digging into her food again.

"Aye," said Ainslie faintly. "I would."

"So you trade with the French and with other clans?" asked Jane.

"Yes, and the English sometimes too," said Ainslie.

"Is that why you all speak English?"

"Aye, all those who travel are expected to speak it," said Ainslie. "Our native tongue is Gaelic, but we know there is a world outside these islands. I speak Norse and French as well. And Arabic." Jane stared at her, feeling suddenly undereducated.

"I only speak English," she said.

"Your Gaelic is coming along," said Ainslie. She ate the lamb and mash with gusto, between swallows of wine. "Tell me about your family at hame."

Jane looked at her, this woman who would one day be the equivalent of a queen. Or a king, she supposed, in the way she thought of the world. Ainslie was still barefoot, and apart from a few social niceties, she didn't seem to care whether she looked prim and proper while eating. Somehow, she still looked like royalty.

"My mother would have a fit if she could see me now," Jane admitted.

"Oh? Why's that?" asked Ainslie, and Jane told her all about growing up in Edinburgh.

* * *

Jane's mother's family was upper crust and had been involved with the woolen textile business at just the right time to take advantage of the madness for tartan after King George's entrance into Edinburgh in 1822. Jane's mother had been raised as one of the lovely daughters of the cream of Edinburgh high society, the type of people who had adopted an accent so ironed of Scottishness that it was nearly English.

She had been, therefore, if not aristocracy, upper middle class and a woman with aspirations for more. She loved Jane's father, but Jane always had the impression she wished that she'd married up instead. Although her mother had never said a word about it, the way she had raised Jane made it clear that she had shifted her aspirations to her daughter. Jane remembered many a lesson at the table—about how to sit properly, to memorise the placement of the cutlery, to speak only when spoken to, the kind of daughter a real aristocrat might have. Of course, real aristocrats had absolutely dreadful children, and no amount of Jane's walking through their modest home balancing a book on her head would change the reality of her social status. Still, her mother had pressed on, with elocution lessons and other mindless knowledge that she thought Jane would need to attract a good husband, but had only marked her as the type of social-climbing aspirational upper middle class girl who was in search of a good match.

Jane, for her part, went along with it, because she had never had a particular desire for anyone and it seemed to make Mother happy. When Jane announced her betrothal to David, her mum had cried tears of joy. Her father had been quietly proud but had told her, "You dinnae need anyone tellin' ye your worth, Janie. Independence is the best part o' your character an' the most important thing in the world."

Her father supported Scottish independence with a fierceness her mother found off-putting and a little backward, but he had grown up in the Highlands, where the aftereffects of Culloden were still felt. He was a *teuchter* by his own admission; although that slightly pejorative name for a Highlander carried some negative connotations with it, he always said he was proud of his origins. He had been a farmer who had met her mother in the city on a trip, and they had fallen in love, leading to the disappointment of her mother's social aspirations.

When her parents married, her mother insisted they stay in Edinburgh, and so her father left the farm behind forever. Jane could not imagine her mother living on a farm, but she did see the wistful look on her father's face sometimes when they traveled anywhere the wide green countryside could be seen in the distance.

Still, it was love, her father had said, and there was nothing to be done about it. "Ye jist canna predict these things, Janie," her father said. "Ye ken when ye ken."

But Jane hadn't. Her entire life had been devoted to scientific pursuits, her mother's tutelage, and her father's kind words. It was enough. When she and the other women had made a splash as the Edinburgh Seven, her mother had despaired—no man wanted a clever wife—and she lamented that all her work had been for naught.

It was 1876, three years after she should have graduated, and her mother's insistence that she had little time left to make a good match had finally gotten to her on that cool, misty afternoon. The Scots married slightly later than their counterparts in England, waiting until their late 20s or early 30s to wed, but her mother argued that Jane's single status at the age of twenty-five meant that she had little time left to find a partner. Jane had lost her temper and shouted at her own mother, behaviour most unbecoming of a lady, in the street in front of hundreds of passersby.

She and her mother had been arguing outside of one of the bookshops on the Royal Mile, and when Jane raised her voice to insist that her mother was an old crone with even older beliefs about women and their roles in life, Jane's mother had left in a huff.

Jane had stood staring despondently after her mother, unsure of what to do or how to make it right.

"If I may be so bold," said a voice at her elbow, "I think I may have a solution for you."

She'd looked up into David's pleasant face. She knew Lord Crichton, of course; they spoke frequently, as he had been at university with her, but he was majoring in political science. He explained that he was having similar troubles with his own family, as he was older than Jane by a couple of years.

"The damned *pressure* of it all, Janie, I swear," David had said, as they walked along the street together. "A man enjoys his tipple, a bit much, yes, but I pushed a policeman off his bicycle only that one time."

David's suggestion was that they strike up a courtship for a number of months, at the end of which he would propose. They would marry eventually, and she would have all the time and money in the world for her scientific projects.

"Yes, this all sounds lovely, David, but it's very one-sided, is it not?" Jane reasoned. "What earthly reason would make you offer me all this?"

David suddenly looked hunted.

"Do you know a place we might be able to go?" he said. "Private, free of judgment? And listening ears?"

Jane smiled.

"I've got something even better," she said.

Edinburgh, for all its faults, is yet one of the most mysterious cities in the world. Its haunting wynds and closes make it one of the most fascinating places for either a mystery or an adventure. Although Jane's mother was ambitious, her father was anything but. Jane recalled many a holiday tramping through the mud in her wellies at her father's family home in the Highlands, happier than she had ever been. This meant that she was more likely to mix with people of all backgrounds, and it was in this way she had found the Edinburgh beneath Edinburgh.

For, you see, the city had many faces, and one of them was the underground population of the working class. In Edinburgh, the town the rich and well-to-do frequented had been built quite literally on top of the one where the working class lived, meaning that these two worlds were more divorced than usual from each other. Jane, endlessly curious, had discovered the belowstreets of Edinburgh and visited often, although if her mother ever found out it would probably be the death of her.

"Blimey, Janie, how'd you ever find out this was here?" asked David, as she escorted him through the milling crowds of people in Mary King's Close. "Absolutely topping! Brilliant!"

"This is where the people who do the real work live," said Jane. "They live too close together and the poverty in this area caused one of the worst outbreaks of the Black Death."

"Hm," clucked David. "Well, we shall look into lending a helping hand down here when we are married."

"Yes," agreed Jane. "Now, then. What is it you wanted to tell me?"

* * *

Here, Jane paused; Ainslie's bright green eyes were attentive, but she felt it prudent not to explain what had happened that evening.

David had looked around, but no one was paying them any attention, aside from general surprise at their presence. It didn't pay to watch anyone too closely in Mary King's Close, after all.

"None of the boys from your club are going to be here," said Jane. "Out with it, David."

And that was when Jane learned that David preferred men but could not be found out if he wanted to pursue a career in politics or keep his inheritance, his family's honour, his personal safety, and his life.

She remembered that she hadn't been particularly surprised or confused by his confession. Although no one had told her it was possible to love someone of the same sex, she was a scientist; it was logical to her and the laws of society were illogical.

"If I agree to your proposition," said Jane, "I'd like to wait until we're both thirty before we marry. There are so many things I'd like to do first."

"My family's wealth will provide for whatever you need," David assured her, smiling. "And you will have all the freedom you desire. But yes, that is the normal custom these days, isn't it? The done thing, waiting until we're established a bit. Thirty is a good round number. We must make the thing believable, after all, and a few years of courtship would make more sense than a few short months."

"Then it's agreed," she said.

"Seconded," said David.

They shared a smile.

"So," he said. "What is it that you'd like time to do, future wife?"

Jane's smile grew.

"Invention."

David and Jane needn't have worried whether others found their courtship believable. They discovered, after a time, that they were both considered eccentrics by their classmates and the world at large. Why shouldn't two of the most well-known eccentrics in Edinburgh high society fall in love with each other? Many people commented about their relationship, but more in the vein of wondering why they hadn't thought of it themselves. Jane and David were a perfect match, and most of the things they got up to were written off as just another eccentricity. Scotland, as always, was fond of its pet eccentrics, and so Jane and David found their marriage an agreeable one, accepted by all. Her mother in particular was over the moon with her daughter's social climbing.

She and David became much closer as friends over their long-pretended courtship and were both delighted to find much to their liking in the personality of the other. They became fast friends, and then best friends, as David in particular was happy to be able to discuss his private interests with someone from whom he feared no repercussion. Their partnership was unbreakable, as she was his only confidant. They visited Mary King's Close more often throughout their courtship, and after their wedding, they set up a charity for mothers and children living in the Close. Jane volunteered there as a doctor from time to time.

And their secret stayed with them, until Joe Bell had witnessed the first flight of her time machine, several years after her marriage to David, in Jane's thirty-seventh year.

Jane didn't think the circumstances were relevant, and it was not really her secret to share, even with a woman born long before either David or herself.

* * *

"He'd had some other troubles," Jane settled on vaguely. Ainslie nodded.

"You must miss him very much," she said, her voice a bit diminished.

"Oh, I do," said Jane. "David is…well, he's really quite foolish, but a sweetheart."

Ainslie reached into the basket she had brought and pulled out a dish.

"What's that?" asked Jane.

"Cranachan," she said. "It's usually for breakfast, but it's a special occasion."

Jane stared at her.

"You have cranachan for breakfast?" she asked.

"Aye," said Ainslie.

"Doesn't it have whisky in it?"

"Aye?" said Ainslie, raising an eyebrow.

Jane shook her head.

"Your Edinburgh doesn't sound much fun," said Ainslie, handing her the dessert. "Here ye are. We'll have it wi' the whisky."

CHAPTER EIGHTEEN

Taste of Honey

"My gran was a great fighter, just like Mum," said Ainslie, as Jane watched her lick the last of the cream off her spoon.

"Your gran that made the pies," said Jane, disbelieving.

"Aye, ye can make pies and kill fowk," said Ainslie. "Why couldn't ye?"

"Because…" Jane started. She thought about it. She really didn't have an answer.

"Was your granddad a—a…" she said, groping for something she considered intimate women's work. "Midwife or something?"

Ainslie grinned.

"Nae, but Aonghus has presided o'er the births o' many clanspeople," she said.

Now Jane was really certain Ainslie was pulling her leg.

"What? Aonghus?" she exclaimed, thinking of the mischievous blond lad.

"Aye, Aonghus!" Ainslie confirmed. "He's sic a gentle soul, oor Aonghus. It's a good thing he's no' in line to be chief. He's interested in becoming a *fáidh*."

"A father?" asked Jane. "So are most men. They aren't doing the work."

Ainslie laughed.

"Nae, a *fàidh*," she said. "A sooth-sayer. A seer. They are...people who find out what is wrong with you, like disease, and make ye better."

"Oh!" she said. "He wants to be a doctor."

"If ye say so," she said. "Mostly he wants to be a midwife, as ye said. He is a gentle wee soul."

Ainslie poured the whisky into two glasses.

"Now, dinnae drink sae fast this time," she advised. Jane smiled.

She put the glass to her lips and tasted the spice of peat and honey, sweet and warming, like drinking a bonfire, like her lips were aflame. She poked her tongue out to catch the escaped drops and saw Ainslie watching her hungrily before she seemed to come out of it and drink her own.

Some time later, the whisky bottle now half-full, Jane collapsed against the side of the bed next to Ainslie.

"You're so smart," she complained. "An'...strong. An' you don't hafta wear shoes."

She clicked the heels of her boots against the floor.

"Ye've nae head for the liquor at a', do ye?" Ainslie smiled fondly.

"I hafta follow all these rules," Jane whined. She stared at Ainslie— for far too long, she slowly realised.

Ainslie looked at her, very seriously.

"Ye dinnae have to here," she said. "There're nae rules here."

She moved closer.

Jane saw her beautiful features lit in stark contrast, as the light from the flames illuminated one side of her face.

"Ye can hae what you want here, Jane," she whispered, staring at Jane's mouth and then her eyes, as if making certain of something.

Jane stared at her, at the curve of her lips, and swallowed.

"What're you—" Jane began, as Ainslie tilted her chin up and brushed her lips across Jane's.

* * *

Jane made a startled noise of surprise, which Ainslie apparently took as approval. She deepened the kiss.

Jane's head was swimming. She tasted heather and honey and the peat-fires burning, the wild and the wet and the mist, the sea and the sound of a thousand swords. She wrapped her arm around Ainslie and pulled her forward, sucking that plush lower lip into her mouth, chasing the taste. She felt so daring and romantic, a new adventurer, maybe even worthy of the clan. Her heart beat as they kissed, her hands drifting into Ainslie's long ginger hair. It was so soft, and she moaned and sighed against her.

Ainslie's kisses became more ferocious by far, and she had started to push off the shoulder of Jane's earasaid, growling through the kiss, little bites to Jane's lips, and—

Suddenly, she was gone, and she took the heat with her. Jane stared up, stupefied, heart wild as the wind in her chest, at the tall, proud woman standing above her in the firelight. She seemed ashamed and cast her eyes away from Jane, her chest heaving with exertion and desire.

"I am sorry," she finally spoke. "How could I behave so? Ye are in your cups, and ye are wed."

And with that, she tore out of the cottage like a woman possessed, leaving Jane to wonder what on earth had happened.

Ainslie had left the remnants of their meal, which Jane packed up. Confused, she set everything on the table and fell into bed, dizzy with confusion, with the taste of honey whisky and the ghost of Ainslie's burning kisses on her lips.

CHAPTER NINETEEN

Finlaggan

Jane had hoped Ainslie would return in the morning for the plates and other vessels, but she was disappointed. Around noon, someone she'd never seen before came to fetch the detritus of the previous evening.

A day passed.

And another.

Jane thought about that night, the events hazy now as most things are on evenings with strong drink. She wondered if it had ever happened.

After some time, she started to become angry when Ainslie didn't show. Instead of working on the machine or talking to the blacksmith about a few possible designs she had in mind, she stewed about the situation. After all, she had never once in her entire life been interested in anyone like that! Sex and romance were all one in her mind, things in which she had detached interest but did not apply to her. She was only a few years away from forty, so she had accepted it—as surely she would have had some inkling before now. She certainly didn't mind other people doing it; after all, she was married to David and was friends with Sophia and Maggie. Society didn't think it was normal to lack desire, let alone for someone of the same sex, but Jane had spent a lifetime being called an eccentric, and she thought society's ideas of normalcy were rather ridiculous. Still, despite her eccentricities, this was something reserved for other people. These savages (there was that word again!) were making her feel things she clearly did not. She was good and worked up when she finally left the cottage to discuss the ideas she had with the blacksmith.

Aileen, as it turned out, was something of an inventor herself. She showed Jane a few different possibilities, and Jane agreed that she should come by the cottage later on and find her, to see if any of the ideas would work.

The cottage was another thing. Jane began to understand that romantic places were not always pragmatic ones. Her initial enchantment with the place had started to wear thin, as most things do when they are no longer fresh and exciting. She'd nearly lit herself on fire a few times when she hadn't been cautious about her skirts, just like so many women had died in her own time period from letting their skirts get too close to the flames. While it was somewhat gratifying to make her own food, chop and haul her own wood, fetch and carry water, and all the other little things that added up to life here in the Highlands in the thirteenth century, it was hard work. She had never thought she might miss the neat clean lines of the manor house she shared with David, or the bright silver serving trays, or the servants who were so unobtrusive as to make things appear as if by magic.

Here, in the wild untamed lands of forest mountains wrapped in mist and the long white strand soft beneath the roaring sea, she was finding that it was one thing to read about the romance of the Highlands and quite another to live it.

She feared, in short, that she had become the exact type of pampered woman her mother had always hoped to make out of her. She held these secrets close to her breast, that she missed the luxury of her own riches and of the future. It seemed ungrateful.

Worse, it made her feel like a snob.

She resolved to push past these feelings of growing dissatisfaction with the crude and often difficult life in this time period. She assured herself that she could, in fact, live without a tea service.

Still, she missed it all the same.

Jane walked by the sea, alone; her thoughts were a tumult. She had convinced herself that Ainslie, or possibly this wild civilisation, had tricked her into thinking she was something she was not. Her emotions were so confusing. She refused to think on the times she'd caught the sunlight off the gold in Ainslie's hair and thought it pretty or the times her eyes had wandered to those soft pink lips, and now she knew how soft they were, and her green eyes, and...

Jane made a noise of frustration in her throat. She'd just have to concentrate harder on getting home. This place was changing her, and the last thing she wanted was to go native.

* * *

Three days later, Ainslie showed up at her door.

Nothing in her expression betrayed that she remembered their experience from earlier in the week.

"Ye'll need to come with me," said Ainslie.

Jane crossed her arms.

"And why should I?" she asked.

"It's time," said Ainslie. Her face was like stone.

"Time for what?" she asked.

"The gathering of the clans," Ainslie said. "We leave for Finlaggan in an hour."

* * *

Jane accompanied Ainslie to the beach, where an impressive fleet of ships awaited. She hadn't really appreciated the military might and political clout of the Dhòmhnaill clan until that moment.

Birlinns and nyvaigs, those old Norse vessels that looked like far larger versions of Malcolm, stood at anchor near the shoreline. The ships were filled with warriors in the process of coming ashore. Jane also recognised those on the Druid Council in one of the ships, escorted onto the sand by a contingent of the clan dressed to the nines in official-looking Highland costume.

And standing beside her parents, in front of the gathered number, was Ainslie, strong and beautiful in the bright sunlight, her hair a waterfall of burnished copper cascading over her shoulder.

"We will be at the Finlaggan outpost for a week," Dòmhnall was saying to the assembled groups. "Food and lodging is provided, but the lodgings are shared. Bathing is possible in the inlets or pools near the site. Directions will be given upon arrival. This is an important event for the clan, perhaps the most important o' the year. It's our chance tae show our strength, but also our kindness and mercy. We look to stave off war, not inspire it. Please do nothing to cause offence at Finlaggan. I know you are all brave warriors and learned people. Let the other clans marvel at our power, but also our mercy."

This said, Dòmhnall gave the signal to start the journey, and they set off down the path, walking towards Finlaggan.

* * *

Several hours later, they reached their destination. Jane and Ainslie had walked together, though little was said between them. Jane kept looking at her, thinking she lit up the sky like the sun, brave and proud. Ainslie preserved a strange silence.

"Ainslie," Jane said quietly. "Can we talk—"

"Not here," Ainslie cut her off abruptly. "Finlaggan."

And so Jane kept silent, a ball of anger simmering in her heart.

* * *

They crested the hill above Finlaggan Loch and were met with the wide views of rolling green hills on either side of the silvery water. In the centre of the loch were two islands, the larger of which held several buildings.

"This is where my family lives for a good part of the year," Ainslie told Jane. "Our time is split between the castle and Finlaggan, depending on the weather and the needs of the people."

The procession wound its way down the hill and across the long wooden footbridge onto the island.

Once everyone was gathered again, Dòmhnall spoke.

"This will be a large gathering," he announced. "There will be little space, and the Dhòmhnaill must be seen as hospitable. There is nothing more important than Highland hospitality. Therefore, you'll be assigned chambers. My family shall set the example and share buildings by twos. Ainslie and Jane, you will be in the far cottage on the loch edge; Aonghus, you'll be sharing with Christina and myself."

"Father—" Ainslie began, but he shot her a look that silenced her. If they were to set an example, Dòmhnall's family would be first.

Jane stared at Ainslie, whose face had drained of colour.

"It's not so bad, sharing with me, is it?" Jane tried to placate her.

"It's no' that, Jane, believe me," said Ainslie.

"Well, what's the matter, then?" asked Jane, temper rising.

Ainslie just shook her head.

The crowd dispersed to seek out their lodgings. The gathering would begin to take place the following day. Rest would be needed, as this was an opportunity to bring issues before the Parliament and Council. Everyone therefore retired immediately, to spend a quiet night of contemplation and get a good night's sleep.

Ainslie pushed the door of the cottage open. It was far smaller than Jane's own in the city, but it was clean apart from a bit of straw on the floor and cobwebs from disuse. Ainslie dropped her parcel of clothes and other necessities in a corner and grabbed a broom, sweeping the floor out. The basket near the fireplace had peat-bricks in it, and Jane went to prepare a fire for the evening. She suddenly froze.

"Ainslie," Jane said. "There's only one bed in this cottage."

"Aye," said Ainslie, without turning around. "I know."

CHAPTER TWENTY

The Gathering of the Clans

The night came on more swiftly than Jane was accustomed to after all her time in the city on Islay. She had expected the same sort of commotion here; after all, thousands of clanspeople were gathered here in Finlaggan, on the island or the surrounding hillsides. Yet it was one of the quietest, most serene evenings she had experienced so far. The silence among such usually raucous people made her contemplative, too.

All too soon, it was time for bed. Ainslie still spoke little, and Jane hadn't felt it prudent to bring up the events of the last evening they had spent together. They had crawled into bed and Jane resolutely faced the opposite direction. In the soft silence of the night, Ainslie had drifted off to sleep.

Jane, for her part, could not sleep. If the place was quiet, her thoughts were loud.

She had rolled over, certain of Ainslie's slumber, to take in the other woman's features. Relaxed in sleep, she looked sweet and almost vulnerable. She studied Ainslie's high cheekbones and blond lashes and thought she looked regal.

Which was the reason she was so badly startled when Ainslie spoke. "Tell me about the future," she said.

"Ainslie—"

"For now," she said. "Just...tell me about the future."

Jane was panicking inwardly; what should she say? All she could think about were words now infamous in Scotland: Culloden, Clearances, Act of Proscription. Everything they'd lost, although Jane only felt echoes of it now herself, having escaped the worst of it.

Then she thought of something.

"You know how it rains here all the time?" Jane asked.

"Mmm," Ainslie agreed.

"Well, one day there will be a man who will invent a fabric," said Jane. "He'll be Scottish, and it will be...a slick sort of fabric to the touch and absolutely impermeable to the rain."

Ainslie cracked open a disbelieving eye.

"It's true," said Jane, warming to her theme. "There will be surgery while you're asleep—"

"Wouldn't ye wake up?" asked Ainslie.

"No, it puts you—you know when you're very drunk and fall unconscious?" asked Jane.

"Nae, but ye would," Ainslie teased.

Jane rolled her eyes.

"So, they put you into a deep sleep and you don't feel anything," said Jane. "There will be instant communications, called the telegraph, and vehicles that will take you across the country in a few hours."

"There must be a lot of treaties with different clans and families to build something on that scale," said Ainslie. "And yet, for all this, there is inequality."

"Yes, I suppose there is," said Jane. "I am one of the first seven women to be educated at the university in Edinburgh. They shouted at us in the streets, threw tomatoes. They blocked us on the day of our exam, but we were able to take the test."

"And did the women do poorly?" asked Ainslie.

"No," said Jane. "Some of us scored in the top percentile of our class."

"Sounds tae me like they were threatened," Ainslie said. "An' ye must wonder, if they were so skilled, what they were threatened by?"

"They think the idea of women 'competing against the opposite sex' is uncivilised," said Jane.

"Ah. So they took our civilisation and thought it less than theirs," mused Ainslie. "Nae wonder ye think us savages, but I cannae think a world in which women are in a separate class is a truly civilised one."

"Well, I do agree with you there," said Jane. "Ainslie. Can we talk about what happened?"

But Ainslie had rolled over, away from her.

"Best ye get sleep," she said. "Tomorrow will be a long day."

Jane wasn't sure how to feel; she was both close and too far away, angry and confused. She did not like to admit it to herself, but she felt rejected. She decided that she would see Aileen the blacksmith on her return to get the missing pieces of the machine and leave as soon as she was able to go.

She wasn't wanted here.

* * *

The following day dawned, but this was only obvious because the mist was a lighter colour. There was a chill in the air, and Ainslie got out of bed to stoke the fire. There wasn't much to be seen out of the windows, but when Jane stood in the open doorway, she saw that many people from other clans must have arrived at different times during the night.

There must have been thousands of them, encamped along the banks of the loch, in addition to the chiefs and chieftains with their families, important Druid members of other councils, and other dignitaries housed in the Dhòmhnaill cottages and halls on the island. There were crowds thronging the place, but the same air of quiet was observed.

Jane would find out later that this was the calm before the storm.

Everyone moved onto the nearby Council Island by way of a stone path raised in the water. Dòmhnall stood at the door to a hall, calling the clans and their leaders by name. They entered the great hall, single file, and sat around the tables set up for them there. Jane watched as the hall filled with what seemed like all the Highland and Island world, chiefs and chieftains from near and far afield, prepared to participate in the day's events.

The council meeting took place in Gaelic, which Ainslie translated for Jane in a low voice. The subjects touched on various matters throughout the Sea Kingdom, including shipping and trade routes, treaties and deals made with other clans, the possibility of peace in the Highlands at large due to a federation of clans, the current issues with the Scottish king, and other aspects of politics and the island economy. Deals were brokered and treaties argued over while they discussed other points of interest raised by their constituents.

There were also matters of law to be decided, something which the Druid Council advised on. Multiple court cases were brought to them from clanspeople near and far. The Druid Council included all the visiting Druids along with the Dhòmhnaill advisors. All in all, it was fascinating, if long. Jane learned a great deal about how the world worked during this time and was intrigued to find how much it differed from her own.

Then Ainslie rose and addressed the assembled group.

"I nominate Lady Jane Crichton for the Druid Council," she announced in Gaelic and then English, so Jane could understand.

Jane gasped and stared up at her.

"She is a brilliant and talented individual," Ainslie went on. "She also has information that will benefit the Dòmhnaill and the clans at large. I realise this is unusual, but so are these circumstances."

"Morag?" asked Dòmhnall. The gathered assembly shifted to look at her.

"I have met her," said Morag. "I agree there is much we can learn from each other. I second the motion. Jane, are you willing to accept?"

Jane's mouth was hanging open. She thought of the men at the society meeting in the Edinburgh of her own time, laughing at her, merely tolerating her presence. Here was a chance to be fully involved as a respected and equal member of a scientific community. And yet she still yearned for her own time and place in history, where she had already made history herself.

"Yes," said Jane in a small voice. "I accept."

She did not mention that she planned on leaving for Edinburgh upon their return to the city.

CHAPTER TWENTY-ONE

Waterfall

If Jane had expected the night following the gathering to have the same quiet, contemplative air of the previous evening, she was very much mistaken.

There was unbelievable noise and revelry, drinking and shouting and carrying on.

"What on earth is going on?" Jane asked, as Ainslie walked up to the doorway of the cottage.

"I was goin' tae ask ye the same, *an Drui*," Ainslie grinned. "We should be out celebratin'."

"We?" asked Jane. "Thank you, by the way. You didn't have to do that."

"Aye," said Ainslie, colour high on her cheeks as she looked at the ground. "We...Both o' us."

She held out a hand, and Jane took it. They walked out into the darkness, where any one of a hundred bonfires were lit that night, and hundreds of clanspeople were in the streets, out on the stone bridge, everywhere they went. People cheered for her, the newest member of the Druid Council, cheered for Ainslie, handed around quaichs of whisky and food and all kinds of delights until Jane was quite silly with it.

She danced with different people around the fires, the flames like Ainslie's hair, her inhibitions loosened by the drink and by being in a culture that drew her in instead of locking her out. She wondered if she had been bewitched by this land, this time, this woman. She told herself she was from a more logical, civilised time. That she should return to a place where proper people wore proper clothes and shoes and walked the city streets and had the benefit of luxuries like running water and macintoshes and wellie boots. Where the train could take you to London in a day, where the transport wasn't entirely by sea. As she watched Ainslie spin around in the dance with her kinsmen, laughing, she wondered if magic was real.

* * *

The sunlight falling across the coverlet woke Jane the following day, and she was surprised not to find Ainslie in the cottage or outside. They'd collapsed in the bed the previous night, exhausted, and Jane hadn't woken until well after noon.

"Do you know where Ainslie went?" she asked a passing clansman, who didn't seem to know English but recognised "Ainslie" and pointed at a grove of trees far above the island on the side of a hill.

Grumbling to herself and wondering what on earth Ainslie was doing so far away from the island, Jane made the long trudge up to the treeline.

She walked into the forest, quiet around her, a small breeze ruffling her hair and clothes. The day was overcast but bright, and the silver light shone through the trees. Jane continued on her way, until she heard a noise off the side of the path and went to investigate.

Pushing aside the branches of a bush, Jane saw a clearing of sorts. And her mouth went dry, despite all the water before her.

For in the clearing was Ainslie, standing naked in a bright, clear pool of water, framed by granite rocks sparkling in the low light reflected off the waterfall coursing down the side of the rock wall and into the pool where Ainslie stood.

The light was silver and blue all around her, a faery-light, unearthly. Her skin glowed white luminous, the freckles across her body like stars in the night sky, and her ginger hair was unbound, flowing dark and wet against the curve of her lower back, water streaming in tiny rivulets down her body, through the cleft in her bottom, down and around her powerful legs. She seemed to hear something and turned slightly, her green eyes glowing ethereal in the pond's reflection, her silhouette aglow, soft curves and hard muscle, the swell of her breasts, and—so like a forest nymph or supernatural creature was she that Jane whimpered in fear and arousal.

"*Halò?*" called Ainslie, and Jane, terrified that Ainslie may have caught sight of her, ran from the clearing as if she were pursued by all the devils of hell.

CHAPTER TWENTY-TWO

Flame

Back on the island, the shouting and celebration went on, and Jane knelt in abject panic on the cottage floor, desperate, not knowing what to do with the tumult of feelings in her heart, her mind. She felt consumed and had no idea what might be happening to her. She thought to pray, but she was an atheist. She thought to argue logic, since she was a scientist. And yet the feelings would not leave her be. She blamed a magic she had never once seen used in her presence but it *must*, it *must* be that, for this woman to have captivated her like no other person in her life. Words sprung unbidden to her mind— "queen," "love," "my sun," "forest goddess"—things her scientific, logical mind should by rights be spurning. She was wild, wild with the terror of it when the door burst open and Ainslie stood there, a storm brewing in her expression as she kicked shut the door and hauled Jane up to her feet.

Ainslie's eyes were all jade fire and her hair a halo, a living flame, as she spoke in a low growl to Jane, who looked down at the floor.

"I ken ye want me," she snarled.

"No," mumbled Jane, "No, you've—you've tricked me, it's a spell, it's…"

Ainslie threw her onto the bed.

"I dinna use magic," she said, crawling over Jane, who refused to look at her. "What you feel, what *I* feel—it's real, Jane, as real as this bed an' my lips on yours. An' if ye absolutely dinna want it, want *me*, even wi' a' the desire in your black eyes, *I will go.*"

Ainslie stared at her. "Tell me, Jane," she said, voice strained. "Is tha' truly what ye want? Shall I go?"

"Savages," Jane muttered. "It must be that. It must be. You've cast a spell."

"If that's what ye want tae believe," muttered Ainslie. "But I saw ye look on me while I bathed."

Jane let out an undignified squeak and glared daggers at Ainslie. "So did you!" she said.

"That's different! Ye were filthy!" Ainslie argued.

Jane sat up, defiant, about to speak, but Ainslie silenced her with a look.

"An' what was it ye were doin' up there, skulkin' in the bushes?" Ainslie demanded, advancing on her again, a waltz, a dance, a war. "Did ye like what ye saw, o' this savage?"

Jane felt herself lean forward, seeking, wanting, instinctively leaning into the heat of Ainslie's fire.

"Fair's fair," said Ainslie. "An' I'm naethin' but a savage, after all."

Ainslie reached forward and snatched at the strings of the corset Jane still wore out of habit, despite the comfort of her new clothing.

Jane gasped, perhaps in horror, perhaps in something else.

"Ye think me savage, and yet ye want me," said Ainslie, hungrily. "Tell me no, Jane, tell me now."

But Jane found herself voiceless, and she was claimed by Ainslie's wild kiss, easy as falling, consumed in her fire, in the flames of her hair unbound falling around them, in the touch of her heated skin.

The strings of Jane's corset were soon untied, the top few pulled loose. The soft white of her breasts rested against the taut fabric, the edges of her areolae just visible above it. Her mouth was open, panting, wanton; Ainslie's hand snaked into her corset and cupped her breast, then she latched onto it with her mouth, teasing a nipple to hardness. Jane cried out, mindless, animal, and Ainslie used it to her advantage, to kiss her and lick into her mouth.

Jane suddenly *wanted*, so blindly there was an ache between her legs.

Ainslie kissed her again, and then a hand suddenly rucked up Jane's skirt, the other pressing her forward onto the bed. Jane's eyes widened; she whined, out of her mind with lust, as Ainslie stroked the insides of her thighs with her fingertips.

"Sae soft," Ainslie moaned and drew breath as Jane spread her thighs apart, just a bit.

Ainslie's eyes fluttered closed at this slight surrender.

"Oh," she sighed.

Ainslie's fingers trailed up her thighs again. Jane held her breath, and Ainslie's fingers touched her—there!—and Jane made an inhuman sound.

"Ready for me," Ainslie said. "Wet and wanton already, ye'll hae ruined your dress."

She pressed a rough thumb to the hood of Jane's clitoris and began a rhythmic motion that made Jane cry out with the new sensations. She had never experienced any of it, being a good Victorian girl who had always obeyed the recommendations against self-pleasure and therefore knew nothing of what Ainslie was teaching her now.

Jane began to rock forward, she couldn't help herself, and a warm wetness drenched the ball of Ainslie's thumb. She let out a strange, long whine she did not recognise as her own voice.

"I ken well how ye look at me." Ainslie's deep voice rumbled across her skin, her tongue and teeth gliding along Jane's bare shoulder to the juncture of her neck, where she sucked bruising kisses, leaving roses in their wake. Jane keened, speechless, head thrown back, cheeks flushed, Ainslie's, owned. "I ken ye dreamed of this, of me taking you, of me bringing ye pleasure with my hands and my tongue."

Jane was an offering, a sacrifice, willing to beg. Ainslie's deft hand loosened more of her corset strings, allowing Jane's round, soft breasts to fall free. Ainslie lifted her, pulled her into her lap as if she were weightless, one hand clutching Jane's breast while making her grind down hard on the hand beneath her skirt.

"A fine lady, sae proper, everything in place," growled Ainslie in her ear. "But you wanted this. You want me. I see the hunger in your eyes. Now, here, underneath my plaidie, you're mine, fine lady, and ye'll do as I say. Anything I say. Won't ye?"

Jane's litany of "Yes, yes, yes" was barely breathed, but Ainslie heard it.

"An' sic a fine, proper lady ye are," said Ainslie, smiling wicked against her skin. "Who'd ken that underneath, ye were sae base, an' sae willing. But I ken what ye truly are, lady. Ye'll no open for just anyone, but ye'll open for me, will ye no?"

And then Ainslie fell into rough-spoken Gaelic growled in Jane's ear, as she slid her fingers deep into Jane's waiting warmth, the first time anyone ever had. Jane screamed as she clutched at Ainslie's shoulder, desperately scrabbling for purchase, and with a great gasp of breath, she came, Ainslie's long sigh of satisfaction mingling with her shout.

"An' again, my lass," Ainslie growled, crooking her fingers. Jane came again, and again, and again, until she lost count. "Aye, ye'll do as I say, won't ye, my little wanton harlot, slave t' my hand."

Ainslie licked and sucked at the shell of Jane's ear as she whimpered, trembling, coming down, the bed soaked.

Ainslie stood.

"An' sae ye call us savages," said Ainslie. "An' yet I ken it'll be you who's a savage for me, when and if I want it. A fine lady, who'll learn well tae beg for what only a savage may give her."

Jane lay panting on the bed, unable to speak, and Ainslie, still fully dressed, left the cottage.

CHAPTER TWENTY-THREE

Aftermath

Jane breathed.

In, out, staring at the ceiling of the cottage, counting the wooden beams.

There were many thoughts crowding at the edge of her consciousness, but right now, she was afloat in a calm sea, surrounded, it seemed, by green and growing things.

She was a scientist. She considered the events as logically as she was able.

David, her husband, preferred men. This was an aspect of their relationship that had always existed and one she had never given much thought. Since knowing Sophia and Maggie, she was aware that women also had the potential to be partners. Her own hangups probably stemmed from her mother's lessons on propriety, and yet she still seemed to have some of the wild in her, which she assumed must originate with her father and his Highland background. She reasoned that while she had not yet felt anything in particular for anyone, male or female, it was possible that she had not yet met the right person. It sounded unlikely, but she was also aware of the multiple permutations of nature in humankind and other animals.

Perhaps, here, Ainslie was that person.

She was lost in this contemplation of events when the door opened again, and Ainslie walked in. She sat down, heavy on the end of the bed, and stared into the fire.

Jane pushed herself up onto her elbows and looked at her expectantly. After a while, Ainslie began to speak in her rough, low voice.

"I shouldnae...I..." she began, halting. Jane watched the strong, supple form of Ainslie, framed by the firelight, shadows dancing on her skin. "I will tak the punishment, if I hae wronged ye. It is the custom of our clan...unwanted advances are punished. I am sorry I said those things, I—"

Ainslie hung her head.

Jane's deep brown eyes sparked in challenge. She stretched out her hand and placed it on Ainslie's arm.

"Don't you dare," Jane whispered, and Ainslie's confused look of misery transformed into one of hope.

"Ye mean...?" Ainslie asked, her tone doubtful. Jane could hardly believe this was the same woman, hunched in on herself and staring at the floor.

"If you don't get over here and kiss me right now," said Jane imperiously, "you *shall* be punished, I will see to it."

"Aye?" asked Ainslie, still hesitant.

"Aye," said Jane, rolling her eyes and physically hauling a startled and befuddled Ainslie on top of her. She smirked impetuously up into those green eyes, where a fire once lit was now rekindling.

"*Och, mo leannan sìth*," she sighed in relief against Jane's lips. "How ye've captivated me, no' a night has gone by I dinna dream o' those bright black eyes. Ye torture me an' I suffer it gladly."

She kept kissing Jane, her lips, her cheeks, her lashes, nuzzling beneath her neck, drinking deeply.

"Ainly let me worship you, *leannan sìth*," begged Ainslie. "I canna live wi'out the touch o' ye, in my dreams, my love, my love, my love."

Jane was bewildered and quite beside herself at this outpouring of passion, though she felt herself grow warm again for the want of it. Still, she needed to know.

"What are you calling me?" Jane asked, between showers of kisses.

"Oh, dinna send me away, please," Ainslie said. "I'll do anything, I shouldnae—I—"

Jane stopped her from kissing again, and Ainslie whimpered. Now Jane was really puzzled.

"Explain," she said, a harsh note to her voice.

"You—you're *leannan sìth*," Ainslie explained, a question mark in her tone. "There's nae ither thing ye could be. An' I touched ye, my apologies, but I ainly ken not tae touch the *gancanagh* and his ilk."

"I'm what?" asked Jane.

"A—one o' the Good Fowk," said Ainslie. "My sincerest apologies for usin' the word, but a—a faerie, the kind that makes ye fall into a passion, an' inspires ye, but ye'll no' live long for it."

Jane was so astounded she could not speak.

"An' it's fine!" Ainslie hastened to say. "I am honoured ye chose me, I dinna mind dying young if I am the pride o' my clan, ainly... dinna send me away, *leannan sìth*. Please. I only ask tae be allowed tae worship ye, an' that all my days, however short they be."

Jane found her voice, as her mind stumbled over the words she wanted to say.

"You think I'm a real faerie?" Jane demanded. "Not a pet name, but an actual faerie?"

"Ye fell oot o' the sky," said Ainslie.

Well, Jane couldn't argue with that.

"Asides," Ainslie continued, wide-eyed. "Why else would I feel this way? I've dallied wi' men an wi' women frae time tae time, an' some hae sported wi' my heart, but...naethin' like this. It's a fire, a hunger, eating me up. I canna sleep or think for the want o' touchin' yer cheek, for one glance frae your eyes, the benediction o' your kisses. I swear I dinna use magic on ye, nor bind ye tae me wi' a spell. This is real an' deep an' aching. I ken ye think us savages but ye live outside o' time an' we canna be expected tae be better than the Fae."

Jane could not think of an answer to any of these things, only that she'd thought it magic herself and she was supposed to be a sceptic.

"Ainslie, I'm not a faerie," said Jane. "I'm a human woman, like yourself."

Ainslie's stern and lovely face fell into a puzzled expression.

"Then why can I think on naethin' but ye?" asked Ainslie. "The night ye first let the pins oot o' your hair, it was like I was blessed. I couldna think o' anythin' else for days. Ye fell frae the sky, Jane. An' ye are my world, I never knew the like o' this feeling. I would gladly throw myself intae the fire for ye."

And Ainslie took Jane's hand and put it on her own chest, where Jane could feel the Highland woman's heart beating rapidly. She cast down her eyes.

"An' sae I only served you," she said in a near-whisper, "not seeking my ain pleasure, as serving you is all I now wish for in the world."

Jane moved her hand from Ainslie's chest, to cup her jaw, and then slide her fingers into that glorious wild halo of hair.

"I've felt the same," she confessed, "and I thought it must be magic, a spell, something turning my mind. But I don't think that's the case."

"You are the *druì*, the clever one," said Ainslie. "I will trust in your wisdom. What is it, then, this thing between us?"

Jane answered by tightening her hand in Ainslie's hair and pulling her forward into a fervent kiss.

CHAPTER TWENTY-FOUR

Leaving Finlaggan

They lay there for a while, afterward. The embers of the fire crackled, the noise outside was subdued somewhat because of the late hour, but it was clear that many of the visitors and the clanspeople of the Dhòmhnaill would not sleep until morning.

Jane traced the intricate patterns on Ainslie's face as she gave her a sleepy smile. The dark tattoo bordered her right eye, curving down the side of her face. It was beautiful and made her look deadly.

"What does it mean?" she murmured. Ainslie seemed bewitched by Jane, just drinking her in.

"Naethin'," Ainslie replied. "It's just somethin' warriors do. Sometimes for coverin' scars."

"It's beautiful," Jane said. "And scary."

"Aye," smiled Ainslie. "That's the idea."

Jane let her fingers brush the labyrinthine design, fascinated by its deep blue colour, like the sea.

"It was done after we were sent tae learn the language," Ainslie was saying. "It was in Glasgow I had the learnin' o' it, Aonghus an' Father too. I think Mum learned English from trading wi' the southerners. She's Norse, y'see."

"Christina's a Viking?" asked Jane, impressed.

"Aye weel, she used tae go viking," said Ainslie. "Granddad always said theirs was an advantageous marriage, but Da said he fell in love an' was nae thinking o' advantages. Mum said she needed a mair consistent occupation when I cam' along, an' o' course there was Aonghus after, sae she became a gallowglass."

Jane shook her head.

"I can't believe women go to war," she said. "Or that men care for children. Right now, the learned men—our Druids, I suppose—say it has ever been thus."

"Then the Council needs to be sacked," said Ainslie. "A lie told for their own ends, although I'm at a loss as to what could be gained from sic a lie."

She stared up at the ceiling.

"Although," she mused, "Adomnán the Saint claimed his mum begged him to stop women fighting. Strange man, calling himself a saint and a 'hero o' women', according to who exactly? The Christians have always been a little mad, if ye ask me."

"Who's that?" asked Jane.

"Oh, an old religious leader from Iona—if you could call him that," said Ainslie. "He gathered the chiefs and chieftains together and they all agreed on this law. Not that it changed much, to be honest. Women still fight. 'Innocents,' my arse."

"You think that's where it started?" Jane asked. Ainslie shrugged.

"All I ken is what my life is like," she said. "Men and women each do as is needed and as matches their talents. I'd hate tae see Aonghus forced t' go tae war, while Mum an' I love the fighting. Some men love the fighting, too, but it's no' a particularly male or female trait. In fact, thinking about it, about the only thing one can do over the other is physically bear a child."

"It does make you wonder who benefits," said Jane.

"Neither," said Ainslie. "Ye've got men an' women both doing things they dinna want, an' a powerful pressure to stay just where they are. I may no' be one o' the *druì*, but even I can see unhappiness there."

"What if a battle comes to you?" asked Jane.

"Ye mean if the clan is attacked?" asked Ainslie. "Everyone must fight. Everyone must protect the children and livestock. There is no one exempt. That would be foolhardy."

Jane was quiet a while, her lips ghosting over Ainslie's skin.

"In my time, this kind of love is illegal," she said. Ainslie's brow lifted.

"Now that is ridiculous," she said.

"It's dangerous," said Jane. "Death and torture are the punishments for it. It's why I married David. I should've told you before. He and I are the best of friends, really, but—"

"But you are not his wife?" Ainslie asked, a desperate hope she could not hide sneaking into her voice. "You wed him because...?"

"David is a politician," she explained. "An important man in our Councils. If he were to be found out, it would end his political career and he would be put in prison. One of Ireland's most famous poets has this reputation. He is not an over-careful man, and I fear that his flippant behavior will one day result in a court case."

Ainslie made a noise of disgust.

"A Council that punishes its poets for love!" she said. "What do they expect poets to do?"

"I really don't know," said Jane.

"The things ye tell me mak me think Mum ought tae go viking an' sack Edinburgh," muttered Ainslie.

"It's not just Edinburgh," said Jane. "It's London, and Paris, and everywhere."

"I think I prefer my world tae yours," Ainslie said. "Waterproof fabric or no."

She lay her head on Jane's breast.

"An' so ye wed your husband tae protect him," she said. "Who's protecting him now?"

Jane smiled and related the story of Joseph Bell to Ainslie, who listened as the noise outside died down to a murmur, and silence came with the dawn.

* * *

The following day was lashing with rain and wind. The visiting clanspeople cringed as they hurried across the stone bridge to the great hall on the Council Island but were happy to be greeted by the enormous, warm fires that had been lit there and the warm food and drink passed around to everyone. As it had been a late night, the Council had not started until mid-afternoon. This was the gentler part of the deliberations. Most of the disputes and serious political discussions had taken place the day before. This was a day of sharing stories, of learning from each other, and of strengthening bonds between clans.

It was an easy sort of peace, and Jane fell into it readily. She smiled as the Irish chiefs told wild stories and insisted they were absolutely true with a cheeky wink and a grin. Christina got up and recounted some tales of when she had gone viking to an enrapt audience. Dòmhnall then talked about the day of their wedding and how he'd cried at it, Christina crossing her arms and blushing in embarrassment as Dòmhnall got choked up again in the telling. The Sea Kingdom's success was not only in military might and political maneuvering, but in the kind of bonds strengthened by days spent on holiday together, talking about the world. Friendship is stronger than anything forged underneath the blacksmith's hammer.

The rest of the week progressed in much the same way, more of a holiday than anything else. People visited each other's cottages and drank together, they taught each other songs and stories, little snatches of language that might help in future trade, and the Druids of various different clans discussed intriguing points of law that had been decided in their time away. It reminded Jane of nothing more than a school holiday with friends not seen in a long time.

However, the time came, as it always did, for good things to come to an end, and Ainslie and Jane packed up their things and said their goodbyes to friends new and old. As the followers of Dòmhnall crested the hill above the islands in the loch, Jane looked back on it with fondness and linked her pinky finger with Ainslie's, if only briefly.

Dòmhnall, who nothing escaped, elbowed Christina and pointed, grinning. Ainslie looked at him in horror and dropped Jane's hand.

"Hush, you fool," Christina said fondly. "You'll only embarrass your daughter."

Dòmhnall grinned.

"Aye," he said. "That's wha' dads are for."

He looked wistfully at the two of them.

"Ah, tae be young an' in love," he said and meant it; his eyes misted over and he gave Christina a soppy look.

"*Da*," complained Ainslie, embarrassed.

Jane laughed, a joyful sound, in the bright sun that shone silver on the clanspeople walking up the path and on the green and bright jewel that was Finlaggan, set in the silver of the loch.

CHAPTER TWENTY-FIVE

The Warmth of Claig Castle

Ainslie let the door of Jane's cottage close with a soft *snick*. Jane was already at the fireplace, working with the bricks of peat, trying to encourage them to flame.

Ainslie took off her earasaid and threw herself across the bed like a contented, smug cat. She propped herself up on her elbow and watched as Jane made sure the fire had caught, bringing warmth to the cottage after a week's absence, chasing out the chill.

"It'll be autumn soon," said Ainslie. "The weather will turn, the nights get darker."

"That hasn't changed," said Jane, sitting on the bed with her. Ainslie gathered her up in her arms and coaxed her to lay on the pillow of her breast, strong arms holding her close. Jane breathed in the scent of her hair, peat-smoke and wild.

"Aye," Ainslie murmured. "But in the isles it's always been different than in Edinburgh, or London, or Glasgow, or any o' the great cities. When the gales come, we'll need tae keep safe, an' that means staying indoors for those as have the luxury o' it."

"Mmm," smiled Jane sleepily. "And you're planning to move in with me?"

"Aye," Ainslie said, grinning. "If ye'll hae me. But I thocht tae warn ye, as the winters can be wicked fierce here, an' the sea-spray on the castle walls, while I need tae be lookin' after the cattle an' sheep."

"But not for a while," said Jane. Ainslie looked at her, and her hand drifted idly into Jane's hair, stroking it.

"Aye, lass," Ainslie agreed. "Not for a while."

They lay quiet, listening to the crackle of the flames in the fireplace.

"If you thought I was a faerie," Jane said, "why would you take me in? The *leannan sìth* are not able to take anything from a mortal if the mortal doesn't agree to it."

Ainslie looked into the flames of the fire.

"Because I saw ye fall from the sky, and I went to investigate," she said. "And there, lying on the cold earth, on the cliffs above the Caimbeul land, was the most beautiful creature I could imagine, in heaven, on earth, or below. Your clothing was strange and I thought you must be Fae, for they are the only ones who could survive a fall like that."

She lightly scratched up and down Jane's back.

"An' I thocht, ah here is what the poets are on about," she said. "For I should gladly throw myself into the sea, into the fire, into the battle, for want o' ye, for a look of love from those shining black eyes."

Jane's breathing had slowed; she was weary from their journey and had fallen asleep.

Ainslie smiled.

"I loved ye afore I knew ye, Lady Jane Crichton," she whispered. "An' now that I do ken ye, I love ye all the mair."

* * *

Jane woke in the morning to the fire already merrily leaping in the fireplace, just as Ainslie came through the door with her arms piled high with food. When she saw that Jane was awake, her face fell.

"Aw," said Ainslie. "An' here I was, gonnae tell ye I cooked it aw mysel'."

Jane sat up in bed, yawning.

"What is it?" she asked.

"Breakfast in bed!" Ainslie announced, as Jane started to get out of the bed. "You stay right there!"

Jane fell back into the downy pillows and warmth, lazily glancing out the window, where she could see clouds moving across a blue sky.

Ainslie was busying herself near the mantelpiece, assembling the plates and cutlery she needed, along with a small tray to set on the bed.

"Here it is!" said Ainslie, with a dramatic flourish.

The plates were piled high with eggs, curds and whey, fish, and rashers of bacon. Tall glasses of milk were placed on the tray, along with knobs of butter on the side and sea-salt in a small dish. There were blackberries and strawberries, much to Jane's surprise. She looked up at Ainslie.

"Are ye fattening me up to eat me?" she asked.

Ainslie appeared to consider this, very seriously, as she dipped a fork into an egg, breaking the yolk and then licking the tines.

"If ye like," she said.

"Oh, you're awful," said Jane, grinning. She began eating her breakfast, the taste of each item unsurpassed in her experience. The food was the freshest she had ever tasted.

"Weel, dinna get too used to it," said Ainslie. "I'm a terrible cook. I had this made for us."

"My compliments to the chef," Jane said. "This is excellent."

"All from Dhòmhnaill lands," said Ainslie proudly. "We are in a place of plenty. Still, nae time to be domestic today."

"Oh? What's happening today?" asked Jane.

"Our presence is requested at the castle," said Ainslie. "There's a man that wants tae have words wi' ye."

Jane looked up from her breakfast, wide-eyed, and gulped audibly.

* * *

They walked along the beach to where Malcolm was waiting to take them across Caol Ile to the castle of Am Fraoch Eilean. The blue waters of the sound were bright beneath the sun, and Jane wondered again about this Scotland, where the weather and winds were warmer and the sun was more consistent than in cold, dark Edinburgh.

"Look, Jane," said Ainslie, pointing to the hills covered in yellow flowers.

"At what? The gorse bushes?" asked Jane.

"Aye," said Ainslie. "Ye ken what they say."

"I have no idea what they say," said Jane. "My 'they' are a few hundred years from today."

Ainslie grabbed Jane and pushed her up against a rock, kissing her senseless.

"When the gorse is in bloom…"

"…kissing is in season," said Jane, breathless. Ainslie narrowed her eyes.

"Apparently *they* haven't changed sae much," said Ainslie. She pulled Jane away from the rock and walked hand in hand with her until they reached Malcolm, and they climbed in.

As Ainslie pushed away from shore and they headed out into the sound, Jane laughed.

"Gorse is always in season," she said.

Ainslie grinned and sent her a wink full of meaning.

* * *

The castle, as always, was a hive of commotion with people going hither and thither, carrying papers or food or random items Jane didn't recognise. Ainslie caught her look of confusion and smiled.

"The Sea Kingdom consists o' most o' the islands between here an' Ireland," Ainslie explained. "It is here, an' Finlaggan, that are the capitals of this country."

"I see," said Jane slowly. "So…Islay is London, in this world. This castle is Buckingham Palace, and Finlaggan is Parliament. The Druid Council here and on the other islands are the House of Commons and House of Lords, members of Parliament, advisors to the king and queen. This is the centre of government, the capital of the Sea Kingdom. Dignitaries from around the world are often visiting, and the Druid Council is made up of those from this island and further abroad."

"I've no idea what those things are," said Ainslie. "But if that's true of your time period, then aye."

"I had no idea the Sea Kingdom was so far-reaching," said Jane. "Nor the kind of travel involved. In my time, I think we don't consider how often people travelled and how far. We think of travel as a new invention."

"Every generation does," said Ainslie. "Everyone thinks they're the first tae invent travel or sex. I always did think the cities an' their strong beliefs in our barbarianism were strange. I am sorry tae hear that prejudice exists in your time as well. We are sae busy that we're building another castle in Dunyvaig as another administrative post."

People think of Highlanders as barbarians in my time because we destroyed your people and culture, Jane did not say. She found tears pricking her eyes, thinking of all that had been lost between this day and those to come.

"Ah, that's just what I wanted tae speak to ye about," Dòmhnall was saying, as he overheard their conversation when they walked through the door of his study. "I'd like ye tae check on Dunyvaig Castle an' the progress o' construction. I'd rather the builders didnae work when the snow comes."

Ainslie nodded, and her father embraced her. Then he turned to Jane and put his hands on her shoulders.

"Welcome tae the family, lass!" he boomed. "I knew it'd happen, didn't I say so, Christina?"

Christina was just entering the room, preceded somewhat by a small, exuberantly bouncing dog that seemed not to walk or run but perpetually levitate in circles around her as she advanced.

"Yes, Dòmhnall, you did," said the tall, broad-shouldered warrior woman. She looked like she could heft her husband in the air and carry him on her shoulders without much effort.

Dòmhnall sat on a gigantic, overstuffed sofa near a fireplace and indicated that they should sit down as well. Jane sat with Ainslie on a similar sofa opposite as Christina perched on the edge of a thronelike chair. The floating dog chose to bounce away from his mistress and investigate Jane.

"Aww," she said, chucking it under the chin. "What breed is he?"

"His name is Madra," said Christina seriously. "He is a small idiot."

"*Mum*," said Ainslie. "Don't talk about him like that!"

She turned to Jane.

"He's of a terrier breed from Skye," she explained. "The Skyemen aren't exactly our friends, but Mum traded for him."

"I've no idea why," said Christina, as Madra made a snortling noise and then began to spin around in place in front of Jane.

"Mum, dinna say that," protested Ainslie. "He's lovely."

Madra sprang into the air, having returned to his levitation exercise once he had deemed Jane worthy of it.

"A Skye terrier, like Bobby," Jane smiled.

Ainslie looked at her, puzzled, but she did not elaborate.

"Madra," Jane said. "That's an interesting name. What does it mean?"

"It's Irish for dog," said Christina.

"You named your dog…Dog?" Jane asked.

"And why not? He is one," Christina said imperiously.

Jane suddenly felt that this conversation may not be going as well as she had hoped. She was saved, however, by Aonghus, whose arrival distracted everyone including Madra, who decided to orbit around him instead.

"So!" said Dòmhnall, after everyone had exchanged greetings and pleasantries. "Tell me how it happened! I want tae hear the whole thing!"

"Da!" said Ainslie, blushing to the tips of her ears.

"Weel I like a guid romance," Dòmhnall said.

"I don't think Ainslie wants to tell you the details, husband," chided Christina. "It's not as if she made to carry her away like we did in my day."

Ainslie, if it were possible, blushed even harder. This did not escape Christina's eagle eye.

"Ainslie nic Dòmhnaill," Christina scolded. "We do not kidnap brides! We do not go viking!"

"It's quite all right," said Jane. "She was a perfect...gentle... woman."

The awkward ending notwithstanding, this seemed to placate Christina, although Dòmhnall still looked keen to hear the whole story.

"I thocht she was the most beautiful thing I ever saw," mumbled Ainslie, "frae the day I found her on Caimbeul lands."

She took Jane's hand but stared at the floor, while Dòmhnall looked absolutely delighted.

"And Jane?" he prompted.

"She is a queen to me," Jane admitted. "And always will be."

"Christina, didnae I tell ye?" he said. "I will send for drinks, an' later we shall have a proper feast."

Jane wondered what on earth "a proper feast" could possibly be, given the feasts she had experienced so far.

"Can we have whitemeats, Da?" Aonghus asked, from where he was playing on the floor with Madra.

"Aye, son," said Dòmhnall. "We'll have everything laid out, an' the entire island will be invited."

"Come on, Da," said Ainslie. "That's an awfu lot o' carry-on just for this. We're no marrying."

A light danced in Dòmhnall's eyes.

"*Yet*," he said.

"Da is a hopeless romantic," Ainslie explained. "Mum no sae much."

Christina regarded her daughter with a steely look.

"I'll have you know I was very romantic in courting your father," she said. "I brought him the finest ale from my clan. We had sex three times the first night."

"Auuughhh!" yelled Ainslie and Aonghus, covering their ears in the way people do when their parents pull that kind of card on them, no matter what age they are. Jane laughed and Madra took this as a sign to start running around the room at top speed, launching himself face-first right into a sofa cushion in his excitement, and everyone laughed at that, too.

The conversation moved on to other topics, and Jane thought about how both she and Ainslie had believed their meeting was borne of some kind of magic.

She was sitting with Ainslie's family by the fire and being spoken to as if their kind of love was the most natural thing in the world; there would be a night of feasting in celebration of their relationship; and she would be on the Druid Council within a few days' time.

Perhaps there was magic in it, after all.

CHAPTER TWENTY-SIX

Aileen's Gift

The summer's last warm breath on Islay was replaced by the first of the gales blowing in from the wide sea. The cottage door banged open and Ainslie came in with a lamb in her arms.

"What's this?" asked Jane, as the wind whistled a vicious tune outside. Ainslie sat down in a chair and showed Jane how to feed milk to the lamb, which she would need to take back out to its mum after a time.

"The wee thing got caught in the mud," Ainslie said, creating a makeshift bottle out of cheesecloth and squeezing milk into the lamb's mouth. It suckled enthusiastically, and Jane grinned up at Ainslie from where she was seated on the floor near the fire.

"You're an auld softie, Ainslie nic Dòmhnaill," said Jane. Ainslie made a *tch* sound.

"Ah, I couldnae leave him oot in weather like that," she said. "He's just a bit malnourished. He'll be right as rain in a few days, an' Aonghus will hae a look at him afore I set him back tae pasture."

Jane petted the lamb, which didn't seem to mind that it was now being cared for by a pair of humans and had fallen asleep in Ainslie's lap.

"Say what ye want about sheep, but intelligence is not their strong point," said Ainslie.

Jane bunched up some blankets and they laid the sleeping lamb on them before turning to their own meal of soup and cheese. This easy domesticity was something Jane had never really known, a life she found herself falling into as naturally as breathing. The give and take of the harvest, the cycle of the seasons, the sound of a storm battering the cottage while they were snug and safe inside—all were the hallmarks of a simple life.

Jane and Ainslie slept, rolled up in the bed together, the rain tapping the windows and the wind seeking entrance, finding the little cottage well-defended, this place that sheltered the two women, their lamb, and the fire that dwindled to embers in the grate.

* * *

Jane's first experience as a member of the Druid Council was a fascinating one.

Many of the Druids were from elsewhere in the world. There were people of many nationalities and colours she would not have expected to see here, in such a powerful position in the holdings of a Scottish clan.

"Wisdom knows no borders," Morag had informed her. "Dòmhnall has sent emissaries far and wide searching for the clever and the wise. Diplomats are more valuable to him than warriors."

Although this may have been the case, the Druid Council was not currently discussing diplomacy. Instead, there was general conversation on the health concerns regarding the Black Plague, which had seen a resurgence in both England and Scotland, all the more terrifying because they did not know its cause.

"If I may," said Jane, who hadn't yet spoken, using her position as a relative newcomer to instead absorb the words of the learned men and women present on the Council.

"The floor is Jane's," said Morag.

"In Edinburgh, I learned from a physic, Doctor Joseph Bell," she said. "He believes that handwashing before surgery can be immensely helpful."

"Agreed," said Morag. "I have long held that handwashing before and after eating is necessary for a healthy life."

"Cleanliness is indeed a virtue," said one of the learned men, a black Moor named Tariq. "This man believes it relates to surgery in some way?"

"Yes," said Jane. "Specifically, he thinks that handwashing before surgery can prevent infection. Could this not also be applied to preventing the spread of the plague?"

This caused a murmur of conversation throughout the Council, and they deliberated on it for some hours. Jane suggested that they would really lose nothing by giving it a try, as it only took moments and not much was lost either way. This the Druid Council agreed on and that they would discuss this development with the *fáidh* to see if it was something that could be put into practice.

Jane had walked home in the overcast chill, grinning to herself. She thought of the Royal Society in Edinburgh, where she was laughed out of the room even though she had built a time machine. She thought of brave Sophia and the other women of the Edinburgh Seven, who had fought so hard simply to be allowed to study, just like men. And here she had her ideas accepted at face value and even deliberated upon. She may have been able to make an impact in a way that she had not back in Edinburgh, if only because women there spent most of their time fighting with other people over the fact that they were women before they even got to the point of scientific enquiry or academic pursuits.

She pushed open the door of her cottage, thinking she might talk to Aonghus personally and see what could be done in regards to this new handwashing concept. She hung up her tartan shawl and went to stoke the fire back to flame, pushing at it with a poker. Ainslie had taken the lamb back out to the fields, it having improved quite a bit overnight, so Jane wasn't expecting her to return for a while. She thought she might speak to Dougal and see if he'd finished her scarf, as the winter looked to be closing in soon, and perhaps the fishmonger would have more of the whitefish that had become a favourite since she moved into the cottage.

She was just thinking of bringing in some of the last flowers of the season for decorating their mantelpiece over the winter when a glint of metal caught her eye. She glanced at it, puzzled, and went over to the table. There, a strange metal shape sat, wrapped up in a note. She unfolded it.

Dear Jane,

My apologies for the time it has taken to render you this. However, it was an odd shape and a tricky one to get just right. I've finished it to your exact specifications. I hope this meets your expectations.

And Jane lifted it out of the paper, a long and complicated piece of metal with three forking ends, glowing in the reflection of the firelight.

It was the missing piece of her machine, the thing that could take her home.

* * *

She pushed the door to the courtyard open.

It had been months since she'd entered the place; the vines were even more overgrown than before, and there lay the machine, forgotten.

Jane stood in front of it, its burnished copper glowing faintly in the late evening light—the nights were drawing in closer with the cold and the red leaves scattered on the ground—and she saw two paths before her, both shining and bright.

In one pocket made from loops of her earasaid she held the piece that Aileen had made, a miracle of design and talent.

In the other, she held another thing Aileen had made, the interlocking rings she'd given Jane as a welcome gift and a display of her own prowess.

She had thought to give one of these rings to Ainslie, when the time was right.

She held these items in her respective fists, buried deep in her pockets, and she watched the reflection of the moon on the machine in the growing darkness.

"Jane?" Ainslie called, as she walked in the front door and closed it. "Are ye hame? I've brocht some o' the *metheglin*, sweetbriar mead frae Ireland. We can hae it wi' dinner. Ah, there ye are."

Ainslie kissed her cheek as Jane came in from the courtyard, shutting the door firmly behind her.

"What were ye doin' out there?" asked Ainslie, pouring the mead.

"Oh, it's an absolute tip," said Jane. "We'll have to clean it out. The vines have grown over everything."

"Aye, an' we shall, when winter is over," said Ainslie, patting the bed, where she waited with glasses of mead and the bottle between them, looking like the wicked promise she was. "It can wait, my lass; it can wait."

And Jane agreed, certainly. It could wait.

Outside, in the moonlight, the machine sat silent. Waiting.

CHAPTER TWENTY-SEVEN

Winter

It was February, when Jane found the man standing outside in the garden.

The snows had fallen, encasing the world in a blanket of ice. The winter had been heavy that year, the winds bitterly cold. Food had grown somewhat scarce, and Dòmhnall had employed hundreds of workers to distribute the venison they had kept in the cold depths of the castle for just such an occasion. Fishing was near-impossible given the strength of the storms. Although it had been a good harvest, the clan relied mostly on dairy and meat. There were not enough animals to go around, and this was becoming clearer as the winter stretched into its deepest darkness.

The long-ago feast night was one of Jane's fondest memories. The entire island had shown up, just as Dòmhnall said, and then the wine and whisky flowed like rivers, the tables groaned with meat and cheese and cream, there were strawberries piled high for dessert, and discussions were had about the latest developments in cuisine from France and further abroad. It was a time of plenty, and yet Dòmhnall was still prudent; he had made allowances for the winter, and the clan was sufficiently provided for despite the multiple feasts of that particular summer.

However, no one had ever seen a winter like this one.

Normally, the winters were divided by squalls and snow, but there were periods of relative sunshine and warmth that allowed people to continue fishing and trade. This winter, they had not been able to sail due to the wildness of the water; if they dared to go out on the sea Dòmhnall warned it would "only return mair dead men an' women."

And so, the clan settled for what was available on Islay. Dòmhnall and Christina ensured that everyone was fed, and Ainslie worked with Aonghus on delivering the meat and fruit to the furthest-flung settlements of Islay, Jura, and Fraoch Eilean. Things were tight, and at the end of February, they were praying for an easy transition into spring. The wild winds usually settled by the end of March, and the tail of April saw summer weather. It had been an unseasonably rough winter, particularly in the harvesting of peat for the firesides, but they had made do. It looked like the entire clan would survive this time.

Unfortunately, this was not the case for the surrounding clans, especially those not under the protection of the Sea Kingdom. During the summer, and before the winds had really come in the fall, Dòmhnall and Christina had organised trade up and down the islands, with Ainslie and Aonghus working as emissaries to their various outposts, ensuring their clanspeople would be taken care of during the winter. The few out-islanders that had managed to get in and out of Caol Ìle before the weather had turned assured Dòmhnall that this was one of the best years for both game and harvest they had experienced, and it looked like they would be able to survive the winter. Because they hadn't been able to leave, or welcome visitors, for some time due to the weather, Dòmhnall and Christina could only hope that the others were faring as well as those on Islay and Jura.

Ainslie was away visiting one of these faraway houses with a fresh supply of meat, and was expected to return that day. Jane walked out of her cottage that morning and saw a man she didn't recognise standing in the garden.

"Hello," she spoke in Gaelic, which she had learned, albeit with questionable results. "Are you looking for Ainslie? She's away at Kilchoman farm, but I'm expecting her back shortly."

The man just stared at her, and she saw, from his hollow eyes and his stare, that he was starving.

Jane was about to speak again when a noise like nothing she had ever heard came from around the corner. Suddenly the man was spit on the end of a long sword, and blood was pouring from his mouth. He had never spoken a word to her, and he fell at her feet.

Jane realised she was screaming and had dropped her basket in the snow.

Ainslie, wild-eyed, was in front of her, holding her face, checking her for injuries, hustling her indoors.

"A sword, a sword, god damn it, a sword!" Ainslie was crying out, searching the cottage, and Jane sat on the bed and the dead man lay out in the snow of the garden. Calls and cries went up outside, disturbing what once was silence, accompanied by the terrible sound of clashing swords and curses all along the city streets.

"What is it, Ainslie, what's wrong?" Jane yelled. This seemed to stop Ainslie's frantic search and pacing.

"The Caimbeulaich, they've come here, Jane," said Ainslie. "They've come here an' I left ye alane, triple ass that I am! Fuck, I ken I left ane here, where is it? Where is the sword? This is our punishment for times of peace!"

"Ainslie!" barked Jane. "The claidheamh mòr is in the pantry, on the side where you left it. I am ready, and I'll fight if needs be. What is going on?"

Ainslie lifted the broadsword from the pantry and handed her own smaller one to Jane.

"The Caimbeulaich are starving and jealous," said Ainslie. "As they ever have been. If they'd only *listen* to Da, they'd have the food they needed. But nae, they're about money, an' they dinna look after the clan! An' sae they're here raiding, instead of sending an emissary tae ask my parents *politely*, nae, they'll murder the island, an' I left ye alane an' undefended…"

"Let's go, Ainslie," said Jane. She grabbed her arm. Ainslie's eyes were filled with the stark terror of what might have been.

"Ainslie! Look at me. I'm fine," said Jane. "But we need to go and defend your people, do you hear me? You cannot let them all die in favour of one! That's not the way a chief thinks."

Ainslie seemed to pull herself together and nodded.

They went out into the snow.

* * *

The riotous scene that greeted them was unlike anything Jane had ever known. The battle raged on for most of the day and the night, but the Caimbeulaich were indeed starving and so not offering much of a fight. Jane felt pity for them and their circumstance; it was unfair that the greed of their chief had made their winter even more terrible than the one experienced in the Sea Kingdom of the Dhòmhnaill clan. The fighting was all the worse for the numbers, as it seemed the Caimbeulaich had an endless supply of what were, at this point, more dead men and women than soldiers. Jane had never needed to pick up a sword, but she had no choice. As she fought by Ainslie's side, with little skill but all the enthusiasm of her headstrong personality, she wondered at the kind of people who would wholesale throw themselves into the slaughter and saw only desperation in the hollow eyes of the people from the other clan. Jane's heart was cut to the quick.

"Could we not call a ceasefire?" Jane shouted to Ainslie. "Help them? They are clearly starving!"

Ainslie glanced over her shoulder as she ran another warrior through.

"Ye be careful o' that bleedin' heart," she yelled back. "Nae, these people dinna want peace. If they did, they'd ask for help instead of raiding."

"But Ainslie—" Jane called.

Ainslie made a sound of disgust.

"I ken ye're no frae these parts, Jane, but I—" She turned around…

And saw Jane lying in the snow, blood from her wound, blood from her mouth, staring into the grey of the late February sky. Fat snowflakes began to fall, on the battle, on Ainslie, on Jane lying there in the snow, as they had on the starving man in their garden.

With a cry set to rend the heavens, Ainslie threw herself on Jane's attacker and slaughtered him. Then she set about destroying anyone else who came close, to keep them away from the place where Jane had fallen. The battle was nearly over, and others took her place in the fight as she fell into the snow beside Jane.

"Aonghus! Aonghus mac Dòmhnaill, you get over here this instant or I swear I'll run ye through myself," screamed Ainslie, holding Jane to her breast, a sound of grief tearing itself from her throat.

Aonghus made a huge furrow in the snow as he threw himself down and collided with the two of them, wrenching open his medical bag.

"Let go!" he shouted in Ainslie's face. "Let go or she'll die as surely as ye'd run her through yourself."

Ainslie stared at him, unseeing.

"I'm yer brother, Ainslie," he said, holding her gaze. "Let me save her life."

Ainslie let go of Jane's body. Aonghus set about checking for vital signs. The battle was apparently over, as the Dhòmhnaill clan were now carrying the bodies of the Caimbeulaich away to stack on a pyre and burn. Tears tracked down Ainslie's face, and she couldn't bear to look at Jane and the sword lying useless by her side, growing cold in the snow.

"She lives," said Aonghus, looking up at his sister. "And she *will* live, Ainslie. I promise ye that."

Ainslie nodded dumbly, and as others made a litter for her to carry Jane back into the castle, she turned and beat the still corpse of the man who had dealt Jane's falling blow.

"Ainslie!" Aonghus shouted.

Ainslie wrenched herself away with great effort. She left the scene and followed the procession of people into the castle, with Aonghus and Jane leading the way.

CHAPTER TWENTY-EIGHT

Snow and Stars

"Where were the pipers, Da?"

"There were nae pipers," said Dòmhnall. "This was a raid, no' a battle."

"It was a massacre," said Christina. "Like no earthly battle I've ever seen."

They were standing in the castle's great hall as Aonghus worked on Jane's wound. Servants hurried back and forth, carrying water, wine, and spiderwebs. He worked on the stitching as his family talked around him. Jane slept through the operation. Aonghus had induced her to breathe from a sponge soaked in a narcotic preparation he had learned about in the medical textbook, *Al-Taisir*, written by the celebrated Arab chirurgeon Ibn Zuhr and considered the absolute latest in surgical procedure.

"They were starving, Da," said Ainslie, pacing back and forth. "They were willing to kill us all. Can ye no speak to the chief?"

"Archie disnae speak to a man without the promise o' coin or the promise o' loss thereof," Dòmhnall said. "His father willingly starves his people. Archie may hae a guid heart, but I wouldnae ken it; he canna stand up tae his da. I'd offer them protection, but the battle is all they ken. It's a sad state o' affairs, an' nane o' us had reckoned on this winter."

"Not much of a man who allows his own clanspeople to starve," said Christina. "Father or son. The man himself isn't starving in this cold, I'm sure."

"Either way," said Dòmhnall, "I'll be glad tae see the back o' this winter. I'll no call for a war wi' the Caimbeulaich for this. If the cold disnae do them in, it'll be a mercy."

"Quiet, all of you," said Aonghus. "I think she's coming round."

Jane's eyes blinked open. The world looked blurry. The first thing she saw when her eyes focused was Aonghus's worried face.

"Aonghus?" she managed, only a whisper, but the word was there. Relief spread across his features.

"Jane," he said. "Welcome back to the land of the living."

Ainslie, for her part, kept well away. Jane could see her standing at the window, staring out at the blizzard that had worked itself up during the night. Jane tried to lift an arm toward her, but failed and dropped it heavily by her side.

"Rest now, Jane," said Aonghus.

"What happened?" she asked.

"A Caimbeul man stabbed you in the back," Aonghus explained.

"As they do," said Ainslie without turning around, and her mother hushed her.

"I've not seen a cut like it before," Aonghus went on to say. "Had he been in possession o' all his faculties, I doubt we'd be having this conversation. As it was, the thrust was weak and superficial. It missed all the primary organs, though you did lose quite a lot of blood. You'll be weak for a while, but should make a full recovery."

"Thank you, Aonghus," said Ainslie. He grinned.

"Anything for my sister," he said, glancing at her. "I'm glad to see you well, Jane. You'll need tae rest for some time."

Jane nodded and fell into a heavy sleep. She did not dream.

* * *

"You see us there, Jane?" Ainslie was saying, in a soft murmur like a running stream. "Like the old stories of the Greeks, up there, amang the stars?"

Jane woke to Ainslie's soft voice, a guttural growl that was at once pleasing and soothing. She opened her eyes and saw that they were in the room of the castle she'd stayed in when she had first arrived and that Ainslie was holding onto her, looking out at the stars above the sea.

"Spring is coming soon, my love," she murmured. "We'll go out a-harvesting thyme an' rosemary, when the weather's better. Aonghus says it'll be—ye'll be awright by then. It's no' sae lang after all, is it? Then we can sleep on the hillsides, an' I can show ye the stars wide across the sky, an' the constellations o' the Greeks whaur the lovers an' the great heroes still live."

Jane felt the tears before she saw them and the slight shudder of Ainslie's body.

"*Please* get better," she said. "Aonghus said—an' I trust him, I do, he is going to be a great *fáidh*, but...God, Jane, I cannae lose ye."

Jane found her hand and took it, squeezing weakly. She made a sound and then winced with the pain.

"Jane? Are ye awake?" asked Ainslie, hurriedly wiping her tears. "What did ye say?"

"*Will ye go, lassie go, tae the braes o' Balquhidder whaur the blueberries grow 'mang the bonnie Hielan heather...*"

This was an overexertion for Jane, who had only whispered the words to the song, but she looked up into Ainslie's green eyes and smiled all the same.

"Where'd ye hear that?" Ainslie asked.

"I had it off some Travelling folk," said Jane. "They sing the songs for a few shillings. I always thought it was beautiful."

"You'll teach it tae me when ye get better, aye?" asked Ainslie.

"Of course," said Jane. "Athena."

Ainslie smiled at her, puzzled, but Jane had fallen asleep.

* * *

For Jane, the days and nights passed much the same.

There wasn't much she was aware of, only that she was fed and she occasionally awoke to Ainslie talking with her or sleeping by her side. Aonghus visited from time to time, checking on her. She felt she must have been asleep for years.

Ainslie's vigil went on through the cold months as the earth turned toward spring.

One fine morning in late April, Jane awoke, and with some difficulty, sat up in bed.

CHAPTER TWENTY-NINE

Spring

It was a few weeks before Jane was able to walk on her own again.

"Ye've had a near escape," said Aonghus, who was around a lot more these days. They'd become firm friends, as April bled into May, and he helped Jane while Ainslie was off on clan errands. She had argued, but he'd insisted; someone needed to work with Dòmhnall and Christina now that the snows had receded, and he *was* the doctor between the two of them, after all.

They sat in the dining hall together, eating lunch. Aonghus was very particular about the food she ate; Jane, being a doctor herself, was impressed at Aonghus's instinctive care of a patient, and she told him so.

"Doctor, heal thyself," she quoted wryly. Aonghus smiled.

"There wisnae much ye could do wi' a sword to the back," said Aonghus. "I'm just glad you survived. Many's a strong young lad or lass o' this clan who haven't, in other battles before this ane."

"How'd you manage it?" asked Jane. "I'd have thought the wound was mortal."

"I'm brilliant." Aonghus grinned and then relented when she saw the look she gave him. "Put ye tae sleep, then stitched ye up. Spiderwebs help close the wound. It's no a perfect science, but I think we did well."

"What did you use for the anaesthetic?" she asked.

"Dwale," he replied. "A mixture of opium and alcohol, among other things."

"We've come far in our research," said Jane. "There are new discoveries—"

Aonghus held up a hand.

"If ye wish tae discuss them," he said, "I willnae stop you, but if you've any concern for the course of history, reconsider what you're about to say."

Jane halted and thought about it.

"I don't know if I could live with myself if I didn't share some of my knowledge," she said.

"All right," said Aonghus. "An' I'll listen to it, but right now we need to focus on you getting better."

Jane nodded, stirring her soup.

"What was the death toll from the battle?" she asked.

"Ah, ye dinna want tae be worryin' yersel—"

"Aonghus," said Jane. "Tell me. Please."

Aonghus sighed, looking into his soup.

"The Caimbeulaich, about two hundred," he said. Jane's mouth dropped open in shock.

"Two hundred?" she exclaimed.

How many of those kills were mine? she wondered. *And how many were Ainslie's?*

She felt herself go pale.

"Aye," he said. "An' it woulda been mair, but I treated many o' them. We're usin' it as a way tae broker peace with the Caimbeulaich, maybe set them up so they dinna starve next winter an' try to take what isnae theirs."

"What about the clan?" asked Jane.

"Nane," said Aonghus. "But tha's no usual. If it had been a normal battle, we'd hae lost more than two hundred. If the Caimbeulaich hadnae been half dead already, we'd been slaughtered tae a man. The Caimbeulaich are fierce as we are, an' they had the element of surprise."

Jane looked out at the glittering water beyond the castle window.

"Would I have been the only casualty?" she asked.

"Aye," said Aonghus. "There are a few ithers injured, but naethin' like what ye had."

"Foolish of me," murmured Jane. "Thinking I'd be able to fight like Ainslie. Then taking someone's life—I'm a doctor, Aonghus. I'm supposed to save lives."

"Now, dinna talk like that, lass," said Aonghus. "It's no yer fault, any mair than it's ours. The death toll is high, but it was their choice tae pillage instead o' bargain. Your death would be on their heads, an' believe me, if ye'd not survived, there would be all-out war."

"What? Over me?" asked Jane. "Just one person?"

"You specifically," he clarified. "I've never seen Ainslie like that. She's usually the one with the cool head, just like Mum. Da's a romantic, an' I've nae head for fighting. But she didna leave your side, not for anything."

Jane thought about this for a while, as she ate her soup. She thought of Ainslie's inheritance and of the danger she was in. How could she ever be the chief her clan needed if her attention was entirely elsewhere? The wheels in Jane's head began to turn, as she began to see herself as a liability instead of an asset. The clan already had a doctor, after all.

"Don't you and Ainslie do diplomatic work in the islands?" Jane asked.

"Oh aye," he said. "But it's Mum goin' tae speak with *na Caimbeulaich*, since Ainslie's in nae mood for that."

And what is going to happen when it's just Ainslie leading the clan? Jane didn't ask.

"Eat all the soup, an' drink as much as ye can," Aonghus advised.

Jane smiled, thinking how she might have offered similar medical advice in her own time period, and she complied with doctor's orders.

* * *

Ainslie returned a few days later, talking about the successful journey she had made to the Small Isles of Rùm and Eigg.

"Malcolm's been lonely these many months," said Ainslie. "Would ye like tae go fishing? Aonghus has given us the all-clear for you tae go about again."

"Nothing too strenuous," warned Aonghus.

"Aye, Aonghus, I ken," sighed Ainslie in exasperation, rolling her eyes. "What do ye say, Jane? Malcolm has missed ye."

"Yes, I'd love to," said Jane. She gave Aonghus a little nod before she accompanied Ainslie down to the water.

* * *

The shallows off of Gigha were beautiful in the sunlight, like tropical paradises Jane had seen painted by returning sailors from the South Seas. She'd never known a Scotland like this one, where the incredible beauty of the islands outshone places far more exotic to her. But then, she'd only ever been to her father's Highland village, never out to the islands.

"Did you know there's a song about a lady who runs off with a Scotsman?" Jane asked, as she waded into the cool water. Little shoals of fish flashed around her legs and her feet sank into the bright white sand. "'Jock o' Hazeldean,' it's called."

"Oh aye?" asked Ainslie. "Why'd she go?"

"I don't know," said Jane. "I think because they were forcing her to marry someone else. They escaped over the border together. She fell in love with the country as much as the man, I think."

"What made ye think o' that?" asked Ainslie. "Are ye gonnae call me yer kidnapper again?"

Jane laughed.

"No," she said. "I was thinking that I also fell in love with a country as much as a woman."

"'Tis a beautiful land," Ainslie agreed. "I've traveled much an' yet never seen its like. I'm sure everyone prefers their ain country."

"This is my country," said Jane. "Only, I've never seen this part of it. I think that's a tragedy."

"Weel," said Ainslie, "ye're seein' it now. It's time ye get back intae Malcolm. They'll be missin' us."

She helped Jane climb over the transom and kissed her as she sat down in the boat.

"All of this is yours," said Ainslie. "As sure as my heart is, too."

Jane smiled into the next kiss, the sun warm on her skin and dancing bright on the water.

Beneath it all, though, she felt doubt creeping in, wondering what purpose she served here.

* * *

Aonghus told Jane that she should be fine to return to her cottage, as she had healed more rapidly than he'd expected. She was given strict instructions for her diet and to take gentle exercise, but he felt she was almost well again. Jane thanked him profusely, but she was glad to return to her own living space.

Jane had expected the accumulation of several months of dust and was surprised to find the house was clean, a merry fire crackling away in the fireplace as if she had never left.

She recognised the part that Aileen had made her sitting on the mantel. To anyone else, it would have looked like nothing much, just some kind of knickknack. But what it symbolised gave her pause.

Ainslie was happily preparing a stew in the pot over the fireplace.

"That smells heavenly," Jane said. "Did you learn to cook while I was away?"

"Och no," said Ainslie, as if that was a sheer impossibility. "Da made this. It's one of his specialities."

"I can't wait," said Jane.

"I dinna want ye tae fight anymore," Ainslie said abruptly. Jane stared at her.

"What? Where did that come from?" Jane asked.

"I canna lose ye, Jane," Ainslie said. "Ye were sae cold, an' thin, an' I lost my heid."

"Ainslie," she said, "I understand that it was hard—"

"You dinna ken what it did tae me!" Ainslie said. "Like my heart ripped out."

"You were distracted because of me," said Jane quietly. "And you'll be reckless because of me whether I fight or not."

"I can protect ye," Ainslie said. "Just…nae mair fighting? I started to understand what Adomnán meant, when he forbade women tae battle."

Jane stood up.

"Ainslie, don't you dare!" said Jane. "You'll be the chief soon. Don't be the reason people in my time period have to fight all the way back to the society you already have. Women aren't the problem. It's that you're afraid to lose someone you love."

"I love my family, an' we've a' been in battles," said Ainslie. "This was different."

"Because you are *in love*," said Jane. "And you're afraid, that's understandable. But you can't forbid me to fight, and you shouldn't start thinking like that! Adomnán and his mother didn't know everything. They were wrong, Ainslie, and you know that."

"But I'm going tae be the chief, an' I canna run off tae the other islands worryin' about you," said Ainslie.

"And refusing to let me fight is going to keep me safe somehow?" Jane demanded. "What exactly do you think would happen if I couldn't? Far worse, I can tell you that!"

"I won't," said Ainslie stubbornly. "I won't allow it."

"If you are so worried about what my existence will do to you, then I'll leave," said Jane. "I'm nothing but a liability to you, Ainslie. Someone to worry about, who needs protecting."

She glanced at the replacement part on the mantel.

Ainslie snorted.

"Leave?" she asked. "An whar will ye go, off tae Barra?"

Jane stared at her. She stood up and walked over to the mantel, picking up the part. Then she went to the door of the courtyard. Ainslie's eyes widened.

"Oh, no," Ainslie said, terrified. "Please, don't leave. We'll talk, it's fine, we—"

"No," said Jane. "I've had a long time to think about this, and I'm only distracting you. Now you want me to hide myself away, and that's no life, Ainslie! I don't mind fighting, if I can be by your side. But I'm not going to be the reason you aren't a good chief for your clan."

She pushed the door open and found the machine buried in the overgrowth. She began to pull the vines away as Ainslie stood in the doorway, sad and strange, as if all the usual fight had gone out of her.

"I thocht I'd lose ye this way, ye ken," said Ainslie. "Back tae yer Edinburgh an' yer husband."

"You leave David out of this!" Jane shouted. "I left him alone and unprotected, in a far worse time for him than this one is for us!"

"Then stay!" Ainslie said. "If you dinna stay, I canna keep you safe, Jane—"

"*Everyone dies*," Jane snarled, startled at her own vitriol. Ainslie froze.

"What?" she asked.

"You! All this!" Jane waved her hand. "The clan system, the Highlands! It's *gone*, Ainslie! They murdered everyone. There are no Lords of the Isles! The Highlands are empty. The Highlanders are poor beggars in the streets of Glasgow and Edinburgh! You can't keep me safe, Ainslie. There is no safe place, not now or then! There is no utopia."

Ainslie's face had drained of colour, and her hands worked, twisting her earasaid.

"I'm sae sorry, Jane," she tried. "Please stay."

But Jane had taken Aileen's gift and pushed it into place.

The machine started up. Jane climbed inside, afire with wrath and fury.

She closed the hatch and started the mechanism.

The last thing she saw before the machine blinked out was Ainslie's mouth forming a single word:

Please.

And Jane faltered, for a moment, but the thing was done.

She thought she heard a sob of grief tear its way out of Ainslie's throat, but then realised it was her own.

It's better this way, she told herself. *She needs to lead her clan, and she can't do that with me there.*

So why do you feel like this is the end of the world? her thoughts replied.

Because I'm selfish, she thought.

Are you? they countered.

And suddenly, there was David's dear face, shouting at her through the small window. He was inexplicably mustachioed and looked haggard, his eyes red.

She opened the hatch.

"Janie!" David cried. "Oh dear God, Janie, we thought you were done for!! Thank God, thank God!"

He lifted her out of the machine and embraced her in a tight hug. He pushed her away from him, holding her shoulders as he looked at her clothing.

"Good God, my girl, what on earth are you wearing?" David asked, inspecting her earasaid. "Dear Lord, are you barefoot?"

"If you keep shouting for God like that, he's going to notice," said Jane, smiling and sniffling a bit. "Why do you have a mustache?"

"Oh, do you like it?" he asked, turning his head left and right. "I think it makes me look rather dashing, don't you?"

"I meant, how long was I gone?" Jane asked, fearing the answer.

"You mean you don't know?" he asked. "How long was it for you?"

"A year, two perhaps?" she said.

David goggled at her.

"Goodness me," he said. "You must tell us everything!"

"Us?" asked Jane.

"Yes, your Doctor Bell took you at your word," said David. "He hasn't left my side except to give lectures at the university. I told him all the fuss wasn't necessary, but he insisted."

"But David," she said, "how long was it for you?"

"Ah, three months, I should think," he replied.

"Three months!" Jane cried. "Oh, you must have been so worried!"

"Yes, yes, but you're home now," said David. "Let's go inside, and I shall make a lovely cup of tea, and you can tell us all about it."

"That sounds wonderful," Jane sighed, allowing herself to be led out of the shed and toward a house she felt she hadn't seen in a lifetime. And perhaps that was true.

Home, she thought to herself, as she followed David up the steps into the manor.

Is it, though? asked her treacherous thoughts, and she willed them into silence.

CHAPTER THIRTY

Up the Airy Mountain

"Dear God, David, it is absolutely freezing in here!" Jane exclaimed, on entering the house.

David gave her a strange look.

"This is how it's always been, Janie," he said. "Perhaps you're catching cold? You *are* barefoot and barely dressed, my dear."

How did we get from there to here? Jane wondered, thinking of her snug little cottage and of the warmth of the great hall of Claig Castle.

"Jane!" Dr. Bell cried upon seeing her. He rushed to embrace her. She smiled at him.

"Sit down, Janie," said David. "You must tell us *everything*."

* * *

It was quite late in the evening by the time Jane had finished her tale, blushing at some of the parts she left out for their sensitivities. She wondered at how spending time in Islay might have changed her, not only in speech but attitude.

She'd been brought her former clothes and her heeled shoes, but she found them restrictive and painful. Her corsets also felt odd, like she couldn't breathe in them. She wondered if it was discomfort from her wound, or if she had grown accustomed to the freer garments of the Dhòmhnaill clan. She was surprised, furthermore, to find that she felt no travel sickness at all after this journey. Perhaps it was because she had spent so long travelling in Malcolm, perhaps it was because this flight had been smoother. Or perhaps more had changed for Jane than she had thought possible.

And so, in her shift and earasaid, barefoot, she sat on the sofa and told her tale, only interrupted for clarifying questions or when David brought more tea and cucumber sandwiches. They tasted wrong to her now—not bad, necessarily, but bland.

She had, however, missed tea quite a bit.

"And this woman, you say she was a clan chief?" asked David, absolutely agog at the story, hanging on her every word as he always did.

"Not yet, but she would have inherited," said Jane. "As long as the rest of the clan agreed, of course. They're very democratic. Her brother Aonghus was second in line and wanted to be a doctor, anyway."

Joe Bell had been somewhat mysteriously quiet during the recital of her tale. When he finally spoke, he shocked the both of them.

"Janie, it hasn't failed to escape my attention that you and this woman love each other very much," he said. "Do you think it was wise to return to us? We'd have managed. My apologies, David. I realise she is your wife, and I may be overstepping here."

"No apology needed," said David. "Janie and I have had a longstanding agreement regarding this marriage. I have to say I agree with Doctor Bell, Janie. It sounds like a much better arrangement for you than all of this."

"She was distracted," Jane said. "I distracted her. There's an entire clan to look after, and she might let them suffer if I am there."

"Look, Janie," said David. "I am the last man to tell you what to do. I know what things for women are like; for that matter, what things are like for people like you and me. It's an opportunity I wouldn't sacrifice."

"I missed you, David," said Jane, resolute. "And I missed home and Edinburgh. Adjusting to that time period was dreadful. I'd like to stay."

But even Jane did not think her words carried much conviction.

"If that is your wish," said Dr. Bell, "then that is your wish. I advise you to think upon it. Since it is getting late, and I must lecture in the morning, I will take my leave of you both for now. I will return in a few days' time to check on you."

"Thank you, Joe," said Jane, kissing his cheek. "For everything."

Dr. Bell bowed to her and then put on his houndstooth travelling cloak as he said his goodbyes to David.

They sat alone, in the enormous cold room that the fireplace seemed to do nothing to warm. The minutes ticked by.

"Janie," David began, hesitant.

"Not tonight, David," she said. "I'm exhausted. Tomorrow?"

"As you wish, Janie," said David. "But we'll hash it out in the morning, do you hear?"

"Yes, husband," she said, smiling, which never failed to coax a smile out of him too.

"Til then, wife," he said and toddled off to his bedroom.

Jane went to hers and found it immaculate; David must have had the servants keep it clean in her absence.

It reminded her of Ainslie, keeping her cottage tidy during her convalescence, and the pain of that memory was swift and sure. She tried to put it out of her mind.

She crawled into the huge bed, skin gooseflesh as it came in contact with the cold sheets. She lay there for a while, staring at the ceiling, a chandelier hanging down from it, high above her head. She wondered how the hell everything could possibly be so cold, when it was hundreds of years later and the houses were nicer, in theory. She thought she couldn't possibly fall asleep in this bed, which seemed as distant and foreign to her as a room in a random hotel.

But she did sleep after all, and she dreamed of bright green eyes, of a voice like smoke and honey, and of red hair like the flames of a fire in a low cottage by the sea.

* * *

David greeted her at the breakfast table the following day.

"I've made you a feast!" he said proudly, gesturing expansively at the table.

The china teapot with the floral design sat atop a silver tray with the china mugs. Individual slices of toast filled several silver toast racks next to piles of butter and marmalade. The china plates were loaded with bacon, slices of ham, Lorne sausage, Stornoway black pudding, baked beans, mushrooms, tomatoes, *bradan rost*, cream cheese, cheddar slices, and tattie scones. Eggs sat in silver eggcups, ready to be cracked with tiny spoons.

"Are we expecting an army?" asked Jane.

David laughed.

"No," he said. "I just didn't know what you'd like to eat, so I ordered everything."

Jane smiled at him and was reminded of another time and place when someone with a rough Scottish burr told her that she'd brought breakfast because she couldn't cook worth a damn.

"Thank you," she said. "This is wonderful, David."

"Right," David said, pouring her a cup of tea. "Now you'll listen to me, Janie, because you never do, and that's fine. You're the smart one, after all. But this time, I can tell you with absolute confidence: you're an idiot, Janie."

Jane was stunned into silence.

"An absolute buffoon," he said, warming to his theme. "A total fool."

Jane's mouth worked.

"How—how dare you—"

"I daresay I do!" David said. "I dare indeed. And I am going to use my right as a husband to do as a husband does and command you, as it may be the only time I shall ever get the opportunity to do so. You have been the clever one during most of our association together, but I feel in my bones that this time I am on the right hoof. As is Dr. Bell, and we know he's one of the cleverest men alive. I don't often find a chance to count myself among the clever men, Janie; you well know I am a dullard and an idiot most of the time, but in this I have an unshakeable conviction."

"David Crichton, you—"

"I shall stop you there, Janie," he said, buttering a piece of toast. "In all our time together, I've thought I was so lucky as to have found a wife with an intelligence far surpassing my own. I admit I have been proud of you for many years and on several occasions. Now, however, Janie, I am for the first time and last time going to tell you what to do."

"And I shan't do it," Jane said.

"Well, in any other circumstance I should say bally to you for that," David said. "But in this one, I certainly hope you will take it to heart. Janie, you get back in that machine and you go back to your fiery Highland chief or so help me God I shall use my husbandly rights to soak your head in the well! I say."

With a final flourish of his knife, he sat back against his chair and crunched down on his toast.

Jane crossed her arms.

"Your mustache is the most ridiculous thing I've ever seen," she told him. He grinned.

"I know. Isn't it just capital!" he said. "You should see the looks I get in Parliament."

"David," Jane said. "I know you're worried about me, but I truly want to be here. This is my home."

David raised an eyebrow.

"I love you, Janie," he said. "You are my dearest friend. We're soulmates of a sort. We always will be. But if *I* had my chance to run off with some wild-haired Highlander who loved me passionately and I didn't take it? Well I should certainly hope, in the name of our long friendship, that you'd call me an idiot too!"

Jane sighed.

"David—"

"Don't you take that tone with me, Jane Campbell," he said. "If you want to be obstinate, that is your right, and we shall say no more about it."

"Your concern is noted," said Jane. "Now, may we breakfast? I am starving."

David nodded, and the conversation moved on to other topics. Jane enquired as to what news and political intrigue had occurred in her absence, and they spent most of the morning discussing the particulars of life in Edinburgh.

CHAPTER THIRTY-ONE

Down the Rushy Glen

Jane sat at the table in the Café Royal, the finest dining establishment in Edinburgh. Kings and queens had dined here. The tablecloths were white, while everything else was silver; the concept of "silver service" was one that this restaurant took seriously.

The ceilings soared overhead, and the wind created by the waiters moving about the room made the chandeliers softly whisper together like crystal wind chimes. The waiters were dressed to the nines in tuxedo suits, standing out against the white and silver surroundings. This was the height of luxury, in the Athens of Scotland, in the fruits of the flower of Scottish Enlightenment, and yet, Jane felt cold.

She felt ambivalent towards the place, certainly, but she didn't understand why she felt cold all of the time. There was really no excuse for it, and she missed her cottage by the sea for the hundredth time in the last week alone.

"May I light your cigarette, madam?" asked a waiter. Jane nodded and waited for flame to touch the end of it before inhaling deeply. Everything was so fancy, including the people invited here. She thought of Mary King's Close and the way the class system separated everyone just as much as poverty. She thought of the loud belly laugh Ainslie would have, seeing all of this. She thought of a time and place where women didn't have to be hogtied into their clothing in order to be seen in fashionable company.

She sighed and shook her head at herself.

The door opened, and two ladies entered, preceded by a couple of dogs. The women were radiant, all smiles. One woman was short and stocky, with her hair pulled into a severe bun, and she seemed ready to challenge anyone who looked her way. The other was tall and willowy, with high cheekbones, a cloud of curly hair, and a dreamy look in her eyes.

"May I take your jacket, madam?" asked one of the waiters.

"Indeed, do!" boomed Sophia, the stocky one. She saw Jane across the room and waved to her.

The two women and dogs progressed through the restaurant, greeting people they knew well. The dogs ran up to Jane, a familiar friend, and wagged their tails.

"Ah, Janie," said Maggie, the willowy one, as Jane stood up to kiss their cheeks Continental-style. "It's been ages! Let's sit."

The women sat down and called for champagne, which was readily brought over in a silver iced bowl. The drinks were poured, a toast was made, and a sumptuous afternoon tea was laid out on the table. Cupcakes of many different styles and designs adorned their plates, along with cucumber sandwiches and other fripperies.

"Sophia. Maggie," said Jane, as they drank and used delicate forks to slice dainty pieces of cupcake. "I must ask you for advice."

"Oh, I do love giving advice," said Maggie. Sophia grinned. She was an imposing figure and often abrasive, but somehow she had browbeaten the entirety of Edinburgh society into accepting the two of them as lovers at face value.

So Jane related her story, in a low voice so only the two of them could hear.

* * *

"You are an absolute idiot."

"Sophia!" scolded Maggie.

"Well, she is!" Sophia said. "That's a once-in-a-lifetime love story! And you came back here to…what, exactly? Spend all your life pushing and shoving to be heard? Go back, Jane. Hell. Take me with you."

"That's just what David said!" Jane replied. "He thinks I'm an idiot, too."

"Well, you have a time machine," said Maggie. "Leaving aside just how exciting it is—and that a woman invented one—it's not as if you can't go back and forth visiting. Like when we leave our families to marry."

"If word got out that Jane invented a time machine," said Sophia, "some man would steal it from her and claim that he thought of it first. Still, Maggie's right. Why don't you make it a point to visit? Then you'll have the best of both worlds—if, indeed, this is the best of any."

"That's just it, you see," said Jane. "I crash-landed there. Something wrong with the motor. I had to give the local blacksmith diagrams to create something that could fit—and what if it happens again, and I'm stranded forever? What if the error that made the mistake in the first place means I can never find my way back accurately? Aileen's not going to be in every time period in the history of…of…"

She smiled sadly. Sophia, who never missed anything (having been taught by Joe Bell herself) latched on to that smile like a dog on a scent.

"What's that look for?" she asked. "Why the blacksmith?"

Jane sighed.

"It's just that…Aileen made some rings to show me that she could do metallurgy too," said Jane. "Intricate designs, like those complicated Celtic knots you see on some of the doorframes around here."

"And you were going to give one of these rings to your Highland chief, I take it?" Sophia asked. Maggie clapped her hands in excitement.

"How romantic!" Maggie squealed. Sophia rolled her eyes good-naturedly. The dogs perked up, but once it was clear that no cupcakes were coming their way, they went back to sleep at the feet of their mistresses.

"Janie, look," said Sophia. "I've got—"

"No, no," Maggie interrupted. "You're all brawn, my love, and while that is very useful in browbeating idiots into letting women study medicine, this is where *I* excel. Romance needs a finer touch, Sophia."

"I'm romantic," Sophia protested, and Jane was reminded of Christina's insistence on the same.

"Listen," said Maggie to Jane. "It's terrifying, when you find out you like women. I mean, not actually—but they don't make it clear that it's possible, so you get confused and maybe frightened. This woman—she comes from a society where they don't think much of it one way or the other, so she's only seeing a lover reject her."

"That's not—" Jane began, then relented. "All right, yes. I was worried and surprised. I've never desired anyone, man or woman, so it was a shock to find it in myself."

"Yes," agreed Maggie. "And from what I've read of the ancient Greeks and other, freer societies, we are not exactly the most open nowadays."

"I've known you and Sophia for years," said Jane. "It's not like I wasn't aware of this sort of thing."

"It's different when it happens to you," said Maggie. "Believe me, I know. But I need you to think very hard about what you want out of life, Janie. Do you absolutely need to be here for some reason? And what is it that you spend most of your time thinking about?"

Jane considered this and realised that nearly everything reminded her of Ainslie—a glimpse of red hair in a crowd, a loud laugh, a woman with a particularly deep voice. She felt a swift arrow of pain in her heart, that nearly felt like her gut; she nearly doubled over with the missing of her.

"There," said Maggie triumphantly. "Trust a writer to know."

"You're a doctor too, Maggie," groused Sophia.

"I am both," said Maggie. "And that makes all the difference."

This mention of their shared education and profession led on to discussion of the current state of medicine in Edinburgh and Sophia's practice, along with the possibility of the University of Edinburgh opening its doors to all female students within a few years' time. Jane told them about her near-miss with death and that Aonghus was a talented surgeon during a time she would never have expected there to be such a thing.

And as pleasant as the conversation was, and the champagne, and the afternoon tea in the overcast shadows of immortal Edinburgh beyond the windows, Jane couldn't shake those memories of walking barefoot in the heather or in the white sands of the shallows with shoals of tiny silver fish flashing round her legs and feet.

CHAPTER THIRTY-TWO

We Dare Not Go A-Hunting

"Hi, Mum," said Jane, as she took her coat off inside her parents' foyer.

"Now, Jane," said her mother, "even after marrying David you still say 'Hi.' It should be 'Hello.'"

Jane held back an irritated sigh. It wasn't that she was unprepared for the rebuke; it was just how early her mum had started in on it. After her wedding, she thought her mother might have backed off a little, but it seemed that her joining the aristocracy had only opened the floodgates for her mother's dubious advice on propriety. The aristocracy, on the other hand, allowed for many more eccentricities than her mother could possibly imagine, but that was the striking difference between the upper and middle classes. There was a freedom in wealth and position, and her mother's ignorance of it marked her out as a poseur rather than someone with fine sensibilities.

"Hello, Mother," Jane corrected herself. Her mother smiled in approval. Jane was glad she'd chosen to wear her finest clothing, including a large hat that tied beneath her chin. She found the entire thing ridiculously chafing and too tight, and her feet hurt in her boots.

Jane had taken to wearing her shift and earasaid around the manor house and going barefoot; David, ever indulgent, had never said a word to her about it. She resented having to go out and squeeze herself into these ridiculous clothes. Not for the first time, she thought about how much of women's lives were decided for them from the moment they woke up. Constraining garments that demanded a certain body shape and shoes that hurt to stand or walk in seemed to be the basis for the idea of the weak, fainting woman. Then she thought of Christina, of Ainslie, of Aileen, and even the men, all ages—from Aonghus, to Dòmhnall, to Dougal—never saying anything about it, as if it were perfectly normal for women to wear and do and say as they pleased.

And, she realised, of course it was.

Unfortunately, her mother had not experienced a similar epiphany.

"Jane," she chided, as they sat down to table. "You haven't been to see us in months. Have you forgotten your parents?"

Jane forced a smile.

"My apologies, Mother," she said. "I have been busy with the Royal Society and the university. Why, did you hear that Doctor Joseph Bell has pioneered handwashing for surg—"

"Oh, tosh," said her mother. "That's no life for a woman. You'll have children soon and forget all about this nonsense."

Jane grit her teeth.

"It's not nonsense, Mother. I've never wanted children. You know that. Besides, I have studied medicine since—"

"Do you have a degree, dear?" her mother asked sweetly.

"Well, no, but that's only because they refused to grant any of the women—"

"Exactly," she said. "And well they did so. The working world is no place for women. You and your friends made such a fuss about it, our names were in the newspapers. How absolutely *dreadful*."

"Mother, do you not think your life is wasted?" Jane demanded. "You float about as if women should be seen and not heard, only useful for producing children! If a man wants decoration he can buy himself a goddamned houseplant."

Jane's mother dropped her teacup. The delicate china smashed against the saucer. She stared open-mouthed. Jane stood from the table and leaned in.

"We dinna need t' pretend t' be English tae be good enough, Mither," Jane growled, as if Ainslie's ghost had a hand on her shoulder.

Her father chose this moment to enter the room.

"Janie," he said warmly, embracing her. "It's good to see you again."

Jane remained on her feet. Her mother hadn't yet regained the power of speech.

"Dad," she said. "I'd like to visit your village with you. Would that be all right?"

He looked thrilled.

"Certainly, Janie!" he said. "That's wonderful. I've no idea why you've changed your mind, but I'm glad you have. You used to love it up there when you were a wee girl."

"Clearly I lost my good senses along the way," said Jane. "This weekend?"

"Aye," her father confirmed. "Shall I come by the manor house with a trap to pick you up?"

"Yes, let's say Saturday morning?" Jane asked.

"How dare you speak to me that way!" her mother finally spluttered. "I am your mother!"

"How dare *you*, madam," said Jane. She turned to her father.

"Make my apologies, please," she said. "I've no patience left, Da."

He smiled.

"Understood," he said. "I shall. Saturday?"

Jane nodded and put her coat on again.

"Saturday."

* * *

The ride in the horse trap with her father down to Waverley Station was a pleasant one. Edinburgh was enjoying one of its rare sunny days. The city, being made of stone, was a marvel of human ingenuity but unfortunately not one with a great deal of greenery. In the last few decades, however, the citizens of that great city had been hard at work draining the Nor' Loch and replacing it with gardens. As the cause of death for many people in places like Mary King's Close and the site of several executions, suicides, and other ghastly events, the Nor' Loch was a place people stayed far away from. The green beauty that was now replacing it made for a lovely ride through the city, and the driver was careful enough that the ride itself was pleasant, without the usual jouncing one experienced when driving over the cobblestones of the Old Town.

The trap pulled up to the station and her father paid the driver. He helped Jane down from it, and they walked into the station together.

Waverley Station had something of the beauty of King's Cross about it; Edinburgh being the capital of Scotland, it enjoyed a similar grandeur in many of its public buildings.

The station, as usual, was bustling; the trains here went to Glasgow, to London, and to points further north. This would be their destination, and changing in Glasgow would be necessary, because her father was from the west coast, too.

They boarded their train's first-class compartment. Jane's mother had money, but Jane's relative wealth meant that she could now support her family in style, especially in the way of living her mother had been accustomed to, through David's generosity. "Well, I'm not using it, old bean," he would tell her with a smile. "Might as well make others happy."

As they settled in the carriage and her father took out his pipe, packing it with tobacco, she removed her gloves.

"Do ye want tae talk about why ye spoke tae yer mam like that?" he asked.

"What, Scottish?" Jane retorted. Her father raised an eyebrow.

She sighed, disgusted.

"I'd like to tell you, Father," she said. "But you must promise me not to tell anyone, especially Mum."

Her father's expression was one of concern.

"Is something wrong, Janie?" he asked. "Has someone mistreated ye?"

Jane looked out the window as the train started to huff its way out of the station.

"No," she said. "I think I may have mistreated someone else."

At that moment, the lady with the trolley arrived at their compartment, and the conversation was abandoned for the time being in favour of ordering tea and sweets.

* * *

The way from Glasgow to Campbeltoun via Inveraray was smooth as it could be. At Inveraray, they alighted and walked along the shores of the sea loch, enjoying an ice cream in the sun.

"See the grey castle over yonder, Janie?" asked her father. "That's been in the Campbell clan for generations."

"It's a pretty town, isn't it?" said Jane. "Charming."

"Aye," her father grumbled. "They put the road in so the military could more easily subdue the clans."

"Oh," said Jane. Suddenly, the winding road and the little bridge did not seem so romantic after all.

They dined at the George, and the medieval decor made Jane's heart hurt.

"Janie," her father said gently. "I ken I'm no a clever man, like your friends at university, but I am your da an' I care about ye. Ye've looked sadder than I've ever seen ye. I thocht ye'd be excited to visit Campbeltoun."

She looked at her father. Barrel-chested, red-cheeked, and brown-haired, he was every Scottish farmer she'd ever seen. He even wore his Wellingtons to dinner.

"Do you love Mum?" asked Jane abruptly.

"What on earth would make ye ask a question like that, Janie?" her father asked.

"Just...I want to know," she said.

Her father glanced down into his dram of whisky.

"Aye, Janie," he said. "I think...she had hoped for a man of higher standing than me."

"Oh, I'm sorry," said Jane. "I wasn't thinking. I'm an idiot."

"No," said her father. "It's not what ye think. She fell in love wi' me as well, despite wanting a fancier sort o' gent. Sometimes, we fall in love wi' someone we never would hae expected. Love's like that."

"It was a rude question," Jane said. "My apologies."

"It's awright, Janie," said her father. "I didna think I'd fall in love wi' her, either. But your mother to me...was like a brilliant star. I'd never seen a woman like her. Still haven't. She only wants the best for ye, an' I ken her tongue is too sharp sometimes, but she loves ye, Janie. We both do."

Jane nodded and drank her wine.

"What was it ye wanted to talk about?" he asked. "It cannae be just the state o' your parents' marriage."

Jane looked around, but they were in a hidden alcove next to a window. No one was listening, and no one took much notice of the two of them anyway.

She leaned forward.

"Da," she said. "I built a time machine."

CHAPTER THIRTY-THREE

For Fear of Little Men

"I dinna ken what to say."

The evening had grown late, and both Jane and her father were fairly in their cups. The tale as told was the kind that needs excessive libations for teller and listener both, especially when it's family.

"You can call me an idiot," said Jane, leaning against the window. "Everyone else has."

The George had, by this time, become fairly rambunctious; the pub was filled with local people enjoying themselves, so none of their conversation had been overheard. Normally, a lady like Jane was frowned upon when drinking, but here in the Highlands, as it ever was, a good drinker was considered a good sort, regardless of gender. The divide between the world of the Highlands and Scotland's Central Belt was always an easy one to see.

Her father sipped his whisky.

"Aye, I could," he said. "An' I can see why they would. An' I'll respect ye when ye say that David's reasons are his ain, for suggestin' ye leave him."

"Oh, I do love David, Da," she said. "Just not like ye love Mum."

Her father smiled.

"But this Ainslie?" he said. "Ye love her like that, don't ye?"

Jane sighed. Her breath made a fog on the window. She pressed her fingerprint into it.

"That's just it, Da," she said. "It wasn't just that I distracted her, or that she needed to lead her clan, or that we fought. All that could be discussed and figured out."

"Then what was it?" asked her father. "This sounds like an ideal situation for ye, Janie, apart frae my missin' ye. Ye're my only daughter. But if ye can visit, I dinna see why it cannae work."

Jane wouldn't look at him.

"But I'm a Caimbeul, Da," she said in a small voice. "And they're at war."

"An' ye never told her?" asked her father.

"No," she said. "I had David's name as a shield, and the more she said, the more I knew I needed to hide it."

"And ye think that if she found out, she'd love ye any less?" he asked.

"I don't know," said Jane. "But she hates the Campbells, Da. I didn't want to find out."

Her father looked into his whisky glass for a while and then drained the last of its contents.

"Weel, there's one way you'll never know," he said. "An' that's if ye dinna go back. It's better than pinin', my lassie."

"What if she hates me?" asked Jane.

Her father shrugged.

"Then she's not as smart as ye say she is," he replied. "Come now, Janie. It's getting late, an' we've got a day ahead of us. The baith o' us will have a sore head tomorrow an' that's no use on a carriage ride. Let's go off tae sleep an' we'll see how things look in Campbeltoun."

Jane nodded and finished her wine. He rose to pay, and she went up the stairs to her room, unlocking the door and pushing it shut behind her.

The room was tiny but nevertheless well-appointed; a water jug sat on a stand next to the single bed. Jane flopped down onto it with the hazy joy of inebriation, at that blessed stage where one is drunk enough to be happy and yet not enough to be ill.

Out the window, Jane could see the moon shining down on the loch and the stars reflected there. She whispered to herself a song she had known since she was a little girl and then fell asleep in the moonlight.

* * *

The carriage ride was long and fairly unpleasant, as those tended to be out in the farthest reaches of the North. Campbeltoun was the westernmost town on the island of Great Britain, and as it was situated near the end of the Kintyre peninsula, getting there was something of a chore.

It was a chore, however, richly rewarded by the town's immaculate beauty and its setting as a jewel on the Campbeltoun Loch, heading out into the sea via the Firth of Clyde. This was their destination for the evening, but not their final one.

Everyone seemed to know Jane's father.

"Archie!" shouted the men at the bar in the pub, and that was how it always began, wasn't it? The rounds would go 'round, and Jane found that out here nobody much minded a woman in the pub or her taking her hair down. She wondered if, once they arrived at her father's village, she'd be able to walk around barefoot again as she once had, all those centuries ago but only a few months in reality.

The singing had begun, as it usually did when it got late enough. Here, the pubs didn't close...not exactly. They locked the front door so the bailiff wouldn't fine them and then the bailiff himself would come in the back door and join them, drinking and smoking around the peat fire.

Oh, Campbeltoun Loch, I wish ye were whisky
Campbeltoun Loch, och aye!
Campbeltoun Loch, I wish ye were whisky!
An I wad drink ye dry!

The men grabbed Jane and danced around in circles across the room, as she shouted with laughter and her father clapped along. It was like another world, and one that was so like Ainslie's that Jane felt at home here. Even with her height and the way she'd always taken up so much space, the men didn't seem to mind. Jane was put in mind of Christina and her height, her muscles, her imposing size, and yet she wore it proudly. Jane decided that she would, too.

Eventually things began to wind down, and Jane found her way to her own narrow bed in a much smaller, humbler hostelry than the George. She fell asleep right away, thinking she was among her own clan and people now.

* * *

The following morning, Jane and her father boarded yet another carriage that would take them to Southend, the village her father hailed from. As they awaited loading, something caught Jane's eye. She froze.

A sign across the street from where they were putting the suitcases into the carriage was advertising a new route offered by MacBrayne ferries, out to the Isle of Islay.

"Da," said Jane, her voice insistent and strained. "Da. Can we go to Islay?"

"We've just finished loading the carriage, Janie," he said, pipe in his mouth, as he climbed down. He walked across the street with her and took a closer look at the sign. "Says they travel on Wednesdays only, an' it's Saturday. But we could go when we return?"

Jane nodded.

"Yes," she agreed. "That would be ideal, I think."

She climbed into the carriage, and the vehicle lurched off towards Southend. Jane kept staring at the sign until it was out of sight.

* * *

Fortunately for Jane, so much went on during their time at Southend that she didn't have much opportunity for impatience. The villagers wanted to see her, hear about her advantageous marriage, learn about all the new advancements in Edinburgh and Glasgow. They were quite poor and didn't venture out of the peninsula much, being occupied with herding sheep and with making the whisky for which that peninsula was known the world over. The inhabitants didn't see the need for leaving but also wanted to hear all the latest news and gossip from abroad, just like people everywhere.

Jane learned more about the centuries-old feud between the Campbells and the MacDonalds, which she actually listened to this time. These old stories had been bandied about since she was a child, but she'd never really paid attention. She'd not known, then, how much of an impact they might have on her life. For some of the people, the feud was one in living memory. The more she learned, the more she despaired of anything working out between her and Ainslie. Later that evening, she said as much to her father.

"Ah, Janie," he said. "Ye canna be listenin' tae old fowk tellin' tales. People want there t' be animosity, because it's somethin' tae do. The only way it's broken is if someone reaches a hand across in friendship first."

"Fat lot of good that did the Scots with the English," Jane muttered. Her father chuckled.

"Aye," he said. "There must be willingness on both sides to come together as equals in an honest fashion. But there's always a chance, Janie. Always."

Jane went to sleep that night and thought over what her father had said. But as much fun as she had out here, she was also a creature of modernity; she missed the hustle and bustle of Edinburgh, her work with the Royal Society, and afternoon tea with cupcakes and champagne. She wasn't made for this life, out here with the sheep on the moors. She was a city person, she told herself, and that was that.

* * *

Their return to Campbeltoun was uneventful, although Jane was looking forward to the ferry trip. She was a bit uneasy about what she would find on the other side of the water. This would not be her Islay, after all.

As she and the other passengers boarded the puffer that took mail out to the islands, she hoped that seeing the place again might enlighten her. Other people could tell her what they thought, but in reality it was a serious decision that would need personal conviction before she knew whether it would be best to stay or return.

The journey was a pleasant one, and the views were breathtaking; she had forgotten that wild Scotland could be such an incredible place. The mountainous islands rising out of the water made for a stern and wild backdrop to the ferry's route through the sea.

Then, beyond a haze of mist, Islay materialised, tall and imposing, green and beautiful, flanked by the Paps of Jura rising up across the strait. The island's houses peeking out from rock outcroppings and the long coastline leading into the port made her feel as though they had crossed over into some other fantastical land. The fresh, cool sea air carried with it a scent of peat and rain peculiar to Islay, and the thought passed through the minds of more than one person aboard the Islay ferry that they had arrived somewhere magical indeed.

CHAPTER THIRTY-FOUR

Where the Brokenhearted Ken

Islay was not what she remembered.

If ever there was a time Jane had experienced culture shock, it was this one. Not when travelling back in time hundreds of years, not when returning to the present and its odd views of women and restrictive clothing, not when seeing Southend again. But now.

Seeing proud, green Islay empty was a soul-sickness that she could never have imagined.

"Da," she asked anxiously, "where is everyone?"

A man sitting outside a shack whittling a piece of wood looked up at her.

"America," he said gruffly.

"America? But why?" she asked.

The man tossed the shavings aside into the grass.

"Nae work here, I'm afraid," he said. "The ferry goes back an' forth, but there's no much in the way o' human habitation. Potatoes took some o' them, the Campbells took the rest."

"The Campbells?" asked Jane, exchanging a look with her father.

"Oh, aye," said the man. "Advantageous marriages, settlin' the auld rivalries, an' so on. The first few Campbells did right by the islanders, but that was a couple generations back. This one never told anybody he'd defaulted on debts, so…nae money, nae trade, nae nothin'. Everybody left."

Jane looked up at the high embankment above Port Askaig.

"There can't be no one left," Jane insisted. "I mean, you're here."

"Aye," said the old man. "It's hame, ye ken. An' yer welcome tae tour the place, just wantin' ye to understand what ye'll be seein'. As a young boy, I saw the island thrivin'. Today…I dinna ken. Maybe history's all that's left for her, puir girl."

Jane's mouth set in a determined frown.

"I shall go and see it," she announced. Her father took her aside.

"Are ye sure about this, lass?" he asked quietly. "Ye dinna ken what ye'll find up there."

Jane looked into her father's kindly, weathered face.

"Yes, Da," she said. "I have to. I must know."

"Awright," he said, sighing. "If ye insist."

He nodded to the carriage driver, and they went up the road from Port Askaig. Jane saw the old man look after them and shake his head before he disappeared indoors.

* * *

She walked the windswept fields with her father, to the city by the sea.

There was nothing left there, just a bothy or two and a few aggressively friendly horses. The view to the sea was the same as ever. It was like nothing had ever been there.

"Maybe this is the wrang place," her father offered. Jane held back tears and shook her head.

"No," she said. "This was it, we…used to walk along the curve of the bay and climb the rocks there—"

She pointed to the side of the bay, with stacks of boulders now rounded from the beat of the sea, from the wind, from time.

"I dinna ken what ye thocht ye might find here, Janie," said her father. "But I think ye need tae hark tae yer heart a bit mair."

And still Jane shook her head, resolute.

"It doesn't matter what I want, Da," she said. "Did you not hear what the old man said? Advantageous marriage to the Campbells brought on this ruin. Should I be involved in that?"

Jane's father put his hands on her shoulders.

"Ye've always been a headstrong one, Janie," he said. "Even when ye were a wee lassie. An' I willna force ye tae mak this decision. It's one ye must decide on wi' yer whole heart. But ken my ain heart breaks, watchin' ye suffer so."

Then he gave her a hug, and the two of them looked out onto the beach and the place that was once a bustling city, so very long ago.

* * *

The carriage ride back to the port was quiet. Jane's father had asked if she would like to stop by the pubs along the way, and she refused. He went in for a few quiet pints and left her alone with her thoughts.

Islay was wild and beautiful, just as it was in Ainslie's time. So much was gone, and yet the curve of the island, the blue of the sea, the white of the sand were all things she held close like a locket over her heart. She hadn't seen the island in its entirety, and the long journey back to the port showed her that it was rich in beauty as well as resources. She knew all things must pass in time, but as a scientist she also knew that nothing ever goes away.

Islay would rise again.

* * *

On the ferryboat, they left behind the peat-scented moorlands of the green isle, queen of the Hebrides. The mist fell back across the island like a shawl over a woman's shoulders, a queen waiting, like Arthur, for her triumphant return.

But Islay now was not Islay then, and there was nothing Jane could do about it. Perhaps the future held promise for the beautiful island in the sea, but it was not the home she had known.

"Look, Janie," her father said, pointing out the window. Everyone had gone to the side of the boat to look out at a smaller island they were passing as the ferry steamed out of the sound.

Jane looked and saw the crumbled ruins of a castle standing sentinel on the island.

"What is it?" she asked.

"Captain says it's an old MacDonald castle," said her father. "Claig Castle, on Heather Island."

Jane stared at the empty ruin off of Jura and buried her face in her hands.

Her father rubbed her back in sympathy as Jane sobbed, while the other passengers studiously ignored her; they were Victorian, after all.

CHAPTER THIRTY-FIVE

Nae Second Spring Again

The return to Edinburgh did not have the same jovial atmosphere as the initial journey.

They stopped off briefly at Inveraray, but Jane elected to stay in her room, staring out at the loch while her father spoke to his friends in the pub below. He'd brought her lunch and dinner, but that was all the communication they had. It was clear to him that she needed time to think, and so he did not pressure her. He understood that there were certain undertakings a father could not prevail upon his daughter to deal with and that she would make her own decision in her own time. Still, he made it clear that he was available, if she should need him.

Jane, for her part, spent a great deal of time thinking, especially about Inveraray Castle, hidden just around the corner behind a grove of trees, as the carriages went up and over the bridge all day. She thought about the Campbells, and the MacDonalds, and Scotland, of feuds and wars and a long winter of starvation that nearly brought destruction upon Islay and the deaths of hundreds who were desperate and hungry. She thought of the city on the island, now reduced to a few bothies next to an empty beach and a roaring sea.

And always, and ever, of green eyes in a pale white face smattered with freckles and of hair like a hearth-fire, red and wild.

* * *

They boarded the train in the first-class compartment again, and as the train whistled, gaining speed as it pulled away from the station in a cloud of steam, Jane's father looked at her.

"Now, Janie," he said. "I've left ye tae yersel a' this time. An' I ken ye may no' want tae speak tae yer auld da, but I hate tae see my little girl in pain."

"Da," Jane protested. He held his hands up.

"All's I'm sayin'," he said. "I'm here, Janie. An' I'm listenin'."

The woman came by with the trolley, and they ordered coffee and tablet as the Highland scenery passed by out the windows, giving way to the rolling hills of the Lowlands and the Central Belt.

"I don't want to want this, Da," she finally said. He nodded.

"That's no' surprisin'," he said. "But if it'll make ye happy, lass, what of it?"

"I'm a Caimbeul, Da," she said.

"Aye, so ye keep sayin'," he said. "An' I'm a Caimbeul too. But Janie, nae clan is evil by nature. Bad choices, feuds, this country's had sic a history o' self-destruction wroucht worse than the English ever could, an' that by themselves."

Jane was silent, sipping her coffee.

"But Jane," he said, "There's naethin' ye can do about it! No' you or me. But sma' tho' we are, we can make a difference. Wee ones, here an' there. The difference is, ye ken already what's in the future, from their perspective, at least. Why make yersel' miserable for things out o' your control in the past?"

He sat back in his seat.

"Be happy, Janie," he said. "However ye can be, an' I'll do what I can tae help ye. But dinna think for a moment tha' this sacrifice means anythin' tae anyone but you. Martyrdom is meaningless without a cause, Jane, an' from what ye told me, ye're only tearin' yerself—an' herself, this Ainslie—apart."

Jane gave him a watery smile.

"Thanks, Da," she said. "Thank you for not judging me, especially for who I love."

"Weel, I wouldna go that far," he said. "I ken I promised I wouldna, but I'll be puttin' my name alongside David and Joe's by sayin': ye're an idiot, lass."

"Da!"

"But ye're *my* idiot," he said, grinning. "An' I'll respect your wishes nae matter what."

Jane wiped her eyes and smiled, while the train pulled into Glasgow Central station and they had to disembark to change for Edinburgh.

* * *

Jane stood on Portobello Beach, alone.

She watched the couples and the children running across the sand. Everything was grey and dark—the sea, the sky, the people. There was little colour in Edinburgh, and people often went into the sea fully dressed. From the grey stone buildings over her shoulder, to the grey beach in front of her, she wondered when and how colour had faded its way out of the city, draining away to other places, to other times. The Highlands, even after the famine, the Clearances, Culloden, still carried a mischief and joy about them that didn't exist in her city.

She loved Edinburgh; it was the city of her youth. Its Gothic labyrinth of passageways and closes were a penny-dreadful writer's dream. There was always an air of mystery in this city shrouded in fog, looking out over the sea. So much of the intellectual flowering of Scotland had happened here, in the arts and the sciences; Robert Burns and Sir Walter Scott had lived here, and she knew how fortunate she was to call Joe Bell a friend.

The summer had also brought news of the gruesome Ripper murders to Edinburgh, a shudder running through the nation that something so awful could happen in London. Joe was considering looking into the case; his deductive skills might be of use to Scotland Yard. Still, it made Jane feel more and more disconnected from this place, where such horrors were perpetrated against women with impunity. She feared that she was romanticising the past far too much, but there was a reason the women in Edinburgh were making sure their doors and windows were locked at night, far from London though they may be. The killer could be anywhere, anyone; travel was not so difficult now as it was in the past, as her recent holiday had shown.

She thought of the past, of the colour of it—the blues and greens of the sea, of the tartan plaidies of the people—and wondered.

CHAPTER THIRTY-SIX

Tho the Waefu' May Cease Frae Their Greetin'

On her way to the museum, Jane passed by the pub where she and her father used to greet the small dog who as "Greyfriars Bobby" earned a worldwide reputation for faithfulness. "Bobby" continued to mysteriously change breeds throughout the years she had known him, and while it became clear to her over time that his story wasn't true and was more a tale of the canny Scot who owned the pub than the faithful dog, she still had liked to bring him treats.

"Best-fed dog in the kingdom," the pub owner used to boast, and she had to agree.

Some time back, they had constructed a statue to the ersatz Bobby, and while he and the story may have been fakes, it gave a few small graveyard dogs a lifetime of luxury in a time that was, for dogs, not an easy one.

Jane stood in front of Bobby's fountain and looked up at the little statue of a Skye terrier sitting on the top, a symbol of the faithfulness of dogs. She was reminded of Madra, whose clear lack of intellect was irrelevant in his place within the Dhòmhnaill household. Like Bobby, he belonged there; regardless of everything, Islay was home.

And despite his being from another place, and so different from the rest, they loved him all the same.

* * *

The museum was quiet in the late afternoon. Jane's boots clicked loudly on the polished floors.

She wasn't exactly sure what she was looking for. Some explanation of what happened to Ainslie, perhaps?

"Excuse me, sir," she asked a man working as a guide. "Could you tell me where I might find information about the Lordship of the Isles in the medieval period?"

He broke out in a grin and shook her hand heartily.

"You're Lady Jane Crichton, aren't you?" he asked. "You're one of the Edinburgh Seven!"

Jane, a bit taken aback, nodded.

"Good for you! Good for all you ladies!" he said. "Stick it to them where it hurts, I say!"

"My goodness," said Jane.

"Ah, my apologies," he said. "I've just followed that story for quite a while, and education is the most important thing anyone can do for this country. It's a way to keep Scotland down, you see. *Saor Alba* and all that, you know."

"Thank...you?" Jane ventured, and he shook her hand again.

"Now, what can I do for you?" he asked. "I assume you're looking into this history as a part of your overall education. I know it isn't medicine, but history is a valid field in itself. If we don't know where we've been, we don't know where we're going, and so forth. Are you looking for something in particular?"

Jane paused.

"I'm looking for any information about Ainslie nic Dòmhnaill," she said. "This would be in the thirteenth century. She'd have been a chief."

"Oh, I see!" he said. "Yes, evidence of the equality of the past may indeed help you in your endeavours. Let's see what we can find, shall we?"

And the man burbled away as he toddled along the halls, talking to Jane about history the entire way.

* * *

"Now let's see," he said, pulling out a large parchment rolled into a scroll. He unrolled it and spread it out on the table. He put on his reading glasses.

"There's record of a Dòmhnall, but his existence is doubtful," he said. "Says here he had two sons, Alasdair and Aonghus. No mention of an Ainslie."

Jane started. She came around the table to look closely at the document.

"No, this can't be right," she said. "Dòmhnall's children were Ainslie and Aonghus, I'm sure of it."

The man shrugged.

"I don't know what to tell you," he said. "Either you had bad information, or this information has been suppressed for some reason, or—"

"Or?" Jane prompted.

"Well," he said. "She may have died young and would not be of much note in history."

Jane froze.

"Is there any way I could find out?" she asked. The air seemed to have been drained from the room.

"Honestly? This far back, we just don't have much," he said. "It's why we don't know for certain if Dòmhnall existed, despite giving his name to the entire clan Donald. Gravestones didn't have names on them, if they were even erected. This woman had status, so it's likely she'd have one, but there's no way to tell. It was just too long ago."

Jane looked at the parchment for any clue, but her search was in vain.

"At least *I* know he was real," she muttered under her breath.

"Pardon?" he asked. Jane smiled and shook her head.

"Nothing," she said. "Thank you so much for your help."

He shook her hand again.

"Anytime, Lady Crichton," he said. "Just you say the word. Any help you need."

Jane nodded to him and walked back through the museum.

Along one of the hallways, something caught her eye. A retrospective on the life of Burns. She slowed and smiled, recalling many times her mother had sung his songs to her. In this time of personal turmoil, a remembrance of her early childhood was a welcome distraction.

As she drew near, she read the lines of a famous poem.

My heart's in the Highlands
My heart is not here
My heart's in the Highlands
A-chasin' the deer.

And something about the poem clicked in her, like a key turned in a lock, and she was flying down the hallway to the door, boots clacking hard against the tile, and she burst through the front entrance like a woman on fire, flagging down a passing carriage.

The ride to the manor house was bumpy, as she insisted on top speed. She threw herself out of the carriage and flung the fare at the driver, who was startled at her impatience. She ran up the steps to the door and pushed it open so hard it banged against the wall.

"David!" she cried, running through the house. "David, I need to go home. She's waiting for me."

CHAPTER THIRTY-SEVEN

High Road

"Are you certain about this, Janie?"

David was watching her work on the machine as he held a plate of cucumber sandwiches in his hand. Off to the side of the shed was a pot of tea and some mugs. Next to Jane was a little packet consisting of more appropriate clothing for her destination. Despite how much she now loathed her corset and high-heeled boots, wearing her Highland dress here would, at best, make her look eccentric, and at worst, cause the kind of scandal David certainly did not need.

"Absolutely," said Jane, reaching for a wrench. David handed it to her as he set down his tray. She grumbled in frustration and gave the machine a good whack with the wrench.

"I say!" David protested, and Jane fell back on her haunches, sighing in disgust.

He knelt down beside her.

"What is it, Janie?" he asked.

"I just—it *crashed* last time, David," she explained. "I'm not quite sure how I got back here, and I was three months late as it was! What if I crash-land again, somewhere that doesn't have a brilliant smith like Aileen? Then I'm stuck between here and there and can't go back!"

David put his arm around her shoulders and she leaned in, sniffling.

"Now, old bean," he said, "it's a terribly difficult business, all this. But you must persevere! If you intend to sweep your chief off her feet, you must keep a steady hand. Is there anything I can do to help?"

Jane shook her head, tears in her eyes. David reached over.

"What about a cucumber sandwich?" he asked earnestly.

Jane looked at the sandwich and then at David. She burst out laughing and David chortled into his mustache.

"You know," David said, after the tension had been broken, "I think I have the very thing."

* * *

Two hours later, the door opened. The shadow of a man in an Ulster stood in the doorway.

Jane turned and looked up into the kindly, genial face of her professor and mentor.

"Joe!" she cried and wrapped her arms around him. "Thank you for coming! But what are you doing here?"

Dr. Bell stepped into the shed, removing his cloak.

"David came 'round to fetch me," he said. "Told me you were having trouble with your machine and thought I might be able to help."

"I'm sorry, Janie," said David. "I know your project is a secret, but since Doctor Bell already knew it…"

"Oh, it's wonderful," she said. "Thank you both."

"Now," said Dr. Bell. "Shall we begin?"

* * *

Jane was able to pinpoint a few of the problems and go through them with Dr. Bell. A few tweaks here and there, and the machine appeared to be ready to make another flight.

"There's no guarantee it'll work," Jane said. "Even with these corrections, I won't know until I try it."

"Well, there's only one thing for it," said Dr. Bell.

"I'm going to do a few short hops across the lawn," she said and climbed in, closing the hatch behind her. A few moments later, she disappeared.

Bell waited, and David was startled by the appearance of Jane and her machine in front of him as he ferried yet another tray of sandwiches to the shed. His quick reflexes meant that none of the sandwiches fell. Jane tried a couple more times before successfully returning the machine to the shed.

"It looks as though all is in order," said Dr. Bell.

"Yes, but these short hops were how I tested it before I made my first long flight," Jane explained. "I have no idea where I am going to end up. Still, the only way to know is to give it a try."

She looked at the machine with trepidation, steeling herself for another long flight.

"I will return as soon as I can, to let you know if it worked," she promised.

She went to kiss David on the cheek, when he addressed her in a low tone.

"Janie," he said. "I know it's awfully bold of me to ask, but I've not asked anything from you since the start of our agreement and throughout our marriage."

"Anything," she promised. "What do you need?"

David glanced back at the house.

"If it's really true that people like me—people like *us*—are more accepted then," he said, "take me with you, Janie. Please."

"The machine only has room enough for one."

"Yes," David said. "But if this flight works, and the machine is dependable, we can rebuild it to make room for two."

Jane looked at the machine and then at the manor house.

"What about all this?" she asked. "You'll lose your beautiful house and all that money."

David shrugged.

"Money is meaningless if you can't have happiness," he said. "It's a small price to pay in order to stop living in fear and to be able to love who you want to love."

His intensity was a surprise to her. She had never seen David like this in all the time she had known him. Gone was the simple and joyful demeanour, replaced with a hunted expression she'd never suspected of him. His stiff-upper-lip dependence upon British flippancy and fortitude had apparently been hiding his fear for a very long time. And Jane knew, all too well, the emptiness of a life lived without the person she loved; although she had not known it before, the loss of it was terrible. David had never even had the chance.

"If this works," said Jane, "I promise I will come back for you. I don't know how I'll be received or even if I'll make it. Keep well, David. I love you."

She kissed him on the cheek again and climbed into the machine. As both Bell and David watched, she flickered out of existence, her eyes filled with fear and locked onto the two men who had helped her to find her way back home.

* * *

Jane was relieved to see the machine had landed gently in the pinewoods. They were both intact.

She opened the hatch and climbed out of the machine.

All around her, birds were singing merrily in the trees. It seemed to be summer. Everything was silent. The pine boughs overhung the little clearing and shaded the machine from the sun.

She went to look outside of the clearing and found that she was at the edge of a cliff soaring some great distance in the air. Below, the waters of a loch glittered silver in the late afternoon sun.

"Who are you?" a voice startled her, speaking in Gaelic, and she turned around to see a young man standing at the head of a group of people and pointing his sword at her.

"Lady Jane Crichton," she replied. "I seek Ainslie nic Dòmhnaill."

The blank looks on their faces confirmed her fears. This was not Islay and perhaps not even the correct time period.

"Come with us," said the young man, switching over to English. "Maybe the chief will like you and ask your hand in marriage."

Jane sighed deeply. They seemed to pay the machine no mind. She thought perhaps they mistook it for a boulder, since it did match the surroundings in colour.

"Go on," said the man, gesturing in front of himself. Jane marched forward, resigned but resolute. She had chosen this path.

She might at least learn from another chief what had happened to Ainslie, if her timing was right.

CHAPTER THIRTY-EIGHT

Low Road

It turned out that they didn't have far to go. An encampment far up the bank above the loch was apparently their destination. Jane walked in front of the group, wary and curious.

They brought her to an overlook, where a lone figure was standing and surveying the land below.

A tall woman with a long ginger braid.

"Chief," called one of the men. The woman turned.

Ainslie's brilliant green eyes danced as she grinned.

"Hello, Jane," she said. "Welcome hame."

* * *

"*You!*" Jane shrieked and pointed. There was mischief in Ainslie's expression. Jane stared in consternation at the soldiers around her, who tried to keep straight faces but broke out in little smiles.

"I'm sorry, Jane," Ainslie said. "I recognised the sound of your machine in the forest an' I couldnae resist!"

"I'm going to throw you off the mountain now," said Jane and rushed up to her—

—only to be grabbed and treated to a searing kiss, right in front of all the soldiers, who whooped and clapped as soldiers are wont to do.

"Back in my arms again," Ainslie murmured. "I didna think I'd see ye again, my faerie."

Jane looked into those features she'd dreamed of for many months. "I didn't either," she said. "Where are we?"

Ainslie looked at her, puzzled.

"Islay, of course," she said. "Ye didna recognise it?"

"But this is a mountain!" cried Jane.

"Aye. Islay has mountains," said Ainslie. "An' down there is Loch Gruinart. Although I suppose I never did show them to ye. We've much to do, Jane. I've much tae show ye."

"Ainslie, what about—" she asked.

"Later," said Ainslie. "No' in front o' the soldiers. Tonight, ye'll dine wi' me."

* * *

There was candlelight in the tent that evening, and the soldiers had retired to their own diversions. A roast sat on the table, along with a few bottles of wine. Jane was famished, for some reason; it'd only been a few hours since David's cucumber sandwiches, but she was as hungry as if she had not eaten for a week.

"Please, eat," said Ainslie. "We're headed back to Claig Castle tomorrow evening. This may be our only chance for privacy, at least for a while. Ye ken everyone will be overjoyed to see you again."

Jane speared a piece of meat on her fork and took a dainty bite. It was delicious; she closed her eyes and hummed in appreciation.

"You keep making noises like that, an' the soldiers'll be talkin' all the way back to Am Fraoch Eilean," teased Ainslie.

Jane smiled but then grew serious.

"How long has it been?" she asked. Ainslie's smile faded.

"Near a year or thereabouts," she said. "I didnae keep track. I didna want tae."

She stared down at her meal and then took a drink of wine for something to do.

"Ainslie, I'm sorry," said Jane. "I was such a fool. I'm sorry I said what I did."

"Was it true?" she asked. "About the clans, about the Lordship?"

Jane swallowed and nodded. Ainslie sighed and sat back in her chair.

"Weel," she said, "it's many years frae now, an' it's no' about tae change anythin' for me, far as I ken. It's sad, but it's out o' my hands, Jane."

She leaned forward on her elbows.

"What's no' out o' my ken is how I feel about ye," she said, putting her hand out, asking silently for Jane to take it.

Jane didn't move. Ainslie stared at her.

"Ye didna come a' this way back tae just be friends?" she asked. "I didna see ye fall this time, but I did hear ye. That boatie o' yours rolls about mair than I'd like. How d'ye no get seasick in that thing?"

"Because I stay still while it is moving," she said. "It's…er. Physics. Design."

"Hmm," Ainslie thought. "Ye'll hafta teach me that someday."

"Of course," Jane agreed.

"Can ye tell me why ye willnae touch me, Jane?" she asked. "Is it because of the fighting? Because ye were right, I admit it. I feared losin' ye sae much that I went mad wi' it, but then I lost ye anyway—I thocht forever. I'm just glad ye've come hame. All is forgiven. If ye canna bring yerself tae forgive me yet, I understand—only I want tae ken why ye won't take my hand."

Jane gathered her courage and took a deep breath.

"I have something I need to tell you," she said. "And if you still want to touch me, to kiss me, to—anything, after you know, then we'll talk about it and I'll kiss you as much as you like, from this day forward. I have forgiven you, and I only ask that you forgive me, not only for being rash that night and running away, but for what I'm about to tell you and for not telling you before."

Ainslie's expression grew serious.

"What is it, Jane?" she asked. "I ken ye're married, but that it's mair in word than deed. I ken ye're from some other time, an' I ken ye're from Edinburgh. If all these impossibilities can be overcome, what can you say tae me that will make me love ye less?"

Jane held her head high, although inside she trembled.

"Ainslie," she said. "I'm a Caimbeul."

CHAPTER THIRTY-NINE

I'll Be in Scotland Afore Ye

Jane lay in her tent, alone.

She didn't know what she'd expected Ainslie to say or do. It certainly was not what happened.

She'd just stood up and left the tent without a word. A soldier had come later and beckoned Jane to follow him. He showed her this tent and that was that.

She was gone. They were together again, and she was gone.

Jane studied the canvas roof of the tent and considered her options. She was too tired to attempt a return to Edinburgh, so she'd make her decision in the morning. She also didn't want to give up so quickly, after coming all this way.

She certainly didn't want to return to David, crying about how foolishly she had squandered her chance. Why tell Ainslie, anyway? She had the Crichton name as a shield. Ainslie didn't know her family; it was unlikely that it'd ever come up.

And yet, she'd partly made her decision to leave because of it, so she wanted to tell the truth. If she was going to boldly ignore the conventions of her own time and enter into a relationship with Ainslie, she wanted it to be on equal ground, with full understanding of what they were both getting themselves into. So, while she was baffled and saddened by Ainslie's response, she had not expected it to go well. This silence was harder to understand than the curses and imprecations she'd imagined or laughter and acceptance. It could mean anything at all.

Despite Jane's concerns, the trip had really taken it out of her, and she fell asleep as she ruminated on the events of the day.

* * *

The following morning, the tents were packed up and carried down the mountain, as they made their way back to the castle. Ainslie still hadn't spoken to her, or even looked her way, as she commanded the soldiers with an expert hand. They walked through the heather and bracken down the paths that led to the sea and the waiting birlinns.

"Malcolm!" cried Jane, as she approached the vessel. She'd missed it, as if it were a family pet.

She saw the corner of Ainslie's mouth quirk up in a slight grin. Jane climbed into the boat and Ainslie followed. The birlinns were out into the sound within the work of a few moments. Ainslie still kept silent.

"Ainslie," said Jane, and when she wasn't interrupted, she went on. "Are you chief? Is that true?"

She nodded once, sharp. Jane felt there was an eggshell cracking around Ainslie's silence. Her position was a delicate one, and so she did not ask anything further as they made their way to the castle.

* * *

Upon reaching Claig Castle, who should greet them but Madra, who was in paroxysms of total joy as he raced around the small group of soldiers. If he'd had wings, he would have taken flight. As it was, he bounced in circles so high in the air that Jane thought he would certainly collide with someone, but he did not.

Inside the castle, Christina welcomed them.

"Jane!" she cried. "You've come back!"

"Yes," Jane nodded. She smiled.

"It's good of you," she said. "Dòmhnall has not been well, and Ainslie is learning the responsibilities of the chief."

Ainslie's head was bowed.

"Have you not told Jane?" she asked. She looked between the two of them with suspicion. "Is something wrong between the two of you?"

"I will take Jane to her cottage," said Ainslie, without answering the question. "I dinna think it's safe tae have her here, under our roof."

Jane stared at Ainslie, openmouthed. The pain of her distrust was more worrying than her silence had been.

Christina raised her eyebrows but didn't pursue that line of enquiry any further.

"Aonghus is with your father," said Christina. "I'm sure they'd both like to see Jane, Ainslie."

Ainslie's eyes flashed, and for a moment, Jane was certain that she'd refuse. Something within her must have persuaded her, as she sagged a bit and then nodded her agreement.

The men were dismissed to go home to their families. Ainslie stiffly indicated that Jane should follow her, and so they went up the stairs to Dòmhnall's chamber.

* * *

Jane had never been into this part of the castle. Dòmhnall and Christina's bed was huge, with sumptuous drapery. There were a few side tables and a desk, but the wall was dominated by yet another enormous window with a perfect view of the sea outside.

"Good to see if anyone is coming," Dòmhnall said from the bed, when he saw Jane looking. "We see most ships that pass by here. Hello again, Jane. It's good tae see ye; we thocht we may never."

Jane blushed and bowed.

"Yes, I'm sorry," she said. "I was away for too long. I hope this isn't a rude question, but—what happened to you?"

Dòmhnall and Aonghus exchanged glances, and Aonghus gave a quick nod.

"My son says I shouldn't do anything that might overexcite me," he said. "An' this story disnae sit well wi' me, even now. I'm lucky tae be livin', I ken that much, but I've nae pride in it. Enough ither men an' women died that I wonder at the luck of it."

He drank from a cup that Aonghus handed him, as he had already grown a bit hoarse.

"Events are happening in Scotland that sound like war," said Dòmhnall. "Then the Skyemen came down for battle, I still dinna ken their reason, and I caught a wound much like yours, Jane."

Jane instinctively put a hand where her scar now existed. Although she had healed well, thanks to Aonghus's ministrations, she would always carry a mark upon her skin showing the way she nearly left this mortal plane.

"An' sae I've been here since," Dòmhnall said. "I've gien the chiefship o'er tae Ainslie, as she's young enough, an' I'd like tae retire, if I'm honest wi' ye. Mair time for fishin', an' bein' taken care of while I drink whisky an' tell auld stories. Yer da is gettin' auld, Ainslie, can ye believe it?"

He smiled and seemed perfectly content.

"What about Christina?" asked Jane. "Would she not be Lord of the Isles in your place?"

"Och weel," said Dòmhnall. "It's really the *Kingdom* of the Isles; the Scots just dinna like us havin' airs, sae we call ourselves that tae make them happy. But everyone out here knows what we really are. An' it's the chiefship handed down; Christina is chief o' her ain clan."

Christina inclined her head slightly.

"I do not plan to retire," she said. "Ainslie has yet much to learn about the ruling of the wider islands. But for now, yes, she is the chief of the Islay MacDonalds. It will be some time before she is Lord of the Isles. I will govern in the interim."

Jane beamed with pride at Ainslie, who still would not look at her.

"Now, please take Jane to her cottage," Christina directed. "And work out whatever is wrong between the two of you. If you intend to lead, Ainslie, you need to communicate with people, particularly your partner. The livelihood of your clan depends upon your fighting prowess as well as your diplomacy. Now, go. Dòmhnall needs his rest."

Aonghus walked over and hugged Jane quickly.

"It's good tae see ye, Jane," he said in a low voice. "An' yer wound, it healed well?"

"Yes," she said. "Thank you, Aonghus. I owe you my life."

Aonghus blushed to the roots of his hair.

"Weel, I dinna ken that," he said, but it was obvious that he was flattered and proud of himself. "Mum's richt, though; ye'll need tae be off, as Da canna tak much excitement in his state."

Jane nodded and then addressed Ainslie's parents.

"I hope you'll feel well soon, sir," she said. "And it is a pleasure to see you again, madame."

She did a little curtsy and turned on her heel.

Ainslie followed her out of the room.

CHAPTER FORTY

I'll Show Ye the Red Deer A-Roamin'

The cottage was clean, just as it had been when she returned after her long convalescence.

Ainslie was crouched by the fire, stirring it into flame.

"Thank you for keeping the cottage clean," Jane said quietly. She stood in the doorway, awkward and unsure.

"Sit," Ainslie said, the first word she'd spoken to Jane directly since the previous night. Jane sat on the edge of the bed.

There was silence again after that, and Jane wondered if that was all she was going to get.

"When I was a child, I swore I would never lay wi' a Caimbeul."

Jane startled and looked at Ainslie, whose back was to her.

"And the Skyemen? They're Caimbeuls too?"

Ainslie sighed and shook her head.

"Nae, they're the Macleans," she said. "An' some o' the Dhòmhnaill, if ye can believe it. I dinna understand why we maun fight a' the time—an' for what? Naethin! Naethin' but the husbands an' wives an' bairns tae weep o'er their graves. Y'see, that awfu' winter wi' the Caimbeulaich? That made sense. They were starving. The men who skewered my father—just greed. Plain greed! They canna keep tae themselves, an' we used tae trade wi' them! Madra is a Skye dog, for God's sake!"

She sat back down on her haunches as the flames licked high in the fireplace, warming the cottage, and bringing back a nostalgia so powerful Jane nearly gasped at the strength of it.

"I'm sorry," she said, for something to say.

Ainslie finally turned to look at her.

"I waited for ye, Jane," she said. "Waited right here. For weeks I wouldna leave this cottage, sae sure ye'd return. An' the weeks turned intae months, an' the Skyemen came, an' I had tae tend tae my responsibilities. Even gone, ye made me mad for the loss o' ye."

"I was a fool," Jane said. "It took me a while to realise it, but… there's a poem, written by a man from a long time in the future, but he'll be the voice of Scotland one day. And reading it made me understand that my heart is, and always will be, right here with you in this little cottage, in this bed before the fire."

Ainslie crawled over to kneel in front of her, and Jane could finally see in her eyes the anguish and terror that had been hidden behind a hard mask the entire day.

"How in God's earth could I hae fallen in love wi' a Caimbeul," said Ainslie. "I fear ye'll be the end o' me, Lady Jane Crichton, an' yet willingly I throw mysel' intae the fire."

She laid her head on Jane's lap and reached for her hands, clutching them with a strength Jane had forgotten she had.

"And I will never leave again," Jane whispered. "I love you, Ainslie nic Dòmhnaill."

The tears were flowing down Jane's cheeks before she realised it, and Ainslie was shaking; after a while, Jane realised that Ainslie was sobbing. She leaned forward and held her, their figures in front of the fire entwined like Celtic knots on the edge of Jane's bed.

* * *

"Ye were like a ghost tae me, Jane," Ainslie said, once the tears had passed. "I was haunted by ye, by the memory o' ye, an' I understood that by yer time I'd hae long passed out o' the world. I didna think I'd see ye again in this lifetime."

Jane stroked her hair as she seemed content to stay in her lap.

"I was an arse," she said. Ainslie snorted.

Jane stared into the fire for a while.

"But…what about…my being a Caimbeul?" Jane asked, hesitant.

Ainslie looked up at her, beautiful red hair matching the flames dancing behind her and her eyes all the brighter green for the tears she had been crying.

"I dinna care, my faerie," said Ainslie. "All God's angels an' devils may conspire tae throw me into the Pit, an' still I'd love ye jist the same."

Some kind of ice around Jane's heart seemed to shatter and melt, and she put her hands on Ainslie's cheeks and kissed those soft lips like her life depended upon it.

* * *

Jane was surprised at their reactions to reuniting. She'd expected arguments, shouting, perhaps a night of passion. This all seemed very tame and strange to her, and she told Ainslie so, the following morning as they walked the moors.

"Weel, we all respond to circumstances differently," Ainslie reasoned. "It may be that we dinna react as we'd expected."

She squinted down the hill, where she could see the red deer leaping across the moors.

"Or," she admitted, "perhaps it hasn't hit us yet."

Ainslie angled a strange contraption in the direction of the deer and lit what looked like a fuse. The resulting explosion was deafening, but one of the deer fell.

"Where'd you get that?" Jane asked.

"Off one o' the Druids," said Ainslie. "From Cathay, this one. Ye tell me tha' people in yer time think Druids do magic, because they never thocht tae write any o' this down. Weel, this is the first time I've seen them produce something tha's like magic tae me. She ca's it a 'hand cannon.'"

Jane looked towards the deer.

"Can I try?" she asked. Ainslie shrugged.

"If ye like," she said. "It's a bit tricky, though—"

Jane closed an eye, sighted down the barrel, aimed, and lit the fuse. Another deer dropped to the ground in the distance. She stood up and gave a proud sidelong glance to Ainslie.

"How on earth did ye do that?" Ainslie demanded. "It took me ages to learn!"

Jane crossed her arms.

"David used to take me hunting," she said. "And clay-pigeon shooting. But my da was the one who taught me how to shoot."

There was pride, shock, and an unidentifiable expression in Ainslie's eyes. Jane flattered herself that it was something akin to lust.

"Best shot in Edinburgh," she said. "I won a prize once, you know."

"Weel, tha's enough meat for today," said Ainslie in a strained voice. "Let's go pick 'em up an' bring 'em back for cleanin'. And then, ah—if ye're not busy…"

"Yes?" Jane asked, mischievous.

"Maybe we can spend some time at your cottage tonight."

Jane gestured towards the fallen deer.

"Go on, then," she said.

"Just as ye say," Ainslie said. She was grinning like a wolf.

After dinner, Jane silently led Ainslie to the bed. She kissed her and started to push her earasaid off.

Ainslie grabbed her hand, a strange look in her eyes. It was something akin to fear.

"What is it?" asked Jane gently. "I've seen your body before."

Ainslie wouldn't look at her.

"Aye, once," she muttered. "An' for a moment. Frae a distance."

Jane sat up a bit.

"Is this why you've always stayed clothed?" Jane asked. "You've seen me naked many times."

Ainslie closed her mouth.

"I won't push," said Jane. "I know I'm only just returned, and I should not have left you, Ainslie. But I would love to see you. My queen."

Ainslie shuddered and suddenly stood up, shedding her earasaid and the rest of her clothing.

"Am I still your queen?" she demanded. "Do ye still wish tae worship me now?"

In the firelight, heavy scars stood out against Ainslie's fair skin, whipmark-wrapped around her entire body. It looked as though there was nothing that had remained untouched aside from her shoulders and her face.

Jane was speechless.

"What happened to you?" she asked.

"A hundred battles," she said, turning in the firelight as she'd once had Jane turn. "A fishing injury. Getting burned when peat-fire fell onto my dress when I was a wean. This is why I made ye turn for me in front o' the fire, when ye first arrived; unlike a waterfall deep in the woods, here, ye can see everythin'."

Ainslie's body was sturdy, corded muscle; she was solid and strong. She spoke to the fire, not looking at Jane.

"An' there ye are, lookin' like a...doll in an Edinburgh shop window," she said. "All smooth an' perfect an' beautiful. How could a faerie like ye look on a mere mortal like me? An' now ye've seen it."

Jane stood from the bed and walked over to Ainslie. With her eyes she asked if she could touch her. Ainslie nodded, and Jane traced the scars, every former wound, every mark on Ainslie's skin.

"They're a part of you," she said. "Like your tattoo. Or a brand. They tell the story of your life, my love."

Ainslie looked up in surprise at her words.

Jane's black eyes burned like the embers of the peat-fire, like coal in midwinter, like coming home.

"And it is the tale of a queen, proud and mighty," she whispered, kneeling down, her fingertips ghosting over Ainslie's inner thighs. "The tale of a queen I would honour all the days of my life."

She pressed a kiss to Ainslie's pubic mound, and a tentative exploration of her tongue had Ainslie's legs spreading even further.

"Lie down, my love," Jane whispered. "Let me worship you."

CHAPTER FORTY-TWO

And as Far as the Bound o' the Red Deer

Ainslie lay supine on the bed. She looked at Jane with curiosity and some fear in her dark green eyes.

Jane kissed her mouth; she kissed down her neck and across her shoulders. Her arms, her breasts, her stomach; the tips of her fingers, the curve of her wrists. Jane kissed Ainslie's thighs, her legs, the tops of her feet. She took her time, lavishing praise and love on her as she went.

"You are the most beautiful thing I have ever seen," Jane murmured. "You are worthy. You are my queen. You will be queen of my heart whether or not you are ever chief of these islands. You make me whole again. You are good, and pure. I love all of you, Ainslie nic Dòmhnaill, and have travelled here, hundreds of years in time scattered like paper across the centuries, just to worship you again."

When Jane returned to kiss Ainslie's lips, she saw tears streaked down her face from the corner of her eyes.

"You are more than a weapon," Jane whispered in her ear. "You are mine."

Ainslie kissed her back, soft and gentle.

"I love ye too, my faerie," she said. "My angel, my doll. Ye are a woman beyond my wildest dreams."

She lifted Jane's shirt and stared at her white, round breasts fallen free.

"It's lang I've dreamt of these," she said. She cupped Jane's breast with her hand as she suckled it with her mouth, laving the point of the nipple with her tongue. Jane whimpered in response and held Ainslie's head close to her breast. Ainslie's hand brushed the other breast and then pulled the rest of the corset-strings free without looking. The corset Jane was wearing fell to the floor.

Ainslie then sat up and pulled the remaining shift and earasaid from Jane, dropping the clothes to the floor. She sat back and drank her fill of Jane's body.

"Ye've the beauty of a ghost," Ainslie said. "When I first saw ye, had tae inspect ye for wounds an' bruises, I…had nae idea what it'd do tae me."

She pulled a pin from Jane's hair and watched it fall, as she had all that time ago.

"Your hair fell and touched the wee bend of your back, an' your perfect arse, an'…I couldnae breathe for your beauty," sighed Ainslie. "I knew I would need tae bathe ye, an' it had tae be all business; I am no ravisher o' women. But it was no easy task."

"Maybe you can bathe me again someday," said Jane impishly. Ainslie's caressing gaze grew hungry.

"Aye," she said. "An' I cannae promise I willnae be savage wi' ye then."

"Will you promise to be savage with me tonight?" Jane asked in a flirty, bold voice she didn't recognise in herself, but it seemed right once she'd said it.

Ainslie was on her in a moment, a tigress pinning her down to the bed.

"Now that I've seen ye again, I must have ye," she growled. "You're *mine*, an' ye'll want nae ither, once I'm done wi' ye."

"I don't know if I can guarantee that," Jane snarked. "What makes you think—oh!"

Ainslie parted her legs and her tongue darted out for a taste. She licked and sucked at the wetness there, and Jane felt a painful hunger between her legs. Swollen and ready, Jane spread her legs a bit more. Ainslie pushed them as far apart as they would go, exposing everything of her obscenely to Ainslie's interested gaze.

Ainslie's tongue suddenly filled her up, and Jane moaned, absolutely surrendering to her lover. The feelings were intense and she tried to squirm away; Ainslie's hand held her hip down with the strength of a vise; such was the fate of one with a warrior woman as a lover. Ainslie, for her part, seemed unabashed. Now that she knew her scars would not disgust Jane, she was wild and uninhibited, her strong body undulating against the bed with her own desire as she pulled Jane closer, pressing a kiss to where Jane was dripping with want.

Jane, for her part, was no longer present; spiraling upwards as she pressed herself down on Ainslie's tongue, she cried out again and again until that crash whited out her vision, and yet Ainslie was relentless, bringing her off again and again, while all Jane could do was hold on and shriek helplessly in her lover's arms.

Ainslie suddenly moaned something in Gaelic and shuddered, while Jane dragged her back up her body and kissed her wild-eyed Highlander. Jane snaked a hand beneath Ainslie and with what she could remember from the first time Ainslie had done this to her, moved her fingers against Ainslie and then dipped them inside.

Ainslie's body bowed and then went taut; lightning seemed to strike her, and she gripped Jane as hard as she could, grinding down onto her hand, they two crying out simultaneously in the night, and Jane breathlessly swearing as she came down only to climax again.

The night continued on, Jane thinking she was suspended between some delicious heaven or hell and wondering if this was the reason they'd outlawed it by her time, because no one could return to what they had once known after tasting the juice of this fruit.

Jane's mind, lost to a bacchanal of pleasure and madness, kept replaying a phrase from Christina Rossetti's cautionary poem again and again. She'd heard it all her life but now it seemed to have a meaning that she may never have known, and she felt she understood why the sister wanted so badly to return to the market, even if it killed her both body and soul:

Then suck'd their fruit globes fair or red:
Sweeter than honey from the rock,
Stronger than man-rejoicing wine,
Clearer than water flow'd that juice;
She never tasted such before,
How should it cloy with length of use?
She suck'd and suck'd and suck'd the more
Fruits which that unknown orchard bore;
She suck'd until her lips were sore;
Then flung the emptied rinds away
But gather'd up one kernel stone,
And knew not was it night or day
As she turn'd home alone.

* * *

The cottage was quiet, after.

The embers made their whispering hiss, and the night went on silent as if it had not been broken with their passion.

Jane lay on Ainslie's chest, the redhead's arm wrapped around her body, as she watched the fire's glow dim.

"Sleep now, my faerie," said Ainslie, without opening her eyes. "Ye are safe here now, in my arms."

And Jane, in defiance of all the Victorian mores flooding through her mind, drifted off to sleep in the arms of her warrior queen.

CHAPTER FORTY-THREE

Yon Moorland an' Mountain Are Mine

Jane awoke alone.

Outside, she could hear the birds cheeping as they really got geared up for the dawn chorus, which other people might love but she found obnoxious, being the product of a big city.

She sat up and rubbed her arms. The fire had been allowed to go out in the grate, and there wasn't even the telltale curl of smoke to indicate that a fire had ever been there. For the first time, the floor was cold as she put her feet onto it and winced. She pulled her long shift on and wrapped her earasaid snugly around her body, fastening it with a pewter brooch for the purpose.

Grumbling, she knelt at the fireside and put new bricks of peat on the grate. She worked at lighting the fire; peat did not always catch properly and could take hours of work just to encourage into flame. She counted herself lucky that she'd had her father teach her how to do necessary things, such as building a fire or shooting, since she would otherwise have been one of Edinburgh's pampered women with no idea how to be useful in this particular place or time period.

Overall, the situation was a strange one. Given their previous evening of passion, Jane expected Ainslie to return at any moment, bearing breakfast foods, all smiles. But Ainslie would not let the fire go out in the grate; that was unlike her. Jane wanted to be angry, especially as she felt exposed and a bit uncomfortable with what they had done the previous night, as she was beginning to learn her upbringing had taught her to feel shame for mornings-after she doubted Ainslie, or anyone else here for that matter, ever had to feel.

But she couldn't shake the feeling that something must be very wrong for Ainslie to abandon her this way. She also did not want to accuse her, or be selfish, after she'd left Ainslie alone for so long, with no way of knowing whether or not Jane would ever return. So she swallowed her own self-doubt and encroaching, useless shame, and she waited.

* * *

When afternoon had near passed to night, and she had not seen or heard anything from Ainslie, Jane left the cottage. She walked the long distance to the shoreline and saw Claig Castle lit up across the water. It was then that she realised she was lost without her own vessel to help her reach it.

Fortunately, someone had pulled a small fishing craft up onto the shore. She recognized it as Dougal's coracle, the tiny boat he used to fish in the shallows and rivers. Jane thought of the many times Ainslie had traversed this very strait and reasoned to herself that it must be easy enough. Besides, she needed to know why Ainslie hadn't returned, and she was furious with herself for allowing things to progress as far as they had without talking about anything, as if nothing had changed between them. And so she was not thinking very rationally when she pushed the boat out into the strait and attempted to row toward the island.

It didn't take long for her to understand that the sound was not one easily navigated by those who were unfamiliar with its currents, and the sun was rapidly losing its light as it vanished beneath the horizon. Jane pulled with all her strength, but she was carried out and away from Claig Castle and the familiar shoreline. She eventually gave up trying for the castle and attempted to land on the opposite shore. Unfortunately, the nighttime currents were not what they were during the day, and the darkness of the land on both sides gave way to the dark of the wide-open sea beyond, as Jane was pulled inexorably closer to the crash and might of the open Atlantic.

* * *

Jane startled awake with real terror.

She realised she must have swooned.

"Fuck," she swore. "Idiot! You could have drowned."

She sat up in her little boat and saw, miracle of miracles, that it had somehow run aground in the night.

"Oh thank fucking everyone and everything," she muttered and tried to step out of the boat.

"Stop right there," said a voice, in Gaelic. She looked up.

A young man held a bow in his hands, arrow nocked, aimed straight for her. She gaped at him.

"Who are you?" he tried, in English.

"Who's asking?" she demanded.

The man bristled at this and shook his head.

"I asked first," he said.

Jane decided to go all out with the woe-is-me-I-am-a-lady act.

"Sir," she said, in a high and mighty tone, "one does not ask such a thing of a lady, not if one is a gentleman."

She tried to look as regal as possible, which wasn't very easy, what with her bare feet and dishevelled hair.

"You don't talk like one of the Islanders," said the man, lowering his bow. He, too, was dressed in the plaid, but his English was as fine as any between the Thames and the Tweed. "My apologies, miss, but you can imagine that we are on high alert, and a woman alone in a rowboat doesn't seem like the most trustworthy of souls. We're expecting an ambush any day now."

He picked his way down the hillside and offered her his hand. She took it, struggling to get out of the boat, but finally she stood by his side. He looked into her eyes, and she saw that he was evaluating her.

"Now that I am close, I can see you are a lady of high bearing," he said. "Please accept my apologies."

He bowed, doffing his cap. Jane was puzzled, having not seen blue bonnets on any of the Dhòmhnaill clan. She then realised his outfit was far more detailed and probably more expensive than any she had seen on the islands.

"Lord Archibald Caimbeul, at your service," he said. Jane's eyes widened. He stood up and looked at her expectantly.

Jane didn't have much time nor any explanation for her existence or sudden appearance on the shore. She panicked and said the only thing that she was certain would save her.

"Lady Jane Campbell," she said, her heart beating a tattoo against her ribs.

CHAPTER FORTY-FOUR

My Heart's in the Highlands

Jane Campbell, you absolute imbecile.

Jane followed Lord Caimbeul up the hill, hoping she could remember how to get back to the boat. Not that it would be of much use; she apparently had zero navigational skills and she well might have been swept out to sea, never to be seen again.

What else was there for it? She followed the man because she had seen the Caimbeulaich fight on Islay, she wasn't about to betray her position, and for once, the Campbell name served as her shield instead of Crichton.

Still she couldn't help the arrow of guilt that shot through her. She was a Campbell, yes, but her lover was not, and that meant something here that she wasn't sure she could ever live down or take back.

I'm staying alive for Ainslie, she told herself, and while this was true, she couldn't help wishing that there was another way.

She followed him down a wide gravel road, which surprised her. Most of the paths on Islay were goat and sheep tracks. She wondered at the extreme difference of the lands and holdings of this clan compared to the Dhòmhnaill and gasped when a carriage arrived to pick them up.

"I take it you've been accustomed to rough and rude living of late," said Archibald. "Well, that is no more as of now. You are one of our kin and will be treated as such. What were you doing out there on that boat, anyway?"

He and Jane boarded the carriage, and the horses were off in an instant. She realised how much she had missed this little luxury, along with many others. She also realised that Archibald was awaiting an answer.

"I was captured by the Dhòmhnaill clan," she said. "I lost my way as I fled."

"And you escaped," he said. "Well done, and a praise to the clan. You seem surprised for one of the landed gentry, at the roads and the carriage."

Jane shrugged, trying for nonchalance.

"They have nothing there of the kind," she said truthfully.

Archibald smirked.

"That's what comes of not having any money," he said. "They are great fighters, but savages all the same."

Jane's mind flashed on the word "savages" and thought of the Caimbeulaich who had attacked them during that long winter. Money apparently did not mean ensuring those in the clan were fed and clothed during inclement weather.

"All that's behind you now," Archibald assured her. "That is, if you really are a Caimbeul."

"What do you mean?" asked Jane, haughty.

"My apologies, miss," he said. "But I cannot take you at your word. I found you alone in a boat on the beach while I was hunting. If I were to take the word of strangers, I should not be in line for the chiefship."

"You're the chief's son?" she asked.

"Yes," he replied. "And I will take you to meet him."

"So I am your prisoner," she said. It was not a question.

Archibald smiled.

"I'm sure you'll find your incarceration much sweeter here than in those savage lands," he said, and the carriage drove on.

* * *

The carriage entered a clearing and Jane was astounded to see a large castle in the centre of a loch.

"That is Innis Chonnel, the seat of my fathers," Archibald said. "We go there to greet the Caimbeul chief, my father. He will know what is needful."

A boat came to pick them up from the carriage depot and carry them across the water. Jane wondered again why the Dhòmhnaill didn't have such wonderful things.

* * *

If Jane had thought Innis Chonnel would be like Claig Castle, in its rustic medieval setting, she was sorely mistaken.

The castle of the Caimbeulaich was lit bright, with some of the most sumptuous decorations she could imagine. The halls were lined with French silks and stuffs, the floors carpeted. Paintings of various different scenes adorned the walls, and maids hurried back and forth down the hallway as Archibald marched through with Jane on his arm. She was reminded powerfully of some of the royal residences she had visited in her youth when her mother was trying to instruct her in regards to attracting a suitor and the kind of residences she should expect to live in, not sell herself short for anything and so on.

It was clear from the start that no expense had been spared. Where the Dhòmhnaill had fortitude and strength, these people had money and more of it than they knew what to do with.

By and by, they came to a throne room. Instead of the large room with a desk that Dòmhnall used to work on matters in his own kingdom, this chief took the concept of ruling quite literally. Jane was surprised he wasn't wearing a cloak of gold.

"My son," said the man on the throne.

"Father," said Archibald, bowing deeply and removing his cap, as he had with Jane.

"What's this you've found?" he asked. "She's dressed like a savage. You know I don't approve of them in my home."

"She was their prisoner, Father," he said. "It's obvious by her bearing that she is one of us, but I thought you might like to see her first. She says she's a Caimbeul, too."

"Hmmm," said the man, grumbling into his beard. "And where do you hail from, miss?"

Jane prayed that her curtsy would finally look like the real thing, as she executed it with a perfection and grace built entirely out of terror.

"Lady Jane Campbell, Your Majesty," she said, tacking on the title in the hopes it would flatter him. "Of Edinburgh."

All of this seemed to be the right thing to say, because the man brightened considerably.

"Ah! Edinburgh!" he cried. "You must have suffered a great deal, my dear! Coming from that great city only to be captured by those Norse savages. They're not Scottish at all, are they, son?"

Archibald dutifully shook his head.

"Now then," said the chief. "I am Lord Colin Campbell, as they style me in English, but you can call me Cailean, my birthname."

"Pleased to meet you, Cailean," said Jane, and he kissed her hand.

"Now, you understand that I still need to keep you under watch for a while," said Cailean. "But once I'm certain you're not a danger to anyone here, you'll be at liberty within the castle grounds. You'll be finely housed in my castle, and you'll want for nothing. I hope this is amenable to you?"

Everything in Jane wanted to spit, to kick and shout, to wrest herself away from him and go running back to the shoreline, to see if Ainslie and Malcolm were on their way to save her. She had been rash and foolish. The only chance she had was staying alive so that the Dhòmhnaill could save her or she could find a way out on her own.

"As you say, Your Majesty," she said instead. He chuckled, still obviously flattered, but shook his finger at her.

"Now, none of that," he said. "Cailean is fine. Archibald, will you show this young lady to her chambers? I'd like to hear everything about what's happened to you, but you'll want to dress yourself properly first. I'll be expecting you both at dinner, and I look forward to hearing more from this charming girl."

With that, Cailean made a motion of dismissal, and Archibald nodded smartly. He took Jane's arm and led her out of the throne room, down the hallway towards the stairs.

How could you have been so stupid? Jane's inner voice kept haranguing her. *Nothing for it now but to wait for Ainslie to save you. That is, if she doesn't assume you were swept out to sea and drowned. Maybe that is what she thinks, and you're lost to her forever.*

Jane narrowed her eyes, and her mouth set.

Well, she thought right back, *then I'll just have to escape and get back to her myself.*

But how?

CHAPTER FORTY-FIVE

My Heart Is Not Here

The dinner that evening was about as far from the ones she had experienced at Claig Castle as it was possible to be.

Everyone was seated according to rank, and servants waited behind those eating. Everyone sat up ramrod straight, and the delicacies distributed were just that: small, artfully arranged foods meant more as a feast for the eyes than the stomach. Jane wondered if this was because they couldn't really afford it or whether they were uncouth enough to throw everything away. She thought of the feasts at Claig Castle, where the champagne and wine flowed, where people burst into song, where the food was devoured by everyone and anyone could share the feast-table with their chief. Here, they were as much removed as the court at Versailles from the needs of the everyday clansman.

Jane made up some story about being taken in by the Dhòmhnaill when a ship she travelled on sank into the sea. This was close enough to the truth, but it was appealing to the listeners, as there may be treasure aboard a ship carrying a woman of Jane's status. She then related, very briefly, that the Dhòmhnaill had taken care of her and she wasn't angry with them in the least.

"Ah well," said Cailean. "Identifying with your captors isn't unheard of, but it must've been a harrowing experience. Forced to walk barefoot! And in that strange shift the islanders wear. You'd swear they were Irish beneath the belted plaid. You're back among civilised folk again, my lass, and you'll find your way back to Edinburgh in no time."

Yet Jane found herself uncomfortable in the restrictive garments she now wore, and she longed for the heather of the island and for her lover. She wished there was some way to communicate with Ainslie and felt a building fear that if she did come to rescue her, Ainslie would wonder if she was with the Caimbeulaich.

* * *

She was given a beautiful room with windows that overlooked the loch and with all the accoutrements a woman of high standing could desire. Mirrors, hairbrushes, even powder for her face. She touched the powder box and thought painfully of Ainslie's sun-freckled face, her green eyes laughing. Not for the first time, Jane wished to know why women were forced into all of this pageantry while men could pick and choose what they wore, where they went, what they did. She had thought, after her experience with the Dhòmhnaill, that perhaps this was not the case for the Highlanders of the past—but the Caimbeulaich were Highlanders too.

She drifted off, in a huge cold bed hung with silk, and thought that the Dhòmhnaill must be a different nation of people indeed.

* * *

In the weeks that followed, Jane was permitted free rein of the castle and then the grounds. She strolled through the paths around the castle, which weren't many, and thought of ways to escape. This was a problem, because like Claig Castle, Innis Chonnel was surrounded entirely by water, and she could not swim. The only way on and off the island was by boat and then God knew how long via the road the carriage had taken. It was a worrying proposition, and she began to despair of ever leaving the shores of the Caimbeulaich holding.

Still yet another fear gnawed at her heart, and that was her love of the finer things. She had been raised to expect them and had grown accustomed to a life of leisure, in her family home and later in David's manor house. The things she had come to terms with missing forever by choosing life on Islay had always been here—just beyond the isles of the Hebrides. She liked the evening sorbet and the strolls in the garden and the damned civilisation of it all. She knew that these people were Ainslie's mortal enemies. Hell, she knew they were her own, having the sword scar to prove it. And yet here she was, not exactly hating her own captivity.

She hadn't known that these delicacies, these luxuries, were so tantalisingly close. And she felt guilty, because she felt that she shouldn't love the things she'd lost in choosing Ainslie and the rude nature of many things about the Dhòmhnaill holdings over her modern life. She wanted to prefer them, she really did—her love for Ainslie still beat strong in her heart—but damn it all, she also wanted to be taken care of and live in sumptuous surroundings. She could even get used to the uncomfortable clothing, if that sacrifice meant she would be able to enjoy the lifestyle she thought she'd bidden farewell to forever.

And what then, she thought, if Ainslie did come? Would she be able to tear herself away? Was Ainslie's love better than the luxury she now knew was available to those willing to seek it out? If Ainslie stretched out her hand, would she then go and leave all this behind as she had left David and Joseph, hundreds of years in the future, and the money and luxury that had been all her life's experience until she fell from the sky into the arms of a rough, savage woman?

There's that word again, she admonished herself, and yet it had returned to her as if it had never left her mind. She wondered what else might be changing, both there and in her heart.

* * *

As she walked along, ruminating on these many things, she saw Archibald in the growing twilight. She often encountered him on her evening walks, and tonight, just like all the others, he doffed his bright blue cap and bowed deeply as she approached him.

"A fine evening, is it not, Lady Jane?" he asked. "Would you do me the honour of allowing me to join you on your walk?"

Jane murmured her assent, and Archibald took her arm. They walked along the path together, Archibald going on about something or the other. Jane paid him no attention, so caught up was she in her own thoughts and concerns, until something he said brought her to a halt.

"Pardon?" she asked politely.

Archibald snatched his hat from his head and started twisting it with his hands.

"I know this is utterly forward," he said. "And yet I must let it be known. Jane, you have walked into my life as if from heaven, and I have not been able to take my eyes from you since. I hope you will forgive me my bluntness, but would you—is it possible you might consider—accepting my courtship?"

His blush stood out high on his cheeks, and Jane stared at him as though she was having trouble encouraging her brain to parse what he had just said to her.

Dear God, she thought, *he's in love with you! And barely into his twenties! Look what you've done! You thought you were in danger before. Now you're really in for it. Step carefully in turning him down.*

Jane offered him a thin smile, and Archibald smiled back, expectant.

CHAPTER FORTY-SIX

A-Chasin' the Deer

Oh no.
What should I do now?

Jane looked at Archibald, colour high on his cheeks, and her pause was turning into an embarrassment he couldn't rightly extricate himself from. Jane had to think fast.

She'd gotten to know him over the time of her gentle imprisonment and found that the Caimbeulaich were not quite the devils that Ainslie thought they were. The long feud had made them enemies from time out of mind, to a point where it seemed neither family could remember what had happened to start everything. Nowadays, the descendants of those with the original complaint continued to war against each other without much reason. It was a born hatred, two warring nations; one could not be said to be more noble than the other.

Don't forget the starving people you saw. Don't forget that the world of this castle is not the world of this clan.

"Jane?" Archibald prompted, and she made a wild decision, staking everything on his feelings for her and his pleasant nature.

"If I tell you something, Archie, will you keep it secret?" she asked. "I need you to know."

"Anything," he agreed, perhaps a bit too readily, but he was already smitten and would have walked to the ends of the earth for her.

Jane wondered what she'd done to attract the attention of not one, but two, red-haired Highlanders.

"Come sit with me," she said, and the two of them sat on a bench in the castle grounds, looking for all the world like two lovers.

"What is it?" he asked, his voice syrupy with love.

"I am very sorry to tell you this," Jane told him, "but I'm afraid I must decline. You see, I am already married."

The wind went right out of Archibald's sails.

"Oh," he said sadly. "Then please accept my friendship and loyalty. They are yours to do with as you please."

Jane turned to him, her dark eyes blazing bright.

"I love a Dhòmhnaill," she said.

His expression was to be expected from one who had been taught all his life that these people were savages, were his enemies.

"Jane," he began tentatively, "I know your captivity may have turned your mind, but believe me when I tell you these savages—"

"Have you ever met one?" she asked. Archibald raised his eyebrows.

"I receive messages from their king," he said, unsure. "Last was about…food for our people, I believe."

"Yes, I was there," said Jane, a cold edge to her voice. "Your kinsmen were starving, because you supply your own castle with riches and let others starve. That battle is the reason I have this."

She lifted the edge of her lèine and showed him the sword-thrust scar; he touched it with terror and reverence.

"This is from a Caimbeul blade?" he whispered.

"Yes," she said. "And their people hold you in horror likewise. I cannot say I blame the man who did this; he was starving, as were perhaps his children. His wife may have been there in the fighting. More than two hundred died."

From the way the blood had drained from Archibald's face, it was clear that he was unaware of the events from that horrible winter.

"I do as my father instructs," he admitted. "I am not yet chief."

"You may never be chief if your father continues to treat his people this way," she said. "Isn't the law of the Highlands one where a chief or chieftain can be deposed and exiled if he or she is not a good leader? What do you think they will do, all those MacDonalds that surround you, to an exiled chief wandering these mountains alone?"

"Jane, your words horrify me," said Archibald. "I should never wish such a fate on my father. Despite his actions, he is still my father, and I love him as a son should. I will speak to him of these atrocities."

"A man who commits atrocities is not a good man," said Jane. "And believe me, if your standard is 'The Campbells Are Coming,' imagine the very dread encompassed in the death and destruction of 'By Sea By Land.' Nothing will be spared, long as you hold me here."

Jane pointed at him and he shrank back as though some avenging angel had come to him in the night.

"And she *will* come for me," Jane said. "Mark my words. And there will be nothing left. The Caimbeulaich will burn to the ground."

"She?" asked Archibald, puzzled.

"Yes, she," said Jane. "And she will come, with all the clan behind her, to wreak vengeance upon you."

She let her arm drop to her side.

"So I ask you, Archibald Caimbeul, my own kin," she said. "Will you help me or no?"

His red-rimmed eyes, dim with tears, gave her the only answer her triumphant heart could require.

* * *

And with Archibald's promise, it seemed that the horizon cleared of clouds. Jane finally began to see a way off the island, maybe permanently, if she played her cards right.

That night, everything changed.

And Jane learned readily that all the subterfuge and feminine wiles she had been taught in Edinburgh and London were for naught, because nothing would remain standing in the face of the pure, unadulterated fury of a Dhòmhnaill who was wronged.

Ainslie had come for her.

CHAPTER FORTY-SEVEN

The Water is Wide

They'd come on boats, through cover of darkness, to surround the island where the castle kept watch over Loch Awe.

No warning signal had been given, because the moon was not yet risen, and an entire fleet of vessels can be silent on the water if they so wish.

From the snatches of shouted conversation Jane heard as she was rushed to her room for safekeeping, the enemy had gained the castle probably by way of the Sound of Jura and Loch Etive, the sea loch that connected the two via the River Awe and the Pass of Brander.

"From the sea, they came," she heard in her mind, as if the Dhòmhnaill were a great sea monster, ready to consume the castle and its inhabitants.

"Stay here, Jane," Archibald said, as he guided her to the bed to sit down. "Don't open for anyone but me, do you understand?"

Jane just looked up at him with a plain and expressionless face.

"She comes for me," Jane said. "As I said she would."

Archibald recoiled; she looked almost supernatural in the dim firelight of the cavernous room.

"Be safe," he said. "For me, won't you, Jane?"

He kissed her forehead and left the room, shutting the door firmly behind himself and probably assuming she would build a barricade. Jane did not move from her place on the bed, and she waited.

* * *

The battle raged on throughout the castle, and the night lit up with the colour of flame. Someone had set the castle alight in their enthusiasm, scaling the walls with torches and knives.

"Where is she?"

Jane could hear Ainslie's voice, a wild animal sound, at a distance and growing closer.

She would have thrown herself out the door but did not want to confuse any of the soldiers in the battle. If she were to die now, she had no hope for the future of her own kin.

The struggle, some moments later, reached the door. Shouting and the clash of swords, fallen soldiers, an absolute bloody din reached Jane's ears. And still she waited.

And Ainslie kicked down the door.

Splinters flew at every angle, and the door was nearly wrested off its hinges.

Jane stared up at an Ainslie she had never seen.

This was a madwoman, a monster, green eyes alight with infernal fire, red hair raised in its braids like ropes of snakes, orange like the fire behind her. Blood and dirt streaked her features and she growled at the sight of Jane, panting.

"The door was open," Jane said, and the Caimbeul soldiers renewed their attack on her lover.

Ainslie was a living flame, roaring at anyone who came near her, and the house was on fire as were her eyes, green dancing in the flying embers. She held a torch in one hand and her sword in the other. A knife was clenched in her teeth and blood poured from her hands, her arms, her clothing soaked in it, and she kicked the door shut in front of the men on the staircase. She threw the torch into the corner, then took the dirk from her mouth and wedged the blade firmly into the hinge side of the door to prevent it being opened from the outside. She slid the lock home.

Then she turned, and Jane shuddered; she had never felt so much like prey as in that moment.

Jane stared up at Ainslie and saw a new, strange light in her bright green eyes. After a moment, Jane realized it was fear. She'd never seen Ainslie afraid before. What was she afraid of? Certainly not the Caimbeul soldiers she had struck down in her fury. Jane realised she feared rejection, feared that Jane had been bewitched by the riches of the Caimbeul estate. All this, she read in the doubt and terror in Ainslie's eyes.

For one quiet, still moment, Ainslie hesitated. Jane held her gaze, and with a slight nod, acquiesced. Ainslie was suddenly in motion again, as if that moment had never happened, wild like a storm at sea.

"Ainslie—" Jane started, but Ainslie dropped her sword onto the floor, grabbed Jane around the waist and threw her onto the bed. Flames began to mount the walls beside the torch as Ainslie tore at Jane's clothing, baring Jane's body as she bared her own, ripping her lèine and earasaid off and discarding them beside the bed. She sat astride Jane, her powerful legs wrapped around her lover's, holding her down with more intent than ever she had, her eyes like cats' eyes, demons' eyes. As she rocked against Jane, as she gripped her breasts in her hands, Jane heard someone slam their body against the other side of the door.

Ainslie snarled at the sound, baring her teeth like an animal, and stayed where she was.

"You knock down that door an' ye'll see me mount your lady as she ought to be mounted," Ainslie roared, all teeth and tongue like a panther, her features contorted into that of a snarling beast, her eyes green burning chips of emerald in the rising flames.

"I lay claim to this woman, she isnae yours, an' she'll scream my name before the hour's through."

The banging at the door became more frantic, and Ainslie turned her attention back to Jane, kissing her so hard she ground her teeth into her lips. Jane, beyond all earthly reason, moaned and bucked up against Ainslie though she saw the fire spiralling out of control beyond the bed.

Anything, anything, Jane thought, delirious, as she spread her legs to allow Ainslie better access, and the flames danced and spun, illuminating Ainslie's body with an infernal glow.

"In yer fine white bed, she'll cry out for me," Ainslie snarled at the door, furious, growling, rocking against Jane. "Body an' soul, she'll be mine. Ye listen well, Caimbeul. She'll be a harlot for me, wanton, wet, ready. Ye can listen to me defile her or ye can save your ain skin. Burn wi' us, or give up an' fight another day."

Jane writhed, insensible, knowing only her desire for Ainslie's body, Ainslie's touch, the pleasure Ainslie alone could give her. The sound of Jane's cries were growing louder, and Ainslie was thrusting against her hard enough to bruise. Jane loved it, begged for it, desperate; she tightened her legs around Ainslie and pushed against her, senseless with need.

"You want this, don't ye, Jane?" Ainslie whispered wicked in her ear. "Ye'd do anything tae feel the way I make ye feel, wouldn't ye? Death, destruction, all is nothing compared to this."

And as an answer, Jane screamed out her climax.

Ainslie's orgasm came on like a hurricane, like a claiming, a triumphant bellow so those on the other side of the door could hear.

She stood suddenly, grabbing Jane by the hair and dragging her roughly from the bed.

"Dress," she commanded and threw her on the ground. Ainslie gathered up her own clothes, the shadows of flames flickering across her strong, scarred body in the firelight, and dressed herself quickly.

Jane stared up at her in shock.

"Dress!" Ainslie repeated. "Or do ye want tae die here, in the fire?"

Jane did as she was told but pushed her skirts up again, touching herself. Ainslie saw this and gave an involuntary shudder.

"Harlot," she sneered. "Later, insatiable one."

Ainslie hefted Jane over her shoulder as Jane squealed in terror, just as the men broke through the door.

They were treated to the sight of an entirely debauched Jane, her skirts hitched up, her long dark hair hanging scandalously down, sated, as Ainslie grinned wicked at them. She put one leg out of the window, winked at them, and disappeared, making a daring escape as she scaled the wall to a boat waiting below in the darkness of the loch. She dropped Jane into it without any kind of warning and then threw herself into it, rowing hard for the opposite shore.

A carriage awaited them at the lochside. Ainslie lifted Jane bodily from the vessel as the furious echoes of the Caimbeulaich echoed across the water. She pushed Jane into the carriage and then joined her, slamming the door.

"Go!" Ainslie cried, and it sped off into the night.

* * *

Jane was gaping at Ainslie, too shocked to speak. But Ainslie was still animal and still desired to confirm her claim on her prize.

"Spread your legs," Ainslie commanded. Jane gaped at her, startled.

"Ainslie—" she began again.

"Spread your legs afore I do it for ye," Ainslie snarled. Jane did so, hesitant; Ainslie pushed her skirts up and pushed her legs apart obscenely, Ainslie's mouth was suddenly on her, sucking at her, licking inside of her, nosing at the juices that had already spent while they had fucked on the bed in the castle. Jane thrust forward, ecstasy overtaking her, as her eyes rolled back up in her head, as her orgasm bolted through her.

Ainslie reared back and stared up at Jane.

"Nae mair runnin' away frae me, Jane. Ye'll do as I say, *exactly* when I say it," she ordered. "Ye'll fuck me as and when I require it, even if it be in the forest, in a burning room, in front of others. Ye will obey me, Jane, as a matter of course, from now on."

"But—" she began, when Ainslie dipped down to taste her again, and Jane cried out, pushing her hips forward, seeking more.

"But naethin'," said Ainslie. "Ye like this, ye wanton little harlot. Ye like me orderin' ye around, tellin' ye what tae do. An' ye're desperate for it, every touch, every taste. Am I wrang?"

Jane whimpered, as her desire overpowered her. She would have promised Ainslie anything, anything to feel the way Ainslie made her feel.

"No," Jane mumbled. She let out a small shriek as Ainslie's deft tongue slipped inside her and blessed the flat roads of the Caimbeulaich as well as the careful driver of the carriage and Ainslie's quick tongue.

CHAPTER FORTY-EIGHT

I Cannot Cross O'er

They were standing at the edge of the forest overlooking the ocean below. Dougal's white coracle stood out in the moonlight, awaiting Jane's return. Nearby, there was another boat pulled up onto the shore. Jane recognized it as Malcolm. She suddenly realized that Ainslie must have found the coracle, washed ashore in Caimbeul country, and made the necessary calculations. She must have decided that she would travel with the rest of her soldiers but leave Malcolm here for the ease of travel should she be able to find and recover Jane—even if it were only her body.

Jane shuddered as she imagined Ainslie's fury and terror upon realizing that Jane had most likely been captured.

"Strip," Ainslie ordered. Jane began to speak, but a hard glance from Ainslie quieted her. Jane began to strip methodically.

"Lay down on that rock," Ainslie directed.

"Here? They'll catch us!" Jane protested.

Ainslie was on her in an instant.

"Did I ask for your opinion, Caimbeul?" she snarled. "Ye're my prisoner. Ye are a faithless, wanton little harlot, a liar and betrayer. What good else are ye but for my pleasure?"

"Ainslie, I—"

"Quiet!" roared Ainslie, suddenly in Jane's face. "Do as you're told. This is what we savages do. I'm ainly fulfillin' your expectations. It's moments afore ye're squirming in my arms, beggin' for what only I can give ye."

She supervised Jane undressing as if she did not believe it would be done.

"These Caimbeul," spat Ainslie, "all proper and prim, ye thocht ye were ane o' them, did ye no? But there's savage in ye now, Jane, an' a' the proof is how readily you'll open your legs for me."

"You don't give me a choice!" Jane finally blurted.

"An' neither did ye gie me a chance!" Ainslie retorted. "Get on the rock. Spread your legs for me. Take your hair down for me. Bare your body tae me."

Jane did all of this, trembling with want.

"You're a witch, I'm sure of it," she whined. "Otherwise, I would never—"

"Ye'd do all this an' more, harlot," Ainslie snapped and came closer to Jane. Jane's hips hitched upwards, inviting, and Ainslie chuckled low in her throat. "As ye are now, as your body begs for me in silence, while ye protest wi' your mouth."

Ainslie dropped to her knees and crawled up the rock, to drink her fill of Jane's sun-dappled skin as the trees moved in the wind. She touched her, pushed her fingers inside, and then licked, sucking around her clitoris, as Jane's body bowed, a slave to her desire, and Ainslie chuckled low again as Jane came helplessly, spread out for Ainslie like an offering.

* * *

"A thousand *claidheamhan-mòra* are behind and to the side of ye," Ainslie snarled. Jane's brows drew together as she stared at Ainslie, puzzled.

Then Jane looked up and saw Archibald standing above them, holding his sword, uncertain. Jane let out a little shriek and covered her nudity as he looked away.

"I don't doubt that you could murder me," said Archibald. Jane could see he was trembling in fear. "But I've come to ask for Jane."

"Never," shouted Ainslie. "She's mine, Caimbeul, do ye no' see? She isnae satisfied wi' the likes o' ye, wha could be?"

"Nevertheless, I—Jane," Archibald addressed her, colouring a pink that was visible even in the moonlight. "I ask that you come home."

Jane, for her part, was dressing hurriedly.

"Hame?" Ainslie demanded, advancing on him. She had not bothered to dress or cover her own nakedness. Such things did not concern her. "What is hame tae Jane, if no' my island? This isnae hame for her. She's mine, Caimbeul! Ye've kept her a captive! For weeks!"

"And what is it that you've done?" Archibald demanded. "Brought her to your rough island, made her think she wants…she wants this?"

"I made her think nae sic thing," Ainslie spat. "She wants it, she wants me, she has come to me o' her ain volition! An' what o' ye, Caimbeul, an' yer robber clan?"

Archibald kept staring at the ground, averting his eyes.

"If—if you wouldn't mind dressing, miss," he said, shyly.

"You ca' me by my name an' give me honour as the chief o' the Dhòmhnaill or I shall skewer ye whaur ye stand," Ainslie hissed. "An' I willnae clothe mysel' for a mind o' yer perversion, ye daft fucking spoon. She disnae want tae go wi' ye, ye glaikit wee cunt."

Archibald stood before this flood of curses stock-still.

"Good Lord," he said, speechless otherwise.

Jane stamped her foot.

"Will you stop arguing over me!" shouted Jane. "I am my own person and will do as I wish!"

The two of them goggled at her. She angrily pulled on the rest of her clothes, lopsided but good enough, aware of her own embarrassment from the heat in her cheeks.

Jane then pushed Dougal's coracle out into the water.

"Jane, don't—" Ainslie started. Jane hopped inside and rowed furiously away from shore.

"Don't what, Ainslie nic Dòmhnaill?" she shouted. "It's always do this, do that with you!"

"You're terrible at seamanship. You're going tae die!" Ainslie yelled. "Come back to shore!"

Jane's silence seethed across the water to her.

"Oh, am I?" shouted Jane. "I'd rather die with my terrible seamanship than spend another moment with either of you!"

"Good God, she really means to do it," marvelled Archibald, but Ainslie was already dressing hastily and then tumbling down the steep brae with a shout.

"She's going to die out there if I don't go, Archie," Ainslie said, her voice panicked.

"You go! I will hold them back," Archibald said, drawing his sword.

This gave Ainslie pause. She turned to him.

"You? Against your kin?" she asked.

Archibald shrugged.

"Time this feuding nonsense was ended," he said. "If I die, I die. Besides…I love her too."

Ainslie was frozen to the spot. She was so startled she wasn't certain what to do.

"Go!" he said. "And save her, for both of us. Goodbye, Ainslie nic Dòmhnaill. May the next time we meet be in peace and friendship."

He smiled.

"And more clothing."

Ainslie's mouth quirked in spite of herself. She nodded to him, and more respect and honour was in that one nod than many words could have expressed. She turned and threw herself into Malcolm, who obeyed his mistress as ever he had and slid calmly out to sea.

CHAPTER FORTY-NINE

Neither Have I Wings To Fly

Jane fumed as she rowed hard toward the land opposite, crossing the body of water again, but this time, with no intent to reach a destination. The sea began to take her, just as last time, but her rage was enough to sustain her over her fear. She figured that she would allow herself to be taken and once the hunger got severe enough, she'd throw herself to the sharks. She was well aware that she was being foolish and suicidal. It felt like the only choice left to her now; between the Dhòmhnaill, the Caimbeulaich, and the deep blue sea, there was only one decision she felt she could make on her own. It was her independence, her intelligence, that brought her here; she'd chosen to return to this time and this woman, but she had felt like a possession for some time now, especially after her imprisonment at Innis Chonnel castle. She had left a time of innovation and reason to return to a place where she was traded back and forth, the reason for war, a bargaining chip.

Typical. It wasn't Helen of Troy who started that war, now was it?

How dare Ainslie talk to her like that, treat her like that? She'd left David, and comfort, and family, and everything she had ever known to return to Ainslie's side, and she treated her as if she was hers to command, hers to…to…

And you love it, at least the sexual aspect.
You loved it since the moment she first yanked on your corset-strings.
You wanted her to be savage, so you could have an excuse.
But this is a thing that lives inside of you.
And it's all right to want.

Jane blushed furiously and refused to listen to her inner voice or to any sort of reason. She was embarrassed and, she slowly realised, a little excited at the memory of Ainslie alive with passion. She hated herself for it—and then wondered why. Is this what the Victorian era had done to people? Convince them that natural things were unnatural and shame everyone for having healthy human appetites? Shame them for the multitude of ways they found their pleasure, some happiness on this earth, before the inevitable end?

This was not the first time she had wondered such a thing, but it was the first time she'd thought about it in relation to herself and her desires. That pleasure—sexual or otherwise—was the thing that made life worth living: laughter with friends, adventure, a night spent in the arms of a lover, however that desire was made manifest.

She realised it was true, everything her inner voice had said, and that half of her initial attraction to Ainslie was a pulse-pounding hope that she would be every bit the savage that people always said the Highlanders would be.

But maybe it was Jane herself that was animal—or rather, Jane too.

The strength of her love for this woman fell almost like a thunderbolt from the sky. Certainly she knew that she loved Ainslie, but the power and eternity of that love, the sheer weight of it, had never come to bear on her before.

She began to regret her choice to leave the shoreline but was sufficiently stubborn to not be able to admit it aloud, even to herself, even in her own head.

Still, the moon had set, and the night had become infernally dark. She couldn't see the outline of the land ahead, let alone the sea in front of her. She only knew the land was there due to a distant crashing, coming nearer.

And then she realised that crashing was not land after all.

Dimly, she could see white water ahead; she wondered if it was some kind of crosscurrent.

"Jane!" a voice came to her across the water; it seemed a million miles away. She turned and was startled to see Ainslie coming up behind her on Malcolm with a speed she had not thought possible in a craft of his type. A lamp hung from Malcolm's dragonhead prow, its light glowing orange and gold upon the dark waters of the sea, as the boat slid alongside her coracle.

"Jane, I need ye to come wi' me now, and I need ye to keep your eyes on me," said Ainslie, careful, tense, as if she was afraid Jane might spook like a horse.

Ainslie reached across Malcolm's gunwale and hooked one strong arm around Jane's waist, lifting her from the boat as if she weighed nothing at all. As Jane was carried aloft between the two vessels, she glanced toward the coracle and what she had thought was white water.

She began to scream.

There in front of them, in the cast of the lamp off Malcolm's bow, was a huge whirlpool, sucking in everything that surrounded it with a noise like thunder. She watched helplessly as Ainslie dumped her into Malcolm, where she sat in the bottom of the boat staring in abject terror at the great maw of the beast. Ainslie's face was hard and expressionless as her strong muscles worked in the swinging light of the lamp, as she worked to get them and Malcolm back to safety.

Some time later, they drew into a secluded bay near the tip of Jura, Ainslie still panting harshly with effort. Ainslie pushed Malcolm up onto the sandy white shore and hopped out with a grace Jane would not have expected.

She didn't speak to Jane, only walked swiftly to the water's edge and stared out in the direction they had come. Her breath began to slow, and Jane realised that Ainslie had been in the throes of the worst kind of panic. She watched the horizon with suspicion, as if she thought the maelstrom could somehow still swallow them whole.

Sunlight was encroaching on the night, the dawn a whisper of gold on the edge of the world.

Jane walked up behind her, wrapping her earasaid around herself. "What was it, Ainslie?" she asked softly.

Ainslie didn't answer for a moment, and Jane thought she might not have heard.

"The Storm Kelpie," she said, in a strange voice Jane had never heard before. "Corryvreckan Pool, the great cauldron of the plaid. If I hadn't—if Malcolm wasn't sae fast, I'd be looking now at your grave frae this shoreline, an' I'd blame myself forever."

Jane felt her heart ache. She took Ainslie's hand.

"It's my fault," she said. "Thank you for saving my life. I'm a fool."

Ainslie turned to her, and Jane was surprised to see tears in her eyes. She crushed Jane to her breast and spoke into the black tresses of her hair.

"I love you, Jane Crichton, Jane Caimbeul, Jane," Ainslie whispered, intense and harsh. "Dinnae even *think* o' doin' that again."

Jane sniffled against Ainslie's chest, as the tears came readily, patterned in courses down her cheeks like raindrops against the cool glass of a windowpane.

"I promise," she said, and she meant it.

CHAPTER FIFTY

Give Me a Boat That Can Carry Two

Apparently Ainslie was loath to get back on the water with Jane after their terror, so she proposed a portage with Malcolm. Carrying a 22-foot wooden boat over land was not the most comfortable style of travel, but as Ainslie explained, she wanted to cross Jura and access the Sound of Islay so that they would find themselves in relatively safer waters, ones she knew well. All her forays to the other shore were either to Gigha or the lower extremity across from Jura; she had never tested herself against the Corryvreckan Pool until that night.

And, as she explained with feeling, she never wanted to again. She knew she'd have nightmares for some time to come, nightmares where she didn't make it to Jane in time, she'd said. And so Jane had agreed to the uncomfortable process of the portage across the Isle of Jura.

The island was stark and lovely, though browner than Islay's green; the deer were plentiful here, and the people they saw raised their hands in greeting. This was safety; this was Ainslie's country once more.

But Jane couldn't help wondering whether there would be retaliation by the Caimbeulaich, thinking the Dhòmhnaill had escaped with their prize, with one of their kin. She could've explained it, although Archibald said it would be useless. She only hoped he'd made it through. She would not soon forget his kindness to her, and she told Ainslie so. Although her jaw tightened at the Caimbeul name, it was clear that she did listen to Jane's experiences and grudgingly admitted that he had been as kind as it was possible to be considering Jane's imprisonment. Jane pointed out that Ainslie had taken her in as well, and no one in the Caimbeul holding made her strip and stand naked before them.

"I had to make sure ye werenae injured!" Ainslie had protested.

"I could've told you," Jane replied. "You just wanted to see me naked. Admit it."

Ainslie huffed a laugh. They looked at each other.

"Weel," she said. "I think we'll need tae build Dougal a new boatie."

Both of them burst out laughing. The tension between them was broken.

* * *

That night, instead of continuing their portage, Ainslie declared she wanted to set up camp because Jane was probably quite tired from their ordeal. Jane had gone along with it, although she knew it was pretence; Ainslie was clearly fatigued from the amount of energy needed to bring Malcolm back to shore and safety.

Jane sat holding a warm mug of broth sourced from Malcolm's stores, sitting in front of the fire Ainslie had lit with a firestriker from the same, beneath a blessedly clear night sky. She could see the stars here, as she never had in Edinburgh: spilled salt across the velvet of the heavens.

Ainslie had gone away to hunt down some dinner. Although she had stores from Malcolm, they weren't fresh. She returned presently with venison, having cleaned the deer some distance from the camp in order not to attract curious animals to their sleeping area.

As the venison roast on a spit over the fire, Jane looked at Ainslie.

"We need to talk," Jane said.

"Oh aye?" asked Ainslie, not looking at her. "About what?"

Jane set down her mug with a sigh.

"You can't keep ordering me around," she said.

This time Ainslie did look at her, confused and a little hurt.

"I—" she began, hanging her head. "I thocht ye liked it."

"I do!" said Jane. "And even admitting it aloud is embarrassing enough. In my time period, we are taught to feel shame about anything to do with sex."

"Then what's wrang?" asked Ainslie, concern colouring her tone.

"It's just…there's a time and a place!" Jane exclaimed. "Not in the middle of a bloody battle with the Caimbeulaich, on a bed in a burning room!"

Now Ainslie did look really ashamed and contrite.

"Aye," she mumbled her agreement. "I just—I saw ye there, on that fine white bed, surrounded wi' all those riches I can never provide, never. I'm a chief an' I'm still no' rich like the Caimbeulaich. I never will be, even as Lord o' the Isles. An'…I dinna ken. I saw red. I wanted, I was—"

Here her voice lowered to a whisper.

"I feared I'd lost ye, an' naething I'd do or say would bring ye back tae me, Jane," she said.

Jane went onto her knees and crawled to Ainslie. She held her face, searching her features in the firelight. Ainslie wouldn't look at her; golden-blond lashes covered the green of her eyes in a demure expression Jane found incongruous on the warrior woman.

"You'll never lose me, Ainslie nic Dòmhnaill," Jane promised. "Never. Never."

"But I *did*," Ainslie suddenly wailed. "I did, aince afore! Then this time, I went tae the cottage, an' ye were gone; the fire was cauld in the grate. I went tae your wee boatie first, did ye ken that, Jane? The round ball, the ship that broucht ye tae me, an' then took ye away!"

Ainslie dropped her head in grief.

"I nearly went mad when ye left, the first time," she said, grinding out the words. "An' I ken we didnae speak o' it, an' I didnae want tae. I wanted it tae be like…like afore. When—before I was afraid, before I knew what it was to fear the loss o' ye, Jane."

Jane stared at her in shock.

"I wouldna sleep, or eat, or hunt," Ainslie confessed, miserable. "I thocht I'd die for the loss o' ye, I was inconsolable, my parents didna ken what tae do for me. Aonghus said I had a wastin' disease, dyin' o' a broken heart."

She looked up, and Jane was surprised, though she also realised she shouldn't have been, to see tears streaking down Ainslie's cheeks.

"An' then ye came back tae me," sobbed Ainslie, her body shaking, the muscles of her strong arms in the firelight moving to cover her face with her hands as she hitched a sob. "An' I thocht…the sun had come out, ye had returned tae me, an' I rejoiced in the joy an' glory o' your bed, an' your arms, my love, my love, my love."

She wept for a while and then calmed a little.

"An' when I had urgent business tae attend, it was the worst timing," she said. "That morning, I crept out o' the cottage for fear o' wakin' ye, an' it took longer than I thocht, an' by the time I came back—"

"I was gone," said Jane, silently cursing herself for it.

"Aye," Ainslie agreed. She lifted her head, defiant. "An' Dougal was complainin' his coracle was gone, an' I thoucht, she couldn't hae done sic a fool thing. But I went searching, Jane, an' I found his wee boatie on Caimbeul lands! I didnae ken what had become o' ye, but I kent where their castle was, an' God help them."

She sighed, fighting the waver in her voice.

"An' if ye ask me never tae touch ye again, I willnae. If ye want tae bring me afore the Druid Council for a tribunal, because ye believe ye hae been wronged in the worst way, do so. Please. I couldna live on thinkin' I'd hurt ye or that my actions had chased ye away."

She pulled a *sgian dubh* out of her clothing, from God knows where, and put the little knife into Jane's hands. She bared her chest.

"Or kill me now," she said. "I willna go on thinkin' I have asked for that which ye havena freely gien. If ye lack the strength, my love, I will do it myself."

Jane held the blade and stared at it, then at Ainslie.

"Oh, you bloody idiot," she said, throwing the knife away and gathering Ainslie up in her arms. "I love you. I was a fool. I will never leave again."

Ainslie, for all her strength, crumpled like paper and seemed to dissolve within Jane's affection.

Jane ran her knuckles along her own cheekbones and was surprised to find her fingers wet when she pulled them away. Apparently, she had been crying too.

She then realised what Ainslie was murmuring against the soft wool of her earasaid.

"Forgive me, forgive me, forgive me," she was chanting in a whisper.

Jane tightened her embrace.

"As long as you forgive me too," she said. "But there's nothing to forgive."

CHAPTER FIFTY-ONE

And Both Shall Row

The following day, they returned Malcolm to the water. Jane was heartily glad to travel again by sea. Although her ordeal had been terrifying, land travel was slow and cumbersome; lugging Malcolm's weight was not on her list of things she wanted to do again.

As they crossed the Sound of Islay, toward Claig Castle, they could see the other birlinns returning home to the island after the battle. Jane glanced down at the seawater passing Malcolm's hull and wondered how many people—both Dhòmhnaill and Caimbeul—had breathed their last, just because of her. She wanted nothing to do with the battle and felt those possible deaths weighing on her conscience with a heavy heart.

* * *

Jane was thrilled to be back in Claig Castle. While it didn't have the accoutrements of Innis Chonnel, despite being a castle of similar size, it had a warmth and homeliness that matched her cottage in the city. She realised that the cold and drafty houses of her time period had much more to owe Innis Chonnel than the merry, dark warmth of the cosiness of Claig Castle.

She wondered if this was the reason castles had a reputation for draftiness and chill. People had followed the method used at Innis Chonnel, rather than Claig Castle, where the money, such as it was, had been used to ensure warmth and friendliness, instead of a show of wealth.

Madra was so delighted to see Jane that his eyes rolled in opposite directions. He leaned back and to the side so that his body was almost bent in two, and then he boomeranged towards her, ricocheting off her leg, such was his extreme delight. He skidded into the wall and recovered almost immediately, shook himself, and then ran in fast circles around her, panting and barking.

Ainslie accompanied her to see Christina and Dòmhnall, who was now up and out of bed with Aonghus's blessing, and the wee dog was in paroxysms of joy, leaping into the air so often he seemed to hover there at waist-height for several minutes at a time.

"What an ugly useless idiot," said Christina fondly.

"Mum," Ainslie complained.

"Congratulations on the victorious battle with the Caimbeulaich," said Dòmhnall. "The warriors have returned, with very few dead among their ranks. Ye've done an excellent job, daughter. Ye are definitely ready to lead this clan."

"Thank ye, Father," said Ainslie, who only used that formality in business situations with him.

"Now then," Dòmhnall said, turning to Jane. "I expect ye didna suffer at their hands? I ken Archie, he's a good sort, if greedy; it's his father I worry about. That man has nae guid thochts on anybody."

"They were kind to me," said Jane. "Archie in particular."

Christina raised an eyebrow.

"And yet, they stole you away as if you were mere chattel," she said, a hard edge to her voice. "Fear not, Jane. You will be avenged. Ainslie and I will organise the war effort, as Dòmhnall is still too weak to be involved."

"Regardless, I'll sign off on it," said Dòmhnall. "Ainslie may now be chief, but I remain Lord of the Isles."

"A diminished title, from those like the Caimbeulaich," said Christina with contempt. "Ye're a king, Dòmhnall, like your forebears. This is the Sea Kingdom, *Dál Riata* as it once was, the Kingdom of the Isles."

"Just so," said Dòmhnall, inclining his head in agreement.

Jane made a sound, something under her breath.

"What was that, Jane?" asked Christina.

Jane raised her head and tried for the same proud bearing she saw in Ainslie and Christina.

"I am a Campbell," she announced.

An explosion could not have caused more of a reaction. Christina's eyes narrowed, Dòmhnall cried out, and all the blood drained from Aonghus's face as if he had seen a ghost.

"Now, I know that spending time with them may have made you think—" Christina began.

Jane shook her head, adamant.

"I'm married," she explained. "My husband is Lord David Crichton. I was born Jane Campbell, of Edinburgh."

"You have brought the enemy into our home!" cried Aonghus, who had found his voice at last. "I cured her of a Caimbeul wound, Ainslie."

Ainslie, at this supplication of her brother, was silent. Her family stared at her.

"And I wish," said Jane, amidst all this weighted silence, "to request that no further lives are taken on my account. I will not go to battle with my own kin, evil or not. My reason for hiding my maiden name is as you can imagine, were you in a strange land, and you were a Dhòmhnaill among the Caimbeulaich."

Madra thought all of this was very exciting and started yapping, wiggling around the room. No one took any notice of him; all eyes were on Jane.

A messenger chose this instant to appear in the doorway. He immediately saw that he was interrupting something and awkwardly stood there, moving his weight from foot to foot.

Dòmhnall finally tore his eyes away from his daughter and her lover to address the messenger, more sharply than he ever had in his long years as ruler. He was known for his gentle nature and his clemency, so the messenger was quite terrified when Dòmhnall spoke to him in this way.

"Weel?" Dòmhnall prompted. "Out wi' it. What could be o' sic urgency, tae interrupt a family affair?"

The boy bowed as low as he possibly could, his face red from embarrassment and shame at being scolded. He spoke in the usual Gaelic, instead of the Lallans Scots the Dhòmhnaill tended to use, as they had learned their English from the same part of Scotland.

"I am very sorry, my lord," the boy squeaked out. "But it couldn't wait, really."

"And?" Dòmhnall asked.

"Lord Archibald Caimbeul is here to see you, my lord," he said. "His ship is laying at anchor in the bay, and he awaits your permission to come ashore."

CHAPTER FIFTY-TWO

My Love and I

Lord Archibald Caimbeul stood in what served as Claig Castle's throne room, where Dòmhnall received guests. There was no throne, only the long table where Jane had first seen him writing, in a large room with enormous windows that reached to the ceiling and overlooked the sea outside.

Archibald bowed deeply. Dòmhnall's face was creased in a frown. Christina was clearly ready to fight as soon as he so much as moved strangely.

Archibald, however, seemed aware of this and stood stock-still. His *sgian dubh* was worn on his right calf in his stocking out in the open, instead of hidden under his arm or another part of his body. This was a statement in itself, because wearing a *sgian dubh* at the calf was the kind of thing people only did when they were among friends. Though his hand was on his sword hilt and the weapon swung by his side, it was with an air of placating formality that expressed the clear intention of peace.

No one present was buying it, apart from Jane. She knew him well.

"My apologies for not sending an advance messenger to you, Your Majesty," said Archibald, stressing the title. Dòmhnall and Christina exchanged glances; it was not like any Caimbeul to make reference to the Dhòmhnaill kingdom, let alone a chief's son. "I felt it necessary to arrive here with haste, to speak with you and answer those messages you have long sent to my clan."

Dòmhnall inclined his head slightly, and Archibald continued.

"Long has it been since our clans were embroiled in this feud," Archibald said. "And long have we lived in enmity, losing lives both Caimbeul and Dhòmhnaill. Shall we forever consider each other this way? Shall we two allow our clans to continue slaughtering each other?"

"What is the meaning of these questions?" Christina demanded. Archibald bowed again.

"Queen of the Isles, it is simply this," said Archibald. "I have long suspected my father's avarice was the cause of the continuation of this feud. If this be the case, then my ascendancy to the chiefship should erase these problems. I come to ask for your counsel. I come, in short, to ask for peace."

Everyone in the room was silent. Ainslie lifted a sceptical eyebrow.

"Hatred between us is foolish," Archibald went on. "Should this be a war you feel needs blood to satisfy, please take the blood that to my father matters most."

Thus saying, he unsheathed his sword; both Christina and Ainslie were there just ahead of him. He made a placating motion with his hands and then turned the hilt toward Dòmhnall.

"Strike, if you will," said Archibald. "I am the only child of Cailean Caimbeul. If I die, he dies without heir. But as you well know, blood is not the only thing that makes the chief; others may retain more enmity than I do for you."

"Why on earth would ye offer sic a thing?" asked Dòmhnall, truly amazed.

Archibald's gaze flicked towards Jane. She nodded to him.

"I've spent some time with one of my kin, these last few weeks," he said. "She has made me see the error of our ways and that we are a stronger force together. Besides, she loves one of your own beyond reason, and I think that tells me all I need to know."

He pushed his sword hilt into Dòmhnall's hands.

"Someone must end the fighting," murmured Archibald. "Or the pendulum will never stop swinging, not for hundreds of years to come."

Archibald knelt on the floor and bared his neck for Dòmhnall to cleave his head from his body. Thus prostrate, he was bathed in a pool of late afternoon sunlight from one of the high windows. This was a show of sacrifice and pageantry the likes of which none of them had ever seen before, all the better for its apparent honesty.

"Rise," Dòmhnall commanded. He shared a look with each member of his family, and they offered a slight nod in return.

Archibald stood.

"Your words have moved me," Dòmhnall said. "If this is an authentic display, so much the better. I and my family shall endeavour tae help ye in any way we can, if it means the end of such mindless bloodshed. Ye canna blame us for expecting some subterfuge; the Caimbeulaich have been dishonest an' money-seeking since time out o' mind."

Archibald nodded in agreement.

"Yes, I am aware of the reputation of my clan," he said. "I can only speak for myself and that what you are seeing now is genuine. I sincerely wish to stop the fighting between us, and as the chief of a large Highland clan, I feel I could learn from those who have not only supported their people but allowed them to prosper."

"This entails sacrifice," said Dòmhnall. "A love of your people that outweighs your love of money. Are you willing to do it?"

"Yes," said Archibald. "I am willing."

"Then ye shall be welcomed here as our brother," Dòmhnall declared.

"However," Christina cut in, "if you so much as look at one of the Dhòmhnaill clan in a way I don't like, you will taste the blade of my sword."

The colour drained from Archibald's face.

"Understood," he said, in a diminished voice.

CHAPTER FIFTY-THREE

Oh Will Ye Be Known as a Poor Beggar's Lady

Jane's cottage was as warm and welcoming as it had been before she had taken to the sea.

She sat on the bed and looked around as Ainslie stoked the fire into leaping flames. She thought the place looked like Christmas; decorated with boughs of evergreen and red leaves, there was nothing quite so cosy and beautiful as her little cottage by the sea.

Archibald had been instructed to stay in the castle, although Jane didn't understand the reason.

"There's nae room for him here," Ainslie grumbled. "Asides, ye cannae trust a Caimbeul."

"How old is that saying?" asked Jane, shaking her head.

Realisation dawned on her.

"Is that why you're here?" she asked. "To guard me, in case I rise up in the night and attack?"

Ainslie turned to her.

"Jane," she said. "The Caimbeulaich are our longtime enemies. Ye've been amang them for a guid few weeks. Do ye think we should be sae foolish as tae trust either o' ye at this point?"

Jane crossed her arms, haughty.

"You trusted me until now!" she said.

"Aye," Ainslie agreed. "Afore I kent ye were a Caimbeul, afore ye disappeared an' reappeared—not only in Caimbeul lands, but in the clan seat! An' now the young Caimbeul heir is here amang us. Now I ask ye, what would ye think in my place?"

"I thought we loved each other," said Jane sadly.

"An' we do," Ainslie said. "But I cannae let my love for ye blind me, an' lose ithers I hold dear. I must think as a chief should. I've nae clue what ye micht me hidin' frae me, Jane."

"I don't think it's fair," Jane protested.

"Weel, it may no be," admitted Ainslie. "An' yet it must be done, until we are certain. I'll ask ye, Jane: what o' the Caimbeulaich o' the future? Did they stop acting the fool? Are they trustworthy? Ye say that 'cannae trust a Caimbeul' is still a saying in your time. Is there a reason for that?"

Jane wanted to argue, but various thoughts occurred to her, not the least the damning event of the Glencoe Massacre. Campbells had broken the law of Highland hospitality by entering Glencoe claiming to need places to sleep, which the MacDonalds granted them. Then they rose up at night during a blizzard and slaughtered most of the clan. It had been done by the command of the king, but it was the subterfuge and the breaking of the sacred law of Highland hospitality that rocked Scotland to its core when the news emerged about the event.

Jane did not reply. She hung her head.

Ainslie went to her and knelt before her. She brushed Jane's hair away from her face and looked into her dark eyes.

"Believe me, Jane," she said. "I love ye, an' I'd sacrifice myself for ye in a heartbeat. But I am also the chief o' my clan. I canna afford tae be sentimental when the safety o' my people is at stake."

Numbly, Jane nodded. Of course she understood, but she did not like the wedge driven between them because of politics, because of an accident of birth.

That night, Ainslie did not join her in bed but kept watch sitting in one of the chairs near the kitchen table. She dropped off eventually in an upright position, leaning on her hand, and Jane watched her drowsily, wondering if it would ever be the same again between them.

* * *

The two of them were startled awake by Jane's cottage door being wrenched open and Archibald thrown onto his knees in front of them.

"Confess!" shouted Christina, all hellfire and war. Dòmhnall and Aonghus stood behind.

Ainslie stood, and for once Jane was thankful they hadn't been in the bed together, as this did not look like a promising development.

"What is it?" Ainslie demanded, looking from Archibald to Jane.

"The Caimbeulaich have declared war on us!" announced Christina. "Do you wish to explain, traitor?"

"I swear," said Archibald. "I swear, I came to you in peace yesterday. This was not my doing."

"The two of you together planned this," Christina snarled. Jane stared at her.

"I have no idea what you're talking about," said Jane icily. She did not like being accused, especially after everything she had gone through.

"Are you telling me that the two of you showing up, one after the other, and then the Caimbeulaich declaring war on the Dhòmhnaill was completely unrelated?" demanded Christina.

"Yes," said Jane coldly. "You are jumping to conclusions. This is not something Archibald would do. I know him well."

"And she defends him, you see?" said Christina. Jane looked at Ainslie, hoping for help from that quarter.

Ainslie looked uncertain, as did both Dòmhnall and Aonghus.

"Bring us before the Druid Council," said Jane, reaching for the only avenue of reason she could think of. "Let them be the judge of us. I am a member; I am owed that much."

"You haven't even returned to the Council!" said Christina.

"Mother," Ainslie cut in. "Please. For me. I need to know."

Christina stared at her daughter and then sheathed her sword. She walked off grumbling.

Dòmhnall and Aonghus hadn't said a word. Two guards came through and arrested both Jane and Archibald.

"Where are you taking them?" Ainslie demanded.

"The castle dungeon," said one of the guards. "They must remain there until trial."

"This is infamous!" cried Jane.

"It's the dungeons or death here on your doorstep," said the guard. "One or the other. Choose."

Jane was incredulous but allowed herself to be led away. She glared at Ainslie, who was looking at the floor.

There was nothing for it but to accept imprisonment and hope for the leniency of the Council she had deserted some months before.

CHAPTER FIFTY-FOUR

And Lie in the Heather Rolled Up in My Plaidie

The doors to their cells clanged shut; Ainslie wouldn't even look at them.

Still, Jane figured, she had to admit the situation looked fairly damning. She didn't blame Ainslie. Or Christina for that matter.

Once their footsteps had echoed away above the stairs, the two of them were left alone in the chill damp of the dungeon, the rhythmic noise of dripping water the only sound apart from their loud breathing.

Their eyes met. When Jane moved, it was sudden and sure.

"Tell me you didn't do this," Jane snarled, her hands on the bars separating their cells.

Archibald moved toward her, lightning fast. He held his head up, tall and proud.

"I swear, on my honour as a Caim—on my honour," he said, changing course mid-sentence, his smile like a rictus. "Will they have the same honour, in judging me?"

"That I cannot say," said Jane. "But I was a part of their Council for a time, and they are usually fair and decent folk. However—you entered the castle on false pretences, and so it is difficult to say what they might do."

Archibald sighed, sagging against the bars of his cell.

"They weren't false," he said. "I truly did mean to make peace with the Dhòmhnaill. I find all this very upsetting and stressful. I prefer friends to foes, and I would like to be a good leader for my clan. I've spent a lifetime watching them starve."

"Why did you not intervene before?" asked Jane.

"I tried," Archibald told her. "Father wouldn't listen."

"Why has he decided to declare war?" asked Jane. "The death toll of the previous winter was far higher. I was there, I remember."

Archibald shook his head.

"The fire," he said. "The fire destroyed many valuable things."

"The fire?" Jane demanded. "What about the cost of human life?"

Archibald shrugged, looking miserable.

"He doesn't care," he said. "He only sees them as swords to help him put more money in his coffers. Otherwise, clansmen could live or die. It matters not to him."

"Infamous," Jane muttered for the second time that day.

"Yes," said Archibald. "That is why I wanted to stop him."

Jane stared at him.

"What is it?" he asked.

"I think I might have a way to get us out of this," said Jane. "A way even the Druid Council could judge in our favour."

"What is it?" asked Archibald. "Oh, if there is anything that would keep me from rotting here in a dungeon forever!"

"I'd think your father would want to avenge you," she said.

"And you would be wrong," said Archibald. "What is it? What have you come up with?"

"You love me, do you not, Archie?" asked Jane.

"Yes. Very much," he replied. "Although I now understand I must love you like a brother, as your heart is not mine."

"This is true," said Jane. "But if you love me, you will follow my lead?"

"To the ends of this earth," Archibald promised.

"Then," she said, "I think it is time that we accept the offer of war with the Caimbeulaich—fighting on the Dhòmhnaill side."

* * *

They had spent an uncomfortable night in the dungeon, and it was with joyful hearts they welcomed the overcast grey skies outside the castle walls. Jane and Archibald kept to themselves, as their plan would only work if it were brought first before the Council.

In the chambers, Morag greeted Jane like a long-lost friend.

"I hope," she murmured to Jane, "for your sake, that you did not do what you are being accused of, Jane. I had looked forward to welcoming you back to the Council, as some of your ideas are quite novel to us."

She released Jane and went to sit with the others.

"Are you certain that you can give an impartial verdict to these two?" enquired Ainslie.

The Druid Council nodded, even Morag. They loved truth and justice above all things, after all.

"If I may?"

Everyone turned to look at Jane. She stepped forward.

"I am, or was, a member of this honourable Council," she said. "You know me to be a woman of science. An inventor. Someone with knowledge beyond your grasp."

Some of the Council were nodding at this, as they did know these things about Jane.

"I am come from the future."

This statement drew laughs, gasps, some disbelief and ridicule.

"That's impossible," said Tariq. "No one can travel in time."

"No one can travel in time *yet*," said Jane. "I am here to offer you a deal: I can adapt the hand-cannon given to the Druids into a weapon of war that will offer sure victory against the Caimbeul clan. I will do this for the Dhòmhnaill, for the Druid Council I once served on, and for Ainslie nic Dòmhnaill, the love of my life, in my time or this."

Ainslie seemed to shiver at this statement but remained resolute.

"What say ye, Council?" asked Morag.

There was much deliberation and discussion. Morag was the one to return the verdict.

"If Lady Jane Crichton is able to adapt the hand-cannon for us," she said, "it is quite obvious that she is on the Dhòmhnaill side. If she is tae answer for Archibald in this, it means fighting against his father in the oncoming war. If these things are done with nae reluctance on the part of either party, baith Jane and Archibald will be excused their punishment."

There were murmurs around the room, and Ainslie had a faint look of something like hope in her expression.

"On the ither hand," said Morag, "if any subterfuge or evil befalls any Dhòmhnaill because o' the dissimulation of *either* Jane or Archibald, they baith will face imprisonment and death."

Jane's stomach turned.

"Are ye baith willing tae speak for each ither?" asked Morag. "Do ye hae enough confidence in each ither's intentions that ye will risk this punishment, should ane o' ye go astray?"

Archibald and Jane exchanged looks.

"Yes," they both said at the same time. Ainslie looked on with jealousy but kept her mouth firmly shut.

"Very well," said Morag. "It is the decision of the Druid Council that these two Caimbeul will remain at liberty in order tae prove themselves in the ways described or baith suffer frae the same fate prescribed tae them. The Council is dismissed. May ye mak the richt choices, Jane and Archibald Caimbeul, or sae much the worse for ye."

With that, Morag dismissed them all.

Ainslie approached the two of them, hesitant. It was clear she was swallowing down a jealousy she had no right to be feeling.

"What do ye want o' me?" asked Ainslie, voice rough with unvoiced emotion.

Jane looked at her, dark eyes burning.

"Lead me to the hand-cannon," said Jane. "I will win you this war."

CHAPTER FIFTY-FIVE

Sky for Your Roof and Your Candles the Stars

Jane was hard at work in the little courtyard of the cottage, where they'd kept the machine. The machine itself had not yet been moved from its landing place in the mountains of Islay, but there were other more pressing concerns at the moment.

Ainslie and Archibald were standing outside in the garden, awkwardly looking at the ground. Jane had shooed them both outside, saying it would be too dangerous for them in the interior courtyard.

They stood together, staring at the ground or at birds wheeling in the sky.

"What do you suppose she's working on in there?" Archibald ventured to ask awkwardly.

Ainslie shot him a look of withering hatred.

"Right. So," said Archibald, for something to say.

Silence went on like a river of syrup between them, sticky and uncomfortable.

"Why d'ye speak like an Englishman?" Ainslie said suddenly.

Archibald looked at her in surprise.

"I, well," he began. "I had an English tutor. Father would have nothing less than the best, you see."

"An' is there somethin' wrang wi' the way I talk?" Ainslie demanded, bristling.

"No!" Archibald said, holding up his hands. "No, it's just…"

He sighed and sat down on the grass.

"All my life, I've been raised to be the chief," he said.

"As have I," Ainslie shot back.

"Yes," agreed Archibald. "Yet you've been raised to rule these islands and the clans on the opposite shore, correct?"

Ainslie gave an abrupt nod.

"Father thinks that England is where we ought to put our hopes for the future and our fortune," Archibald explained.

"My da trades wi' the English as well," said Ainslie. "Took their side in a few battles against the Scots."

"Against the Scots?" asked Archibald, puzzled. "Aren't you Scots yourselves?"

Ainslie drew herself up.

"Nae," she declared. "We are the Dhòmhnaill."

"You certainly sound Scottish to me," said Archibald.

"We learnt our English in Glasgow," said Ainslie. "But we are the Dhòmhnaill, all the same. I can also speak in Norse, Arabic, Gaelic—what would ye prefer? My father has prepared me for the chiefship, too."

Archibald nodded, pulling at the grass. He was still young and somewhat gawky, barely out of his teens, while Ainslie, like Jane, was at the other end of thirty or so.

"I apologise for the contempt my clan has always held yours in," he said. "If they had spent any time among you, they would know that none could be matched for intelligence, loyalty, or warrior spirit."

Ainslie crossed her arms, but it was clear her heart was melting a bit.

"An' now that ye have come here?" she prompted.

"I will fight by your side," he swore. "Always and forever, Ainslie nic Dòmhnaill, consider me your friend."

"My goodness, the two of you make a racket," said Jane, finally emerging from the courtyard.

Ainslie and Archibald looked up guiltily; they hadn't realised that their words could be overheard, it seemed.

"It's ready," Jane said and showed them the hand-cannon.

It was still small, but with a longer barrel, and it had a stock for putting against the shoulder.

"The percussion lock firearm and the breech-loading rifle were both invented by Scots," said Jane proudly. "I just kind of…hurried up the production of the thing."

Ainslie examined the weapon. She looked up at Jane.

"And what does it do?" she asked.

"The same thing as the hand-cannon," Jane explained. "Except you can reload it easily, it's portable, and you can shoot for distance."

Although Ainslie was impressed, she did not seem pleased.

"We will use it for this battle and no other," she said. "Afterwards, it will be destroyed. Nane o' us will speak a word of it."

Jane stared at Ainslie, hurt and confused.

"I thought you'd be proud."

"An' I am, lass," said Ainslie. "Ye hae the mind o' a Druid, an' let nae man no' mark it. But this…"

She stared at the adapted hand-cannon as if it was something hateful.

"This is a weapon of indiscriminate destruction, like an explosion, like lightning," she said. "Nae man should have a weapon such as this."

"The hand-cannon was the precursor to the gun," Jane said. "Later models would be even more deadly."

"All the better for us no' to have the thing," said Ainslie. "Ye said the gun, as ye call it, was developed later? I take it this was *much* later than now?"

Jane nodded.

"Weel, *now*, I prefer that my soldiers look their enemy in the eye," said Ainslie. "It provokes mercy an' restraint."

"You don't trust your own men to be prudent?" Jane asked.

"I trust no man who is gien the Hand o' God tae make war with," said Ainslie. "This battle, an' nae ither."

Jane nodded.

"Understood."

* * *

The Caimbeulaich had made good on their promise and were sailing their ships to Islay and Jura to participate in the battle. Horns sounded, and the clash of *claidheamhan-mòra* could be heard echoing across the water. The shouts of the men and women in battle were mingled together with sword thrusts, and the almighty din was eventually drawn into a glen where Ainslie, Jane, and Archibald stood together on a small promontory.

"Everyone!" Ainslie shouted in Gaelic. "This is the voice of the Dhòmhnaill chief! I ask that you put down your weapons!"

There was a blessed, incredulous silence for a moment as the Dhòmhnaill paused, and then derisive laughter as the Caimbeulaich did not stop fighting and the clank of swords resumed.

"Jane," said Ainslie. Jane took aim. She knew that her skill with the gun meant that the man she had targeted would not be mortally wounded, and she had already accepted that life during this time period was far more violent than her own. Understanding that she would be accepting this kind of environment if she chose to return to Ainslie, she had given it a great deal of consideration. This was a part of her life here, and acting the wilting flower about it would only endanger them all. This was the way she could be a valuable partner to a woman who would be the chief.

She fired into the crowd. The shot echoed. One of the Caimbeulaich fell.

This miraculous felling of one of their own made the Caimbeulaich hesitant.

"Again, I ask: put down your weapons!" Ainslie shouted again.

She was ignored. Jane reloaded.

The second *crack* of the gunshot echoed through the glen, and another of the Caimbeulaich fell.

The warriors were now hesitant to start the attack anew; it seemed like their compatriots had been felled by some supernatural instrument.

"Listen to me!" Ainslie cried, in Gaelic. "I am the chief of the Dhòmhnaill; I stand here with one of your own! I stand here with Lord Archibald Caimbeul, the chief's son!"

This definitely got their attention, but the battle raged closer still, close enough that Archibald could see his father in the fight.

Ainslie nodded to Jane.

Jane raised the gun.

"No, don't!" cried Archibald, but it was too late.

When the next *crack* rang out across the glen, a man fell within thirty yards of their outpost.

"Father!" cried Archibald, rushing to his aid.

It was true. Cailean Caimbeul had fallen among the ranks of his warriors.

CHAPTER FIFTY-SIX

My Love for a Fire

Archibald rushed to throw himself over the prostrate body of his father.

"Archie, are you mad?" his father demanded from the ground. Jane was relieved to note that the bullet had only winged his shoulder.

"I will not let you die this way, Father," Archibald said, resolute.

"All right, that's enough!" boomed another voice from the field of battle.

Dòmhnall stood grinning among the warriors as if he were out for a picnic.

"Da, ye're no supposed tae be out o' bed yet!" Ainslie said.

"Aye, Aonghus said the same," Dòmhnall agreed. "An' I said he'd no stop me, so he came wi' me instead."

"Aonghus?" asked Ainslie, astonished. One of the warriors turned around, and sure enough, her brother stood there in the field.

"I ask the Dhòmhnaill to lay down their weapons," Ainslie announced, in Gaelic. "This is the word of your chief. Will the Caimbeulaich do the same?"

Archibald nodded and rose.

"I beg you to preserve the life of my father," he said. "This feud has gone on long enough, and I tire of battles. Let us beat our swords into ploughshares, and go forward as friends."

Neither the Caimbeulaich or the Dhòmhnaill wanted to continue fighting, so they made a half-hearted grumble of protest but put away their weapons and withdrew.

Cailean Caimbeul tried to rise, furious in his defeat, only to find Dòmhnall standing above him.

"Now, then," said Dòmhnall. "I think it's time that you and I retire, don't you? The children are doing all right for themselves, and I think they will both be great leaders."

He looked at Ainslie and Archibald, who were speaking to their respective clans; peace seemed imminent.

Dòmhnall held out his hand and helped the man up.

"Your son has not your greed, and my daughter is warlike," said Dòmhnall. "Does retirement sound like a good plan to you, Cailean Caimbeul? You are welcome at my castle for the evening. I have a fine collection of whisky."

The Caimbeul chief looked like he was going to argue.

"But I insist," said Dòmhnall, pushing him away from the field of battle, Aonghus trailing in his wake.

* * *

There were very few dead from the battle, which was a fresh occurrence for both clans.

Aonghus followed Dòmhnall and Cailean to the castle, in order to help in the man's healing. He'd never seen such an expertly placed wound in his life, and told Jane so.

Jane, according to her promise, destroyed the hand-cannon for good.

* * *

The sun shone bright on the water, on the green hills around, and on the golden flames of Ainslie's hair.

She quirked a smile at Jane, who approached her as the warriors went their separate ways.

"A fine strategy," she said. "Ye'll be a warrior yet."

She cast her gaze toward the ground and did not seem to know what to do with herself, fidgeting.

"We have much to discuss, Ainslie nic Dòmhnaill," she said.

"Aye," muttered Ainslie, still looking at the ground.

"But first," said Jane. Ainslie lifted her head in surprise.

"Aye?" she ventured, hope stealing into her expression.

Jane grinned. Ainslie, still cautious, grinned back.

"Take me home."

* * *

Later that evening, the fire made the cottage warmer still; and Jane's body was bare, a sacrifice to Ainslie, her queen.

Ainslie wrapped a strong arm around Jane's waist and pulled her down the bed, ensuring Jane's bare bottom was supported on a pillow.

"I hunger for ye, little harlot," Ainslie said in a strangled voice and cupped Jane's bottom, nosing her legs open. She pressed kisses to the insides of Jane's thighs, which became licks, trails of her tongue until Jane was shivering with want.

Ainslie touched her, gently, spread her open with fingertips soft and nimble. Jane was already wet, as she always was for her queen— ready and waiting.

Suddenly, Ainslie lifted her, hauling her forwards with her hands under her bottom, and buried her face between Jane's thighs. Ainslie's tongue darted out to fill her, and Jane moaned at the onslaught of sensation, plundered by Ainslie's quick tongue. Impatient, Ainslie let out a moan and pulled her closer, crushing her, sucking her clitoris into her mouth as Jane screamed and kicked lightly against her shoulders. Within seconds, Jane was coming, and she thought this time would be as it always was, where Ainslie would leave her, but it seemed her queen was willing to exhaust her, until it seemed there would be no end to it.

The amount Jane would give to this woman was itself endless; this woman who had granted her pleasure unlike any she had ever known. Jane willingly offered herself up, pushing herself down on Ainslie's tongue, and she shrieked in delighted abandon as Ainslie sucked at her one last time, the bed soaked through, her thighs wet with it. Jane was nothing but animal, rocking against Ainslie, and her last thought before her world went dark was about the wildness of the women of Dionysus.

* * *

In the morning, the cottage was quiet, and the embers flickered and hissed in the grate.

Jane rolled over and saw Ainslie there. Ainslie smiled, all freckles and bright green eyes, and pulled Jane to pillow her head on Ainslie's breast, lazily stroking her arm until Jane fell asleep again in the safety of her lover's arms.

* * *

"Ainslie."

"Aye," Ainslie said, as she brought in the peat from the garden. It was later that morning, and the day had dawned bright and warm, a blessed rarity.

"I need you to take me to the place where we left the machine."

Ainslie stared at Jane, openmouthed, the peat forgotten in her arms. She clearly wanted to argue but could not summon the strength.

"Please. There's something I have to do."

Ainslie nodded, quick and sharp, and set the peat down next to the fireplace. She pinned her earasaid over her shoulder in preparation for the journey.

CHAPTER FIFTY-SEVEN

She Has Led Her High Up on a Mountain

Jane saw the sad determination in Ainslie's expression and moved quickly to correct her own error.

"No," Jane said, cradling Ainslie's face in her hands. "No, I am not leaving you. Not now, not ever again."

She kissed Ainslie, soft and slow, loving her Highland warrior's plush lips. She deepened the kiss. Ainslie moaned and clutched at Jane's earasaid, pulling her into a tight embrace.

Jane was the first to pull away, panting softly.

"Then why do ye go?" Ainslie asked, her emerald eyes burning bright with tears.

"I have to—for a little while," said Jane. "There's a promise I need to keep."

"An' ye'll return tae me?" asked Ainslie.

"Yes," Jane said, with all the force she could muster behind the words. "I know it's a lot to ask, but—will you trust me, Ainslie?"

The redhead looked as though she might not.

Then, with a great deal of courage and heart, she breathed deeply and nodded.

"Then show me the way to the machine."

* * *

The machine was undamaged, and possibly untouched, since she had landed here.

Jane had followed Ainslie up the mountainside. The day was a rare one—sunny and beautiful, through the broom and the heather down to the loch sparkling blue and silver below. It was a breathtaking view, and Jane was pleased that she had landed in such a beautiful spot.

She finished the pre-flight check of the machine; all seemed to be in order.

It was time to go.

"Wait," said Ainslie. She drew her lover to her breast.

She stared into Jane's dark eyes for a long time, saying nothing.

Ainslie ran her hands down Jane's arms and smiled.

"I've never been sae afraid in battle as I am the now," said Ainslie. "I fear I shall never see your beautiful face again, Jane, my love, my life, my everything."

She pulled her into a kiss, sweeter than their last; this was the kind of kiss given as a mark of farewell, the kiss a soldier gives their partner before going to war.

"You have nothing to fear," whispered Jane, dizzy with Ainslie's kisses. "I will come back to you."

Ainslie sighed and then knelt down, plucking some of the heather from the ground.

She fixed it to the brooch holding up Jane's earasaid.

Jane looked at her curiously.

"Sae ye remember," Ainslie murmured.

"I could never forget," said Jane, her hand combing through Ainslie's long hair.

Ainslie pressed her forehead to Jane's.

"I love ye, Jane Caimbeul," she said fiercely. "I love ye tae distraction an' madness, an' wi' all my heart."

Jane's heart beat fast; her eyes fluttered closed.

"I love you too, Ainslie, chief of the Dhòmhnaill," said Jane. "And through hell or heaven, I will return to you. I promise."

Jane kissed Ainslie once, hard, and then flew to the machine, disappearing into it and pulling the hatch closed, as if she feared she would lose her nerve.

The machine's engines started up, and it flickered out of existence, as if it had never been. Only the pressed-down heather and broom gave any indication that it had been there at all.

* * *

The machine blinked into existence, but not where Jane had expected.

She poked her head out of the hatch to survey her surroundings. This wasn't the manor.

She'd never seen this place before. It was some kind of research lab, judging by the microscopes and other instruments on various tables.

She climbed out of the machine, careful of her bare feet on the cold floor. She wondered how she was going to get back to the manor house like this; she'd cause a riot in the streets of Edinburgh.

She was inspecting a microscope when a voice behind her startled her nearly out of her wits.

"I see by your clothing that you have recently been in battle," said the voice. "And the cuts on your hands indicate it was the kind fought with swords. Judging by your dress, I'd say you were just returned from the thirteenth century."

Jane turned around and crossed her arms, raising a mocking brow. Dr. Joseph Bell grinned at her, and she grinned back.

"Oh, Joe, I'm so relieved it's you!" she exclaimed, throwing herself into his arms. "I had no idea where I was. The machine has a mind of its own sometimes."

"Indeed," Joe Bell said. "There may be something in what you say, my dear lady. If such a thing weren't the stuff of dreams, I'd say perhaps it has grown a sentience—or always had it."

"That's not possible," Jane shook her head. "I calibrated everything perfectly. I just keep ending up in unexpected places."

"Last year, I'd have said time travel was not possible," said Bell. "And yet—"

"Yes, yes," said Jane. "Whatever remains, however improbable, must be the truth. You have said so, many times."

"She hears, but she does not listen," Bell chided her gently. Jane smiled and rolled her eyes good-naturedly.

"Have you seen David?" she asked. "How long have I been gone?"

"This time, around a year perhaps?" said Bell. Jane's mouth dropped open.

"A year?" she cried. "Oh, he must be so worried."

"Don't trouble yourself," said Bell. "He's had a splendid time imagining you off on your adventures, your feats of derring-do, and all that sort of thing."

Jane smiled; she was really quite fond of David.

"I'm glad," she said. "But I need your help, Joe."

"I am at your service," he replied.

"I need to adjust the machine," Jane said.

"Because of its inaccuracy?" he asked.

"We'll look at that as well, yes," she said. "But it's primarily to adapt the machine so it can carry two."

A light danced in Bell's eyes.

"I see," he said, smiling.

"Yes," Jane replied to the question he didn't need to ask. "I'm bringing David home."

CHAPTER FIFTY-EIGHT

An' Bade Her Look O'er the Sea

The door to the manor opened, and Jane stepped inside.

It had the same strange chill she had noticed after her first return and she wondered again how anyone survived it. She longed for the warmth of hearth and home.

"David?" she called out, her voice echoing through the empty house. Not even a serving-girl was there; the place was deserted. It felt like a museum, without life in it; her own cottage felt cosy even when she was there alone.

Joe had helped bundle her into a carriage so that her presence in Edinburgh wearing medieval Highland dress could not be remarked upon. Returning to the manor house was always strange, and if the cab driver talked, well, Jane's eccentricity was well known.

Jane walked up the grand staircase to her bedroom and went into her wardrobe. She sighed as she removed her clothes and began to pick out more modern things to wear. She spent ages choosing the right pieces and then time pinning up her hair, which had grown much longer in her absence. She placed a hat on her head and her feet into the restrictive high-heeled boots, which now chafed at her, so accustomed was she to the glorious joy of barefoot freedom on Ainslie's island.

She looked at her reflection in the full-length mirror. She was every bit the proper Victorian lady, but her heart ran wild and Highland— she remembered a snippet of song that went that way—

From the lone shieling of the misty island
Mountains divide us, and the waste of seas;
still, the blood is strong! the heart is Highland
and we in dreams behold the Hebrides.

Jane stared at herself in the mirror.

"I will return to you, Ainslie, my love," she whispered.

Her reverie was broken when she heard the downstairs front door bang shut.

"Janie? Janie!" David's voice called from downstairs. "Are you here?"

Jane rushed out to the landing.

"Yes! Yes, I am here!" she said and met him halfway down the staircase, where he threw his arms around her with joy.

* * *

"Good Lord!" David was saying as he poured the tea. "And they just—put down their swords? At her word?"

"Yes," said Jane, her eyes shining. "She had to say it more than once, but it happened."

"Ah, Janie, I envy you your adventures," said David, whose mustache had become really quite ridiculous in her absence. "I've missed you this long year, and your stories."

"Well," said Jane. "That's what I've come back for."

"What, to tell me stories?" asked David, guffawing into his mustache. "I say, old thing, you needn't interrupt your sex life for me!"

"David!" said Jane, scandalised more because it was David speaking than actually offended.

"Oh now, Janie, that's the best part!" David said. "Passion! Love! A warrior woman! All this sounds absolutely brilliant. Top hole."

Jane laughed. She had missed David quite a bit.

"David, I came back to ask if you'd like to join me," Jane said, setting her teacup back in its saucer.

David's eyes were round. He stuttered for a moment.

"Are you quite—I mean I wouldn't be in the way—would I? Perhaps—but no." David voiced a string of nonsensical words.

"It's all right, take your time," said Jane. "If there's anything we have left to us, it's that."

"It's just—Janie, I know I have no claim on you as a husband," said David. "Nor do I want to assert any such thing. Would I not be cumbersome to you?"

"David," said Jane, moving to sit next to him on the settee, "while we may be married only in name, you are my best friend. I would not want to leave you here, unless you wanted to be left. Remember, you asked me to come back for you."

"A foolish man's wish," said David, shaking his head. "Janie, I'd only be a burden."

"You are no burden to me," she replied. "And I'd like to think you safe and sound, instead of roaming this enormous house alone."

David looked around, and it was clear he agreed with the sentiment.

"Isn't there only room for one in your machine?" he asked, scarcely daring to hope.

"Joe Bell helped me with the alterations," she said with a grin. "It's now a boat that can carry two."

"Won't our families miss us?" he asked, the last of his doubts fading away like Highland mist in the summer sun. "What if I don't find it to my taste?"

"The time machine works in both directions, David," said Jane. "It will be as if we moved to America; we'll be far away, but we can always visit. If you decide it's not to your taste, I can return you here as if you had never left at all."

David sat and appeared to think about this for a very long time, chewing on his mustache a bit.

He quite suddenly and firmly replaced his teacup in its saucer with a clatter.

"Right-ho," he said. "Let's go to America."

CHAPTER FIFTY-NINE

These Isles Ye Behold Are MacDonald's, My Own

The machine blinked into existence on the top of the same mountain where Jane had left Ainslie.

Jane pushed the hatch open and the cool air swept into the machine's interior, dusting it with falling snow.

Amazed, she stepped out of the machine, her heels crunching lightly in the coverlet of white.

She stared around her for a moment; it was dark and clearly winter.

"I say!" said David, his head appearing in the hatch. "This is—what's the word—absolutely smashing, Janie! Excellent work."

"It's winter," Jane said, as David climbed out of the machine.

"Aye," David agreed, trying out a Scottish word, as he was Scottish himself despite how much his parents had hoped education and elocution would help him forget it.

He stood beside her as large snowflakes fell in lazy drifts at their feet. It was fresh snow and newly fallen; the chill in the air was one of late autumn and early winter, and so not unpleasant.

Jane touched the heather she still wore on her chest, heather that had not yet withered.

"I left her in the summer, David," she said.

"Hmm," David said, chewing his mustache. "That is a sticky problem. The machine performs more as an approximation, it seems."

"Mind of its own," Jane murmured.

"Do you know the way to civilisation, Janie?" David enquired.

Jane nodded.

"I do," she said. "I fear it might be uncomfortable, given these clothes, and that we will cause quite a stir in the city, looking this way."

David laughed.

"I certainly hope so," he said. "These clothes are rather ridiculous. Well, lead on, my girl; I look forward to the peat whisky fires and kilted men dancing round the fluffy cows and all that tosh."

Jane smiled at him with an affectionate look of exasperation and began to carefully pick her way down the mountain.

* * *

As it turned out, the only excitement either of them caused was that Jane had returned. People were running to her from their houses, embracing her, asking where she'd been, and who was the man beside her? She told them David was her husband, blushing, but this didn't seem to matter to any of them for some reason.

They made their way to Jane's cottage, where she pushed the door open.

She was surprised to find the fire burning, the peat-scent strong in the cottage, and the dark silhouette of someone familiar asleep in one of the chairs that had been pulled in front of the flames. Lamb was roasting on the spit, and the crackling of the fire echoed softly in the warm room. Shadows danced on the walls with the bright orange of the fire, throwing the hazy shapes of the cottage's furniture into relief.

The long braid of ginger hair glowed bright in the firelight, and the sight of her strong body made Jane's heart skip a beat. The person in the chair startled awake as the door swung in, and she turned to look at the doorway.

Jane smiled at Ainslie.

"Jane?" Ainslie whispered, hardly daring to believe it.

"Yes, it's me," said Jane. "I've come back."

Ainslie threw herself into Jane's arms, kissing her soundly. She kept kissing her, everywhere she could reach, her cheeks, her eyelids, the edges of her ears...

And then noticed David standing behind her, an amused look on his face, though he tried to hide his smile behind his moustache.

"Oh, don't mind me," he said. "Carry on."

Ainslie backed away from Jane and looked at him curiously.

"Ainslie," said Jane. "This is my husband, David. Can we talk?"

* * *

The three of them sat around the table in the cottage. The dinner had been excellent, and David was leaning back in his chair, drinking as much whisky as he could get inside of himself.

"I say," he said. "I say. I say, indeed."

He squinted at his glass.

"What was I saying?" he said.

"I never left the cottage," Ainslie murmured to Jane. "I trusted ye'd come back, an' I wanted a warm welcome for ye. I've lived here ever since."

"You didn't have to do that," Jane gasped. "What about your father? Your mother? Aonghus?"

Ainslie shrugged, gazing on Jane with a dreamy smile.

"They can tak care o' themselves," she said. "I never doubted ye, Jane. Never."

"Capital!" roared David, startling them. "Absolutely capital! I give you my blessing. All four of you! Six? Janie. How many of you are there?"

Jane plucked the glass of whisky out of his hand.

"I think that's enough for the evening," she said.

"Quite right," said David and then announced, "I'm off to bed."

He stood, saw the bed on the other side of the room, staggered over to it, and flopped onto it face first.

"That's your husband?" Ainslie said. "He's daft as a brush."

"Oh, hush now," said Jane. "Husband in name only. He's far more like a brother than a husband. He's a good man and has always been good to me."

Ainslie smiled.

"Then he is welcome in the land of the Dhòmhnaill," she said. "In the morning, we will go tae fetch your wee boatie an' bring it here. Tonight is for talking and telling stories."

"Is that so?" asked Jane, touching Ainslie's face and drawing her in for a kiss. "I'm not sure what more we can do, since David's commandeered the bed."

"I think we may have enough to keep us until the dawn," said Ainslie. "I've news, an' I think it micht be enough to warrant a sleepless night."

She kissed Jane again.

"News an' ither things," she said, her hand in Jane's hair, her heart beating time with Jane's own.

"Other things?" asked Jane, teasing her as she took Ainslie's lip between her teeth, sucking gently, kissing her softly as Ainslie stifled a moan.

Nevertheless, Ainslie sat back, though she still looked at Jane's mouth hungrily.

Jane sensed there was something important in the air and settled back, looking at Ainslie expectantly.

"The truth is," Ainslie began, "we may no need the cottage after all, if David wants it."

Now Jane was really confused.

"What?" she said. "But I adore this cottage."

She looked meaningfully at the bed.

"And the bed," she said, grinning.

"The reason we won't need it is because we'll baith be moving intae the castle," said Ainslie. "On my da's orders."

"Why does he want us to do that?" Jane asked.

"Because," said Ainslie, looking up from her clasped hands, "Da has decided to retire as part o' a deal wi' Cailean Caimbeul."

The implications of this statement dawned on Jane. She stared at Ainslie, her eyes shining.

"So that means—"

"Aye," said Ainslie. "I am to be the new Lord o' the Isles, ruler o' the Sea Kingdom."

There was silence in the cottage, broken only by the crackling of the fire, while the gravity of this statement sank in.

"Capital," David's muffled voice announced from the bed, where his face was still mashed into the mattress. "Absolutely spiffing. Top hole."

The two women burst out laughing, and Jane threw herself into Ainslie's arms, shouting congratulations, before the two of them melted together into a passionate kiss.

CHAPTER SIXTY

An' My Bride an' My Darlin' Are Ye

The following morning the snow was still falling.

Ainslie had asked Jane to follow her, and Jane had done so, trailing behind her in the snow, heart filled with curiosity.

Outside of the city, the woodlands were quiet in the early-morning darkness. A few birds sang in the trees as they walked past, as it seems birds are the first to know of the approach of dawn, but otherwise the only sound was their footsteps in the snow and the slow whistling of wind.

"Winter's no' yet come," Ainslie remarked as they walked. "Ground's got a bit o' the snaw-cover, but the earth's still soft below."

"It's still quite warm," Jane agreed. "I didn't bring warm clothing as I thought I'd be right back."

Ainslie shot a wry smile over her shoulder.

"Aye, a mind o' its own," she said. "Sometimes I think it puts ye where ye need tae be."

Jane sighed.

"It's not sentient," she muttered.

"Weel, either it's sentient or ye're a terrible inventor," said Ainslie. "An' I ken at least ane o' those things isnae true."

Jane grinned.

"I cannot argue with that logic," she said.

"Aye, and don't ye forget it," Ainslie said, proudly puffed up like the fat little robins that weighed down the nearby branches with their rotundness.

"An' here we are."

They stood on a crest in a valley, and the mountains around them were tall and imposing in the early-winter snow. The overall impression was one of the Highlands, of the wilderness of Scotland, of the *sublime* that so many artists had tried to capture over the years.

Ainslie turned to Jane, looking nervous. Jane raised an eyebrow.

The first rays of dawn began to colour the world again, piercing the tendrils of fog still curling around the tops of the mountains, and the mist that rolled along the ground below.

"What is it?" Jane asked.

Ainslie stretched out her hand.

On top of her palm lay a pair of rings.

"I wanted t'wait until I had somethin' tae offer a great lady," Ainslie said, in a shy voice Jane had never heard from her before. "I had Aileen forge these for me, but I was waitin' for the richt opportunity. Somethin' that would make ye consider my offer, somethin' that would compare tae the riches ye may be accustomed to in the future."

She blew out a breath, all fog and smoke.

"I am soon tae be Lord o' the Isles, an' I am chief o' the Dhòmhnaill," said Ainslie. "I ken it's no a fine house in the city, but these lands an' these people are mine, an' I've a thousand *claidheamhan-mòra* waitin' at my word."

Ainslie gestured, to indicate the mountains and the oceans around them, at the lights in the village below, to the inlets where the clan castles stood in stern majesty overlooking the distant waters.

She got down onto her knees as the sun rose above the snow-covered mountains, bathing the world in light.

"All o' these things will be yours as well, if ye want them," she said.

Ainslie held up the rings.

"Lady Jane Crichton, born Caimbeul," said Ainslie, her voice quavering with emotion, "will ye do me the honour of accepting my marriage proposal?"

Jane was so astounded she couldn't speak.

Ainslie's eyes took on that old determined shine, in war or in feasting.

"Will ye marry me?" she asked, loud and clear as a Highland spring.

Jane collapsed into the snow in front of Ainslie as if someone had cut her strings. She scooped up one of the rings from Ainslie's outstretched palm.

"Yes, of course I'll marry you," said Jane.

"Oh, thank—" Ainslie began in relief, but she was silenced by Jane's kisses.

* * *

The door of the little cottage opened. David turned around from where he had decided to sample a bit more of the whisky to see if he still enjoyed the taste. He found that he did, but further tests were clearly necessary.

The whisky glass was nearly obscured by his enormous mustache as the two women made their way into the room.

"Good heavens!" he exclaimed, when he saw the state of them. "What happened to you?"

Their hair was full of snow and their clothing sodden, as if they'd both lost a rather vigorous and energetic snowball fight.

Jane, cherry-cheeked and beaming, displayed her ring.

"Ainslie asked me to marry her, and I said yes!" Jane cried.

David stared at them and then laughed.

"Congratulations, old thing!" he said. "Shall we get a divorce, then?"

"Hmm," said Jane, kissing Ainslie, who was now red as a cherry as well, but more from embarrassment. "Perhaps we should. I don't want to be a bigamist."

"Just say ye don't," said Ainslie.

"What's that?" asked Jane.

"If ye don't want tae be married, ye just say ye dinnae," said Ainslie. "In my lands, it's easy as that, an' asides, the Druid Council has better things tae do than debate your marriage or ours."

David gently took Jane away from Ainslie to speak to her privately.

"All jokes aside, Janie," he said seriously. "If this is really what you want, I won't stand in your way. I will get a divorce for us, even in the future, but I don't want to disturb anything we've built together. I want you to inherit from me if it comes to that, and I don't think we can do that divorced. However, it's up to you and whatever you choose. I support you all the way."

"I love you, David," said Jane. "Thank you for being such a wonderful man. Will you let me think about it? I am sure we'll have time before the wedding."

David nodded, his eyes sparkling as he smiled behind his mustache. He embraced her.

"And I love you too, my friend," he said. "I'll await your decision. Never feel obligated to me, Janie. I only want the best for you."

Jane returned the hug and then crossed the room to Ainslie, where they fell onto the bed together laughing, happy in each other's arms.

CHAPTER SIXTY-ONE

Red Her Cheeks as Rowans Are

News of the impending wedding rang out from the major city on Islay to every village and town in the surrounding area.

Lord Archibald Caimbeul, now chief, had been sent an invitation. Indeed, so had the entire Clan Caimbeul.

The marrying of the future Lord of the Isles, let alone a Dhòmhnaill chief, was the event of a lifetime.

It was also a time of great feasting, drinking, and carousing such as had never been seen before in the lives of many from the new generation, as they could not recall the marriage of Dòmhnall and Christina, having been too young.

The unique aspect of this particular wedding of two women made the affair a promising one indeed.

Those greyhairs who remembered the weddings of previous Lords looked forward to it all the more for the fond memories of those celebrations, and those who had not yet had the experience looked forward to it as their first. They'd heard all the stories before, of course, and the tales made their anticipation all the greater.

This meant that the upcoming event would need to be one of the greatest ever held in their history, living or dead, and preparations began months ahead of time to ensure the marriage of Ainslie nic Dòmhnaill and Jane Caimbeul was the spectacular of the century.

* * *

One day, as they were preparing bouquets of roses and thistles and Dougal was showing off the extravagant flower display he had arranged in and around his new wee boatie, the crowd of laughing, chatting clansmen suddenly parted.

Christina of the Isles, strong and beautiful, stood there in their midst.

"Mum!" cried Ainslie, going to hug her. Christina smiled, a softer look on that stern warrior face.

"I've come to speak to your intended," Christina announced.

Everyone was silent. Jane stood and hoped she wasn't trembling too much.

Then, Christina knelt down on the grass and offered the hilt of her sword.

"Please accept my apologies for my behaviour," she said. "Our clans will now be joined. I was foolish and using the prejudice of long centuries past to dictate my actions and my distrust. I offer you the hilt of my sword in good faith, a promise which I intend to keep."

Jane was astounded and had no idea what to say.

"Say ye accept," Ainslie whispered to her.

"I accept," Jane repeated automatically.

Christina lifted her head and stood. She then embraced Jane.

"Then I welcome you into our family," she said. "Long may you rule by my daughter's side and bring a time of peace and plenty to these lands."

Aonghus let out a whoop, which gave everyone else permission to clap and cheer. Christina grinned at her subjects and then left them as majestically as she had arrived.

Jane let out the breath she had been holding, sagging in relief.

"That could've gone badly," she said. Ainslie nodded.

"Aye," she agreed. "But it didn't. An' now, the weeks count down tae the day we wed."

She gave Jane a dazzling smile and went back to making bouquets.

* * *

The day finally came.

While Ainslie and Jane had helped where they could, most of the work was done by the joint effort of both clans.

Claig Castle looked like it never had before.

The interior was lit with thousands and thousands of candles. Flowers, wreaths, and bouquets lined the walls, chairs, and tables. Roaring fires in every fireplace of the castle warmed the rooms, and everyone had turned out to see the wedding. They milled throughout the castle, enjoying drinks and the endless supply of delicious food that was available to everyone. Never had the riches of the Dhòmhnaill been so conspicuous, and never had the riches of the Caimbeulaich been spent so well. Instead of money for yet another war, this time it was invested in love, which might prevent future wars from occurring.

And in the midst of it, the pipers played and the harpists' music echoed sweetly through the castle. Those who were able to sit sat down; the rest stood and watched. There were crowds even outside, on the island, peering into the castle; one person standing at each window gave a rundown of what was happening inside to the waiting crowd.

The music swelled and then calmed.

Ainslie stood in the doorway, breathtaking. Her red hair was down, flowing loose against her back. She wore a simple, yet beautiful, costume of white satin and lace, chiffon and netting. The dress alone was something that people of that time period had not yet seen, so opulent was the fabric and the design. Her cheeks were rosy, and her lips were tinted pink for the ceremony. She wore her golden circlet upon her brow, and the golden torc that emphasised the graceful curve of her neck. She looked romantic and delicate for the first time in her life.

She walked forward, to the front of the room, a bouquet of heather and roses held in her hand.

She turned to look out over the enormous number of clanspeople she now ruled and hoped they would fall in love with Jane as much as she had.

The music swelled again. Ainslie swallowed in anticipation.

Jane was both her hope and her shield. Jane was now her reason for everything.

Ainslie awaited Jane's arrival, knowing that soon, the woman she loved beyond reason would be someone she could call "wife."

CHAPTER SIXTY-TWO

Bright Her Eye as Any Star

There was an audible gasp from all present. Even those outside paused in their narration to stare at the otherworldly woman who graced their presence.

Jane and David appeared in the archway, as they had agreed David giving her away made the most sense in the context of their situation. Few noticed the handsome, bright-eyed man standing in his 19th-century small kilt, a gift from Jane's family he had brought along as an item of clothing he thought appropriate to the time period.

Those present only had eyes for the woman on his arm.

Proud and haughty as any queen, Jane stood in the archway at the end of the long hall. Her eyes were bright, and her long, dark hair fell in waves around her face. Long sections of her hair were tied with ribbons, crisscrossing along her dark locks. She wore a circlet like the one Ainslie had worn on their first meeting, gleaming silver against the snowy white of her skin. Her collarbones were dusted with shadows beneath, and the swell of her breasts were a promise below tight, white fabric. Her corset outlined her narrow waist, and the bloom of her hips below led to the long white skirt of the dress losing her shape in the deep folds of chiffon, only allowing the outline of a shapely leg when Jane walked forward toward her bride.

She stood before Ainslie and was amazed to see the tears standing in her lover's eyes, so proud and happy. She'd never seen Ainslie look so beautiful or so blessed.

"We are gathered here," announced Dòmhnall, for it was he who would preside over the wedding, "to join these twa in an eternal bond."

Ainslie took Jane's hands, and both were beaming with ridiculous smiles.

"Ainslie has some words she wishes tae say tae Jane."

Ainslie brushed her hair to the side, nervous. She couldn't let go of Jane's other hand.

"When I met ye," she said, "ye were ane o' the Fair Fowk, fallen frae the sky. I learned, over time, that ye were a brilliant, beautiful soul, an' I am honoured that ye chose tae be my wife. I am sae fortunate tae have ye, my wee faerie; I canna imagine life without ye. I promise tae be everything ye need, an' that ye'll want for naethin' a' the days o' your life."

Ainslie blushed, staring at the ground; she was unaccustomed to displays of emotion.

"And now Jane will say a few words," Dòmhnall announced.

"Ainslie," Jane said, and Ainslie lifted her head to look into Jane's eyes, "you have changed everything I knew about the world. You have shown me peace, and war, and passion; you have shown me equality, forgiveness and steadfast love. I never thought I would know anyone like you. My love for you is deep and enduring, endless as the sea."

Dòmhnall grinned at them, but they only had eyes for each other.

"Ainslie nic Dòmhnaill," he said, "do you take Lady Jane Crichton, born Caimbeul, to be your wife?"

The tears were running freely down Ainslie's cheeks now, and she made no move to release Jane's hands to wipe them away. Her emerald eyes burned bright.

"I do," said Ainslie, her voice strong and sure.

Dòmhnall turned to Jane.

"And do you, Lady Jane Crichton, born Caimbeul, take Ainslie nic Dòmhnaill, Lord of the Isles and chief of Clann Dhòmhnaill, as your wife?"

Jane's blinding smile and matching tears said everything already, but Jane nodded her head anyway.

"I do," she said.

"Then, by the power vested in me as the patriarch of this clan," said Dòmhnall, overjoyed, "I now pronounce you wife and wife."

The silence that rang out after this proclamation was merely the eye of the storm.

"You may kiss the bride."

Ainslie and Jane fell into it as though they were no longer bound by the laws of gravity, and though Dòmhnall raised his arms in triumph and the entire castle along with the surrounding island erupted in roars, cheers, and whistles, the two of them may as well have been alone in the universe.

* * *

Confetti fell from the ceiling as Ainslie and Jane ran out, laughing, hand in hand, to greet the people.

The party was already underway, with whisky and wine passed around from person to person. The food was plentiful, and everyone was welcomed into the castle, both Caimbeul and Dhòmhnaill, to participate in the feast. Some of the birlinns had been roped to the posts on the island for the purpose, and the celebration was one truly Dhòmhnaill: by sea, by land.

After receiving thousands of kisses and well-wishes from clanspeople of both families in the receiving line, it was time for the great feast. While everyone was welcome in the castle, it was a squeeze, with all the rooms and grand staircases full. Some people elected to stay outside and cavort in the birlinns, Dougal waving joyously from his little boat decked with flowers for the occasion.

Jane and Ainslie sat on the raised dais, the place of prestige, while food and drink were brought to them. There was singing, drinking, and feasting on all the plumpest lambs and delicacies that could be sourced both near and far. There was so much food to go around that many of the Caimbeul clan, who remembered the previous winter, were absolutely delighted to find that they now seemed to be a part of a clan so wealthy that all its people ate and drank ambrosia and that this unexpected windfall guaranteed a prosperous future for chief and clansperson alike.

Dòmhnall stood and waved his hand for quiet. The entire castle eventually quieted down to hear what he had to say.

"When I met Jane," he said, "I knew. I just knew she was the one for my Ainslie. Didn't I, Christina?"

Christina inclined her head in agreement.

"So there are few present who are as thrilled at this union as I am," he continued. "Well, excepting Ainslie herself."

Everyone cheered, and Ainslie ducked her head, blushing.

"And sae, my daughter," he said, "I make ye a gift, a wedding-dowry for her whom you love."

Ainslie stared at him, startled; she looked to her mother and Aonghus, as this was unexpected.

"Now that ye will be the leader o' baith clan an' island," Dòmhnall said. "I ken ye'll mak me proud, as chief, an' soon, as Lord o' the Isles."

He turned to her, smiling.

"An' sae I mak a present tae ye o' Finlaggan Castle," said Dòmhnall. The entire assembly gasped; Finlaggan had only recently been completed.

"An' I hope ye'll allow your auld man his grey years in the castle o' his youth, Claig, where we are now staundin'," said Dòmhnall. "But a new marriage needs a new hame, an' Finlaggan is tae be the centre o' the kingdom frae this day forward."

Shocked whispers travelled through the crowd, and Ainslie stared at her father.

"Da, I cannae accept that," she whispered. "It's—"

"It's tae be your legacy, my daughter," said Dòmhnall. "An' ye'll have Jane tae help ye. Dunyvaig still needs completing, but Finlaggan is ready, an' it was always my intention tae mak it the centre o' the kingdom."

He opened his arms.

"It's yours, lassie," he said. "If ye want it."

Ainslie stood, and to the surprise of everyone, threw herself into her father's arms, overcome with emotion.

"Oh, thank ye, Father!" she cried, hugging him. He gave her a kiss on the cheek, and Ainslie sat down next to Jane.

"And now—we dance!" Dòmhnall announced. The band struck up, and everyone cheered.

Ainslie squeezed Jane's hand under the table and looked into her eyes.

"Now I'll hae somethin' tae offer ye that equals what ye deserve," said Ainslie. "A castle, an' a kingdom, for my faerie queen."

Jane kissed her soundly, causing another riotous cheer, and then Ainslie drew back with a mischievous look on her face.

"Shall we dance, my love?" asked Ainslie, her pretty copper hair falling around her pale face, cheeks high and rosy with love, delight, and wine.

"Yes," said Jane and delicately put her hand in that of her lover. Her wife. When she thought of that word, a thrill ran through her.

Jane and Ainslie danced, first together, then apart, then with family and friends and strangers.

And tall Jane, too-much Jane, too-*everything* Jane, was a beautiful, delicate, graceful queen of the Fae that night, and everyone danced Strip the Willow with her and always returned for more.

CHAPTER SIXTY-THREE

Fairest o' Them A' by Far

The night grew late, and the revelry even louder, as Jane found her way to where David was sitting on a barrel, watching the stars. Fires had been lit across the island, a constellation fallen to the earth, and the dancing and shouting had continued to increase throughout the night. She would be taking a tour of the island with Ainslie soon enough, so that everyone who hadn't been able to attend the wedding could offer their congratulations. For the moment, though, she'd asked her new wife for a moment alone to speak with the husband she had left behind.

Jane sat down beside him and saw his eyes twinkle, a smile hidden beneath his mustache.

"Congratulations, old thing," he said.

"I hope you aren't going to be too lonely," she said.

"Lonely!" he said. He turned to her and took her hand. "Janie, I love you like a brother. But seeing you find love—*real* love—here, in the past? I think this may be the happiest I've ever been."

"I don't want you to think I've abandoned you," she said.

David laughed.

"You brought me here, didn't you?" he asked. "I don't feel abandoned at all. I'm here with the person I probably love best in all the world."

Jane leaned against him, and they sat in companionable silence for a while, watching the celebrations.

"They offered me your cottage, you know," he said. "I hope you don't mind."

Jane shook her head.

"I do love the place," she replied, "but if we've got a castle to run, I can't be in two places at once, and you need somewhere to live until we can find you something more suitable."

"More suitable?" asked David. "Janie, I've always wanted something like this—a simple life. That big old manor house only felt full when you were in it. Damn thing's like a mausoleum otherwise. Still, it is home, I suppose, after a fashion. Promise we'll go back and visit from time to time?"

Jane smiled.

"I promise," she said.

There was a loud whoosh of fire and then a cheer; everyone was getting quite rowdy by this time of the night.

"Do you think—" Jane began and then hesitated.

"Out with it, my girl," said David, patting her hand.

"Do you think this marriage is the reason the Caimbeulaich took over later on?" asked Jane, guilty.

David sighed.

"We cannot really know these things," he said. "But it'd be foolish to spurn a love like that because you fear for the future, which to these people is so far away as to be meaningless."

"Yes, but *we* know," Jane insisted. "Is my happiness really worth all the sadness to follow?"

David turned and looked into her eyes. He squeezed her hands.

"Look, Janie," he said. "This might turn out to be a time of plenty for these people. It may be the flower of their civilisation. It might be that later marriages caused the problems we both know about; it's impossible to be sure. Perhaps it was this wedding; perhaps it was a wedding two hundred years in the future. Are you really willing to sacrifice Ainslie because the Dhòmhnaill might, someday, go to war with the Caimbeulaich again?"

Jane stared at him and then made a noise of frustration.

"Why are you being so…logical?" Jane grumbled.

"Learnt from the best," David said and elbowed her. She snorted.

"David, I've brought the whisky," said a voice. "I could only get a bottle from the—why, hello there, Jane! Congratulations!"

Lord Archibald Caimbeul stood before them, awkwardly clenching the neck of a bottle of whisky in his right fist. Everything seemed normal enough, apart from the red blush Jane could faintly see staining the young man's cheeks.

Jane looked from Archibald to David and clapped a hand over her mouth.

"David! You didn't!" she scolded, as he looked a bit out of sorts as well.

He stared at the ground.

"Well," he muttered, "I always did have a weakness for Caimbeuls."

Jane gaped at him, then threw back her head and laughed and laughed.

* * *

"If I didnae ken better, I'd say ye were conspiring," said Ainslie, walking up to the three of them sharing the whisky bottle.

Archibald and David looked up at her with guilty expressions, and Jane threw herself into her wife's arms, covering her with kisses.

"Hello, wife," Jane said, as she pulled back, her eyes shining like stars.

Ainslie beamed.

"Hello, wife," she replied and kissed her again. "The dawn's comin' soon, my love. An' our bed's waiting."

Everyone in earshot cheered at this loudly.

"Shall I carry ye there?" Ainslie asked.

"Should you—!" Jane began and then squealed as Ainslie hefted her into a bridal carry.

The warrior chief looked over her shoulders.

"See ye in the mornin', laddies," she said, and winked.

Jane waved goodbye to them, and they lifted the whisky bottle in salute.

Then she put her arms around Ainslie's neck as she walked away from the men and stared up at her wife, enraptured.

CHAPTER SIXTY-FOUR

Mo Nighean Donn Bhoidheach

The dawn made itself known on the horizon, washing the world in a pale blue light.

The room they were given had windows that stretched from floor to ceiling. It was also hung with rich tapestry; the beaten-copper bath was there, along with fresh pressed thick towels and robes. It was the kind of appointment that would satisfy even the most exacting queen's taste.

They hadn't yet consummated their marriage due to the lateness of the hour and the effort of the celebrations, along with greeting their people, but the two women lying in the bed were now more than two women: they were two queens, waking together for the first time as wives.

Ainslie, asleep on her pillow, turned all white and burnished gold as the sun rose over the horizon, the red ribbon of her hair like a flag across the white of the cotton.

Jane smiled, humming that old song Ainslie had taught her, as she gazed upon her new wife with an ache of love that could not be denied.

Ainslie's scars created patterns on her skin, smattered here and there with freckles. The early morning light illuminated the blue knotwork of the ink across her cheekbone. She lay naked, unashamed, her strong, muscular body outside the sheets she had kicked off the night before. Her breasts were round and lovely in the early morning sunlight, nipples pink and soft after the way of red-haired people. Jane gazed upon this visual feast of Ainslie at rest and considered how this woman thought of love as just another sort of war and wondered.

For Jane had brought her a wedding gift, too.

She caressed her awake, thoughts of strawberries and cream on her mind as Ainslie's sleepy eyelids opened to let in the sunlight she bathed herself in—and in that sunlight, the refracted gemstones of her green eyes shone deep and bright.

"Mornin'," she murmured.

"Good morning," replied Jane and kissed her languidly.

After a few moments, Jane pulled back, though Ainslie tried to chase her with her lips.

"I want to try something," said Jane. "But I need to know if you want it."

Ainslie cocked a brow at her, then cuffed her arm around Jane's waist and dragged her forward.

"Anything wi' ye, I want," she growled in a low voice.

"Teach me how it is ye want me tae touch you."

Jane bit her lips and shook her head, mischief in her eyes.

"No," she said. "I want to show you the way *I* want to touch you."

Ainslie's eyes grew round.

"If you're frightened or want me to stop at any time," said Jane. "Let me know, all right?"

Ainslie nodded, curious now.

Jane worshipped her, as she had always wanted to, with kisses everywhere on her body, caressing every part of her. She nosed at Ainslie's copper pubic hair, kissing her mound, laving her clitoris with her tongue, all gentle, gentle, with the love she had to offer, and Ainslie permitted it, a little confused as to the quiet steadiness of Jane's attentions.

"I love you," said Jane, planting soft kisses on the insides of Ainslie's thighs. "My queen. My forever. My everything."

"I love ye too, ye mad thing," said Ainslie and chuckled.

"All right," said Jane. "I've brought you a gift. An invention of my own design. I would like to try it."

"Aye," said Ainslie. "Go on then."

Jane may not have been a military woman like Ainslie was, but she was brilliant. As a doctor, scientist, and inventor, Jane was more than familiar with the advancements of her own time: electricity, batteries, medicine, and, in this particular case, recent innovations in the world of massage treatments. Whilst she had been momentarily in her own time, Jane had thought that there were a few things that might be adjusted and possibly appreciated in Ainslie's time as well. Jane had already had occasion to enjoy this invention. She hoped Ainslie would enjoy it just as much.

A soft buzzing sound startled Ainslie; she looked at Jane with suspicion.

Jane gentled her with her hands.

"Trust me," said Jane. "Please."

And she placed the vibrator against Ainslie's clitoris.

Ainslie gasped and tried to wriggle away from the sensation, but Jane held her still with a hand on her hip. Ainslie stared down at Jane in wonder as she drew Ainslie up, lifting her bottom, and kissed her belly. Then Jane moved forward until she held the vibrator in place with her hips.

She dipped down to taste Ainslie's lips as Ainslie started to cry out, sharp little staccato moans, and the thought wandered across Jane's mind again. *Strawberries and cream*—the taste of her lover's mouth, the scent of her lover's arousal in the air—*strawberries and cream*.

Suddenly Ainslie jackknifed into a sitting position and sank her teeth into Jane's shoulder, grinding hard against the vibrator as she shrieked her release into the meat of her wife's skin. She nudged against it again and came violently, rocking against it as if she were addicted, shameless, luxuriant, radiant in her joy, chasing her own pleasure until a later thrust pushed the vibrator against Jane, who was so turned on and sensitive that her orgasm was instantaneous and fierce. They cried out together and ran to exhaustion in their exultation.

* * *

Some time later, Ainslie awoke.

Jane smiled, brown eyes twinkling. She hadn't slept, only rested and watched her wife in repose.

Ainslie, exhausted, threw an arm around her. The two women, both naked on the wide white bed and bathed in the silver Highland sunlight pouring through the window like a blessing, were content.

"My faerie queen," Ainslie murmured, "an' her magic. That must have been magic, whatever it was."

"So you liked it," Jane said.

"Liked it?" Ainslie repeated, astonished. "I dinna ken how anyone wouldn't!"

"I'm glad," Jane said. "I wanted to make you feel as good—as *wild*—as you make me feel."

"Och, Jane," Ainslie murmured, tracing the features of her beautiful face. "You already do."

Jane flushed with pleasure, and Ainslie kissed the tip of her nose.

"*Ho ró, mo nighean donn bhoidheach,*" she began to sing, pushing Jane's hair behind her ear.

"*Hi rì, mo nighean donn bhoidheach,*" Jane replied, having learnt the words by now.

"*Mo chaileag lagach bhoidheach,*" Ainslie replied, and then grinned as she sang:

"*Cha phòs mi ach thu.*"

Jane sighed in happiness.

"'I will marry nane but you,'" Ainslie repeated. "And I did," she said proudly, twining her fingers with Jane's.

Outside, the birds began to sing, and the clanspeople to wake and go about the business of the day.

In the quiet of the castle room, in the sunlight, Jane kissed Ainslie on their marriage bed and smiled.

"You did," Jane agreed.

CHAPTER SIXTY-FIVE

The Mist-Covered Mountains of Home

Finlaggan was beautiful, the island and the mountains breathtaking in the mist.

The new castle stood on the island in the loch, much like Claig Castle sat on its island in the Sound.

"It reminds me of hame," said Ainslie, taking Jane's hand.

"It is home," said Jane.

They stood together on the hill above Finlaggan, awaiting their new life. They both wore their long shifts and their matching earasaids held at the shoulder with pewter pins. A circlet with a gemstone embedded in it shone upon each brow: for Ainslie, a golden circlet with an emerald to match her eyes, and for Jane, her silver wedding-circlet with a blood-red garnet that shone like a captive sun.

They made their way down to the island, where they were surprised to see everyone waiting for them. A cheer went up, and provisions were rolled out. It seemed that the wedding party had not yet ended.

Jane mentioned this to Ainslie, and she nodded, as if it were the most natural thing in the world.

"Wedding celebrations can last months," she said.

"Months?" Jane cried. "You mean everyone is going to be drunk for months?"

"Ye say that like we weren't already," said a voice. "An' Hogmanay is worse, ye ken."

Ainslie was overjoyed to see the bright eyes and blond hair of her brother.

"Aonghus!" she cried.

"O' course," said Aonghus, puzzled. "Ye didna think I'd miss the opportunity tae see ye oot o' the house forever?"

Ainslie cuffed him, and he cuffed her right back, both of them laughing.

"Nae," he said. "I wanted tae be here. What kind o' brither wad I be if I didna help wi' the housewarming? Asides, Mum an' Da wad kill me."

He waved at Christina and Dòmhnall, standing a ways off among their people, with Madra going absolutely mad and leaping around their feet.

The new brides walked into the waiting crowd, and Jane was overwhelmed to be greeted by the congratulations and gifts from so many people she had met. Aileen hugged her and was thrilled to see that her rings had been put to good use.

"I'll be hangin' a sign on the shop sayin' I provide custom for the royal family," she said, grinning. "Business will be booming, I'll tell ye that!"

Jane was astonished to see Morag and others from the Druid Council approach her. Morag bowed.

"I hope your elevation to royalty will no' prevent ye frae returning tae the Council," Morag said. "My deepest apologies for our trials, but we'd lang been at war wi' the Caimbeulaich."

Jane curtsied to her.

"I understand," said Jane. "All is forgotten. Are you certain you'd still like me to form a part of your Council?"

Morag nodded; the others, including Tariq, nodded too.

"You have much to say about the world and medicine," she said. "And, from what I understand, you've created another invention?"

Jane stared at her, puzzled, and then turned to give Ainslie a good whack.

"Ainslie!" she chided. Ainslie looked at her and shrugged.

"Ony invention like that needs tae be known," she said, bursting with pride, "an' my wife is a magician! If ye truly are Fae, it wouldna surprise me."

Jane smiled, shaking her head at Ainslie's brazenness.

"I'd be happy to return, Morag," she said. Morag, delighted, bowed and went away to make preparations for the housewarming.

David was the next to emerge from the crowd. He sidled up to Jane and whispered in her ear conspiratorially.

"And how was it, hey?" asked David. "Bit of the old saffron massage?"

"David!" Jane gasped, but she laughed anyway.

"Do you know," said David, "they've started saying 'smashing' because of me?"

"Have they?" said Jane, merriment dancing in her eyes.

"Yes, but they haven't the right sound of it," said David. "Something like ''s math sin,' I think."

"I'm glad you've had a positive impact here already."

David smiled.

"Thank you, Janie," he said, kissing her cheek. "And may good fortune be yours, all of your days."

"And good luck to you," said Jane, catching the eye of Lord Archibald Caimbeul, "and Archibald."

David blushed; she smiled up at him and they embraced. Then David released her back into Ainslie's waiting arms.

"What do ye think?" murmured Ainslie, as her lips brushed Jane's ear. "A kingdom, a castle, all my islands an' lands for ye, my love? An' we brokered peace with the Caimbeulaich. A fine dowry, on baith sides."

"It's breathtaking," said Jane, as they were led hand-in-hand to the entrance of Finlaggan Castle for the very first time.

The crowd drew back and left the two of them standing there on the precipice.

The two women stood together and turned to one another. Ainslie put her hands in Jane's.

They kissed, to the uproarious celebration of the crowd, which threw all manner of hats, papers, and other items into the air and then caught them. A piper played somewhere in the background, marking this glorious occasion.

A new lord.

A new chief.

A new queen.

A new castle.

A bright new future.

Chief Ainslie nic Dòmhnaill and Lady Jane Caimbeul turned toward the castle door, with both their clans waiting behind them, and they stepped forward together as one.

THE AUTHOR'S GUIDE TO MATTERS OF HISTORY, CULTURE, AND GEOGRAPHY

Overview

As a Scottish historian, cultural anthropologist, and folklorist, I have tried to remain faithful to the general history, culture, and geography of Scotland. As you read, keep in mind there is a tendency to look at history with modern eyes—to assume, for example, that the role of women in society has always been the same, that oppression has always been the reality. This also goes for the role of LGBTQ people.

History is not so much written by the victors as ignored by those in power, and so much of the history of women and LGBTQ individuals is hidden. (History, as they say nowadays, is often gayer than you think.) This does a great deal of disservice to movements fighting today for rights and freedoms. It's easier to defy appeals for change when people believe something they are striving for "has never existed" rather than "these are things we used to have that need to be restored."

That said, this is a work of fiction, so there are places where I have embellished the facts.

The Time Periods

Edinburgh of the 1880s was the product of the earlier Scottish Enlightenment. More details are known about this period in London than in Scotland as far as popular culture is concerned, mostly due to the popularity of stories about Peter Pan and Sherlock Holmes (both, incidentally, written by Scotsmen, J.M. Barrie and Sir Arthur Conan Doyle respectively). Edinburgh and Glasgow made enormous contributions to the sciences and the arts of the time period.

The historical realities of the Highlands and Islands of the 13th century are less well known, and much of what is seen in popular culture about this part of the world tends to be from the 16th century onward. These notes are meant to fill in some details for those interested and provide resources for further research if readers would like to know more.

The Sea Kingdom or Kingdom of the Isles

By the time this narrative takes place, Dál Riata (Kingdom of the Isles) no longer exists. However, the islands that formed a part of the Norse-Gael Sea Kingdom were still ruled over by the Dhòmhnaill (called Donalds or MacDonalds today, and in modern Scottish Gaelic,

Clann Dòmhnaill). The kings of Dál Riata were previously known as "Kings of the Isles" and later as "Lords of the Isles." This was a downgrade, but the MacDonalds would later adopt this terminology themselves.

The original kingdom of Dál Riata was an entirely separate nation from Scotland and England and included hundreds of islands, parts of Ireland, and the Isle of Man. This meant that the Dhòmhnaill were an independent nation, free to trade and treat with anyone they liked. They took the side of the English in some battles and the side of the Scots in others.

In those times, the sea was like a highway; travel was far easier between islands than on land, giving the islands power equal or greater to that of Scotland, England, Wales, or Ireland as nations. Despite the efforts of the Scots and the English, the Sea Kingdom remained under control of the Dhòmhnaill for centuries.

John MacDonald of Islay, Earl of Ross, forfeited his ancestral lands and the title of Lord of the Isles to a later Scottish king, James IV of Scotland. The title has belonged to the crown ever since, despite the MacDonalds trying to get it back to this day.

Women can be chiefs and chieftains in Scotland, and this has always been the case throughout all of Scottish history. In the Scottish clan system, "chief" is higher than "chieftain" in the hierarchy. Ainslie's ascension to the title of Lord of the Isles in addition to the chiefship of the Dhòmhnaill while her father was still living was not an uncommon thing in the Highlands and Islands. While it was often the case that the descendants of the current chief became the next leader, the system was a democratic one, and if it was believed that the new chief or proposed chief was a bad ruler, the clan would seek out someone new. There was no concept of divine right of kings in their world. Respect and chiefship had to be earned, continually, throughout a leader's lifetime. Therefore, the title passing to someone else while the former chief was still alive (whether or not the successor was their own descendant) was a frequent occurrence before the chief became too old or infirm to tend to his or her duties.

Scots Language

I have tried to be sparing in my use of the Scots language, mainly for reasons of clarity. Ainslie's family using Glaswegian Scots is literary license, as they most likely would have spoken English in a much different way. However, their speech is meant to serve as a counterpoint to Jane and David's, just as David's is clearly far more upper-class English than Jane's. Just before Jane's time, there was a push to speak in what became known as Scottish Standard English. Around the same time, writers Robert Burns and Sir Walter Scott wrote in Scots language to preserve it.

This dichotomy continues to this day, with a great deal of controversy about the Scots language, and code-switching between Scottish Standard English and broad Scots depending on the circumstances of the individual. There are many regions of Scotland in which the Scots language consists of different vocabulary, so there is no one overarching way of speaking in Scots.

Here, the choice was a lighter version of the Glaswegian Scots dialect, because Glasgow is still the usual destination of islanders even now. However, it is highly unlikely they would have spoken anything like this on Islay in the 13th century.

Scottish Historical Events of Note

A few events are mentioned throughout the story, because they are known to all Scots. These are the major historical matters of note.

Glencoe—In 1692, the king sent to Glencoe a contingent of Campbell soldiers, who pretended they were overflow from Fort William. Under cover of this lie, they accepted the hospitality of the MacDonalds and then rose up in the middle of the night in a blizzard to slaughter the clan. There were worse massacres in the Highlands, but this one is notorious because of its flouting of the ancient law of Highland hospitality. See commentary on Chapter Twenty-seven and Chapter Fifty-three for more.

The Battle of Culloden—The last battle fought on Scottish soil occurred in 1746. The Jacobites had followed Bonnie Prince Charlie to the muddy waste of Drumossie Moor, now called Culloden. They were hungry, they didn't fight well on flat ground, and it was raining and muddy. William Cumberland (the Butcher), on the opposing side, had trained his soldiers to defeat the famous Highland charge.

Although people like to paint this battle as Scots vs. English, there were Scots on both Cumberland's side and Charlie's. Both Highlanders and Lowlanders were on Charlie's side, and there were also English and French soldiers on both sides of this battle. Those on Charlie's side were massacred, and the result of Culloden was the razing of the Highlands to new heights of cruelty. The Battle of Culloden took less than an hour and changed Scottish and British history forever.

Culloden also led to the Act of Proscription and the Dress Act, which banned many of the things that made the Highlanders who they were. The effects of Culloden echo down throughout history, but many feel that much of the blame lies squarely with the reckless behaviour of Bonnie Prince Charlie, much less a hero than people would like to make him out to be. He died a drunk without legitimate issue in Italy. Scotland would never be the same.

Act of Proscription—After Culloden, many things considered Highland Scottish were outlawed, including various forms of Highland dress and also weaponry. The Highland Dress Act was eventually repealed, and on King George's visit to Edinburgh in 1822, during which he dressed in a very ridiculous traditional Scottish costume, the wool merchants of Edinburgh discovered a moneymaking scheme that has persisted to modern times. This was the invention of clan tartan, which had not previously existed.

Clearances—The populations of the Scottish Highlands and Islands were destroyed by two Highland Clearances. The Clearances were the forced removal of clanspeople from their own lands, by their own chiefs. This was the true end of the Highland clan system, and occurred during two different points in history, the first happened primarily after the battle of Culloden in 1746. However, Campbells of the Kintyre peninsula were the first to change over to the new system even prior to the Rising in 1745. Prior to the Clearances, clanspeople lived on and farmed the agricultural land and swore fealty to the chief, who in turn gave them care and protection. The second Clearances were even more severe, lasting through most of the 1800s and into the 1900s, with the chiefs pushing their clanspeople out via assisted emigration. This and the potato famine that struck Scotland as well as Ireland in 1845 emptied the Highlands of people.

The Clearances inflicted some of the worst damage on Scotland in all of its history, and they were done by Scots to other Scots. After Culloden in 1746, the clan system was disbanded forever. The clans had operated on a barter system, and with that gone, money became more and more important. Many chiefs evicted tenants to make room for a hardy breed of sheep, Cheviot. Unfortunately, this coincided with the sudden craze for all things "Scottish and romantic," which meant that Highlanders were starving while the rest of the UK was celebrating tartan, along with what was ostensibly "Highland" culture.

Today the mountains and glens of the Scottish Highlands are frequently empty, something many scholars note when writing about the sublime imagery of the Highlands in paintings and photographs, which often lack people. Much of today's Scottish Diaspora is the result of the Highland Clearances.

Historical Figures

A Word about Naming Conventions—People living under the Highland clan system referred to themselves as "first name, daughter/son of first name," therefore "Ainslie nic Dòmhnaill" and "Aonghus mac Dòmhnaill" are "Ainslie, daughter of Dòmhnall" and "Aonghus, son of Dòmhnall" respectively.

Women did not take the last name of their husbands in Scotland because they trace lineage in a different way. Clan affiliation was extremely important. Sometimes men would take their wives' names if the wife's family was more powerful or influential. (Female clan chiefs today have to find husbands who are "confident enough in their masculinity" to take on their wife's surname because she is the chief of her clan.)

Mac/Mc are exactly the same and interchangeable. They have nothing to do with Irish vs. Scottish background, as some believe; usage just depended on what the person writing it down for the first time chose to do.

Not all Scottish surnames are patronymic. People could join a clan in various ways, whether by treaty or coercion or the spread of that clan into new lands, so people bearing a certain surname are not necessarily lineal descendants. However, when the administration of an area was no longer Gaelic-speaking, these names were applied in a blanket fashion to those of the clan.

Listed Alphabetically by First Name

Adomnán the Saint—Irish spiritual leader who created the Law of the Innocents, agreed to by many clan chiefs and frequently ignored. As the full text of this law, available online, illustrates, he thinks very highly of himself, calling himself "the saviour of women." The Law of the Innocents also provides written proof that women went to war in this culture—if they didn't, why would you need a law against them doing so?

Aonghus Mòr mac Dòmhnaill—son of Dòmhnall mac Raghnaill, the first person to use the last name MacDonald

Archibald Caimbeul/Campbell—son of Cailean Caimbeul, inheritor of the lands at Loch Awe

Cailean Caimbeul/Campbell—one of the first chiefs of the Campbell clan

Christina of the Isles—chief of the Clan Ruaridh (Rory/ MacRory) and a famous historical character in her own right. She is an anachronism here, given that she was born in 1290.

Dòmhnall mac Raghnaill—first chief of Clan Donald (Clann Dòmhnaill), although historians are not sure if he really existed. He is considered a Hebridean Sea-King.

Joseph Bell—inspiration for Sherlock Holmes, educated both Sir Arthur Conan Doyle and Robert Louis Stevenson in Edinburgh. His pioneering research into handwashing before surgery, along with his deductive methods of diagnosis, made him famous in the medical community. Like Holmes, he was often seen in an Ulster coat. Bell was also consulted on the Ripper murders in London.

Margaret Todd—Dr. Sophia Jex-Blake's partner, a novelist and doctor; see Chapter One notes that follow.

Somerled—the Norse progenitor of Clan Donald, grandfather of Dòmhnall mac Raghnaill, and ruler of the Kingdom of the Isles.

Sophia Jex-Blake—the originator of the Edinburgh Seven and a doctor; see Chapter One notes that follow.

Cultural Norms

Speaking of Language—Scotland has three official languages: Scottish Gaelic, Scots (Lallans), and English. Other extant languages in Scotland were Norn (a form of Norse) and Norman French. A Pictish language would have predated most of these, but we have little information about it.

The Highlands today are fairly quiet, but Islay was a booming place at more than one time in its history. Ainslie speaks Gaelic, Norse, Arabic, and French as well as English by way of Lallans (Lowland) Scots. Her English would have sounded more lilting than the way the people of the aristocracy spoke, as is the case with islanders today.

Ainslie's family speaks Glaswegian Scots, which for their time period would be highly unlikely. This was an artistic choice to contrast between Archibald's English and Ainslie's English, and to illustrate the difference between their priorities and the kinds of things they want for their respective clans. Archibald was raised to speak English as the English do, which is something that still happens in Scotland and Ireland today if a family has the money to pay for elocution lessons or to send the child away to boarding school. There are as many types of Scottish accents as there are Scots; today's Highland and Island

Scots are often mistaken as Irish or English, even by other Scottish people. The "movie Scottish" accent is not all that common, and in some cases, entirely invented.

Gaelic is a complicated and difficult language for many reasons, and due to how the words change with tenses and a variety of other things, the language is utterly untranslatable without the help of a truly Gaelic-speaking person. Scottish Gaelic and Irish are two distinct languages. Scottish Gaelic is pronounced GAL-ick and Irish is pronounced GAYLE-ick, but usually just called "Irish."

The Roles of Women—The Sea Kingdom and indeed much of the Highland clan system overall was egalitarian. Ainslie would be surprised at the idea of a culture where women were forbidden to do anything. Theirs was a primarily Norse-Gaelic culture, and the Norse were known for their egalitarian beliefs.

Sex—Sexual assault was punishable by "outlawry," the removal of the protection of law for the individual, or death. Outlawry meant social ostracization, expulsion from the clan, exile, and the removal of civil rights. Due to these harsh punishments, sexual assault was extremely uncommon, despite popular misconception.

Exile for a clansperson was already equivalent to death. Enemy clans would take any opportunity to kill someone from an opposing clan who was alone. This withdrawal of the protection of law meant that everyone was in their legal rights to persecute or kill the individual without fearing punishment.

Customs regarding same-sex unions were hazier, because of the dearth of records from this time period. Even then records on homosexuality in the extant sagas only discussed men. However, it was likely that no one cared all that much. Sex itself was a matter openly discussed. Many things changed with the introduction of Christianity. As a result, many stories—far too many!—that are set in the past make it look like rape was commonplace. Authors then claim they are including it to make their tales "gritty and realistic to the era," when they achieve the exact opposite.

In fact, it is likely that rape and sexual assault are far more common today, because of this misconception of history and misunderstanding, because of Victorian ideals and mores that we still live under, and because this is the narrative that most readily fits the belief system that has created our modern world. People do not like to face challenges to their narratives; they have built their own identities up within them. Facts and history do not care about belief, however, only about reality, which has always been multifaceted in every nation and generation.

Tea—Despite its current status as the "most British of drinks," in the 1800s coffee was the British drink of choice. The proliferation of coffeehouses, especially in London, was often lamented in the media. Interestingly, arts, research, and education in the United Kingdom flourished during this time of coffeehouses.

Then pub culture began, changing the drug of choice from a stimulant to a depressant; many people believe this contributed a great deal to the diminishment of the UK on the world stage. Tea came in later on when the British were encouraged to drink tea as a display of patriotism, because British colonies had tea plantations while coffee originated from the colonies of other nations.

COMMENTARY ON SELECTED CHAPTERS

CHAPTER ONE

Edinburgh

Doctor Joseph Bell worked at the University of Edinburgh. He is famous for several medical advancements, including washing the hands before and during surgery. His deductive methods of diagnosing patients caused quite a stir in the medical community. He taught Robert Louis Stevenson and Sir Arthur Conan Doyle, and was also Conan Doyle's inspiration for Sherlock Holmes.

The Edinburgh Seven were, in 1869, the first women to be educated as doctors in Great Britain. The women were not granted degrees when they should have graduated in 1873 by the University of Edinburgh despite passing the course with flying colours, so Dr. Bell is showing Jane a great deal of respect and flouting the social mores of the time here in calling her "Doctor."

In 2019, the Edinburgh Seven were finally granted their degrees posthumously, and female medical students at the University of Edinburgh accepted on their behalf.

CHAPTER TWO

Up The Waverly Steps

The Waverley Steps—a long set of stairs leading into Edinburgh's Waverley Station.

Sophia and Margaret—Sophia Jex-Blake wanted to attend the University of Edinburgh to study medicine, but she was told they wouldn't admit just one woman, so she took out an ad in the paper and found six others. Among these was her partner, Margaret Todd, a novelist as well as a doctor. They lived openly as lesbians during a time period when it was frowned upon.

CHAPTER THREE

In The Manor House

Homosexual Relationships between women were only grudgingly accepted in 19th-century Scotland, but were outright illegal between men.

The **"Scottish Cringe"** is a recently named phenomenon in which Scottish people try to distance themselves entirely from overt expressions of Scottish cultural identity, such as tartan.

Elocution—Both Jane's and David's parents sent them to elocution lessons in order to iron out their accents, or in David's case, make sure he sounded English before he had a chance to acquire a Scottish one. This remains an issue in Scotland to this day.

CHAPTER FOUR
Highlands

Earasaid/Arisaid—This is technically a blanket, as were all the kilts of former times. Men and women wore the same garment, just differently; men's great kilts bisected the knee, while women's fell to the ground. Underneath this item, a saffron shirt/long shift/*lèine* was worn. During this particular time period, it is doubtful whether they would have worn the blanket part of the costume, but it is included because it is easily recognisable as Scottish.

Caimbeul/Campbell, Caimbeulaich/Campbells—*Caim beul* means "crooked mouth" in Gaelic, and the clan was seen as crafty and devious. This clan had famously been at war with the MacDonald clan since time out of mind; some even think it was the MacDonalds that gave them their name.

Dòmhnall/Donald. Clan Donald/Dhòmhnaill, conversely, means "the ruler of the world." Dòmhnall mac Raghnaill was the famous ancestor and originator of Clan Donald, though historians dispute whether he really existed.

CHAPTER FIVE
Island

Somerled/Somhairlidh/Somhairle (SORE-ly) was the Norse progenitor of Clan Donald and the ruler of the Kingdom of the Isles.

Footwear—Highlanders of this time period went barefoot by choice. If they did wear shoes, they were soft, thin leather similar to ballet slippers, which made it easy to feel the ground beneath their feet. They were called *ghillie brogues* and had laces up the legs and holes in the sides so the shoes would empty of water when they walked through a river. Today's usual formal kiltwear includes modernised *ghillie brogues*.

Boats and Ships—Ainslie's boat, Malcolm, is a *faering*, a personal vessel, smaller than the *birlinns* used by her clan but clinker built, with a tall dragon's head prow similar to those placed on the longships to protect against evil at sea. The dragon's head also indicates that the ship's owner is the chief or king. *Birlinns* were larger cargo ships, also called "galleys"; *nyvaigs* were the same type of ship but smaller than the *birlinns*. Sometimes the names were interchangeable. They were the kind of vessels people think of as Viking.

CHAPTER SIX
Islay

Kingdoms—Ainslie refers to herself as different than the Scots and the English because, as noted above, the Dhòmhnaill saw themselves as a separate kingdom.

CHAPTER SEVEN
Heather Island

Claig Castle, located on Am Fraoch Eilean (the Heather Island), was the stronghold of the Clan Donald. Located off the isle of Jura, in the Sound of Islay, it allowed the clan to maintain its superiority over the waters of the islands for hundreds of years. Today, there is nothing left of the castle but a ruin.

CHAPTER EIGHT
Castle

Bathing was incredibly important in Norse cultures, which were extremely fastidious about their cleanliness and their hair. The Dhòmhnaill are Norse and Gaelic and shared those cultural traits.

In Jane's time, bathing would not be as frequent. She would have had a private bathtub, as she was upperclass, but it wouldn't have been used as frequently as Ainslie's people would bathe. Bathing in general wasn't an uncommon thing for Victorians; a strip-bath was normal and done frequently. Victorian people also enjoyed public baths in the cities. Even so, by Norse standards Jane wouldn't be considered clean.

Sanitation during Jane's time period wasn't at its best either. In Edinburgh, the cry of "gardyloo!," a bastardisation of the French *garde á l'eau* ("watch out for the water") was all the warning anyone would get if the people in the upper apartments (that is, the wealthy) were emptying their chamber pots out the window into the street. This practice, incidentally, was one of the contributing factors that led to the use of high heels in European cities, originally a men's shoe style, to keep their feet out of the muck. Edinburgh smelled so terrible because of all this that in Boswell's famous biography of Samuel Johnson he recounts that as they were walking up the Royal Mile Johnson leaned in and said to him, "I smell you in the dark!"

CHAPTER NINE
Feast

The Hebrides were extremely well-stocked with many different kinds of foods; game was and is plentiful in Scotland. Fruit was a delicacy, as it was difficult to keep fresh during transport.

CHAPTER TEN
Moonlight on Caol Ìle

Jane is demisexual and demiromantic, a person who does not experience sexual or romantic attraction unless she/he forms a strong emotional connection with someone, and whose love interest is then focused on that person alone. She previously believed herself to be asexual and aromantic.

CHAPTER ELEVEN
Fishing off Gigha

Scotland is often cloudy, but when the sun is out, the light has a strange and quite beautiful silver quality to it. Beaches in Scotland are often white sand and the water is very clear, much like the tropics (but only in appearance). So much so, in fact, that an advert for holidays in Thailand once used a photo of a Scottish beach and claimed it as one of their own!

CHAPTER TWELVE
Crossing the Sound

Pronunciation key to the song (approximate):
Ho ro, mo nean down voy-ach

Hi ri, mo nean down voy-ach
Mo (*ch* throat sound) alluk lach voy-ach
Ha fos mi ach oo.

CHAPTER THIRTEEN
Return from Barra

Aonghus, usually written "Aonghas," means "One-Choice." The "Mòr" added to his name means "big."

Ainslie is usually a surname, but if it is used as a first name, it is unisex. The name, like many other Scottish names, is transferred from combining the Æne placename and the Old English word lēah, meaning "hermitage in the wood clearing." (This was entirely unintentional, but those who are familiar with my other work, *Caledonia*, will find it amusing.)

CHAPTER FOURTEEN
The Women of Innse Gall

Innse Gall, the Gaelic name for the Hebrides, means "foreigners' islands." This further serves to illustrate that the Norse-Gaelic Sea Kingdom was a different country from Scotland at that time. Islay and Gigha are a part of the Inner Hebrides, while islands like Barra and Skye are part of the Outer Hebrides. The islands are collectively referred to as the Western Isles, and all islands of the Hebrides are considered a part of the Highlands despite some, like Islay, being less mountainous and on a latitude with Glasgow in the Lowlands. This is because the term refers to the Gaelic-speaking parts of Scotland, which includes all of the Hebridean islands. These islands are the last strongholds of the Gaelic language and culture today.

Women fought and, much like in other Norse societies, were accustomed to equality with men.

Sexual Assault—As noted above, punishment for crimes like sexual assault were extremely severe, exile from the clan or death, which were the same thing for the most part. This kind of behaviour brought shame not only on the perpetrator, but on the entire clan. Rape was extremely uncommon in that time period due to these practices, and indeed anyone could kill a rapist without fearing punishment. The Norse-Gaelic Sea Kingdom of the Dhòmhnaill was separate from Scotland and England as well, so it followed its own rules.

Again, the question of "Who is civilised?" arises. In many ways,

Jane's time period is far more brutal than Ainslie's—as, indeed, is our own.

CHAPTER FIFTEEN
The Druid Council

Druids are always a topic of contention when it comes to modern interpretations. There are even arguments that the Druids never existed at all. Briefly: we know absolutely nothing certain about them. We don't even know if they were religious in any way. They left no records behind. NeoDruidism was made up of whole cloth around the 18th century or so, as a part of the Romantic movement.

The best guess we currently have is that Druids were a council of learned people, similar to a group of university professors. A religious person or two may have been involved in said council, but they would form a part of the whole. Historically speaking, however, the only thing we know for certain is that they were of relative importance to society and that they practiced human sacrifice on a wide scale, although the purpose for this is also unknown. There is currently argument among historians as to whether this was projection by the Greeks or Romans, but there is a fair amount of archaeological evidence available regarding the practice.

CHAPTER SEVENTEEN
Whisky and Cranachan

Whisky is spelled *whisky* in Scotland and *whiskey* in Ireland; both words are an Anglicisation of *uisge beatha* (Scottish Gaelic) and *uisce beatha* (Irish), "the water of life." No whisky in Scotland is ever referred to as "Scotch," and neither are the people. They are "Scots" and so is their language.

Mary King's Close—During Jane's time period, the poor lived beneath the streets of Edinburgh. The crowded conditions there made disease thrive; families would sleep 10-20 to a room. It was a way to keep the serving class out of sight and out of mind. It was also a place to go when someone didn't want to be seen. Mary King's Close in Edinburgh is still open to visitors today, for those interested in seeing how the poor lived at the time.

CHAPTER EIGHTEEN

A Taste of Honey

Peat—one of the most important products in both Scotland and Ireland. It was, and in some places still is, used as fuel, as a heat source, as flavour for whisky, and as an item to harvest and sell. It is dug up from peat bogs. It is also one reason that the land itself in these regions can be dangerous; the peat underfoot could be on fire all along the entire bog but you wouldn't know it until you stood on it. Islay produces a whisky that has the highest degree of peatiness out of all the whiskies in the world.

CHAPTER NINETEEN

Finlaggan

Finlaggan, the ancient seat of the Lords of the Isles and the Clan Donald, was the centre of power for many centuries in the Sea Kingdom. During the heyday of the Lords of the Isles, the larger island had a castle and many cottages, buildings, storehouses, etc. The smaller Council or Parliament island nearby was where the clans would gather for council meetings. Visitors today can visit the ruins by walking past the visitor centre and across a narrow bridge to Eilean Mòr, the larger island; the Council Island is just beyond it in the water but there is no access to it. Today, the seat of the MacDonald clan is Armadale Castle on Skye.

Creative Commons ShareAlike
Aerial photo of Eilean Mòr, Council Island, and Loch Finlaggan by Gunther Tschuch

CHAPTER TWENTY
The Gathering of the Clans

Scottish Ingenuity—Even as a small, oppressed nation, Scotland has always had a long history of invention and innovation. The Macintosh raincoat Jane is talking about was named after a Scottish man, named, unsurprisingly, Charles Macintosh, who invented waterproof fabric. She also discusses general anaesthetic, the telegraph, and the steam engine train, all products of Scottish innovation and design.

CHAPTER TWENTY-TWO
Flame

Victorians and Sex—Victorians were not as repressed as we make them out to be. Still, they had some interesting ideas (read: bizarre) about the sexuality of women. This was the time of the temperance movement, which didn't only relate to alcohol: graham crackers were invented as a way to stave off masturbation, for example. For a woman of Jane's time, avoiding self-pleasure was recommended as a way to keep her mind on her work. Her reactions to everything here are very much her first time in every way.

CHAPTER TWENTY-THREE
Aftermath

Faeries—Ainslie assumes Jane must be *leannan sìth*, a sort of faerie succubus, since she fell out of the sky just like in her clan's old faerie tales and because she feels such intense desire for Jane she doesn't have another explanation for it. The *leannan sìth* are also big on consent. So when Jane clarifies that she wanted Ainslie's attentions, Ainslie believes that her fairy-lover has accepted her and is relieved—even though the lovers of the *leannan sìth* die of eventual thirst and starvation because they are so captivated by their lover. The *leannan sìth* is also a kind of muse and brings great success to their lovers, but they usually die young due to the vampiric nature of the faerie. The Irish *gancanagh* is a similar creature that appears as a handsome man whose skin is addictive. Those who touch it become completely obsessed and die pining shortly thereafter. Belief in faeries was not so much religious as a fact of life to people of that time period.

This is also why the idea that Jane is a time-traveller doesn't seem to bother Ainslie. Everyone knows that time passes differently in Faerie than elsewhere and that the Fae can walk between worlds. **"Good Fowk"**—Nobody wants to get on the bad side of the Fae. Faeries aren't happy when you say bad things about them, so they are called the Good Folk, the Good People, etc.

CHAPTER TWENTY-FOUR
Leaving Finlaggan

Adomnán the Saint wrote the Law of the Innocents, agreed upon by several Irish and Scottish clans. One of the directives, to stop women from fighting, was included because his mother saw a dead woman with a baby on a battlefield and it made her sad. As you can imagine, the law did not stop women from doing anything, including participating in war.

"One of Ireland's Most Famous Poets"—This is a reference to the famous Oscar Wilde case, which landed Wilde in prison for two years. Jane is living in 1888, and her prediction will come true with his trial in 1895.

Highland Hospitality—This law was a sacred one, and the idea of breaking it was horrific to anyone living in that part of the world at that time. Highland hospitality consisted of taking care of any person that ended up in the household, instead of outright murdering them, which was also common in Ainslie's time period. Highland hospitality helped strengthen the bonds of a clan and its allies over time. There is a story of a visitor to a clan who argued with a chief's son while awaiting the chief's return; during the argument, the visitor killed the son. The chief escorted the visitor back to his clan himself in order to protect him. Such was the intense importance of bonds and clan ties along with Highland hospitality.

CHAPTER TWENTY-FIVE
The Warmth of Claig Castle

Travel—As noted before, people were extremely well travelled during this time period, and people of all colours and creeds lived in and around these islands. Tariq on the Druid Council stands as an example; at the time, the contributions of those from Islamic cultures in mathematics, the sciences, and medicine were known all over the world. This means it is extremely unlikely that any of these regions were 100 percent "white." "White" is in quotes here because the concept is a modern one. Place of origin mattered more, and even to this day in the UK, prejudice runs along class/place of origin lines rather than colour-coded ones.

Same-Sex Relationships—Dòmhnall and Christina's acceptance of their daughter's same-sex relationship was not uncommon in medieval times and cultures. A lot of what we think of as normal, in the sense of that kind of oppression, is far more based on Jane's time than Ainslie's.

CHAPTER TWENTY-SIX
Aileen's Gift

The Wide Sea: Jane's cottage is in a fictional, nameless settlement in what is now Saligo Bay. Islay, a physically large island with a very small modern population, is much changed since Ainslie's time when it was the centre of her world and of a vast kingdom that reached from the Isle of Man to Ireland. Most of the settlements there today weren't founded until the mid-1700s.

Aileen is an extremely talented blacksmith and metallurgist. She is also a savvy businesswoman. She knew that people would come to her from all the other islands for custom if she was serving the royal family, and so she acted accordingly.

CHAPTER TWENTY-SEVEN
Winter

Feuding Clans—The longtime enmity of the Dhòmhnaill and Caimbeul clan is famous. The Clan Donald looks noble nowadays because they are "the stronghold of the Gael," who were, as you can see in this story, not even considered Scottish at the time, but a separate kingdom. However, they preserved Gaelic tradition. Clan Campbell has yet to live down the reputation it earned due to the famous abuse of Highland hospitality at the Massacre of Glencoe. (Even there, however, there were Campbell soldiers who broke their swords over their knees and refused to participate in the slaughter. Nothing in history is black and white.)

CHAPTER TWENTY-EIGHT
Snow and Stars

The Greeks—Ainslie is referring to the love story of Perseus and Andromeda, who were put into the sky as the constellation Andromeda.

Travelling Folk—These are the native nomads of Scotland and Ireland and the British Isles as a whole; they are all that remains of the clan system. They are the people who retain the old folk songs, stories, and customs of the past, frequently winning singing and storytelling competitions. Despite this, Travellers experience some of the worst treatment and prejudice of any group in modern-day Britain and Ireland.

Jane's Wound—there is an old saying that Highlanders are "clean-fleshed," meaning they heal well from wounds that should have been fatal.

CHAPTER TWENTY-NINE
Spring

What's to Come—Jane's outburst informs Ainslie of the swift and brutal future destruction of the clan system, of the Lords of the Isles, and of the Scotland that existed at the time. Jane was living at a time in which people were celebrating Scottish romance, but while the upper class was playing Highland dress-up, actual Highlanders were suffering.

CHAPTER THIRTY
Up the Airy Mountain

The Second Half of the Book features chapter titles that relate to a song or poem. This one is based on "The Fairies," a poem written by William Allingham.

Breakfast at the Manor House—The breakfast consists of eggs, bacon, baked beans, Lorne sausage, link sausage (bangers), black pudding, toast, a cooked tomato, tattie scones (potato pancakes, a bit like hash browns), toast, and fried mushrooms. Tea and coffee are also served, and the tea is drunk with milk. Also called a "fry-up," this is a "full English" or "full Scottish" or "full X" breakfast, depending on the region where it is served and its regional variations. The entirety of the UK and Ireland have a variation on this huge breakfast with regional differences. Most of the utensils mentioned here are still used in Britain, including the toast racks and the tea service. Blood pudding, a fried tomato, and tattie scones are breakfast foods even to this day in Scotland. "Egg and soldiers," that is, a softboiled egg served in a little cup with strips of toast for dunking, is still a common British breakfast. The bacon common in the UK is loin bacon, more like slices of ham than the crispy belly bacon preferred by Americans. The UK also has "streaky bacon," which visually resembles American bacon, but is not the same.

"My Right as a Husband"—Wives didn't have many rights during this time period. The laws and public opinion were changing during Jane's lifetime, but wives could not own property or their own wages until the mid-to-late 1800s, and women could not vote. Once married, they were considered the property of their husband in every way.

Many of our ideas about how the different genders behave and what they are capable of originate in Victorian mores and social thought. David and Jane are extremely eccentric for their time, but they're rich, and money excuses everything. However, many of these laws changed during Jane's lifetime because so many "eccentric" people decided those rights were worth fighting for.

Parliament—At this time, Scotland had no Parliament. Following the Treaty of Union that united Scotland and England as "Great Britain," the Scottish Parliament dissolved and did not return until 1999. David is Scottish, but serves as an MP in London. Scottish and Irish Home Rule became important during this time. The Crichton name was a solid one in Edinburgh, and David's family connections along with his wealth would make him the kind of candidate the English of the time could accept. Even though Jane and David lived in relative wealth, their very Scottishness made them something like second-class citizens, just as describing things as "British" when they are Scottish hides the ingenuity and invention of an entire nation of people. While Scotland is a part of "Great Britain," the entire world hears "British" and thinks "English."

CHAPTER THIRTY-ONE

Down the Rushy Glen

The Athens/Paris of Scotland—Edinburgh is often referred to in this way, due to its history in the arts, culture, and literature, and the beauty of its architecture.

Smoking, Dogs—Paying customers could smoke or bring their pets if they wished into many establishments that catered to the rich, something which remains true today.

Scottish Universities finally opened their doors to women in 1892.

CHAPTER THIRTY-TWO

We Dare Not Go A-Hunting

Scottishness—Jane speaks in Scots here (Lallans) to emphasize not only her own Scottishness, but her mother's. Much of the cultural aspects of her upwardly mobile mother are affectations; Jane is underlining the fact that they are all Scots and her mother married a Highlander. Speaking this way would be far more shocking to her mother than Jane's swearing.

CHAPTER THIRTY-THREE

For Fear of Little Men

"Campbeltown Loch" is a famous song, although sung quite a while after the events take place here. It referenced how expensive whisky was in Campbeltown although it was one of the most prolific producers of whisky in Scotland in the past. It's the age-old story of how those who produce things don't always have the money to afford them.

CHAPTER THIRTY-FOUR

Where The Brokenhearted Ken

Emigration—Some of the worst ravages of famine visited Ireland and the Hebrides. Faced with starvation or transportation after failed battles and the Clearances, many people in Scotland had no choice but to go to America or Canada, never to return. In the 1800s, the population of Islay was near 15,000. Today, the island has 3,000 inhabitants and nine whisky distilleries, with plans for more.

Claig Castle—Islay and Jura no longer have any complete castles. Claig Castle has almost vanished completely.

CHAPTER THIRTY-FIVE

Nae Second Spring Again

The Ripper: Jane's time period is roughly 1888, when these murders occurred.

CHAPTER THIRTY-SIX

Tho' The Waefu' May Cease Frae Their Greetin'

Greyfriars Bobby—Famous story of a faithful dog that waited at its master's grave, now known to be a hoax. The hoax was well-known even during Bobby's lifetime. The story is still so well loved that most don't like to disabuse anyone of the notion. However, Bobby was played by at least two different dogs. His/their collar and bowl are on display at the Edinburgh Museum.

"Saor Alba"—This slightly odd way of saying "Free Scotland!" was meant as a command; Gaelic-speakers differ as to whether this is accurate or not. It is a recognised motto of the Scottish Independence effort.

CHAPTER THIRTY-NINE

I'll Be In Scotland Afore Ye

Scottish Wars of Independence—The events Dòmhnall is referring to are the first stirrings of this conflict, a series of military campaigns fought between the Kingdom of Scotland and the Kingdom of England in the late 13th and early 14th centuries. "Scotland" is different to Dòmhnall's kingdom; he sees England, Scotland, Wales, and Ireland as separate countries to the one he rules (the Sea Kingdom, formerly Dál Riata).

The Skyemen—People on Islay frequently fought those from Skye, but it depended on circumstances; sometimes they were allies. The old joke, "the Scots and their worst enemies, the other Scots," is true.

CHAPTER FORTY-ONE

I'll Show Ye The Red Deer A-Roaming

Chapter Titles here are taken from the folk song "Will Ye Gang Tae The Hielands, Leezie Lindsay?"

CHAPTER FORTY-TWO

And Far As The Bound O' The Red Deer

Christina Rossetti, an English poet of renown, wrote "The Goblin Market," a narrative poem published in 1862.

CHAPTER FORTY-THREE

My Hearts In The Highlands

Seamanship—Jane was incredibly lucky that she ended up anywhere near land at all during this episode. Her craft drifted from south of Port Askaig (on the Islay side of the Sound, near Jura, where Am Fraoch Eilean is located) to the inlet almost directly across from it on the mainland, where the sea-loch goes into the Kintyre Peninsula. This is also roughly where her machine first landed. Saligo Bay, where the nameless "city" is located, is on the opposite shore of the island, and is a six-hour walk from Port Askaig.

Castles—Innis Chonnel and Kilchurn are both Campbell seats in Loch Awe, although Kilchurn is more likely to be featured on the covers of shortbread tins.

CHAPTER FORTY-FIVE

My Heart Is Not Here

Courtship—Archibald Caimbeul is exactly the kind of man Jane was expected to marry. This, coupled with the tantalising temptation of a life much like the one she'd left in Edinburgh, makes his offer not an easy one to turn down, despite Jane's love for Ainslie.

CHAPTER FORTY-SIX

A-Chasin' The Deer

"The Campbells are Coming" is the pipe song of the Campbells. Their motto is "Ne Obliviscaris," "Forget Not"; variations on this motto are shared by a few other Highland clans.

Clan Donald/MacDonald/Dhòmhnaill—The clan's motto is "By Sea By Land," invoking the vast Sea Kingdom ruled by the Lords of the Isles.

CHAPTER FORTY-SEVEN
The Water Is Wide

Chapter Title—Titles are from the folksong "The Water is Wide."

Supernatural Fury—The Dhòmhnaill, and indeed most Highland clans, were not known for their pacifist ways. The fury inherent in this kind of incident, where the Dhòmhnaill felt that the Caimbeulaich had stolen one of their own, especially one who the chief loved, would be felt keenly. The Dhòmhnaill would do anything to be seen as the most terrifying enemy possible, almost to a level of the supernatural.

CHAPTER FORTY-NINE
Neither Have I Wings To Fly

Corryvreckan is the third largest whirlpool on earth. Scottish folklore refers to it as the Storm Kelpie, where the Cailleach, a Storm Hag and the Old Woman of Winter, also called Beira, Queen of Winter, washes her plaid to usher in the cold season. "Corryvreckan" (*Coire Bhreacain*) means "the cauldron of the plaid." It lies between the islands of Jura and Scarba, between the land and the wild Atlantic. It is Corryvreckan that made Claig Castle advantageous for the Dhòmhnaill clan, making the only safe passage in from the Atlantic one in which ships had to pass the Castle and allowing the Dhòmhnaill control of the seaways for hundreds of years.

CHAPTER FIFTY
Give Me A Boat That Can Carry Two

Jura today is still brown vs. Islay's green. Claig Castle would have technically been a part of Jura, not Islay. There are more deer on the Isle of Jura than there are people. The Paps of Jura (large mountains) are prominent and visible from a large portion of Islay. This is somewhat hilarious because "paps" means "breasts." There are three Paps of Jura, so whoever named them knew some interesting women. Either way, the backdrop of Jura is partly what gives Islay its sublime charm. George Orwell wrote *1984* while living on Jura.

Sgian Dubh (SKEE-an DOO) means "black dagger." In this case, the word "dubh" means "concealed." The dagger is worn secretly on the body if the person distrusts their company and on the outer calf of the stocking when among friends. When Archibald appears at Claig Castle with the sgian dubh visible, it is a gesture of friendship and trust. The sgian dubh is a weapon of last resort. All Scots used a claymore, a dirk, a targe (type of shield), and a sgian dubh/sgian achlais, depending on their circumstances. These people were armed to the teeth 100 percent of the time. This proliferation of weaponry was noted by foreign contemporaries as "ridiculous," but they lived extremely violent and dangerous lives.

CHAPTER FIFTY-ONE
And Both Shall Row

The Lord of the Isles—As noted above, the history of this title is a complicated one. The original kingdom, which included parts of Ireland and the Isle of Man, was called Dál Riata. The Lord of the Isles title, while it sounds impressive and romantic, was in fact a diminished one for a people who had once had a kingdom. In reality, the kingdom still existed, but the Dhòmhnaill were still forced to adopt this lesser name.

CHAPTER FIFTY-TWO
My Love And I

Archibald has placed himself in mortal danger in order to broker peace between the clans. All present must agree to his words, not only Dòmhnall; a clan chief's rule is not absolute, and since Ainslie's ascension her opinion is as valuable as Dòmhnall's. Archibald is aware that the enmity existing between their clans is really one between Dòmhnall and his own father at this time; therefore, he asks forgiveness of Dòmhnall first.

CHAPTER FIFTY-THREE
O Will Ye Be Known As A Poor Beggar's Lady

Chapter Title—from "Tibbie Dunbar"
"Ye Canna Trust a Campbell" is an old Scottish saying. Nowadays, the old feud is played up for tourists, but it is not really an existing issue.
Glencoe Massacre—The famous massacre of the Glencoe MacDonalds in 1692 was a historical sore spot even in Jane's time

period. Some MacDonalds managed to escape over the mountains to their allies, the Stuarts of Appin, but the rest of them were killed. The MacDonalds of Glencoe were notorious thieves and their destruction would not have caused much of a stir. There were other far worse massacres in the Highlands. However, betraying the law of Highland hospitality was one of the most egregious behaviours possible at the time, and despite being done by order of the king, opinion at the time was that the Campbell soldiers involved in the massacre used subterfuge and had committed the crime of "slaughter under trust." When the news got out, it turned the MacDonald-Campbell feud into a general distrust of the Campbells that lasted for centuries.

Traitors—Both Jane and Archibald are very lucky to not have been killed on the spot. Certain rules were upheld with swift violence, and this kind of traitorous behaviour was punished severely. The law of Highland hospitality was too important to be ignored and provided safety to both Jane and Archibald until they could prove their good intentions.

CHAPTER FIFTY-FOUR
An' Lie In The Heather Rolled Up In My Plaidie

The Percussion Lock Firearm and the Breech-loading Rifle were invented by Scots, Alexander John Forsythe, whose percussion lock replaced the earlier flintlock, in the early 1800s, and Patrick Ferguson in 1770 respectively. The hand-cannon was a Chinese invention and probably unknown in most of the world at the time. However, cannons and explosives existed, and a council of scholars would readily understand some of the concepts behind the gun itself. Handheld guns would become a part of regular warfare somewhere around this time period in Western Europe.

The Druids' Verdict—This kind of Solomonic judgment is dangerous, but also wise, because it asks both parties to believe in and trust the intentions of the other. From Morag's perspective, it will pit them against each other, should they be evil; it will cause the downfall of both if one of them is evil; it will be a boon to the clan if both of them have good intentions and will work in tandem for the betterment of the clan. In all three scenarios, the Dhòmhnaill will benefit.

CHAPTER FIFTY-FIVE

Sky For Your Roof, An' Your Candles The Stars

Invented by a Scot—Scotland punches well above its weight for a nation of its size, particularly an oppressed and colonised one, in the world of scientific enquiry and invention. Ainslie disapproves of the way Jane's adaptation of the hand-cannon will give an unfair advantage to anyone who uses it. As a warrior herself she can appreciate the damage it will do one day.

CHAPTER FIFTY-EIGHT

An' Bade Her Look O'er The Sea

Chapter Title—from "Will Ye Gang Tae the Hielands, Leezie Lindsay?"

"From the Lone Shieling"—"The Canadian Boat Song," of disputed authorship, is one of many famous songs and poems about Scottish exiles.

CHAPTER FIFTY-NINE

These Isles Ye Behold Are MacDonald's, My Own

Ainslie's upcoming ascension to the title of Lord of the Isles in addition to the chief of the Dhòmhnaill while her father is still living was not an uncommon thing in the Highlands and Islands. See opening note for details.

CHAPTER SIXTY

An' My Bride An' My Darlin Are Ye

"Somethin' Tae Offer a Great Lady"—Ainslie isn't only offering Jane her hand in marriage, but also trusting her with her lands, her people, everything she holds dear, and all of which are both her kingdom and her responsibility. Ainslie's offer here is a pact in itself, a way to tell Jane that she is willing to offer her the world.

CHAPTER SIXTY-ONE
Red Her Cheeks As Rowans Are

The Wedding of Any Chief was an enormous celebration that lasted for months. The wedding of the Lord of the Isles was the kind of event where people would remember exactly where they were when it happened so that they could talk about it in their old age. This kind of wedding, and the festival that followed it, could last a year or more—partly because when all the allies who were further afield would show up with gifts the whole party would start again. This particular wedding, of this particular Lord of the Isles, would be the kind of event people would remember for many generations. The Caimbeulaich and the Dhòmhnaill are, and were, the two largest and richest clans in all of Scotland. A wedding-feast hosted jointly by these clans would be an incredible sight.

Christina of the Isles—A clan chief in her own right, Christina is offering Jane the blade of the Ruaridhs, long since joined with the Dhòmhnaill clan through her union. Christina was not a woman to be trifled with; she led the armies of the Ruaridh clan and frequently that of the Dhòmhnaill as well. If she hadn't offered her blade to Jane, enmity may have arisen between the Dhòmhnaill and the Ruaridh; where one animosity ended with Ainslie and Jane's wedding, another would have begun if Christina had decided it was the correct course of action.

CHAPTER SIXTY-TWO
Bright Her Eye As Any Star

Finlaggan would come to be the centre of the Kingdom of the Isles, both governmental and social; the population of Islay would eventually move there and settle around the banks of the loch.

CHAPTER SIXTY-THREE
Fairest o' Them A' by Far

The questions and implications of time travel are always difficult. Jane's actions might have changed the course of history, or perhaps this had always been its course.

CHAPTER SIXTY-FOUR

Mo Nighean Donn Bhoidheach

"My Beautiful Brown-Haired Girl"—The phrase itself means "my beautiful brown-haired girl" (meaning young woman), although some have anglicised it to "My Nut-Brown Maiden", despite the fact that there is another unrelated English folk song of the same name. Jane learning the song that Ainslie sang to her months before is something of a feat. Many Gaelic speakers will listen to make sure the singer knows the actual words and isn't just parroting.

The Vibrator—There is a *lot* of argument as to whether the vibrator was really invented during Jane's time or whether it was just meant to be a massage device. Clever women have been adapting things for their own use for quite some time, so whether or not this is a little anachronistic, Jane's personal love of invention would definitely lend itself to adapting something that might make her lover happy.

CHAPTER SIXTY-FIVE

The Mist-Covered Mountains of Home

"Saffron Massage"—a euphemism for lesbian sex from a medieval Arabic text, because saffron is ground into the cloth when dying fabric. For David, this is the height of rascally talk, which is why Jane is so surprised.

'S Math Sin (SMAH-shin)—Linguists are divided on the truth of this, but it is true that "'s math sin" and "smashing" sound very similar and also mean the same thing.

FOR FURTHER READING

These recommendations are for books on Scottish history and culture that are entertaining rather than academic. There are many academic caveats about these books, but they provide a good general overview, along with more controversial takes on Scottish history. Readers will find that these books are a good jumping-off point to discovering more about the history and culture of Scotland.

Scottish Highlanders by Charles Mackinnon

How the Scots Invented the Modern World: The True Story of How Western Europe's Poorest Nation Created Our World and Everything in It by Arthur Herman

Wild Scots: 400 Years of Highland History by Michael Fry

The Druids by Stuart Piggott

The Invention of Tradition: the Highland Tradition of Scotland by Hugh Trevor-Roper, in *The Invention of Tradition* edited by Eric Hobsbawm and Terence Ranger

FOR FURTHER LISTENING

Videos of many of the songs referred to in *My Heart's in the Highlands* can be found on YouTube. Here is a list of links to them and related songs that were active in March 2020.

"The Water is Wide"—https://youtu.be/d32rALuwRtQ
Also called "O, Waly, Waly," a folk song of Scottish origin, 1600s.

"Will Ye Gang Tae the Hielands, Leezie Lindsay?"—https://youtu.be/7677MLq0ZhQ
A folk song about a poor Lowlands woman enticed away by a Highland chief of the MacDonalds; Robert Burns recorded the initial fragment, which now has many lyrical variants.

"The Braes o' Balquhidder"—https://youtu.be/KOK3cAZCSoM
An original folk song that would later be adapted into "Wild Mountain Thyme." Balquhidder was the home and now burial place of Rob Roy MacGregor, whose last name was outlawed during his lifetime, and whose epitaph reads "MacGregor Despite Them."

"Ho Ro Mo Nighean Donn Bhoidheach"—https://youtu.be/NKsrYk-KGsoY
"Ho Ro, My Beautiful Brown-Haired Girl" (Mo = my, nighean = girl, donn = brown-haired, bhoidheach = beautiful)—A Scottish Gaelic folk song. This song is sometimes anglicised into "My Nut-Brown Maiden", but that is more an approximation than a translation. In fact, some English translations of this song are also approximations and entirely change its meaning. Adding to the confusion, there is also a different popular English folk song called The Nut-Brown Maiden / Nut-Brown Maid.

"Tibbie Dunbar"—https://youtu.be/C-zDgMF_q3A
A Robert Burns love song.

"Campbeltown Loch (I Wish You Were Whisky)"—https://youtu.be/x-ozEeBb4LI
Humorous folk song pointing out that although Campbeltown was a major producer of whisky, the people living there couldn't afford to drink it. The song is anachronistic here as it was written long after Jane's time, but is reflective of a part the Scottish vaudeville music

hall scene that was popularised during her time period, and would eventually gain worldwide fame through performers like Sir Harry Lauder, who was followed in later years by Andy Stewart and others. Harry Lauder is said to have been the first Scottish performer to sell over a million records, and it is unfortunate that these contributions to Scottish song tend to be overlooked today.

"Mull of Kintyre"—https://youtu.be/OrbuDWit1Co
Song by Paul McCartney about the Kintyre Peninsula, where he lived with his wife Linda.

"Loch Lomond"—https://youtu.be/MjNwsTbixbc
Scottish folk song about two soldiers imprisoned in Carlisle castle. One will be killed, one released. The condemned soldier is telling the other not to worry about him because by dying he will reach Scotland first.

"Mairi's Wedding/Lewis Bridal Song"—https://youtu.be/qgiRY0rYuu4
Folk song originally written in Gaelic by John Roderick Bannerman for Mary McNiven when she won the gold medal at the National Mòd.

Puirt-a-beul—https://youtu.be/fze5krlgBDw
An example of "mouth music," rhythm for working.

ALPHABETICAL GLOSSARY AND PRONUNCIATION GUIDE*

Pronunciation of *ch* as in *loch*: the voiceless velar fricative, a soft *ch*, the same sound as the Spanish J in words like Julio. Spelling here adheres to the spelling used in Scotland and England, e.g., "watercolour" rather than "watercolor." Punctuation follows the conventions of American English.

Act of Proscription—see Author's Guide

Argyll (ARE-gyle)—A region of the Highlands, or people from the Argyll region, most often Campbells, who later held the title of Dukes of Argyll. Most of the action in this story during Ainslie's time period takes place in modern-day Argyll and Bute.

Auld Alliance—the longstanding friendship between France and Scotland

beul (BALE) —Scottish Gaelic word for "mouth"

birlinn / nyvaig (BER-lin / NY-vayg)—larger clinker-built boats of a design similar to *faerings*, propelled by sail and oar, also called "galleys." The boats looked like those traditionally imagined as "Viking," but did not necessarily owe their design to Viking ships as they differ in various ways. These were used for transport of troops and cattle as well as warfare and were of varying sizes. There is also some evidence they were used for mercantile transport between the various centres of the Sea Kingdom. The MacDonalds of Islay were the strongest regional naval power. *Birlinns* (larger) and *nyvaigs* (smaller) were both peculiar to the Hebrides. These vessels were particularly noted for their speed. Depictions of these in Scottish heraldry, especially that of the Lords of the Isles, are called *lymphads*.

black pudding—very popular breakfast food, sausage made of congealed cow's blood. Stornoway black pudding is considered the best.

blue bonnets—Prior to the kilt, a blue bonnet dyed with woad was the most recognisably Scottish item of clothing. In later years, blue bonnets signified Covenanters and afterwards, Jacobite support.

bradan rost (BRAH-dun RAHST)—Scottish Gaelic for "roast salmon," *bradan rost* is a very specific type of smoked salmon dish native to the Highlands of Scotland. It is a method of smoking salmon hot, which simultaneously cooks and smokes the salmon. *Bradan rost* is a speciality of Loch Fyne.

brat / plaid / lèine (Brot/PLAYd/LEY-nah)—The *lèine* was the long saffron shirt worn beneath the plaid. During Ainslie's time, the *brat* would have been the predecessor to the plaid/earasaid, more of a tartan cloak or cape, but worn in a similar fashion. The earasaid/plaid (great kilt) evolved from the *brat*. Both men and women wore one, but used different words for it (earasaid for women, plaid for men). "Plaide" is Scottish Gaelic for "blanket." These characters dress in a somewhat-anachronistic way, as the plaid and kilt only really became a thing in the 1500s. The plaid was used as a sleeping blanket as well as an article of clothing and was similar to a sleeping bag in its use.

bothy (BAWTH-ee) a basic shelter, available to anyone and usually left unlocked for public use

"By Sea By Land"—the motto of the Donalds

Caimbeul/Campbell/Caimbeulaich (KAYM-bl/CAM-bell/CH (soft ch)AYM-bl-ach)

Caledonian MacBrayne—ferry company that still operates in Scotland

"Campbells are Coming"—the song of the Campbells, anachronistic here as it was written many years later

"Campbeltoun Loch"—a fun folk song based on the fact that while Campbeltown produced a lot of whisky, it was often too expensive for locals to afford

Caol Ìle (CULLEELA)—Sound of Islay

chirurgeon—surgeon, archaic

claidheamh mòr (CLIYVE-Mor)—Gaelic for "great sword," a two-handed broadsword. Called "claymores" in English, during Ainslie's time period, these would have been a bit shorter than the later swords of the same name.

Clearances—see Author's Guide

clinker-built boat—Scandinavian boat-building style using interlocking wooden beams

close—the inner courtyard of an apartment building or a narrow alleyway, surrounded by tall buildings, often private property not open to the public

coracle—The rowboat that Jane attempted to reach Claig Castle in is tiny, the nautical equivalent of sailing in a teacup. Dougal would have been using it to fish in the shallows or the rivers. It is not a seagoing vessel.

Coracle, Public Domain photo, Wikimedia.org origin

cranachan (KRAN-a-(soft ch, as in *loch*) en / KRAN-a-ken)—delicious Scottish dessert of raspberries, whipped cream, oatmeal, heather honey, and, of course, whisky

Crichton (CRY-tin)

Culloden—KULL-odden

Dál Riata (DAHL-ree-ah-da) the original name of the Norse-Gaelic Sea Kingdom; see Author's Guide for more

Dòmhnall (DOHL, like saying "doll" through the nose)

dreich—wet, damp, grey, miserable weather

drui—singular of Druid

dwale—English anaesthetic made from alcohol and opium, used from 1200-1500

earasaid/arisaid (ara-SITCH/are-is-AIG)—Spelling is interchangeable. This is technically a large blanket, as were all the kilts of former times. Men and women wore the same garment, just differently; men's great kilts bisected the knee and hung over the shoulder, while women's *earasaid/arisaid* could be used as a hood and also fell to the ground.

Edinburgh (EDIN-bra)—capital of Scotland

faering (FARE-ing) clinker-built personal vessel with a square sail

fat little robins—In Scotland, robins are tiny and round, very unlike North American robins.

fáidh (FOY)—The term means "seer" or "prophet" but covers a number of abilities, including divination and the diagnosis of disease, and here describes what we could call a doctor.

gallowglass (GALLOW-glass) mercenary soldiers of the Norse-Gaelic Sea Kingdom in 13th-century Scotland

gancanagh (GONE-ka-na)—Irish faerie resembling a handsome man. He has addictive skin; once his lover touches it, they will pine away for him into nothingness.

Gigha (GEE-ah, with a hard G)—A small island between Islay and the Kintyre Peninsula, with a mild climate and sunnier than other parts of the country, Gigha has some of the clearest blue water and whitest-sand beaches in Scotland. Its name derives from Norse, Good Island or God's Island.

glaikit wee cunt—"stupid little fucker," basically

Glencoe—GLEN-ko

gloaming—time after sunset where the world turns lavender. In the Highlands and Islands, the sun rises as early as 3 am, and after it sets late at night, the world is filled with a lavender light. Gloaming is a Scots word for the long purple twilight peculiar to the Highlands and Islands. It is not a synonym for twilight, but a word for the extended middle ground between night and day in this part of Scotland. Light remains in the sky, but no sun; the world is lavender for hours and hours, and this quality of light is difficult to photograph. During the summer, Scotland can see over 18 hours of light during a day. This contrasts with its winter, in which there are often less than 6 hours of light during the daytime.

gorse—a perennial bush in Scotland with yellow flowers, very flammable and often used in heating brick ovens. The joke is that gorse is always in season.

Greyfriars Bobby—see Author's Guide

Halò—also written as *hallo*, etc. An English loanword into Gaelic from *hello*, it is pronounced as it is written (*hallo*).

hand-cannon—Chinese invention, precursor to the gun

hobgoblin stool—Or "broonie stool." This is a small stool placed near the hearth for the house goblin or brownie, and no one is allowed to sit in it as its sole purpose is for the hobgoblin or brownie of the house. These creatures appreciated a bowl of milk and a stool to sit by the fire, but would fly into a rage if given food or gifts. The Fae were real to everyone in those days, so there were accommodations made for these creatures.

Innse Gall (INN-yis GOWL / INN-sha GALL)—"islands of the foreigners," the Western Isles, the Hebrides.

Islay (EYE-luh)—island in the Inner Hebrides, the former seat of Clan Donald and the "capital" of the Sea Kingdom.

Leith (LEETH)—A maritime burgh near Edinburgh, it is part of Edinburgh today.

Lord of the Isles—diminished title of the Sea Kingdom royalty, usually the head of the Dhòmhnaill clan. Today that title belongs to Prince Charles, but these titles no longer really correspond to their original usage.

Lorne sausage—a square sausage of minced meat, rusk, and spices from the Lorne area of Scotland

metheglin (MA-theg-lin)mead with added spices or herbs. *Metheglin* is a Welsh word, but all kinds of places were producing mead by this time in history. Mead was a honey wine that was a very popular drink in the region at the time, along with Atholl Brose. Legend has it that a king once won a battle simply by offering the Atholl Brose recipe to the enemy. Atholl Brose is an ancient drink-variant of the cranachan dessert, and is somewhat similar to the far more modern Bailey's Irish cream and Scottish heather cream (1974/1980 respectively), which add chocolate.

na Caimbeulaich (Na CAYM-bl-ach)—the Campbells

nyvaig—see *birlinn*

Och, mo leannan sìth (Lennan-SHE)—"Oh, my faerie lover." *Leannan sìth*, a kind of succubus, were said to take human lovers who then led short but very inspired lives. Consent is important to these creatures, and if the intended turns them down, the faerie becomes their slave; if they are accepted, the human enjoys a brief if highly talented life before their faerie-lover drains them.

plaidie (PLY-dee)—an affectionate Scots term for the tartan wool blanket called *féileadh-mór, breacan an fhéilidh*, belted plaid, earasaid, or great kilt. It forms the larger part of the Highland outfit, and was a multipurpose article of clothing. They are somewhat incongruous in Ainslie's time period.

"*Pòg mo thòin*" (POK ma-HON (Scottish Gaelic), POGUE ma-HO-EN(Irish)—"Kiss my arse."

portage—carrying a boat over land. It is unpleasant, especially in the case of Malcolm, whose size and weight would be significantly more than that of a canoe.

puffer—The Clyde puffer was a type of coal-powered steam ship used in Glasgow and the west coast of Scotland for transferring cargo and passengers.

Image of Quaich
CC Share-Alike photo by Apie / CC BY-SA 3.0

quaich (QUAKE, with a *ch* as in *loch*)—Two-handled drinking vessels that were often used for ceremonial purposes or to toast friends, but they could be used at any time.

's math sin (SMAH-shin)—It's good!

saffron massage—Saffron cloth is made by grinding saffron firmly into the material. This was a euphemism for lesbian sex as described in medieval Arabic text.

"Saor Alba" (SOOR AH-la-pa)—slightly odd way of attempting to say *Free Scotland!* meant as a command; Gaelic-speakers differ as to whether this is accurate or not. The adjective should be after the noun and feminised, for example. *Saor* also means "cheap" and "joiner/carpenter." Regardless, this is a recognised motto of the Scottish Independence effort, and in the narrative is said by a man who is not a Gaelic speaker.

sgian dubh, sgian-achlais (SKEE-an DOO, SKEE-an OCH-lush)—This literally means "black dagger," but in this case *dubh* refers to its normally being hidden rather than a colour. The sgian dubh was hidden on the body when among enemies or worn on the calf on the side of the dominant hand when among friends. This knife probably evolved from the sgian-achlais (sleeve or armpit dagger) which was worn beneath the armpit as a weapon of last resort.

"Silver service"—five-star food service, where the food is served at the table instead of plated in the kitchen, and always served from the left. It is a tradition from upper-class 19th-century Britain.

Small Isles—Canna, Rùm, Muck, and Eigg, a group of islands in Lochaber, Inner Hebrides. Despite their name, they are not particularly small.

Smoking and society—In Jane's time period, smoking was extremely common, and cigarettes were available everywhere.

sonsie—a Scots word meaning strong and healthy, with connotations of beauty.

tablet—a traditional sweet made from sugar, condensed milk, and butter, cut into small squares. Despite resembling fudge, the two are nothing alike. Tablet is very hard, dry, and crumbly. It travels well and has a unique consistency. It is often flavoured with whisky.

tattie scones—potato pancakes

tattoo—This word is familiar to many as "an indelible mark or figure fixed upon the surface of the body by the insertion of pigment under the skin." Ainslie's facial tattoo is of arguable historical merit. Many records talk about facial or body tattoos or paint on the Norse, the Celts, the Picts (hence the name), the Britons, and more. These tattoos were blue in colour and some historians believe they were bodypaint rather than indelible. Either way, if they were tattoos, they weren't made with woad, which does not work for tattooing. Ainslie's facial tattoo in a blue knotwork pattern is based on Pictish and Norse knotwork but is primarily artistic license here.

teuchter (CHOO (soft *ch*) ter, sounds like *chookter*)—This is a pejorative term that means "Highlander" or "Islander" but it can be used in an endearing way by those who are themselves *teuchters*.

The Edinburgh Seven—the first women to attend university for medicine in Great Britain; see Author's Guide.

tip—garbage dump

torc—a circular neck ornament that usually opens from the front, made from a single piece of either straight or twisted metal. A golden torc signified a leader or person of high ranking among the Iron Age Celts; they were later also worn by warriors. Many people wore their personal wealth on their bodies. For Ainslie, this is probably an ancient family heirloom.

Travelling folk—Native people to Scotland and Ireland, Travellers live nomadic lives and retain most of the folk songs and stories of both countries. They experience extreme prejudice even today, despite their culture being arguably descendent from the older clan system.

Viking—This was a job description rather than a descriptor of a people or culture. To "go Viking" was to pillage, loot, raid, explore, etc. The word is probably something more akin to "pirate" than a nationality.

Wellie boots—Popularised by the Duke of Wellington, these are tall rubber rain boots. Just about everyone in Britain has a pair of wellies.

whitemeats—cheeses and curds, an Irish delicacy.

wynd (WINED, as in "wind a watch")—a pathway between buildings, sometimes covered, sometimes not, usually larger than a close, but the words "wynd" and "close" can be interchangeable.

* A NOTE ON THE GAELIC LANGUAGE: Pronunciation of Scottish Gaelic varies wildly from the cities to each individual island. Irish Gaelic, called *Irish* in Ireland, is not all that similar to Scottish Gaelic. However, those islands closest to Ireland, such as Islay, tend to have Scottish Gaelic speakers with a more "Irish" accent and pronunciation to their words. The sea was the highway in the past, so the islands and Ireland tend to share more things in common with each other.

This dialectical difference is also true of the Islanders' accents when speaking English, because they often have a unique lilt that sets them apart from the rest of Scotland. There are so many ways to pronounce Scottish Gaelic, no one can settle on a universal pronunciation. People will often find there are more variants on accent and pronunciation across the country and in the Highlands and Islands than would be expected of a small nation. This is one of the reasons Scottish Gaelic is difficult to acquire and preserve. The pronunciations listed in this guide will have variants throughout the country, and in other places where Scottish Gaelic is spoken, like Cape Breton, Nova Scotia.